5/17/10.
$24.99
B+T

5/10

the
TRADE
of
queens

TOR BOOKS BY CHARLES STROSS

The Clan Corporate
The Family Trade
The Hidden Family
The Merchants' War
The Revolution Business
The Trade of Queens

THE
TRADE
OF
QUEENS

BOOK SIX OF THE MERCHANT PRINCES

CHARLES STROSS

A TOM DOHERTY ASSOCIATES BOOK
New York

This is a work of fiction. All of the characters, organizations, and events portrayed in this novel are either products of the author's imagination or are used fictitiously.

THE TRADE OF QUEENS: BOOK SIX OF THE MERCHANT PRINCES

Copyright © 2010 by Charles Stross

A Tor Book
Published by Tom Doherty Associates, LLC
175 Fifth Avenue
New York, NY 10010

www.tor-forge.com

Tor® is a registered trademark of Tom Doherty Associates, LLC.

Library of Congress Cataloging-in-Publication Data

Stross, Charles.
  The trade of queens / Charles Stross. — 1st ed.
    p. cm. — (Merchant princes; bk. 6)
  Book six of The merchant princes.
  "A Tom Doherty Associates book."
  ISBN 978-0-7653-1673-8
  1. Clans—Fiction.   2. Nuclear weapons—Fiction.   3. Washington (D.C.)—Fiction.
4. Boston (Mass.)—Fiction.   I. Title.
  PR6119.T79T73 2010
  823'.92—dc22

                                                                    2009040696

First Edition: March 2010

Printed in the United States of America

0 9 8 7 6 5 4 3 2 1

To peace activists,
everywhere

acknowledgments

The Trade of Queens is the sixth book in an ongoing series—
and the final one in this story line. It wouldn't exist without help
from a multitude of people; no novelist works in a creative vacuum, and whatever we do, we owe a debt both to the giants
upon whose shoulders we stand, and to our test readers and editors. Giants first: This book—indeed, this whole series—would
not have happened if I hadn't read the works of H. Beam Piper
and Roger Zelazny.

But literary giants aren't the only folks I want to thank. This
series wouldn't have been written without the intervention of
several other people. My agent, Caitlin Blaisdell, nudged me to
make a radical change of direction from my previous novels.
David Hartwell and Tom Doherty of Tor encouraged me further,
and the editorial process benefited from the valuable assistance of
Moshe Feder and Stacy Hague-Hill, not to mention Tor's outside
copy editors. My wife, Karen, lent me her own inimitable support

acknowledgments

while I worked on the series. Other friends and critics helped me in one way or another; I'd like to single out for their contributions my father; also Steve Glover, Andrew Wilson, Robert "Nojay" Sneddon, Cory Doctorow, Sydney Webb, and James Nicoll. Thank you all. And then there is my army of test readers, who went over early drafts of the manuscript, asking awkward questions: Soon Lee, Charles Petit, Hugh Hancock, Martin Page, Emmet O'Brien, Dan Ritter, Erik Olson, Stephen Harris, Larry Schoen, Fragano Ledgister, Luna Black, Cat Faber, Lakeland Dawn, Harry Payne, Marcus Rowland, Carlos Wu, Doug Muir, Tom Womack, Zane Bruce, Jeff Wilson, and others—so many I've lost track of them, for which I can only apologize. Thank you all!

Finally, I'd like to thank the Office of the Under-Secretary of Defense for inviting me to talk at the Highlands Forum in Washington, D.C., thereby giving me the opportunity to do my reconnaissance.

the
TRADE
of
queens

NORThwOODS

Morning, July sixteenth.

In a locked store room on the eighth—top—floor of a department store off Pennsylvania Avenue, a timer counted down towards zero.

Another timer matched its progress—in a janitor's store on the top floor of a museum building near the Mall, behind a door jammed by cyanoacrylate glue in the lock and hinges.

And unfathomably far away, on a scaffold by the swampy banks of a slow-moving river, two men labored over a third timer, readying it for delivery to a target in the looking-glass world of the United States of America.

Nobody understood yet, but the worlds were about to change.

Four hundred miles from D.C., in a quiet residential street in Boston, the first bomb of the day detonated.

It wasn't a very large bomb—just a repurposed concussion grenade—but it was right under the driver's seat of the parked Saturn it was attached to. There was a bright flash; every window shattered as the car heaved on its suspension. Mike Fleming, standing in his doorway with keyfob remote raised, had no time to blink; the pressure wave shoved him backward and he stumbled, falling against the doorframe. In the ringing moment of silence after the blast, car alarms went off up and down the street and panicking dogs added their voices to the chorus. The hot yellow light of burning plastic and seat cushions filtered through the empty windows of the car, warmth beating on Mike's face as he struggled to work out why he was sitting down with his legs askew, why the back of his head hurt—

They want me dead, he realized, coldly. Then: *Dr. James screwed up.* It was an easy mistake to make. The technician who'd planted the bomb had meant to wire it to the ignition circuit, but they'd got the central locking instead. The fine art of car bombing had gotten positively esoteric in the past few years, with the proliferation of in-car electronics, remote-control engine starters, and other bells and whistles; and US government agents were more used to defusing the things than planting them. Then: *But that means they're complicit for sure.* The thought was shocking. *It's Operation Northwoods, only this time they're doing it for real.*

Mike reached up gingerly and felt the back of his head. There was going to be a nasty lump in a few hours, but his fingers came away dry. No bleeding. Taking stock, limb by limb, he took deep breaths, pushing down the wave of impending panic. *I'm alive,* he told himself. Shaken but intact. He'd been lucky; if he hadn't changed the batteries in his keyfob remote three months ago he might have been closer to the car, or even reduced to using the door key, with fatal results. As he stood up, something crunched underfoot. Fragments from the rear window, pea-sized pellets of safety glass. Bending down stiffly, he picked up his go-bag. His leg twinged hard inside its cast. What now? *Clear the killing zone,* the instructors had insisted, years before. But they'd been talking about a different kind of ambush—a car bomb was a passive trap. *Probably they were relying on it. Probably* . . . Mike pulled his pistol from the bag and duck-walked towards the street, edging around the burning car as he scanned for threats. In the distance, a siren began to scream.

Less than twenty seconds had elapsed.

"Duty Chief? This is the major. I have some orders for you. The day code is: Echo, Golf, Zulu, Xray, five, nine, Bravo. Did you get that?"

"Yes, my lord. One moment . . . yes, that is correct. What do you have for me?"

"Flash priority message to all Internal Security posts. Message begins: Traitors to the Clan have activated Plan Blue without authorization. Any security officers in possession of special weapons are to secure and disarm them immediately. Anyone not in possession but with knowledge of the disposition of special weapons must report to me immediately. Use of lethal force to secure and disarm special weapons in the possession of unauthorized parties is approved." Riordan swallowed and shifted his grip on the cell phone. "Anyone who is unaware of Plan Blue or the nature of the special weapons—you should execute Plan Black *immediately*. I repeat, Plan Black, immediate effect. Order ends. Please copy."

The stunned silence at the other end of the connection lasted almost a second. "My lord. Plan Blue? Plan Black?"

"Copy, damn your eyes!"

"Sir." The duty officer pulled himself together: "I copy . . ." He repeated Riordan's orders. "I'll put that out immediately, by your leave?"

"Do it. Riordan out."

He closed the phone with a snap and glanced sidelong at Lady Olga. She was staring across her seat back at Miriam, who was talking intently into her own phone, her face a study in strain. He opened his mouth, but she raised a finger. Half a minute passed as their driver, Alasdair, carried them ever closer to the turnpike; then Miriam held the phone away from her face and shook her head. "Trash," she said, holding it out to Brill, who popped the battery before sliding it into a waste bag. "We are so fucked," she said tonelessly.

"Plan Black?" Olga raised an eyebrow.

"What did Mr. Fleming say?" asked Riordan, ignoring her to focus on Miriam.

"It's—" Miriam shook her head, punch-drunk. "Crazy talk. He says Dr. James works for the vice president! And *he's* been in collusion with someone in the Clan for years! It's insane! He said something about tapes, and about them *wanting* an excuse, a Pearl Harbor."

"Can Fleming do anything for us?" Riordan stared at Miriam as she shook her head again. "Why not?"

"He says he's disposable. He's going to try and find someone to talk to, but there's no point going through the chain of command. We're trying to negotiate with people who want us dead— tell me it's not true?"

"Figures," Olga said tartly. Everyone stared at her—even Sir Alasdair, by way of the rearview mirror.

"What do you mean, my lady?" Riordan's return to exaggerated courtesy was a sign of stress, screamingly clear to Miriam even in her punch-drunk state.

"We've been looking for a second mole, ever since Matthias went over the wall, nearly a year ago. But we haven't been looking very *hard*, if you follow. And I heard rumors about there being a former politician, now retired, chief executive of a major logistics corporation, who was cooperating with us to provide doppelgangered locations and distribution hubs, back in the good years, in the late eighties and early nineties. The West Coast operation— back when WARBUCKS was out of politics. Before his comeback as VP. The crown fits, does it not?"

"But why—" This from Brilliana, unable to contain her curiosity.

"We don't work with politicians," Riordan said tiredly. "It's too hard to tell good from bad—the ones who stay bought from the ones who don't. There's too much potential for blowback, as the CIA can attest. But WARBUCKS was out of politics, wasn't he?"

Miriam nodded, brooding. "He was in the wilderness until . . ." Her eyes widened. "Oof. So, he got a second start in politics, and the duke would have pulled the plug. Am I right? But then Matthias went over the wall, and his report would have ended up where WARBUCKS—or one of his people—could read it, and he'd have to take out Matthias and then try to—oh *no*—"

"He'd have to try to kill us all," Olga finished the sentence, nodding, "or not even BOY WONDER could keep him from impeachment, yes? Our mole, for whom we have not been looking with sufficient vigor, isn't a low-level functionary; he's the vice president of the United States. And now he fears exposure."

Riordan reached over to tap Sir Alasdair on the shoulder. "Do you know where your Plan Black site is?" he asked.

"Yes, my lord." Alasdair nodded, checking his side mirror as he floored the accelerator to merge with the traffic on the interstate. "I'm taking us there."

"What's Plan Black?" Miriam tried to make eye contact with Olga.

Riordan cleared his throat. "My lady, we need to get you to a place of safety. But it's not just you; in light of the current situation we *all* need to get clear. Plan Black is a defensive measure, put in place by his grace after the mess last year. It's a pull-out—everyone in this world is to proceed to a safe site, collect essential equipment, and cross over."

"But that's—" Miriam paused. "What about the conservative faction? Earl Hjorth, the duchess, whoever took the bombs and activated Plan Blue, will they—"

"No." Riordan bared his teeth. "And I'm counting on it. Because if they disobey a directive from the acting head of Clan Security in the middle of an emergency, that's all I need to shoot them."

"It's the civil war, my lady, all over again." Olga whistled tunelessly. "They've been begging for it—and now they're going to get it."

In another world, in a mansion overlooking a lawn that swept downhill to the banks of a small river, an elderly man sat at a writing desk in a room off to one side of the great hall. It was a small room, walled in bare stone and floored with planks, which the tapestries and rugs failed to conceal; the large window casements, built for light but featuring heavy oak shutters with peepholes and iron bolts, suggested the architect had been more concerned with security than comfort. Despite the summer heat he held his robes of office tight about his shoulders, shivering as he stared at the ledger before him with tired eyes. It was a balance sheet of sorts, but the items tallied in its columns were not quantities of coin but the living and the dead. And from time to time, with the slow, considered strokes of his pen, Baron Julius Arnesen moved names from one column to the other.

Arnesen was a survivor of seventy-some years, most of which he had experienced in a state of barely suppressed existential terror. Even now, in a house his security chief assured him was securely doppelgangered from both the known alternate worlds (in the United States by a convenient interstate off-ramp, and in New Britain by a recently acquired derelict warehouse), and at the tail end of yet another civil war (this one between the Clan and the rival noble houses, rather than between Clan families) and at the tail end of his years, he could not bring himself to sit with his back to door or window. Besides, an instinct for trouble that had served him well over the decades whispered warnings in his ears: Not all was right in the Gruinmarkt, or within the uneasy coalition of Clan radicals and conservatives who had agreed to back the baroness Helge Thorold-Hjorth and her claim to bear the heir to the throne. *It's all going to come apart again, sooner or later,* he told himself gloomily, as he examined the next name in the ledger. *There are too many of them. . . .*

The civil war in the Gruinmarkt, torched off by the conservative Baron Henryk's scheme to marry the troublesome Helge—who had grown up in the United States, calling herself Miriam—to the king's second son, had left an enormous mess in its wake. Crown Prince Egon, paranoid by disposition, had sensed in the betrothal the first stirring of a plot to assassinate him; he'd moved against the Clan with vicious speed and ruthless determination, and in the three months they'd run wild his followers had destroyed the work of decades.

Egon was dead now, blown to bits along with most of his army when they tried to take a Clan castle, and Helge—pregnant as a result of the gynecological skullduggery of one of the Clan's own doctors—was acknowledged as the dead Prince Creon's widow. But a goodly chunk of the backwoods nobility wouldn't believe a word of it, even if she presented them with a baby who was the very spitting image of Creon in six months' time. To them, Helge was simply an impostor, willing puppet for the Clan's avarice and ambition. They were keeping their mouths shut right now, out of fear, but that wouldn't last forever; and weeding out the goats from the sheep was proving to be a well nigh impossible task. As magister of the royal assizes, Julius had considerable freedom to arraign and try hedge-lords whom he might suspect of treasonous intent; but he also had to walk a fine line between rooting out threats and conducting a witch hunt that might itself provoke another uprising.

Here in the countryside eight miles outside the capital Niejwein, in a house seized from the estate of the lord of Ostrood—conveniently missing with his sons since the destruction of the royal army at the Hjalmar Palace—Julius had established a crown court to supervise the necessary unpleasantness. To arraign and execute nobles in the capital would be inflammatory; better by far to conduct the grim job beyond the city walls, not so far out of sight as to invite accusations of secrecy, but distant enough to deter casual rubbernecking. With selected witnesses to testify to the fairness of the proceedings, and a cordon secured by imported American security devices as well as armed guards, he could proceed at his leisure without fear of the leading cause of death among judges in the Gruinmarkt—assassination by an angry relative.

Take the current case in hand, for example. Sir Euaunt ven Pridmann was a hedge-knight, titular liege lord to a village of some ninety souls, a house with a roof that leaked, three daughters with dowries to pay, one son, and a debt run up by his wastrel grandfather that exceeded the village's annual surplus by a factor of fifteen. Only a writ of relief from usury signed by the previous king's brother had spared him the indignity of being turfed out of his own home.

For such a man to show up in the army of the late pretender to the throne might be nothing more than simple desperation, for Egon had promised his followers a half share in the Clan lands that they took for him—not that ven Pridmann had done much looting and pillaging. With gout and poor eyesight he'd spent three-quarters of the war in his sickbed, and another fourth groaning with dysentery. That was why he hadn't been present at the destruction of the Hjalmar Palace by the god-cursed "special weapon" Clan Security had apparently detonated there, and his subsequent surrender and protestations of loyalty to the true heir were just another footnote to the whole sordid affair. But. *But.* Julius squinted at the ledger: How could you be *sure*? Might ven Pridmann be what the otherworld Americans called a *werewolf*, one who stayed behind to fight on in secret, after the war? Or might he have lied about his culpability, claiming innocence of very real crimes?

Julius sighed and laid his pen down beside the ledger. You couldn't be sure; and speculation about intangibles like loyalty in the absence of prior evidence was a good way to develop a raging case of paranoia. You could end up hanging thousands, as a preventative measure or in the hope of instilling a healthy fear in the survivors—but in the end, would it work? Would fear make them keep their heads down, or provoke a further uprising? *He's got gout,* Julius reasoned. *And he's too poor to buy a gun or pay a lance of infantry. Low risk.* And reasoning thus, he crossed ven Pridmann off the death list.

There was a knock.

"Yes? Yes?" Julius said querulously, looking up.

An apologetic face peeped round the door. "Sorry to bother you, my lord, but you have a visitor? Philip ven Holtz-Hjalmar from the Office of the Post, with dispatches from the Crown."

"Tell him to leave them—" Julius paused. *That's funny, I wonder what it is?* The post office in question was the Clan's courier service, manned by members of the six families and their close relatives who held in common the talent of walking between worlds. Normally he could expect at most one courier delivery a day, and today's had arrived some hours ago. "Show him in."

"At once, my lord."

The manservant withdrew. After a moment's muted conversation, the door opened again.

"My lord Arnesen." Julius didn't recognize the courier. He was a young fellow, wearing a dark business suit, conservatively cut, standard uniform for the couriers who had to travel in public in American cities. The briefcase he held was expensive and flashy: brushed aluminum with a combination lock and other less obvious security measures. "May we speak in private?"

"Of course." Julius waved at his servant: "Be off, and keep everyone away from the door."

"Thank you, my lord." The courier didn't smile.

"Well? What is it?" Julius strained to sit up, pushing back against the weight of his years.

"Special message, for your eyes only, from her grace the dowager Thorold Hjorth." He put the briefcase down on the side table.

This should be good, Julius thought. The duchess Hildegarde, Helge's grandam, one of the mainstays of the conservative faction, hadn't had the time of day for him since the disaster at the Summer Palace three months ago. *If she's decided to kiss and make up now it must mean—*

He was still trying to articulate the thought when the messenger shot him in the face, twice. The gun was fitted with a suppressor, and Baron Arnesen was seated; there was barely any noise, and the second bullet was in any case unnecessary.

"She sent her best wishes," said the courier, sliding his pistol back into the padded sleeve and picking up his briefcase in his left hand. "Her *very* best wishes."

Then he rolled his left sleeve up, focused his eyes on the temporary tattoo on the back of his wrist, and vanished into the locked and derelict warehouse that Julius Arnesen had been so reassured to hear of from his chief of security.

Meanwhile in another world, a doctor of medicine prepared himself for his next house call—one that would destroy families, rewrite wills, and quite possibly generate blood feuds. *They deserve it,* he thought, with a bitter sense of anticipation. *Traitors and bastards, the lot of 'em.*

For Dr. Robard ven Hjalmar, the past six months had brought about a disastrous and unplanned fall from grace and privilege. A younger child of the same generation as the duchess Patricia, or Angbard ven Lofstrom, born without any great title or fortune to his outer-family-derived name, Robard had been quick-witted and ambitious enough to seize for himself the opportunity to study needful skills in the land of the Anglischprache, a decade before it became the common pattern of the youth of the six families. In those days, the intelligent and scholarly were viewed with circumspection, if not outright suspicion: Few paths were open, other than the military—a career with direct and useful benefits to the Clan's scions.

Robard aimed higher, choosing medicine. In the drafty palaces of the Gruinmarkt, the allure of Western medicine held a mesmeric attraction to the elders and the high ladies. With open sewers in the streets, and middens behind many houses, infection and disease were everyday killers: Childbed morbidity and infant mortality robbed the Clan of much of its vigor. Robard had worked hard to convince Angbard's dour predecessor of his loyalty, and in return had been given some slight experience of life in America—even a chance to practice medicine and train after graduation, so long as he packed his bag and scurried home at the beck and call of his betters.

Antibiotics and vaccines raised many a soul from death's bed, but the real returns were quite obviously to be found in obstetric medicine. He realized this even in premed; the Clan's strength lay in its numbers, and enhancing that would find favor with its lords. As for the gratitude of its noblewomen at being spared a difficult or even fatal labor . . . the favors so endowed were subtler and took longer to redound, but no less significant for all that. One day, Robard reasoned, it was likely that the head destined to wear the crown would be there solely by his intervention—and the parents of that prince would know it. So for two decades he'd worked at his practice, patiently healing the sick, attending to confinements, delivering the babies (and on occasion discreetly seeing to the family-planning needs of their mothers), while keeping abreast of the latest developments in his field.

As his reputation burgeoned, so did his personal wealth and influence. He bought an estate in Oest Hjalmar and a private practice in Plymouth, growing plump and comfortable. Duke Lofstrom sought his advice on certain technical matters of state, which he dealt with discreetly and efficiently. There was talk of an earldom in his future, even a petty barony; he began considering the social advantages of taking to wife one of the ladies-in-waiting who graced the court of Her Majesty the queen-widow.

Then everything inexplicably and rapidly turned to shit.

Dr. ven Hjalmar shrugged, working his left shoulder in circles to adjust the hang of the oddly styled jacket he wore, then glanced at the fly-specked mirror on the dresser. His lip curled. *To fall this far . . .* He glanced sidelong at the battered carpetbag that sat on the hotel room bed. *Well, what goes down can come right up again,* he reminded himself.

It was all the Beckstein women's fault, mother and daughter

both. He'd first heard it from the mouth of the haughty dowager duchess herself: "The woman's an impostor of course," Hildegarde voh Thorold-Hjorth had snapped at him. "Do you really think it likely that an heiress has been living secretly in exile, in the, the barbarian world, for all these years? Just to surface *now*, when everything is finally settling down again? This is a plot, you mark my words!"

Well, the Beckstein woman *wasn't* an impostor—the dowager might not know a DNA paternity test from a rain of frogs, but he was under no such illusions—but the emergence after so long of her black-sheep mother certainly suggested that the dowager was right about it being some sort of conspiracy. And the bewildering ease with which Miriam had destroyed all the obstacles set in her path and then taken on the Clan Council like some kind of radical reformist firebrand was certainly suggestive. *Someone* was clearly behind the woman. And her exposure of the lost cousins, and this strange world which they had made their own, was a thunderbolt out of the blue. "She's a loose cannon," Baron Henryk ven Nordstrom had muttered angrily over a glass of port. "We shall have to take her out of play, Robard, or she's going to throw the board on the floor and jump on the pieces."

"Do you want me to neutralize her permanently?" ven Hjalmar had asked, cocking his head slightly to one side. "It seems unsubtle. . . ."

Henryk snorted in reply. "She's a woman, we can tie her down. If necessary, you can damage her a little." He didn't mention the other business, with the boy in the palace all those years ago; it would be gauche. "Marry her off and give her some children to keep her busy. Or, if she won't back off, a childbed accident. Hmm, come to think of it, I know a possible husband."

Well, *that* hadn't worked out for the best, either. Robard snorted again, angry and disquieted. He'd seen what the Pervert's army had left of the pretty little country house he'd bought, kicked the blood and ashes of Oest Hjalmar from his heels for a final time after he'd made the surviving peasants build a cairn from the ruins. He'd done his bit for Henryk, insuring the rebellious cow got knocked up on schedule for the handfasting after she stuck her nose in one too many corners where it didn't belong; how was he to know the Pervert would respond by committing regicide, fratricide, patricide, homicide, and generally going apeshit?

But after that, things went even more askew. Somehow Angbard's minions had conspired to put her *on the fucking throne*, the throne!—of all places—with a Praetorian guard of hardline progressivist thugs. And she *knew*. She'd dug and dug until she'd turned up the breeding program, figured out what it was for—almost as if she'd been pointed at it by someone. Figured out that Angbard had asked him to set up the liaison with the clinic, no doubt. Figured out that what was going on was a power struggle between the old bitches who arranged the marriage braids and the macho phalangist order of the Clan Security organization. Figured out that *he* was the fixer, the enabler, the Clan's own medic and expert in reproductive technology who had given Angbard the idea, back when he was a young and foolish intern who didn't know any better. . . .

His idea. The power of it still filled his age-tempered heart with bitter awe: The power to raise an army of world-walkers, to breed them and train them to obedience could have made him the most powerful man in the six—now unhappily seven—families. If he'd waited longer, realized that he stood on the threshold of his own success, he'd never have sought Angbard's patronage, much less learned to his dismay how thoroughly that put him under the thin white duke's thumb.

Stolen. Well he had, by god—by the Anglischprache's dead god on a stick, or by Lightning Child, or whichever thrice-damned god really mattered (and who could tell)—he had stolen it back again. The bitch-queen Helge might have it in for him, and her thugs wouldn't hesitate with the hot knives if they ever discovered his role in Hildegarde's little gambit—but that was irrelevant now. He had the list. And he had a copy of the lost, hidden family's knotwork emblem, a passport for travel to New

Britain. And lastly, he had a piece of paper with a name and address on it.

James Lee had done his job well, during his exile among the Clan.

Finally satisfied with his appearance, Dr. ven Hjalmar walked to the door and opened it an inch. "I'm ready to go," he said quietly.

Of the two stout, silent types standing guard, one remained impassive. The other ducked his head, obsequious—or perhaps merely polite in this society; Robard was no judge of strange mores—and shuffled hastily towards the end of the corridor.

The doctor retreated back to his room to wait. These were dangerous times, to be sure, and he had nearly fallen foul of muggers on his way here as it was; the distinction between prison guard and bodyguard might be drawn arbitrarily fine. In any case, the Lees had done him the courtesy of placing him in a ground-floor room with a window overlooking a walled garden; unless Clan Security was asleep at the switch and the Lees had been allowed to set up doppelganger installations, he was free to leave should he so choose. Of course, that might simply be yet another of their tests. . . .

There was a knock; then the door opened. "Good afternoon, Doctor."

Ven Hjalmar nodded affably. "And the same to you, sir." The elders were clearly taking him seriously, to have sent James Lee to conduct him to this meeting. James was one of the principal heirs. One-quarter ethnic Han by descent, he wouldn't have raised any eyebrows in the other Anglische world: but the politics of race and ethnicity were very different here, and the Lee family's long sojourn on the west coast of the Clan's world among the peasants of the Middle Empire had rendered them conspicuous in the white-bread northeast of New Britain. "Chinese gangsters" was perhaps the nicest term the natives had for them, and despite their considerable wealth they perforce kept a low profile—much like Robard himself. "I trust it *is* a good afternoon?"

"I've had worse." Lee held the door open. "The elders are

waiting to hear your proposal in person, and there's always the potential for—misunderstandings, in such circumstances. But we are all men of goodwill, yes?"

"Yes." Ven Hjalmar smiled tightly. "And we all hold valid insurance policies. After you, no, I must insist. . . ."

The Lee family had fallen out of contact with the rest of the Clan most of two centuries ago—through betrayal, they had thought, although the case for cock-up over conspiracy was persuasive— and in that time they had come to do things very differently. However, some aspects of the operation were boringly familiar: an obsession with the rituals of hierarchy, pecking order, and tiresome minutiae of rank. As with the Clan, they relied on arranged marriages to keep the recessive genetic component of the world-walking trait strong. Like the Clan, they had fractured into a loose formation of families, first and second cousins inter-marrying, with a halo of carriers clinging to their coattails. (Again, like the Clan, they practiced a carefully controlled level of exogamy, lest inbreeding for the world-walking trait reinforce other, less desirable ones.) *Unlike* the Clan, Mendelian genetics had made a late arrival—and actual modern reproductive gene-tics as practiced in the clinics of America was an unknown black art. Or so ven Hjalmar believed; in fact, he was betting his life on it.

"Speak to me of this breeding program," said the old man on the mattress.

Ven Hjalmar stared at his beard. It straggled from the point of his chin, wispy but not too wispy, leaving his cheeks bare. *Is that spirit gum?* he wondered. The cheeks: There was something unnatural about their smoothness, as if powdered, perhaps to conceal the pattern of stubble. It would make sense perhaps, in an emergency, to be able to shed the formal robes, queue, and beard, to dissolve in the crowd. . . . "It was established by the

Clan's security division a generation ago," he said slowly. "Normally the, the braid of marriages is managed by the elder womenfolk, matchmakers. But with a civil war only just dying down, the Clan's numbers were diminished drastically." It was surprisingly easy to slip into the habit of speaking of them as a third party, as *them* not *us*. Another creeping sign of exile.

"In America, to which they have access, medical science is very much more advanced than in the Gruinmarkt—or in New Britain. Childless couples can make discreet use of medical services to arrange for a child to be born, with one or other parent's *genes*"—he used the alien word deliberately, throwing it into conversation without explanation—"to the wife, or to a host mother for adoption. The duke came to an arrangement with such a clinic, to discreetly insure that a number of such babies were born with the ability to pass on the world-walking *gene* to their own offspring. Records were kept. The plan was to approach the female offspring, as adults, and offer to pay them to be host mothers—paid handsomely, to bear a child for adoption. A child who would, thanks to the clinic, be a true world-walker, and be fostered by the Clan."

The old lady to the right of the bearded elder tugged her robe fastidiously. Despite the cultivated air of impassivity, the stench of her disapproval nearly made the doctor cough. "They are unmarried, these host mothers?" she asked querulously.

Ven Hjalmar nodded. "They do things *very* differently in the United States," he added.

"Ah." She nodded; oddly, her disapproval seemed to have subsided. *Must be some local custom. . . .* He took note of it, nervously.

"As you can imagine, the Clan's, ah, matchmakers"—he'd nearly said *old women* but caught himself at the last moment—"did not know of this scheme. It undermined their authority, threatening their rank and privilege. Furthermore, if it went to completion it would hugely undermine the noble families, for these new world-walkers would be brought into the Clan by the duke's security apparatus, with no hereditary ties to bind them to the braids. The scheme found favor with the radical reformers who wished to integrate the Clan more tightly into America, but to those of us who had some loyalty to the old ways"—*or who preferred to be bigger fish in a smaller pond*—"it was most suspicious."

The old man—Elder Huan, James Lee had whispered in his ear as they approached the chamber—nodded. "Indeed." He fixed ven Hjalmar with a direct and unwavering gaze that was entirely at odds with the image he had maintained throughout the audience up to this point, and asked, "What do you want of us, Doctor?"

Ven Hjalmar did a double take. "Uh, well, as a doctor, the duke commanded my attendance. I obeyed, with reservations; however, I consider myself to be released from his service by the occasion of his death. The family loyalists and the radicals are currently tearing each other apart. I come to you in the hope that you might better exercise the wisdom needed to guide and integrate a generation of new world-walkers." He smiled tightly. "I do not have the list of host mothers on my person, and indeed it would be no use to you without a physician licensed to practice in the United States—which I happen to be. There will be expenses, and it will take some time to set up, but I believe my identity over there is still secure. And I have in any case taken steps—"

Elder Huan glanced sideways at the sour-faced old woman. "Aunt Mei?"

Aunt Mei sniffed. "Get to the *point*, boy. We don't have all day!" Elder Huan produced a pocket watch from one sleeve of his robe and glanced at it. "You are trying to sell us something. Name your price."

Sweat broke out on Robard's hands. *Not so Chinese,* he realized. Either that, or the directness was a snub, unconscionable rudeness to someone of professional rank. "I can give you world-walking babies," he finally admitted. "I will have to spend some time and considerable money in the United States, and it will take at least eighteen months to start—this can't be hurried, not just the pregnancies but the appearance of legitimate medical practice—but once the operation is up and running, I can deliver up to fifty new world-walkers in the first two years, more later." *Lots* more with harvested eggs and sperm and an IVF clinic; times had moved on since the first proposal to use AID and host mothers. "The money . . . I believe on the order of two million US dollars should cover start-up costs, and another hundred thousand per baby. That would be eight thousand pounds and eight hundred pounds. You'll need to build a small shipping operation along similar lines to the Clan's to raise the money—but you have the advantage of being utterly unknown to and unsuspected by the federal agencies. If you stay out of their exact line of business you should thrive."

Aunt Mei's eyes narrowed. "And *your* price?" she asked.

It was now or never. "I want somewhere to live," he admitted. "My patron is dead, the Clan is in turmoil, and I doubt their ability to survive what is coming. I know the Americans—I've worked among them for years—the Gruinmarkt will not be safe. If the loyalist faction wins, they will try to continue as before, a big mistake. If the progressives win . . . they'll want to live here." He smiled, as ingratiatingly as he could. "We are distant cousins. Can we put past misunderstandings behind us and work together? Consider me a test case."

"You ask of us accession to our family," declared Aunt Mei. "Money and status besides, but principally refuge from your enemies." She turned and nudged Elder Huan. "Is that *all*?" She sounded mildly scandalized.

Elder Huan stared at ven Hjalmar. "Is that all, indeed?" he echoed ironically. "You would betray your own family . . . ?"

"*They* betrayed *me*!" Ven Hjalmar was beyond containment. "I was placed in an intolerable position! Obey the duke and earn the undying hatred of a woman who was to be married to the heir to the throne, or disobey the duke and—well!" He swallowed. "I gather there is a curse: *May you come to the attention of important people.* At first it looked like a simple problem to solve. The girl was an idiot, naive, and worse, was poking her nose into places it did not belong. But then the civil war started, the duke was incapacitated, and she . . . well. My household was destroyed in the war: My parents are dead, I have no brothers or sisters. What is a man at the end of his affairs to do?"

There it was, on the table. Spun as neatly as he could manage, admittedly, no hint that his own actions had been motivated by aught but the purest obedience to his elders and betters; but soon there would be no one alive to gainsay his account. (The duke was reliably dead, and as for the dowager Hildegarde, she had followed the most insane imaginable strategy of tension with the Americans, obviously lacking even the remotest idea of the magnitude of their inevitable response—she would follow him soon, and certainly long before she'd move to New Britain, of that he was certain.) Robard sweated some more, waiting for the elder Huan to give some indication of his thoughts. Then, after a moment, the elder inclined his head, and looked at Aunt Mei. "As you will."

Aunt Mei looked at ven Hjalmar. "We shall consider your proposal," she said slowly. "Such matters are best decided on after full discussion: You may enjoy our hospitality while we search for consensus. But I shall tell you this minute that if we agree with it, there will be another price you must pay."

"Another . . . ?" Ven Hjalmar was at a loss.

"Yes." She smiled, a crinkling around the eyes that hinted at amusement. "If you are to stay with us, you will have to find a wife." She clapped her hands. "Nephew." James Lee bowed. "Take the doctor back to his room."

Erasmus Burgeson strode through the portico of the People's Palace as if he owned it, his brown leather duster swinging around him. His usual entourage followed him—a pair of guards in the black peacoats and helmets of Freedom Riders, a stenographer and a pair of messenger boys to race his orders to the nearest telautograph, three secretaries and assistants. It was impossible to fart without his entourage recording the event and issuing a press release to reassure the masses that the commissioner of state propaganda had eaten a healthy breakfast and his bowels were in perfect working order. *Such is the price of being on the winning side,* he reminded himself whenever it got a bit much; the alternative—a short walk off the end of a long rope—was far less attractive.

Just one month had wrought great changes. The pompous neoclassical building was crawling with Freedom Riders and guards from the newly formed Security Committee, checking passeportes and getting underfoot: but with some justification, for there had been three assassination attempts on members of the Radical government by Patriot renegades in the past week alone—one of them successful to the extent of having cost Commissioner of Industry Sutter half the fingers on one hand and the use of his left eye, not to mention a secretary and a bodyguard. Erasmus had made much of this shocking martyrdom, but it was hardly the most onerous fate the Patriot mob had in mind for any commissioner who fell into their hands, as the full gibbets in rebel-held Rio de Janeiro could attest.

But the guards didn't impede Burgeson's progress through the entrance and up the stairs to the Avenue of Ministries; they stood aside and saluted with alacrity, their faces expressionless. It was only at the door to the receiving room that he encountered a delay: Commissioner of Security Reynolds's men, of course. "Citizen Burgeson! You are expected, but your colleagues must identify themselves. Your papers, please!"

Erasmus waited impatiently while the guards confirmed that his aides were indeed on the privileged list, then nodded amiably to the underofficer on door duty. "If you please?" he asked. The man practically jumped to open the door, avoiding eye contact: Erasmus was of the same rank as the head of his entire organization. Erasmus nodded and, not waiting for his entourage, walked through into the outer office. It was, as usual, crammed with junior people's commissioners and bureaucrats awaiting instruction, cooling their heels in the antechamber to the doctor's surgery.

Not pausing for idle chatter, Burgeson walked towards the inner door.

A stout fellow who overtopped him by a good six inches stepped sideways into his path, blocking the doorway. "You can't—" he began.

Erasmus stopped and looked up at him. "Don't you recognize me?" It was genuinely curious, to be stopped by anyone—even a bruiser in the uniform of the Security Committee.

The bodyguard stared down at Erasmus. Then, after a second, he began to wilt. "No sir," he admitted. "Is you expected by 'is citizenship this mornin'?"

"Yes." Burgeson smiled, showing no teeth. "Why don't you announce me?"

The ability to intimidate secret policemen didn't come easily or lightly to Erasmus; he still found it a thing of wonder as he watched the big bodyguard turn and push the door ajar to announce his arrival. He'd spent years in the camps, then more years on the run as a Leveler underground organizer in Boston, periodically arrested and beaten by men of this selfsame type, the attack dogs of power. It was no surprise after all these years to see these people rising in the armed wing of the revolutionary democratic cadres, and leaders like Reynolds gaining a certain reputation—especially in view of the unfolding crisis that had first provoked an abdication and then enabled the party to hold its coup—but it was a disappointment. *Meet the new boss, just like the old boss*: Erasmus remembered the Beckstein woman's cynical bon mot. Then he dismissed it from his mind as the thug threw the door wide open before him and stood aside.

"Hail, citizen." Sir Adam Burroughs smiled wearily at him as the door closed at his back. "Have you been keeping well?"

"Well enough." Erasmus lowered his creaking limbs into one of the ornate chairs that faced Sir Adam's huge, gilt-tooled leather-topped barge of a desk. And indeed, it was true: With the tuberculosis that had threatened to kill him cured by Miriam's magic medicine, he felt like a new man, albeit a somewhat breathless one upon whose heels middle age was treading. "Drowning in paper-work, of course, but aren't we all? My staff are just about keeping on top of the routine stuff, but if anything out of the ordinary comes up they need their reins holding." Barely a square inch of Sir Adam's desk was occupied, but that was one of the privileges of office: There was another, discreet servants' door in the opposite wall, and behind it a pool of stenographers, typer operators, and clerks to meet his needs. "What can I do for you, citizen?"

"It's the French business." Sir Adam sounded morose. "I've asked Citizens Wolfe and Daly to join us in a few minutes." Wolfe was the commissioner for foreign affairs, and Daly was the commissioner for the navy: both cabinet posts, like Burgeson's own, and all three of them—not to mention Sir Adam—were clinging on to the bare backs of their respective commissariats for dear life. Nobody in the provisional government knew much about what they were supposed to be doing, with the question-able exception of the Security Committee, who were going about doing unto others as they had been done by with gusto and zeal. Luckily the revolutionary cadres were mostly used to living on their wits, and Sir Adam was setting a good example by ruth-lessly culling officials from his secretariat who showed more pro-ficiency in filling their wallets than their brains. "We can't put them off for any longer."

"What are your thoughts on the scope of the problem?" Erasmus asked carefully.

"What problem?" Sir Adam raised one gray eyebrow. "It's an imperialist war of attrition and there's nothing to be gained from continuing it. Especially as His Former Majesty emptied the coffers and mismanaged the economy to the point that we can't *afford* to continue it. The question is not whether we sue for peace, it's how—ah, John, Mark! So glad you could join us!"

So am I, Erasmus thought as the two other commissioners exchanged greetings and took their seats. Being seen to proceed by consensus on matters of state was vital—at this point, to take after the king's authoritarian style would be the quickest way imaginable to demoralize the rank and file. "Are we quorate?" he asked.

"I believe so." Wolfe, a short, balding fellow with a neat beard, twitched slightly, a nervous tic he'd come out of the mining camps with—Erasmus had had dealings with him before, in Boston and parts south. "Is this about the embassy?" he asked Sir Adam.

"Yes." Sir Adam reached into a desk drawer and withdrew a slim envelope. "He insisted on delivering his preliminary list of demands to me, personally, 'as acting head of state' as he put it." He made a moué of distaste. Wolfe grunted irritably as Sir Adam slid the envelope across the desk towards him. "I don't want to preempt your considered opinion, but I don't consider his demands to be acceptable."

Erasmus raised an eyebrow: Daly, the naval commissioner, looked startled, but Wolfe took the trespass on his turf in good form, and merely began reading. After a moment he shook his head. "No, no . . . you're absolutely right. Impossible." He put the paper down. "Why are you even considering it?"

Sir Adam smiled with all the warmth of a glacier: "Because we *need peace abroad.* You know and I know that we cannot accept these terms, but neither can we afford to continue this war."

"May I?" Erasmus reached for the letter as Sir Adam nodded.

"But the price they're demanding—" Erasmus scanned quickly. After the usual salutations and diplomatic greetings, the letter was brusque and to the point. "It's outrageous," Wolfe continued. "The money is one thing, but the loss of territory is wholly unacceptable, and the limitation on naval strength is—"

"Choke them," Erasmus commented.

"Excuse me?" Wolfe stared at him.

"There is stuff here we can't deal with, it's true. War reparations . . . but we know we can't pay, and they must know we can't pay. So buy them off with promissory notes which we do not intend to honor. That's the first thing. Then there's the matter of the territorial demands. So they want Cuba. *Give* them Cuba." He grinned humorlessly at Wolfe's expression. "Hasn't the small matter of how to put down the Patriot resistance there exercised us unduly? It all depends *how* we give them Cuba. Suppose we accede to the French demands. The news stories at home will run, the French have *taken* Cuba. And to the Cubans, our broadcasts will say, sorry, but the Patriots stabbed us in the back. And there is nothing to stop us funneling guns and money to the Patriots who take up arms against the French, is there? Let it bleed them, I say. They want Nippon? Let them explain that to the shogun. It's not as if he recognizes our sovereignty in any case."

"What naval concessions are they demanding?" asked Daly. "We *need* the navy, the army isn't politically correct—"

"They want six of our ships of the line, and limits on new construction of such," Erasmus noted. "So take six of the oldest prison hulks and hand them over. Turn the hulls in the shipyards over to a new task—not that we can afford to proceed with construction this year, in any case—those purpose-built flat-topped tenders the air-minded officers have been talking about." Miriam had lent Erasmus a number of history books from her strange world; he'd found the account of her nation's war in the Pacific with the Chrysanthemum Throne most interesting.

"These are good suggestions," Sir Adam noted, "but we cannot accede to this—this laundry list! If we pay the danegeld, the Dane will . . . well. You know full well why they want Cuba. And there are these reports of disturbing new weapons. John, did you discover anything?"

Daly looked lugubrious. "There's an entire *city* in Colorado that I'd never heard of two weeks ago," he said, an expression of uneasy disbelief on his face. "It's full of natural philosophers and artificers, and they're taking quantities of electricity you wouldn't believe. Something about a super-petard, made from chronosium, I gather. Splitting the atom, alchemical transformation of chronosium into something they call osirisium in atomic crucibles. And they confirm the French intelligence." He glanced at Erasmus: "I mean no ill, but is everyone here approved for this news?"

Sir Adam nodded. "I wouldn't ask you to report on it if I thought otherwise. The war is liable to move into a new and uncertain stage if we continue it. The French have these petards, they may be able to drop them from aerodynes or fire them from the guns of battleships: a single shell that can destroy a fleet or level a city. It beggars the imagination but we cannot ignore it, even if they have but one or two. We need them likewise, and we need time to test and assemble an arsenal. Speaking of which . . . ?"

"I pressed them for a date, but they said the earliest they could test their first charge would be three months from now. If it works, and if ordered so, they can scale up production, making perhaps one a month by the end of the year. Apparently this stuff is not like other explosives, it takes months or years to synthesize—but in eighteen months, production will double, and eighteen months after that they can increase output fourfold."

"So we can have four of these, what do you call them, corpuscular petards?—corpses, an ominous name for an ominous weapon—by the end of this year. Sixteen by the end of next year, thirty-four by the end of the year after, and hundreds the year after that. Is that a fair summary?" Daly nodded. "Then our medium-term goal is clear: We need to get the bloody French off our backs for at least three and a half years, strengthen our homeland air defenses against their aerodynes, and work out some way of deterring the imperialists. In which case"—Sir Adam gestured irritably at the diplomatic communiqué—"we need to give them enough to shut them up for a while, but not so easily that they smell a rat or are tempted to press for more." He looked pointedly at Erasmus. "Finesse and propaganda are the order of the day."

"Yes. This will require care and delicacy." Erasmus continued reading. "And the most intricate maintenance of their misconceptions. When do you intend to commence direct talks with the enemy ambassador?"

"Tomorrow." Sir Adam's tone was decisive. "The sooner we bury the hatchet the faster we can set about rebuilding that which is broken and reasserting the control that we have lost. And only when we are secure on three continents can we look to the task of liberating the other four."

An editor's life is frequently predictable, but seldom boring.

At eleven that morning, Steve Schroeder was settling down in his cubicle with his third mug of coffee, to work over a feature he'd commissioned for the next day's issue.

In his early forties, Steve wasn't a big wheel on the *Herald*; but he'd been a tech journalist since the early eighties, and he had a weekly section to fill, features to buy from freelance stringers, and in-depth editorial pieces to write. He rated an of-fice, or a cubicle, or at least space to think without interruption when he wasn't attending editorial committee meetings and dis-cussing clients to target with Joan in advertising sales, or any of the hundred and one things other than editing that went with wearing the hat. Reading the articles he'd asked for and *editing* them sometimes seemed like a luxury; so he frowned instinc-tively at the stranger standing in the entrance to his cubicle. "Yes?"

The stranger wore a visitor's badge, and there was some-thing odd about him. Not the casual Friday clothes; it took Steve a moment to spot the cast on his leg. "You're Steve Schroeder?"

"Who wants to know?"

The stranger shrugged. "You don't know me." He produced a police ID card. Steve sat up, squinting at the badge. *Drug En-forcement Agency? Mike Fleming?*

"Not my department; Crime's upstairs on—"

"No, I think I need to talk to you. You commissioned a bunch of articles by Miriam Beckstein a couple of years ago, didn't you?"

Huh? "What's this about?" Steve asked cautiously.

"Haven't heard from her for a while, have you?"

Alarm bells were going off in his head. "Has she been arrested? I don't know anything; we had a strictly business relationship—"

"She hasn't been arrested." Fleming's gaze flickered sidelong; if Steve hadn't been staring at him he might not have noticed. "She mentioned you, actually, a couple of years ago. Listen, I don't know anyone here, and I've got very limited time, so I thought I'd try you and see if you could direct me to the right people." He swallowed. "She pointed me at a story, kind of, before she disappeared. I need to see it breaks, and breaks publicly, or *I'm* going to disappear too. I'm sorry if that sounds overdramatic—"

"No, that's all right." *Jesus, why me? Why now?* Steve glanced at his workstation for long enough to save the file he was reading. *Do I need this shit?* Building security mostly kept the nuts out with admirable efficiency; and paranoids invariably headed for Crime and Current Affairs. If this guy *was* a nut . . . "Mind if I look at that?" Fleming handed him the badge. Steve blinked, peering at it. *Certainly* looks *real enough.* . . . He handed it back. "Why me?"

"Because—" Fleming was looking around. "Mind if I sit down?"

Steve took a deep breath and gestured at the visitor's chair by his desk. "Go ahead. In your own time."

"Last year Miriam Beckstein lost her job. You know about that?"

Steve nodded, guardedly. "You want to tell me about it?"

"It wasn't the regular post-9/11 slowdown; she was fired because she stumbled across a highly sophisticated money-laundering operation. Drug money, and lots of it."

Steve nodded again. Trying to remember: What had Miriam said? She'd been working for the *Industry Weatherman* back then, hadn't she? Something wild about them canning her for uncovering—*Jesus*, he thought. "Mind if I record this?" he asked.

"Sure. Be my guest." Fleming laughed as Steve activated his

recorder. It was a hoarse bark, too much stress bottled up behind it. "Listen, this isn't just about drugs, and I know it's going to sound nuts, so let me start with some supporting evidence. An hour ago, my car was blown up. The news desk will probably have a report on it, incident in Braintree—" He proceeded to give an address. "I'm being targeted because I'm considered unreliable by the organization I've been working for on secondment. You can check on that bombing. If you wait until this afternoon, I'm afraid—shit. There's going to be a terrorist strike this afternoon in D.C., and it's bigger than 9/11. That's why I'm here. There's a faction in the government who have decided to run an updated version of Operation Northwoods, and they've maneuvered a narcoterrorist group into taking the fall for it. I'm—I was—attached to a special cross-agency task force working on the narcoterrorist ring in question. They're the folks Miriam stumbled across—and it turns out that they're big, bigger than the Medellín Cartel, and they've got contacts all the way to the top."

"Operation—what was that operation you mentioned?" Steve stared at his visitor. *Jesus. Why do I always get the cranks?*

"Operation Northwoods. Back in 1962, during the Cold War, the Chiefs of Staff came up with a false flag project to justify an invasion of Cuba. The idea was that the CIA would fake up terrorist attacks on American cities, and plant evidence pointing at Castro. They were going to include hijackings, bombings, the lot—the most extreme scenarios included small nukes, or attacks on the capitol; it was all 'Remember the *Maine*' stuff. Northwoods wasn't activated, but during the early seventies the Nixon administration put in place the equipment for the same, on a bigger scale—there was a serious proposal to nuke Boston in order to justify a preemptive attack on China. This stuff keeps coming up again, and I'd like to remind you that our current vice president and the secretary for defense got their first policy chops under Nixon and Ford."

"But they can't—" Steve stopped. "They've just invaded Iraq! Why would they want to do this now? If they were going to—"

"Iraq was the president's hobbyhorse. And no, I'm not say-ing that 9/11 was stage-managed to drag us into that war; that would be paranoid. But there's a whole new enemy on hand, and a black cross-agency program to deal with them called Family Trade, and some of us aren't too happy about the way things are being run. Let me fill you in on what's been going on. . . ."

EVACUATION

The marcher kingdoms of the East Coast, from the Nordt-markt south, were scantily populated by American standards: The Gruinmarkt's three to four million—there was no exact census—could handily live in New York City with room to spare. The Clan and their outer families (related by blood, but not for the most part gifted with the world-walking talent) were at their most numerous in the Gruinmarkt, but even there their total extended families barely reached ten thousand souls. The five inner families had, between them, a couple of thousand adult world-walkers and perhaps twice that many children (and some seniors and pregnant women for whom world-walking would be a hazardous, if not lethal, experience).

At one point in the 1930s, American style, the inner families alone had counted ten thousand adult world-walkers; but the Clan's long, festering civil war had been a demographic disaster.

To an organization that relied for its viability on a carefully husbanded recessive gene, walking the line between inbreeding and extinction, a series of blood feuds between families had sown the seeds of collapse.

Nearly twenty years ago, Angbard, Duke Lofstrom, the chief of the Clan's collective security agency, had started a program to prevent such a collapse from ever again threatening the Clan. He'd poured huge amounts of money into funding a network of fertility clinics in the United States, and the children of that initiative were now growing to adulthood, ignorant of the genes (and other, more exotic intracellular machinery) for which they were carriers. Angbard's plan had been simple and direct: to approach young female carriers selected from the clinics' records, and pay them to act as host mothers for fictional infertile couples. The result was to be a steady stream of world-walkers, raised in the United States and not loyal to the quarreling families, who could be recruited in due course. Miriam, Helge, had been raised in Boston by Angbard's sister as an experiment in cultural assimilation, not to mention a political insurance policy: Other children of the Clan had been schooled and trained in the ways and knowledge of the exotic West.

But Angbard had planned on being around to coordinate the recruitment of the new world-walkers. He hadn't expected Matthias's defection, or the exposure of the clinics to hostile inspection, and he hadn't anticipated the reaction of the Auld Bitches, the gaggle of grandmothers whose carefully arranged marriages kept the traditional Clan structure afloat. Their tame gynecologist, Dr. ven Hjalmar, was a stalwart of the conservative club. He'd been the one who, at Baron Henryk's bidding, had arranged for Helge's involuntary pregnancy. He'd also acquired the breeding program records for his faction and, most recently, taken pains to ensure that Angbard would never again threaten their prestige as gatekeepers of the family trade. And now the surviving members of the Clan's conservative clique—the ones who hadn't been massacred by Prince Egon at the ill-fated betrothal feast—were cleaning up.

On that July morning, approximately one in every hundred world-walkers died.

In his private chambers in the Ostrood House, Baron Julius Arnesen was shot dead by Sir Gavaign Thorold.

Lord Mors Hjalmar, his eldest son Euen, and wife Gretyl were blown up by a satchel charge of PETN delivered by a courier who, not being a member of the clique responsible, also died in the blast—neither the first nor the last collateral casualty.

There were other, less successful assassination attempts. The young soldier detailed to slay Sir Helmut Anders had second thoughts and, rather than carrying out his orders, broke down and confessed them to his commander. The assault team targeting Earl-Major Riordan arrived at the wrong safe house owing to faulty intelligence, and by the time they located the correct headquarters building it had already been evacuated. And the poison-pen letter addressed to Lady Patricia Thorold-Hjorth—lightly spritzed in dimethyl mercury, a potent neurotoxin—never left the postal office, owing to an unusual shortage of world-walkers arriving to discharge their corvée duties that day.

In fact, nearly two-thirds of those targeted for assassination survived, and nearly a third of the would-be assassins were captured, were killed, or failed to carry out their missions. As coup d'état attempts went, this one might best be described as a halfhearted clusterfuck. The conservative faction had been on the back foot since the betrothal-night massacre, many of their most effective members slain; what remained was the rump of the postal committee (cleaving to the last to the trade that had brought them wealth and power), the scheming grandmothers and their young cat's-paws, and a bedraggled handful who had fallen upon hard times or whose status was in some other way threatened by the new order.

Only one element of the conspiracy ran reliably to completion. Unfortunately, it was Plan Blue.

In a humid marsh on the banks of a broad river, there stood a scaffold by the grace of the earl of Dankfurt. The scaffold lacked many of the appurtenances of such—no dangling carrion or cast-iron basket of bones to add to the not inconsiderable stench of the swamp—but it provided a stout and very carefully surveyed platform. Here in the Sudtmarkt most maps were hand-scribed in ink on vellum, and accurate to the nearest league. But this platform bore stripe-painted measuring sticks at each corner, and had been carefully pinned down by theodolites born by world-walkers. Its position and altitude were known to within a foot, making it the most accurately placed location in the entire kingdom.

Five men stood on the scaffold beside a cheap wheelbarrow that held an olive-drab cylinder the size of a beer keg. Two of them wore US army fatigues, in the new desert pattern that had come in with the Iraq war: outer-family world-walkers both, young and more tenuously attached to the Clan than most. The other three were clad in fashions that had never been a feature of that time line. "Are you clear on the schedule?" demanded one fellow, a thin-haired, thin-faced man whom Miriam had once likened to a ferret.

"Sir." The shorter of the two uniformed men bowed his neck formally.

"Tell us, please," said one of the other fellows, resting his hand on the pommel of his small-sword.

"At T minus eight minutes, Erik takes his place on the barrow. I then cross over. Emergence is scheduled for level two, visitors' car park block delta three. There will be cameras but no internal guard patrols inside the car park—active security is on the perimeter and at the doors."

The ferret-faced man nodded. "Kurt?"

The tall, sandy-haired soldier nodded. "I dismount. We have sixty seconds to clear down any witnesses. Then we wheel the barrow to the stairwell. By T minus six the payload is to be emplaced in the place of the red fire extinguisher, which we will place in the barrow. We are then to proceed back to our arrival point, whereupon Jurgen will take his place in the barrow and I will bring us home no later than T minus five."

"What provisions for failure have you made?" asked the fellow with the small-sword.

"Not much," the Ferret admitted. "Jurgen?"

Jurgen shrugged. "We shoot any witnesses, of course." He tapped one trouser pocket, which was cut away to reveal the butt of a silenced pistol peeping out of a leg holster. The uniforms weren't very authentic—but then, they only had to mislead witnesses for a few seconds. "If we can't cross back because of a surveyor's error, we turn the barrow upside down and Kurt stands on it. I ride him. Yes?"

The Ferret nodded to his companion. "My lord earl, there we are. Simple, sweet, with minimal room for things to go wrong."

The earl nodded thoughtfully. His eyes flickered between the two soldiers. Did they suspect that the thumbwheel on the payload's timer-controller had been modified to detonate six minutes earlier than the indicated time? Probably not, else they wouldn't be standing here. "If we'd been able to survey inside this, this five-sided structure . . ."

"Indeed. Unfortunately, my lord Hjorth, it is the most important administrative headquarters of their military, and it was attacked by their enemies only two years ago. The visitors' car park is as close as we could get. The payload"—the Ferret patted the stubby metal cylinder—"is sufficient to the job."

"Well, then." Earl Oliver Hjorth managed a strained smile. "I salute your bravery. Good men!"

Jurgen's cheek quirked. "I'm certain that there will be no trouble, my lord."

"Everyone in the witch-kingdom expects to see fire extinguishers in stairwells," added the Ferret, not bothering to explain that the keg-sized payload looked utterly unlike a fire extinguisher. "And it won't be there long enough for anyone to tamper with it." Strapped to the detonation controller, it weighed nearly ninety kilos; there was a reason for the carefully surveyed crossing point, the wheelbarrow, and the two strong-backed and incurious couriers.

"Good," the earl said briskly. He pulled out a pocket watch and inspected the dial. "Fifty-six minutes, I see. Is that the time? Well, I must be going now." He nodded at the Ferret. "I expect to see you in Dankfurt by evening."

"And the men, sir," prompted the Ferret.

"Oh yes. And you." Hjorth glanced at the uniformed couriers. "Yes, we shall find a suitable reward for you. I must be going."

With that, he turned and clambered down the ladder, followed by his bodyguard. Together, they squelched towards the rowboat that waited at the water's edge. It would carry them to the other side, and thence to the carriage waiting to race him away down the post road, so that he would be a couple of leagues distant before the clocks counted down to zero.

Just in case something went wrong at the last moment. You could never be too sure, with these devices.

The Explorer rumbled slowly down a narrow road near Andover, thick old-growth trees blocking the view to either side. Harold Parker State Forest wasn't exactly the back end of nowhere, but with thousands of acres of hardwood and pine forest, campground and logging roads, and day trippers moving in and out all summer, it was a good place to disappear. Miriam sat back with her eyes closed, trying to fend off the sickening sense of impending dread. It was happening again: the sense of her life careering out of control, in the hands of—*Stop that*, she told herself. Half the occupants of the big SUV were sworn to her, bound by oaths of fealty; the rest were—*If I can't trust them, I can't trust* anybody.

It was turning into a recurring motif. Just as she tried to get a handle on her life and steer a course for herself, someone would try to *look after* her, usually with disastrous consequences. Betrayal, destabilization, chaos, and—as often as not—deaths. She'd thrown a party two days ago, inviting friends and possible allies to sound them out about a new venture—a whole new political program, in fact, not simply a business idea—only to receive heavy-handed hints about matters more properly handled by Clan Security. And today she'd come to talk to Earl-Major Riordan about them, only to learn that her worst suspicions were if anything an understatement of the problem: that the stick-in-the-mud faction, fearful of change, were on the edge of all-out revolt—

—had in fact revolted, that event possibly triggered by the very fact of her absence from the royal court; and other matters out of nightmare were in train, the Clan's stolen atomic weapons lost and possibly deployed. So here they were, bumping along a logging road towards a secret, undisclosed location where Clan Security maintained a cache of equipment and a doppelgangered transfer house—

The SUV was slowing. Miriam opened her eyes. "Nearly there," Sir Alasdair grunted.

Riordan was still glued to his cell phone, nodding occasionally between bursts of clipped hochsprache. Miriam tapped him on the shoulder. He held up a hand. "Be right back," he told his absent conversationalist. "What is it?"

"If there's a mole inside ClanSec, how do you know your Plan Black site hasn't been rigged?" she asked. "If I was trying to mousetrap you, I can't think of a better way to do it than scaring you into running for a compromised rendezvous."

Riordan looked thoughtful. Miriam noticed Sir Alasdair's shoulders tense. Brilliana chirped up from the back row of seats: "She's right, you know."

"Yes," Riordan said grudgingly. "But we need to evacuate—"

"It can be booby-trapped here, or in the Gruinmarkt," Olga pointed out, her voice icy cold. "If here, we can deal with it. Over there—we shall just have to reconnoiter, no?"

"Sounds like a plan," said Sir Alasdair. "Who are we expecting here, my lord?"

"This site is meant to be held by Sir Helmut's second lance."

Riordan sounded thoughtful as he stared at the screen of the tablet PC in his lap. "Two over here, six over there with two active and four in recovery or ready for transfer. The site on the other side is a farmhouse, burned out during the campaign, I'm afraid, but defensible."

"Can you identify them?" asked Brilliana.

"By sight, yes, most probably. Outer-family aspirants, a couple of young bloods—I can show you their personnel files, with photographs. Why?"

"Because if I see the wrong faces on duty I want to be sure before I shoot them."

The Explorer was slowing. Now Sir Alasdair took a sharp left onto a dirt trail barely any wider than the SUV. "We're about two hundred yards out," he warned. "Where do you want me to stop?"

"Right here." Riordan glanced at Brilliana. "Are you ready, my lady?"

Brill nodded, reaching into her shoulder bag to pull out a black, stubby gun with a melted-looking grip just below the muzzle and a box magazine stretching along the upper surface of the barrel. "Sir Alasdair—"

"I'm coming too," rumbled Miriam's head bodyguard. He pulled the parking brake. "My lord, would you care to take the wheel? If a quick withdrawal is required—"

"I can drive," Miriam heard herself saying. "You don't need me for anything else, and I'm sure you need your hands?"

Riordan glanced at her, worried, then nodded. "Here's the contact sheet." He passed the tablet PC back to Brill, who peered at it for a few seconds.

"Okay, I am ready," she announced, and opened her door.

For Miriam, the next few minutes passed nightmarishly slowly. As Alasdair and Brill disappeared up the track and into the trees alongside it, she took Sir Alasdair's place behind the wheel, adjusting the seat and lap belt to fit. She kept the engine running at a low idle, although what she'd do if it turned out to be an ambush wasn't obvious—backing up down a dirt trail while under fire from hostiles didn't seem likely to have a happy outcome. She sighed, keeping her eyes on the road ahead, waiting.

"They know what they're doing," Olga said, unexpectedly.

"Huh?" Miriam swallowed an unhappy chuckle.

"She's right," added Riordan. "I would not have let them go if I thought them likely to walk into an ambush."

"But if they—"

Someone was jogging down the track, waving. Miriam focused, swallowing bile. It was Brill. She didn't look happy.

"Wait here." Olga's door opened; before Miriam could say anything, she was heading towards Brill. After a brief exchange, Brill turned and headed back up the path. Olga returned to the Explorer. "She says it's safe to proceed to the shack, but there's a problem." Her lips were drawn tight with worry.

"You'd better go," Riordan added. "We're on a timetable here."

"We're—" *Oh.* Miriam put the SUV in gear and began to crawl forward. *It's an evacuation plan; they've got to figure on hostiles blowing it sooner or later, so . . .* She'd seen enough of the Clan's security machinations in action to guess how it went. Wherever they were evacuating through, the safe house—shack?—would be anything but safe to someone arriving after the cutoff time.

The track curved around a stand of trees, then down an embankment and around another clump to terminate in a clearing. At one side of the clearing stood a windowless shack, its wooden slats bleached silvery gray by the weather. Brilliana stood in front of the padlocked door, white-faced, her P90 at the ready in clenched hands. "Park here," said Olga, opening her door again.

Miriam parked, then climbed down from the cab. "Where's Alasdair?" she asked, approaching Brill.

Brill shook slightly. "Milady, he's gone across already. Please *don't go there*—" But Miriam had already seen what was round the side of the shack.

"What happened?" she demanded. "Who are they?" Riordan

had also seen; he knelt by the nearer of the two bodies, examining it. Lying facedown, dressed in hunting camouflage jacket and
trousers, they might have been asleep. Miriam stared at Riordan,
then back at Brill. "What happened?" she repeated.

"They were waiting for us." Brill's voice was robotic, unnat-
urally controlled. "They were not the guards we expected to see.
That one"—Riordan was straightening up—"I recognized him.
He worked for Henryk."

Riordan was holding something at arm's length. As he came
closer, Miriam recognized it. "Silenced," Riordan told her, his
voice overcontrolled as he ejected the magazine and worked the
slide to remove the chambered round. "An assassin's weapon."

Brill nodded, her face frozen; but something in the set of her
shoulders unwound, slumping infinitesimally.

"Oh my god." Miriam felt her knees going weak. "What's
Sir Alasdair walking into?"

"I don't know." Brill took a deep breath. "I wouldn't want
to be in their shoes. Don't worry, my lady, he'll try to save one of
them for questioning."

Miriam shivered. Her sense of dread intensified: not for herself, but for Alasdair. The man-mountain had already saved her
life at least once; deceptively big and slow, he could move like an
avalanche when needs must. "What are they doing here?"

"If I had to guess, I'd say the conservatives think they're inside our OODA loop." Olga looked extremely unhappy. "This
has to have been planned well in advance. My lady, I beg your
indulgence, but would you mind waiting in the truck? It has
been modified—there is some lightweight armor—it would set
my mind at ease."

"Really?" Miriam fought back the urge to scream with frustration.

"Lady Olga, allow me." Brill touched Miriam's arm. "Walk
with me."

Brill led Miriam back up the track, just beyond the bend.
"What's going to—"

Brill cut across her, her voice thick with tension. "Listen, my lady. In a couple of minutes, two of us—I would guess the earl and myself—will have to cross over, piggyback. *If* the map is truthful, *if* Sir Alasdair has been successful at his task, I will return. Then Lady Olga will have to carry you across, while the returnee recovers their wits. If I don't come back you should assume that we are both dead and that before we died we betrayed your presence here to your enemies. In which case you and Lady Olga must *drive like hell* then go to ground and lose yourselves as thoroughly as you can imagine. Because if Earl-Major Riordan is dead or captured, our enemies will have accomplished their end, and all they need you for is to bring the heir to term and then . . . they won't need you anymore. Do you understand? Do you *understand*?"

Brill's grip on her wrist was painful. Miriam nodded, jerkily. "How long?" she managed.

"About . . . hmm. No more than five minutes." Brilliana's lips quirked. "If Sir Alasdair ran into trouble and we can't fix it, we'll come back. No false heroics. So you see? If I don't come back soon, it's because I can't."

"You could be walking into an ambush." Her heart was going too fast, Miriam realized distantly.

"We could but we won't." Brill nodded her head at the uphill slope. "What do you think that is?"

"That's a—" Miriam stopped. "Oh. *Clever.*"

"Yes." The ground level in the Gruinmarkt didn't always match the level in this world. World-walking tended not to go too well if the world-walker arrived several meters above ground level; and it didn't work at all if they tried to cross over inside a solid object. "The shack is the primary location, but there's a secret secondary. At the crest of the ramp, step off the track to the left, about six feet, then cross over. There's an outhouse, and you come out at roof level with a clear field of fire." Brill hefted her gun. "Listen, go back to the truck and wait with Lady Olga." She smiled diffidently: "It will work out, you see."

Near a small town in Pennsylvania, six miles north of Camp David, Highway 16 runs through rolling hills and open woodland, past the foot of a low mountain called Raven Rock.

A casual visitor turning off the highway onto Harbaugh Valley Road wouldn't see much: a wire mesh fence and a narrow track off to one side, and a sign warning of a restricted area. But if they drove up the road a couple of miles it would be another story—assuming the armed guards didn't stop them first. Tucked away behind the trees on top of the mountain there was a huge array of satellite dishes and radio masts. And beneath the ground, buried under many meters of bedrock, lay the Raven Rock Mountain Complex, home of the Alternative National Military Command Center, the 114th Signal Battalion, and the emergency operations centers for the army, navy, air force, joint staff, and secretary of defense.

Of course, a casual visitor wouldn't have seen the visitors arriving in the back of unmarked black Lincoln Town Cars with smoked windows, that sat oddly low on their suspension. They wouldn't have seen the thick steel doors that opened inside the low, windowless buildings, or the downward-sloping tunnel that cut into the ground, or the elevators and cranes and the blast doors set into the side of the tunnel. Indeed, there was no such thing as a casual visitor at the concrete-and-steel-lined installation embedded in the ground beneath the motel and golf club buildings.

Welcome to the Undisclosed Location.

In a compact, brightly lit conference room ninety feet below the ground, the vice president sat with his advisors, watching television. They had a lot of television to watch; a rack of six sets covered half a wall, flicking through channels on a twenty-second cycle. Bloomberg, CNN, Fox News, and C-SPAN played tag with the Cartoon Network and Discovery Channel on four monitors; two others were permanently tuned to NBC and the view from a traffic camera overlooking a street intersection in Dupont Circle.

The vice president leaned back in his chair, stretching his arms, and glanced at the skinny Yalie with his lapel-pin crucifix and rimless spectacles. "This is the boring part," he confided. "We used to come down here and game these scenarios every month or so during the nineties, you know. All weekend long. Used to be the Russkies on the other side, or the Iranians. They'd set up their opening move, we'd set up our response, and then we'd see how it all played out, whether or not we locate and kill the threat before it activates, which branch of the crisis algorithm we go down. The trouser legs of terror." He chuckled, a throaty laugh that terminated in a bubbling cough. "So. Do you think they're bluffing?"

Dr. Andrew James glanced past his boss, at the empty chair where State's assistant secretary ought to be sitting if this session wasn't classified FAMILY TRADE–only. "I couldn't say for sure, sir, but that phone call sounded promising." He gestured at the desk telephone in front of him, beige and stuffed with buttons with obscure labels that only made sense to the NSA eggheads who designed these gadgets. "The call terminated promptly."

"Good," WARBUCKS said vehemently. "Gutless bastards."

"We don't know for sure that it terminated as intended, sir," James warned. "The adversary's INFOSEC is pretty good for an amateur operation, and the bugging transcript from contact FLEMING indicates at least one of them was concerned about the bait phone."

"They got the message, either way. Bart, is there any noise on the Continuity side?"

"Nothing new, sir." Bart, a graying DISA apparatchik, was hunched over a laptop with a trailing cable patched into a wall jack—a SIPRNet connection. "They're all just standing by. SECDEF is aboard KNEECAP on the ramp at Andrews AFB, standing by for JEEP with short-notice takeoff clearance. BOY WONDER is in the EOB as usual. Uh, message from SECDEF. He wants to know if you've got an update."

"Tell him no"—WARBUCKS stared at the wall of televisions, then reached behind his left ear to adjust the multichannel earpiece—"but if they don't send us a message within the next twenty-four hours I think they're probably going to fold. I just want him where—want backup. This *could* go wrong."

Dr. James's BlackBerry buzzed for attention. Glancing down at its screen, he froze. "Sir."

"Speak."

"SIGTRADE just issued a RED FLASH—some kind of coded signal. It's running through their network—" The machine buzzed again. "Uh, right. Something is going on. Post six reports surveillance subjects all just freaked. They're moving, and it's sudden."

WARBUCKS closed his eyes. "Round 'em up, then. That's plan—which plan—"

Another aide riffled hastily through a ring binder. "Would that be HEAD CRASH, sir? Track and disable immediate, then hood and ship?"

"That's the one." WARBUCKS nodded. "Send it," he told Bart. "And tell them I want hourly head counts and updates on everything—misses as well as arrests."

In private, behind locked doors, the discussion took a different shape.

"Sit down, Jim. Have a whisky?"

"Yes, please." James Lee settled into the overstuffed armchair and waited while his father—Elder Huan's nephew Shen—filled two crystal tumblers from a hip flask and ensconced himself in the room's other armchair. His den was furnished in conventional Western style, free of exotic affectations or imported reminders of the Middle Empire here; just two overstuffed armchairs, a battered mahogany bureau from the inventory of a retired ship's captain, and a wall of pigeonholes and index files. The Lee family's decidedly schizophrenic relationship with New Britain was tilted to the Occident, here; but then, Dad had always been a bit of an Anglophile. "How's Mother keeping? And Angelina? I haven't seen them lately—"

"Neither have I, Jim. We write, regularly—Xian says all is well and they're enjoying the peace in the summer house near Nan Shang." Nan Shang in what would be California, two worlds over—or the Middle Empire in the world where the eastern seaboard belonged to the marcher kingdoms. With the fiscal crisis in full flow, and latterly the riots and disorder, many of the family's elders had deemed it prudent to send their dependents away to safety. While the Lee extended family were nothing like as prominent in the West as the six Eastern families had become in the East, their country estates were nevertheless palatial. "The postal service is still working. Do you want me to—"

"No, I'm sorry, Father. Just curious. You wanted a chat?"

"Yes." His father was silent for a few seconds. Then: "What is your opinion of the doctor? Did you have an opportunity to form an opinion of him during your stay with the cousins?" During the six months during which James had been a pampered hostage.

"I didn't know him well, Father. But—you want my honest opinion? He's a worm. A most dangerous, slimy, treacherous worm."

"Strong words." The lightness of his father's tone was belied by his sour face. "Do you have reason for it?"

"I believe so. I don't think he told Eldest any outright untruths, but nothing he said was quite right, either. He was telling the truth when he said he was the personal physician to many of the Eastern cousins' womenfolk, but he was also . . . not as put-upon as he would have you believe. He said he earned the undying hatred of the woman Helge—and he was telling the truth there, too. But Helge didn't impress me as being anybody's fool. She's neither naive nor stupid, and when we had time to talk— there's something unpleasant underneath this excess of servility on his part, Father. I can't tell you precisely what he's hiding, but he's hiding *something*."

"That much was obvious from his performance." Shen took a sip of whisky. "I don't think Mei is serious about finding him a wife—unless she means to set the Widow Ting on him." James flinched; avoiding cousin Ting and her dangerous games had been one of his wiser moves. "I gather she's itching to marry again. That would make . . . three? Four? No matter. It is perfectly clear that the doctor is as twisty as a hangman's noose. What your uncle would like to know is—can he deliver what he offered?"

"I don't know." James paused. "You may know more than I, Father. Is it true that Helge is with child?"

For a long moment his father stared into his tumbler. "It might be so."

"Because." James licked his lips. "Before the Per—before the youngest son's rebellion, she was held prisoner and securely chaperoned. And I met the heir to whom she was betrothed. *He* wasn't going to do any begetting on her. There was unsavory whispering about some of ven Hjalmar's works, among the servants I cultivated. Some said that the man was an abortionist. Others accused him of drugging and raping noblewomen—a story I find incredible, under the circumstances described. What is true is that the Clan's ladies, whom he served, made use of a hospital or clinic in the United States, which he helped run. I know *that* much. And Helge was leashed for poking her nose into some business that sounds very like this baby clinic he offered to elder Yuan. So: I believe he is mostly telling the truth—again, only mostly."

"What do you think he plans ?"

"What he—" James stopped. "You can't be thinking of working with him! He's a viper. He's stung two masters already, why would he stop short of making it three? It's in his nature!"

"Calm down, boy, I'm not making that decision!"

"I'm sorry, Father."

"That is good. Don't worry unduly—we trust him no more than you do. But we need to have some idea of his goals before we can decide whether to make use of him or not. If he can deliver what he offers—perhaps as many as five hundred world-walkers within ten years—that is a matter of enormous significance! We would not have to worry about the Eastern cousins after that. It would open up new business possibilities, ways of making ourselves useful to those in authority—whoever they may be, when the current incivility dies down—new blood in our thinning arteries. *Can he do it?* That is what my brother asks. If he can, then we can use him: tie him down, shadow his work, and eventually take it over. But if he's a mere charlatan"—Shen made a dismissive gesture, casting the shadow of ven Hjalmar over his left shoulder—"we know how to deal with that, too."

James tried again: "I think it's unwise—"

"You have made that clear already!" his father snapped. "Your opinion is *noted*. But the decision-making is for your elders; they must balance the safety and needs of the family against the risks involved in taking this asp to our breast. All my brother needs from you now is an assessment—is what he says *possible*?"

James took a deep breath, embarrassment and anger warring. "I . . . I can't deny it. From what the Eastern cousins were saying, when they had no reason to guard their tongues—yes, very possibly."

"Thank you." Shen lifted his tumbler. "I think it best if we do not include you in the discussion; you are, perhaps, too close to its subjects. I agree with your assessment of the doctor's character—but even serial traitors may be useful to us on occasion. Especially if we know their weaknesses. Which is why I ask again: What do you believe his goals are?"

James frowned. "What goals? Beside keeping his head on his shoulders?"

Shen leaned forward. "Has it gone that far?"

"He did something to Helge that angered her greatly. And she is pregnant, with an heir to the throne of Gruinmarkt that is universally acknowledged as such by the Eastern cousins, who say something about a, uh, *DNA paternity check*, whatever that might be. Are they fools, Father? Is *she* a fool? I think those rumors about drugs and rape are . . . not true, exactly, but close. Ven Hjalmar got Lady Helge pregnant with seed from the royal line—then his patron died, and he must run for his life. He wants money, sanctuary, and time to continue his work—which is this breeding program. He wants to use us, Father, that's what I think."

"Ah." His father relaxed, smiling at last. He raised his glass. "And you think that's all?"

"I wouldn't swear to it, but—"

"It'll do." Shen took a sip. "Thank you, son. I think I can discuss this with Eldest now."

James's shoulders sank. "You think Uncle will take Dr. ven Hjalmar on."

"Yes." Shen's smile widened. "But don't worry. He will be under control. . . ."

The second thing to catch Miriam's attention was the mingled smells of scorched wood and warm blood. The first was managing to control her fall; being carried piggyback was hard enough when the steed was a strapping young soldier, never mind a physically fit but lightly built younger woman. As Miriam and Olga disentangled themselves, Miriam looked around curiously. They'd come through in the target area once a deeply relieved Brill had confirmed that the zone was secure, and it was Miriam's first chance to see the havoc that the Pervert's army had inflicted on the Clan's outlying minor steadings.

One farmhouse looked much like another to her eye—in the Gruinmarkt they tended to be thick-walled, made from heavy logs or clay bricks depending on the locally available materials— but this one bore clear signs of battle. The roof of one wing was scorched and blackened, and the window shutters on the central building had been wrecked. More to the point—

"Who—" she began, as Olga raised a hand and waved at the armed man standing guard by the door.

"My lady!" He went to one knee. "Lord Riordan awaits you in the west wing."

"Rise, Thom. Where are Knuth and Thorson?" Olga was all business, despite what had to be a splitting headache.

"We haven't seen ear nor tail of them since they crossed over yesterday." The guard's eyes widened as he looked at Miriam: "Is this—"

"Yes, and you don't need to make a scene over me," she said hastily. Turning to Olga: "The other two—they're your missing guards?"

"Let us discuss that indoors." Olga nodded at the farmstead's front door, which stood ajar. Thom followed behind like an over-eager dog, happy his mistress was home. "I think Knuth and Thorson are probably dead," she said quietly. "The two who were waiting for us definitely weren't them."

Miriam nodded, jerkily. "So they were assassins? Just there to kill whoever turned up?"

"Whoever turned up at the duty staff officer's primary evac-uation point, yes." The picture was clear enough. The evac point had been guarded by a lance of soldiers, two on the American side and six in the Gruinmarkt. The assassins had murdered the two guards in the state park, then planned on catching Earl Ri-ordan and his colleagues as they arrived, one by one. They hadn't anticipated a group who, forewarned, arrived expecting skullduggery. "I expect Lady d'Ost will try and find where they hid the bodies before she comes hither to report. Come on in-side, my lady."

The farmstead was a wreck. The guards had made a gesture towards clearing up, pushing the worst of the trashed furniture and shattered kitchenware up against one wall and sweeping the floor—the pretender's cavalry had briefly used it as a stable—but the scorch marks of a fire that had failed to take hold still streaked the walls, and there was a persistent, faint aroma of rot-ting meat. The guards had brought out camp chairs and a folding table, and Riordan had set up his headquarters there, organizing the guards to man a shortwave radio and track unfolding events on a large map. He looked up as Miriam arrived. "Welcome, Your Majesty."

"How bad is it?" Miriam asked.

"We're getting reports." He grimaced. "The evac plan is running smoothly and I've ordered all stations to check out the other side for unwelcome visitors. Didn't want to say why—things will be chaotic enough without setting off a panic about a civil war. The trouble is, we're fifteen miles out of Niejwein—the eye of the storm—half a day's ride; and I'm not happy about disclosing your location. In the worst case our enemies may have direction-finding equipment, and if they've got their hands on Rudy's ultralight . . . we've got to sit tight as long as possible. I've ordered Helmut to bring a couple of lances here as soon as he's nailed down the Summer Palace and I've put orders out for the arrest of the entire postal committee and, I regret to say, your grandmother. We can weed that garden at our leisure once we've got it fenced in. Unless you have any other suggestions?"

"Yes." Miriam swallowed. "Is there any word of my mother? Or, or Dr. Griben ven Hjalmar? I think they're in cahoots. . . ."

Riordan glanced at one of his men and barked a question in hochsprache too fast for Miriam to follow. The reply was hesitant. "No reports," he said, turning to Miriam. "I'll let you know if anything turns up. I assume you're talking about the duke's special, ah, medical program?" Miriam nodded. "I'm on it. Now, if you wouldn't mind—" He looked pointedly at the security guard with the radio headset, who was waving urgently for attention.

"Go to it." Miriam shuffled awkwardly aside, towards the doorway into the burned-out wing of the farmhouse. "What do we do now?" she asked Olga.

Olga grimaced. "We wait, my lady. And we learn. Or *you* wait, I have orders to send. Please." She gestured at the bedrolls on the hard-packed floor. "Make yourself comfortable. We may be here some time."

Twenty years ago, in the rookeries of a town called New Catford, Elder Huan had known a young and dangerous radical—a Leveler and ranter called Stephen Reynolds.

In those days, Huan had been the public face of the family's business involvements—a discreet railroad for money and dispatches that the underground made use of from time to time. Reynolds had been Huan Lee's contact, and for a while things had gone swimmingly. Few organizations had as great a need for secrecy as the Leveler command, and indeed Huan had toyed with the idea of disclosing the family's secret to him—for the family's singular talent and the needs of the terrorists and bombthrowers and other idealists were perfectly aligned, and the pogroms and lynchings of the English, tacitly encouraged by the government (who knew a good target for the mob's ire when they saw it—and skin of the wrong color had always been one such), did nothing to endear the authorities to him. At least the revolutionaries preached equality and fraternity, an end to the oppression of all races.

A series of unfortunate events had closed off that avenue before Huan started down it; raids, arrests, and executions of Leveler cells clear across the country. He, himself, had been forced to world-walk in a hurry, one jump ahead of the jackboots of the Polis troopers. And that had been the end of *that*. The first duty of the family was survival, then profit—martyrdom in the name of revolutionary fraternity wasn't part of the package. In the wake of the raids he'd thought Stephen Reynolds dead—until he heard the name again, in a broadcast by the revolutionary propaganda ministry. Reynolds had survived and, it seemed, prospered in the council of the Radical Party.

This didn't entirely surprise Elder Huan. As he had described it to his brothers, some time later, "The man is a rat—sharp as a wire, personally courageous, and curious. The Polis will have a hard time taking him." And now the fox was in charge of a hen coop of no small size, having emerged in charge of the Annapolis Freedom Riders, then promoted to organize the Bureau of Internal Security that the party had formed to replace the reactionary and untrustworthy Crown Polis.

Now Elder Huan—through conduits and contacts both esoteric and obscure—had arranged for a meeting with the man himself. The agenda of the meeting was to be the renewal of an old alliance. And Elder Huan intended to make Reynolds an offer that would secure the safety of the family throughout the current crisis.

For his part, Reynolds—a thickset fellow with brown hair, thinning at the crown, and half-moon pince-nez that gave him an avuncular appearance even when supervising interrogations—was looking forward to the meeting for entirely the wrong reasons.

"I want you and two squads to be ready outside the front door. Place another squad round the back. Plain clothes, two steamers ready for backup." He smiled, not warmly. Brentford, his secretary, nodded and scribbled in his notebook. "You should arrest everyone in the building or leaving it after my departure, *unless* I indicate otherwise by displaying a red kerchief in my breast pocket. Special Regime Blue, with added attention. The charges will be resisting arrest, treason, membership of a proscribed organization, and anything else that occurs to you. Have the Star Tribunal ready to sit on them and I'll sign off on the execution warrants immediately. Do you have that?"

Brentford nodded, impassive. These were not unusual orders; Citizen Reynolds took a very robust approach to dealing with subversives. "The, ah, exception, sir? Do you have any other instructions to deal with that case?"

"No." Reynolds made a fist, squeezing. "If anything comes up I'll handle it myself."

"The danger, sir—"

"They're petty smugglers and racketeers, citizen. I dealt with them before, during the Long Emergency; it's almost a certainty that they want to deal themselves a hand at the table, in which case they're in for a short, sharp surprise. I merely reserve the final judgment *in case* there's something more serious at hand." He stood, behind his desk, and straightened his uniform tunic, flicking invisible dust motes from one black lapel. "Plain clothes, I say again. I'll see you at eight."

Reynolds strode to the door as Brentford saluted. He didn't look back. Brentford was a reliable party man, a typical functionary of the new organization: He'd do as he was told, and look up to Reynolds as a bluff fellow who led from the front, as long as he occasionally indulged in eccentricities such as periodically going into the field to gather up nests of vipers and traitors with his own hands.

Reynolds didn't smile at the thought. There were risks attached to this behavior, and he didn't hold with taking risks unless there was something he held to be personally important at stake. Maintaining his carefully constructed public image was all very well, but placing himself in front of a desperate fugitive's knife was . . . it was *undignified*. On the other hand, sometimes it was necessary to deal with former Polis informers himself, to insure that they fell downstairs or swallowed their suicide pills. He considered it to be a small mercy—far less unpleasant than what fate held in store for them in the ungentle hands of his enthusiastic staff in Interrogations and Inquiries.

Citizen-Commissioner Stephen Reynolds was more than willing to go into the field in person and meet past friends— especially if it meant that he could silence them before they could spill their guts to the interrogators in the BIS basements.

The venue Eldest Huan had chosen for the meeting was a tiny front-room bar in a public house in Menzies Gate, a run-down suburb on the edge of what, in another world, would be called Brooklyn. His foot soldiers had paid the owner handsomely to take his wife and six children and two servants and move out for the night: a three-month amnesty from protection money, *and* a wallet bulging with ration coupons. "I want privacy," Huan had told One-Eye Cho, "and I want a safe exit. See to it." The pub, unbeknownst to its owner, was colocated with a trackless forest clearing in the northern Sudtmarkt—one carved out with sweat and axe and saw by Cho's sons. Eldest had dealt with Reynolds before, and with the Polis, and was under no illusions about the hazards of dining with devils in Secret Security Police uniforms. "Place two reliable bearers in the exit, and two armed guards. Find someone who can pass as white, and put him behind the bar with a shotgun to cover my retreat. He can be the bartender. Put another in the kitchen, who can at least provide cold cuts and soup if our guest is hungry."

The pub was a theater: Reynolds and Huan had both prepared scripts for the other's benefit. The only question remaining was that of whose review would be more favorable.

Eight o'clock; the sky was still bright, but the shops were mostly shuttered, the costermongers and peddlers and rag-and-bone men and beggars had mostly slunk away, and the front windows of the pub were dark. Reynolds surveyed it professionally as he approached along the pavement. He'd swapped his uniform for a suit of clothes as ill-fitting—even moth-nibbled—as any he had worn during the long desperate years on the run. On the far side of the road, a couple of dusty idlers clustered near a corner; he glanced away. Down the street, a steamer sat by the curb, curtains drawn in its passenger compartment. All was as it should be. He nodded, then turned back towards the door and rapped the head of his cane on it twice.

A spy-slot slid aside. "We're shut."

"Tell your master an old friend calls." Reynolds kept his voice low. "Remember New Catford to him."

The spy-slot closed. A moment later, the door opened. Reynolds slid inside.

The pub was indeed short on customers, but as the barman shot the bolts and returned to his place, Reynolds was intrigued by the appearance of the couple sitting at the one sound table, each with a glass of beer to hand. The old Chinaman he recognized, after a pause: It was indeed the gangmaster and smuggler from New Catford who had called himself Cheung. But who was the middle-aged white man? *Questions, questions.* Reynolds smiled broadly as he approached the table and Cheung stood.

"Ah, Citizen Reynolds!" cried Cheung—Reynolds suppressed a wince—and the other fellow stood, somewhat slowly. "How wonderful to see you prospering so in these harsh times. Please, this is my associate Dr. ven Hjalmar, a physician. Please have a seat. Beer? Spirits? Have you eaten?"

Reynolds negotiated the social minefield and sat, without glancing at the bartender—whose impassivity told him more than he needed to know about his loyalties. *Most professional,* he decided: Cheung clearly knew what he was about. Which suggested a simple wrap-up might be difficult—but then, the presence of the doctor implied that this might be rather more complex than the usual pathetic blackmail attempt. "A beer would be welcome. I gather you had a business proposal you wanted to bring to my attention?"

"Oh yes, indeed." Cheung smiled happily. "To your very good health!" He raised his glass. Reynolds perforce followed suit and submitted to another five minutes of trivial niceties. "We considered putting some elements of this proposal to you all those years ago, in Catford, but the unfortunate excess of zeal displayed by the Polis impressed upon us the need for discretion. Now, however, anything we choose to confide in you is unlikely to be beaten out of you by the royalist inquisitors. So: another toast, to our future business success!"

Reynolds blinked as he answered the toast: This was very much *not* what he'd been expecting. "I'm afraid you have the better of me," he admitted. "What business do you have in mind?"

Cheung glanced around before he replied. "You must have realized that I had a most effective way of moving dispatches and contraband between locations, without fear of interception." Reynolds nodded. "Well, that . . . mechanism . . . is still available. And I believe that, given the nature of your current engagement, you might very well find a use for it." Reynolds nodded again, slightly perturbed. *What's he on about?* he wondered. Cheung beckoned at the bartender. "Scott. Please come and stand in front of Citizen Reynolds, then make yourself scarce. Have Ang report to me in five minutes."

The bartender—Scott—bowed slightly, then stepped in front of the table. "Observe," he told Reynolds. He looked away, in the direction of the archway leading to the kitchen. Then he vanished.

"This is our family secret," Reynolds heard Cheung saying behind him as he waved his arms through the thin air where Scott had stood: "We can walk between worlds. We have had to hold this to ourselves, in utter confidence, for generations; I'm sure you can imagine the consequences if word were to leak out in public. However, I know you to be a man of utmost probity and integrity, and in your new and elevated rank, I am certain you will recognize the desirability to keep this a secret as close to your chest as any matter of state. I brought the doctor along because he can explain to you the origins, transmission, and limits of our family talent better than I; it is hereditary, and we have never met any people to whom we are not blood kin who can do it. . . ."

Reynolds swallowed: His heart was hammering. "Business," he said hollowly. "*What* business?" He turned round slowly. Where had Scott gone? Was he behind him? Waiting with an axe—

"I want to put my family at your service," said Cheung. His expression was bland. "I am certain you will find our unique talent very valuable indeed. These are dangerous times; the party has many enemies. I hope that you—we—will better be able to defend it if we can come to a working agreement?"

Reynolds licked suddenly dry lips. "How many of you are there?" he asked.

"Seventy adults, able to perform at will, and their children. Two hundred other relatives, some of whose offspring may be able to do so. And Dr. ven Hjalmar has a proposal that will, I am sorry to say, strike you as something out of a philosophical romance, but which may revolutionize our capacity in the longer term, ten years or more."

Reynolds glanced round again, just as a young man—half a head shorter than the absent Scott—appeared out of thin air, bowed deeply to him, and moved to take up his station behind the bar. He swallowed again, mind churning like a millrace. "How much do you want?" he asked.

Cheung smiled. "Perhaps Dr. ven Hjalmar should start by telling you exactly what is on sale. We can discuss the price later . . ."

7/16

On the ninth floor of a department store just off Eighteenth Street NW in Washington, D.C., there was a
locked janitor's closet. Earlier that morning the police
had been busy downstairs. A security guard had been found
dead in a customer restroom, evidently the victim of an acciden-
tal heroin overdose. Nobody, in the ensuing fuss, had felt any
need to fetch cleaning supplies from this particular closet, and
so, nobody had discovered that the door was not only locked but
the lock was jammed, so that the key wouldn't turn.

Because nobody had visited the room, nobody had called a
locksmith. And because the door remained locked, nobody had
noticed the presence of an abandoned janitor's trolley, its cylin-
drical plastic trash can weighted down by something heavy. Nor
had anyone, in an attempt to move the trolley, discovered that its
wheels were jammed as thoroughly as the lock on the door. And
nobody had raised the lid on the trash can and, staring inside,

recognized the olive-drab cylinder for what it was: a SADM—storable atomic demolition munition—in its field carrier, connected to a live detonation sequencer (its cover similarly glued shut), a very long way indeed from its designated storage cell in a bunker at the Pantex plant in West Texas.

The janitor's store was approximately 450 meters—two blocks—away from Lafayette Square and, opposite it, the White House; and it was about ten meters above the roofline of that building.

The detonation sequencer was, at heart, little more than a countdown timer—a milspec timer, with a set of thumbwheels to enter the permissive action codes, and more thumbwheels to enter the countdown time and desired yield. Beneath the glued-down cover were additional test and fault lights and switches. From the timer emerged a fat cable that screwed onto a multi-pin socket on the outside of the bomb carrier. Inside the carrier nestled one of the smallest atomic bombs ever assembled, so compact that a strong man with a suitable backpack frame could actually carry it. But not for much longer.

Eleven-sixteen and twelve seconds, on the morning of July 16, 2003.

Stop all the clocks. All of them.

It was a regular summer day in Washington, D.C. Open-topped tourist buses carried their camera-snapping cargo around the sights on Capitol Hill—itself something of a misnomer, for the gentle slope of the Mall was anything but mountainous—past the reflecting pool, the Washington Monument, the museums and administrative buildings and white stone–clad porticoes of power. In hundreds of offices, stores, restaurants, and businesses around the center ordinary people were at work.

Like Nazma Hussein, aged twenty-six, daughter of Yemeni immigrants, married to Ali the cook, cleaning and setting out tables in the front of her family's small lunch diner on K Street NW, worrying about her younger sister Ayesha who is having trouble at school: Papa wants her to come and work in the restaurant until he and Baba can find her a suitable husband, but Nazma thinks she can do better—

Like Ryan Baylor, aged twenty-three, a law student at GWU, hurrying along H Street to get to the Burns Law Library and swearing quietly under his breath—overslept, forgot to set his alarm, got a reading list as long as his arm and a hangover beating a brazen kettledrum counterpoint to the traffic noise as he wonders if those cans of Coors were really a good idea the evening before a test—

Like Ashanda Roe, aged twenty-eight, working a dead-end shelf-stacking job in a 7-Eleven on D Street NW, sweating as she tears open boxes of Depends and shoves them into position on an end galley, tossing the packaging into a rattly cage and whistling under her breath. She's worrying because her son Darrick, who is only seven, is spending too much time with a bunch of no-good kids who hang out with—

Six thousand, two hundred and eighty-six other people, ordinary people, men and women and children, tourists and natives, illegal immigrants and blue bloods, homeless vagrants and ambassadors—

Stop all the clocks.

In the grand scheme of things, in the recondite world of nuclear war planning, a one-kiloton atomic bomb doesn't sound like much. It's less than a tenth the yield of the weapon that leveled the heart of Hiroshima, a two-hundredth the power of a single warhead from a Minuteman or Trident missile. But the destructive force of a nuclear weapon doesn't correspond directly to its nominal yield; a bomb with ten times the explosive power doesn't cause ten times as much destruction as a smaller one.

Oliver Hjorth's first bomb detonated at twelve seconds past eleven-sixteen, on the ninth floor of a steel-framed concrete department store about a third of a mile from the White House.

Within a hundredth of a second, the department store building and everything else on its block vanished (along with fifty-seven staff and one hundred and fourteen shoppers), swallowed by a white-hot sphere of superheated gas and molten dust. The department store's neighbors, out to a radius of a block, survived a fraction of a second longer, their stone and concrete facades scorching and beginning to smoke, until the expanding shock wave, air compressed and flash-heated to thousands of degrees, rammed into them like a runaway train.

Beyond the immediate neighborhood, the shock wave dissipated rapidly, reflecting off concrete and asphalt and thundering skywards in a bellowing roar that would, a little over a minute later, be audible in Baltimore. And beyond a couple of blocks' radius, only the most unlucky bystanders—those standing where they were caught with a direct line of sight down Seventeenth Street or H Street—would be exposed to the heat pulse, their skin charring and their eyes burned out by the flash.

But within a third of a mile, the destruction was horrendous.

Nazma Hussein saw a flash out of the corner of her eye, like a reflection from the noonday sun, only more brilliant. Looking up, she glanced at the window: But it was nothing, and she looked back at the table she was laying out cutlery on, and deposited another fork on the place mat just as the shock wave arrived to throw a thousand glittering plate-glass knives through her face and abdomen.

Ryan saw a flash on the ground in front of him, and winced, closing his eyes as a wave of prickly heat washed over the back of his head and neck. He inhaled, his nostrils flaring. Flashes sparkled inside his eyelids as he smelled burning hair. His scalp ablaze, he drew breath to scream at the excruciating pain. But then the wind caught him with one hand, and the law library building with another, and clapped them together. And that was all he knew. A small mercy: He would not live to suffer the slow death of a thousand REMs that he had been exposed to, or the fourth-degree burns from the heat flash.

Ashanda was lucky. Working in the back of the store, she saw no flash of light, but heard a roar like a truck piling into the front of the building. The ground shook as the lights failed, and she fell to the floor, screaming in alarm. The rumbling went on for much too long, and she closed her eyes and prayed that it wasn't an earthquake; but who in D.C. had ever imagined an earthquake striking here? As the vibration faded, she pulled herself to her knees, then up to her feet. People were moaning in the front of the shop, but without lights she might as well be blind. She began to fumble her way back to the stockroom door, still shaky, praying that Darrick was all right.

The White House, although originally built in the late eighteenth century, had been reconstructed in the mid-twentieth around a steel load-bearing frame. With stone walls and a steel skeleton, it was by no means as fragile as its age might suggest; but the Truman-era structure wasn't designed to withstand a nuclear blast at close range, and in time of war the president was supposed to be elsewhere.

The White House survived the heat flash, but the shock wave took barely a second to surge down the street. By the time it hit the West Wing it was traveling at just over three hundred miles per hour, with an overpressure slightly over six pounds per square inch—funneled by the broad boulevard—and the force of a tornado.

BOY WONDER, the forty-third president of the United States, was chatting informally with his deputy chief of staff and special assistant (whose windowless office in the middle of the first floor of the West Wing was perhaps the most eavesdropper-proof location in the entire federal government) when the shock wave hit.

It would never be determined precisely why the president was visiting his campaign manager, chief political strategist, and senior advisor, rather than vice versa; it was perhaps a reflection of the importance of this secretive political operative to the administration. But the location of R's lair, in the middle of a warren of offices on the first floor, meant that none of its occupants could have had any warning of the catastrophe. Perhaps the lights flickered and dimmed as the White House's backup power supply kicked in, and perhaps they stared in annoyance at the dead phones in their hands; but before anyone had time to walk as far as the office door, the masonry, concrete, and stone of the West Wing was struck by a pile driver of compressed air. Just over six pounds per square inch sounds far less impressive than just under nine hundred pounds per square foot, but they are the same thing. Worse: The compressed air in the wave had to come from somewhere. As the shock wave passed, it left behind an evacuated zone, where the air pressure had dropped precipitously, swinging the strain on the building's structure from positive pounds to negative. It was a lethal whiplash of pressure, five times worse than a direct strike by a tornado.

Had the West Wing been built of modern reinforced structural concrete it might have survived, albeit with severe damage. But it wasn't, and the falling ceiling respected neither rank nor titles of nobility.

Eleven seconds later, the second bomb detonated. This one had been planted on the top floor of the Holocaust Museum on Fourteenth Street SW, just off Independence Avenue and two blocks away from the Mall.

Perhaps Earl Hjorth had meant to target Congress; if so, he'd been overoptimistic—situated over a mile away, the Capitol suffered external blast damage and many of its windows were blown in, but aside from shrapnel injuries, a number of flash fires ignited by the detonation, and severe damage to the outside of the dome, the Capitol was not seriously affected.

Not so the cluster of federal agencies around the Mall. FEMA and the FBI were both less than three thousand feet from ground zero; and pity the employees of the Department of Agriculture, across the road from the museum. More than eleven thousand people, mostly government employees and tourists, were directly affected by the second bomb, half of them killed by heat flash or shock wave as the rippling blast tore the heart out of the federal government.

And then there was the third bomb.

Eleven-sixteen and thirty-eight seconds. Two figures in desert fatigues bearing sergeant's stripes—Kurt and Jurgen, who were in fact, by grace of his lordship Baron Griben ven Hjalmar, sergeants-at-arms of the post—appeared out of nowhere on the second floor of a car park adjacent to the Pentagon, one of them standing and the other sprawling atop a wheelbarrow that also contained an olive-drab cylinder.

"*Scheisse,*" said Jurgen, as Kurt swung his feet over the side of the barrow and stood up. Beneath the low concrete roof half the theft alarms of half the vehicles in the park were shrilling in an earsplitting cacophony that filled the head and threatened to overflow when he opened his mouth, a profoundly unnatural counterpoint to the low rumbling from outside.

"This way." Kurt, eyes flickering side-to-side, pointed along a line of parked trucks and SUVs towards a bare concrete wall with a fire door. Jurgen swallowed bile, picked up the handles of the wheelbarrow, tried to ignore the nausea in his stomach. His feet lurched side-to-side as he shoved the heavy load towards the stairwell. "*Two minutes.*"

"Two? Okay." Jurgen nodded. Everything was crystal clear, suffused with a luminosity of migraine. The Boss couldn't be blamed for taking these little precautions, he could see that. "How about here—"

"No, we want a stairwell—"

"You! Freeze!" Jurgen stumbled. The guard who had just stepped out of the stairwell—*Why is there a guard here?*—had his M16 raised. "Identify yourselves! Sir!" The military courtesy didn't in any way detract from the pointed message of the assault rifle. This wasn't in the plan. Jurgen's head pounded.

"What's happening?" called Kurt.

"Full lockdown. Badges, *now!*" Another siren joined the

clamoring car alarms—this one full-voiced and deep, the stentorian honking of a building alarm.

Kurt raised his left hand, then reached inside a trouser pocket.
Time slowed to a crawl as he rolled sideways towards a parked
F250. Jurgen dropped the barrow's handles and broke right, div-
ing for the opposite side of the row to take cover behind a Toyota
compact. As he reached for his Glock, an earsplitting crackle of
full-auto fire echoed from one end of the car park to the other.
Grounded behind the Toyota, he rose to kneel, raised his pistol,
and returned fire through the car's windows—not aimed, but sup-
pressive. He winced with each pull of the trigger as the reports
rammed ice picks into his already aching head. He couldn't be
sure, but Kurt seemed to be shooting, too. Another hammer-drill
burst of automatic fire, then the guard's weapon fell silent.

"Kurt, wer ist—"

The harsh bang of another pistol shot was followed almost
immediately by the irregular snap of rifle fire, and Kurt ducked,
heart hammering and mouth dry. *There's more than one of
them,* he realized, icy horror settling into his belly. The plan was
simple enough—he'd brought Kurt over, Kurt was to carry him
back—but with him pinned down behind this automobile, there
was no way that was going to work. He swallowed and rubbed
his left sleeve against the car, trying to expose the temporary tattoo on his wrist. If world-walking twice in five minutes didn't
kill him, there was a good chance a three-floor fall would do the
job, but the ticking nightmare in the barrow was an even more
certain exit ticket.

"Ish' vertrich nu!" He shouted, then stared at the knot on his
wrist until it expanded into a white-hot pain between his eyes.

Falling. Into silence.

Behind him, ten meters up the aisle from where Jurgen's bleeding body lay, twenty meters from the sentries crouched behind a
Humvee, the thing in the wheelbarrow emitted a click, then a muffled bang, and finally a wisp of smoke that coiled towards the ceiling. The detonation sequencer had done its job, but this particular
FADM had missed its last maintenance check due to a book-

keeping irregularity. The constant warm rain of neutrons from the high-purity plutonium pit had, over the years, degraded the detonators distributed around its shell of high explosives. Overdue for tear-down and reconstruction half a decade ago, the bomb failed to explode; instead, the long-term storable core began to burn, fizzing and smoldering inside its casing.

Not all the detonators had degraded. When the high explosive sphere finally blew seventy seconds later, it killed four marine guards as they advanced from truck to truck, closing in on the hostiles' last known location. But the blast was unsequenced and asymmetric. Rather than imploding the weapon's pit and triggering a fission chain reaction, it merely fragmented it and blasted chunks of hot plutonium shrapnel into the surrounding cars and concrete structure of the car park.

July 16, 2003, eleven o'clock and thirty minutes, local time; fighters roared, circling overhead. Beneath the leaden, smoldering skies the clocks had stopped, the telephone exchanges dead and muffled by the electromagnetic pulses. And though the survivors were stirring, shocky and dazed but helping one another shuffle away from the burning holes of the city in every direction—north, south, east, and west—nothing now would ever come to any good.

Stop all the clocks.

ÐAMAGE CONTROL

I
t had taken Steve nearly an hour to get Fleming out of his office, during which time he'd gotten increasingly irritated with the skinny, intense agent's insistence that some insane conspiracy of interdimensional nuclear narcoterrorists was about to blow up the Capitol. *Why do the fruitcakes always pick on* me? he kept wondering.

Of course the explosion in Braintree checked out—gas mains, according to the wire feed. But that was no surprise: It was the sort of detail a paranoid would glom onto and integrate into their confabulation, especially if it happened close to their front door. One of the first warning signs of any delusional system was the conviction that the victim was at the center of events. Tom Brokaw wasn't reading the news, he was sending you a personal message, encrypted in the twitches of his left eyebrow.

Sure Fleming didn't seem particularly unhinged—other than

insofar as his story was completely bugfuck insane and required the listener to suspend their belief in the laws of physics and replace it with the belief that the government was waging a secret war against *drug dealers from another dimension*—but that meant nothing. Steve had been a beat journalist for years before he found his niche on the tech desk. Journalists attract lunatics like dog turds attract flies, and he'd listened to enough vision statements by dot-com CEOs to recognize the signs of a sharp mind that had begun to veer down a reality tunnel lined with flashing lights and industrial espionage. So he'd finally cut Fleming off, halfway down a long, convoluted monologue that seemed to be an attempt to explain how Beckstein had got his attention—not without qualms, because Fleming sounded halfway to stalkerdom when he got onto the subject of rescuing her from some kind of arranged marriage—and raised his hand. "Look," he said wearily, "this is a bit much. You said they made you translate tapes. And there are these lockets they use for, what did you call it, world-walking. Do you have any kind of, you know, physical evidence? Because you can appreciate this is kind of a complex story and we can't run it without fact-checking, and—"

Fleming stood up. "Okay." He looked exasperated. "I got it."

Steve peered up at him owlishly. "I don't want to blow you off. But you've got to see—they'll laugh me out of the meeting if I can't back this up with something physical. And this isn't my department. I'm not the desk editor you're looking for—"

Fleming nodded again, surprising him. "Okay. Look," he glanced at his watch, "I'll phone you again after they make their move. I don't think we'll have long to wait. Remember what I said?"

Steve nodded back at him, deadpan. "Atom bombs."

"You think I'm nuts. Well, I'm not. At least I don't *think* I am. But I can't afford to stick around right now. Let's just say, if a terrorist nuke goes off in one of our cities in the next week, I'll be in touch and we can talk again. Okay?"

"You got it." Steve clicked his recorder off. "Where are you going?"

"That would be telling." Fleming flashed him a feral grin, then ducked out of the cubicle. By the time Steve levered himself out of his chair and poked his head around the partition, he was gone.

"Who was that?" asked Lena from real estate, who was just passing with a coffee.

"J. Random Crank. Probably not worth worrying about—he seemed harmless."

"You've got to watch them," she said worriedly. "Sometimes they come back. Why didn't you call security?"

"I wish I knew." Steve rubbed his forehead. The shrill buzz of his phone dragged him back inside the cubicle. He picked up the receiver, checking the caller ID: It was Tony in editorial. "Steve speaking, can I—"

"Turn on your TV," Tony interrupted. Something in his tone made Steve's scalp crawl.

"What channel?" he demanded.

"Any of them." Tony hung up. All around the office, the phones were going mad. *No, it can't be,* Steve thought, dry-swallowing. He moused over to the TV tuner icon on his desktop and double-clicked to open it. And saw:

Two lopsided mushroom clouds roiling against the clear blue sky before a camera view flecked with static, both leaning towards the north in the grip of a light breeze—

"Vehicles are being turned back at police checkpoints. Meanwhile, National Guard units—"

A roiling storm of dust and gravel like the aftermath of the collapse of the Twin Towers—

"Vice president, at an undisclosed location, will address the nation—"

A brown-haired woman on CNN, her normal smile replaced by a rictus of shock, asking someone on the ground questions they couldn't answer—

People, walking, from their offices. Dirty and shocked, some of them carrying their shoes, briefcases, helping their neighbors—

"Reports that the White House was affected by the attack cannot be confirmed yet, but surviving eyewitnesses say—"

A flashback view from a surveillance camera somewhere looking out across the Potomac, *flash* and it's gone, blink and you've missed it—

"Residents warned to stay indoors, keep doors and windows closed, and to drink only bottled—"

Minutes later Steve stared into the toilet bowl, waiting for his stomach to finish twisting as he ejected the morning's coffee grounds and bile. *I had him in my office,* he thought. *Oh Jesus.* It wasn't the thought that he'd turned down the scoop of a lifetime that hurt like a knife in the guts: *What if I'd listened to him?* Probably it had been too late already. Probably nothing could have been done. But the possibility that he'd had the key to averting this situation sitting in his cubicle, trying to explain everything with that slightly flaky twitch—the man who knew too much—that was too much to bear. Assuming, of course, that Fleming was telling the truth when he said he wasn't the guy behind the bombs. *That* needed checking out, for sure.

When he finally had the dry heaves under control he straightened up and, still somewhat shaky, walked over to the washbasins to clean himself up. The face that stared at him, bleary-eyed above the taps, looked years older than the face he'd shaved in the bathroom mirror at home that morning. *What have we done?* he wondered. The details were in the dictaphone; he'd zoned out during parts of Fleming's spiel, particularly when it had been getting positively otherworldly. He remembered bits—something about mediaeval antipersonnel mines, crazy stuff about prisoners with bombs strapped to their necks—but the big picture evaded him, like a slippery mass of jelly that refused to be nailed down, like an untangled ball of string. Steve took a deep breath. *I've got to get Fleming to call in,* he realized. A faint journalistic reflex raised its head: *It's the story of a lifetime.* Or the citizen's arrest of a lifetime. *Is a nuclear unabomber even possible?*

J. Barrett Armstrong's office on the tenth floor was larger than Steve Schroeder's beige cubicle on the eighth. It had a corner of the building to itself, with a view of Faneuil Hall off to one side and a mahogany conference table the size of a Marine Corps helicopter carrier tucked away near the inner wall of the suite. It was the very image of a modern news magnate's poop deck, shipshape and shining with the gleaming elbow grease of a dozen minimum-wage cleaners; the captain's quarters of a vessel in the great fleet commanded by an Australian news magnate of some note. In the grand scheme of the mainstream media J. Barrett Armstrong wasn't so high up the totem pole, but in the grand scheme of the folks who signed Steve's paychecks he was right at the top, Thunderbird-in-chief.

Right now, J. Barrett Armstrong's office was crowded with managers and senior editors, all of whom were getting a piece of the proprietor's ear as he vented his frustration. "The fucking war's *over*," he shouted, wadding up a printout from the machine in the corner and throwing it at the wall. "Who did Ali get the bomb from? There's the fricking story!" A bank of monitors on a stand showed the story unfolding in repeated silent flashbacks. "How did they smuggle them in? Go on, get digging!"

Nobody noticed Steve sneaking in until he tapped his boss, Riccardo Pirello, on the shoulder. Rick turned, distractedly: "What is it?"

"It's not Iraq," said Steve. He swallowed. "It's narcoterrorists, and the nukes were stolen from our own inventory."

The boss was belting out orders to his mates and boatswains: "Bhaskar, I want an in-depth on the Iranian nuclear program, inside spread, you've got six pages—"

Steve held up his dictaphone where Riccardo could see it. "Scoop, boss. Walked into my office an hour ago."

"A—what the fuck—" Riccardo grabbed his arm.

Nobody else had noticed; all eyes were focussed on the Man, who was throwing a pocket tantrum in the direction of enemies both Middle Eastern and imaginary. "Let's find a room," Steve suggested. "I've got my desk line patched through to my mobile. He's going to call back."

"Who—"

"My source." Steve's cheek twitched. "He told me this would happen. I thought he was crazy and kicked him out. He said he'd phone after it happened."

"Jesus." Riccardo stared at him for a moment. "Why *you*?"

"Friend of a friend. She went missing six months ago, investigating this, apparently."

"Jesus. Okay, let's get a cube and see what you've got. Then if it checks out I'll try and figure out how we can break it to Skippy without getting ourselves shitcanned for making him look bad."

The atmosphere in the situation room under Raven Rock was a toxic miasma of fury, loss, and anticipation: a sweaty, testosterone-breathing swamp of the will to triumph made immanent. From the moment the PINNACLE NUCFLASH alert came in, WARBUCKS hunched over one end of the cramped conference table, growling out a torrent of unanswerable questions, demanding action on HEAD CRASH and CLEANSWEEP and other more arcane Family Trade projects, issuing instructions to his staff, orders for the Emergency Preparedness and Response Directorate and other sub-agencies within the sprawling DHS empire. "We're still trying to raise the EOB, sir," said one particularly hapless staffer.

"I don't want to hear that word *trying*," snarled WARBUCKS. "I want *results*. Success or failure. Clear?"

The TV screens were clear enough. Andrew James couldn't help staring at the hypnotic rewind footage from time to time, the sunny morning view of downtown D.C., the flash and static-riddled flicker, the rolling, boiling cloud of chaotic darkness shot through with fire rising beyond the Capitol. The close-ups replaying every ten minutes of the Washington Monument blow-down, chunks of rock knocked clear out of the base of the spire as the Mach wave bounced off the waters of the reflecting pool, cherry trees catching fire in a thousand inglorious blazing points of light. Inarticulate anchormen and women, struggling with the enormity. Talking heads, eyes frozen in fear like deer in the headlights, struggling to pin the blame on Iraqi revenants, Iranian terrorists, everyone and anyone. *Northwoods,* he thought. *He made it work.* Nobody else in the national command structure had ever had the sheer brass balls to pull that particular trigger, to play power chords in the key of the Reichstag Fire on the instrument of state—

"Dr. James."

He tore his eyes away from the screen. "Sir?"

WARBUCKS grinned humorlessly. "I want to know the status of SCOTUS as of this morning. I very much fear we'll be needing their services later today and I want to know who's available."

James nodded. "I can find out. Do you want me to expedite the draft order on Family Trade just yet?"

"No, let's wait for confirmation. BOY WONDER will want to pull the trigger himself once we brief him, assuming he survived, and if not, I need to be sworn in first. Otherwise those bastards in Congress will—"

"Sir?" Jack Shapiro, off the NSA desk just outside the conference room, stuck his head round the door. "We've got eyeballs overhead right now, do you want it on screen?"

WARBUCKS nodded. "Wait one, Andrew," he told Dr. James. "Put it on any damn screen but Fox News, okay?"

Two minutes later the center screen turned blue. Static replaced the CNN news crawl for a moment; then a grainy, gray, roiling turbulence filled the monitor from edge to edge. A flickery head-up display scrawled barely readable numbers across the cloudscape. Shapiro grimaced, his face contorted by the telephone handset clamped between neck and shoulder. "That's looking down on the Ellipse," he confirmed. "The chopper's standing off at six thousand feet, two thousand feet south of ground zero—it's one of the VH-3s from HMX-1, it was on station at Andrews AFB when . . ." He trailed off. WARBUCKS was staring at the picture, face frozen.

"Where's the White House?" he demanded hoarsely.

"About"—Shapiro approached the screen, pointed with a shaking finger—"there." The splash of gray across more gray was almost unrecognizable. "Less than six hundred yards from ground zero, sir. There *might* be survivors—"

Dr. James quietly pushed his chair back from the table, turned away from the screens, and stood up. A DISA staffer took over the chair even before he cleared the doorway. The corridor outside was cramped and overfull with aides and officers busily waiting to see the Man. All of them showed signs of agitation: anger and fear and outrage vying for priority. *Patience,* James told himself. *The end times haven't begun—yet.* WARBUCKS would be a much better president than BOY WONDER (the bumbling dry-drunk scion of a political dynasty had inherited his dad's presidential mantle but not his acumen); and in any case, a presidential martyrdom pardoned all political sins.

Dr. James headed for the communications office. His mind, unlike almost everyone else's, was calm: He knew exactly what he had to do. Find out where the surviving Supreme Court Justices were, locate the senior surviving judge, and get him here as fast as possible to swear in the new president. *Then we can clean house.* Both at home and in the other world God had provided for America, as this one was filling up with heathens and atheists and wickedness. *There will be a reckoning,* he thought with quiet satisfaction. *And righteousness will prevail.*

Steve Schroeder had barely been back at his desk for ten minutes when he received another visit. This time it was Riccardo, with two other men Steve didn't recognize but who exuded the unmistakable smell of cop. "Mr. Schroeder," said the tall, thin one. "Mr. Pirello here tells me you had a visitor this morning."

Steve glanced at Riccardo. His boss's forehead was gleaming under the fluorescent tubes. "Tell him, Steve."

"Yes," Steve admitted. "Do you have ID?"

The short fireplug in the double-breasted suit leaned towards him: "You don't get to ask questions," he started, but the thin man raised a hand.

"Not yet. Mr. Schroeder, we're from the FBI. Agent Judt." He held an ID badge where Steve couldn't help seeing it. "This is my colleague, Agent Fowler. It would make things much easier if we could keep this cordial, and we understand your first instinct is to treat this as a news investigation, but right now we're looking at an unprecedented crime and you're the first lead we've found. If you know anything, *anything* at all, then I'd be very grateful if you'd share it with us."

"If there's another bomb out there and you don't help us, you could be charged with conspiracy," Agent Fowler added in a low warning rumble. Then he shut up.

Steve took a deep breath. The explosions kept replaying behind his eyelids in slow motion. He breathed out slowly. "I'm a bit . . . freaked," he admitted. "This morning I had a visit from a man who identified himself as a DEA agent, name of Fleming. He spun me a crazy yarn and I figured he was basically your usual run-of-the-mill paranoid schizophrenic. I didn't check his ID at the time—tell the truth, I wanted him out of here. He said there'd be nukes, and he'd call back later. I've got a recording"—he gestured to his dictaphone—"but that's about it. All I can tell you is what he told me. And hope to hell he gets back in touch."

Agent Fowler stared at him with an expression like a mastiff contemplating a marrowbone. "You sent him away."

Fear and anger began to mix in the back of Steve's mind. "No, what I sent away was a *fruitcake*," he insisted. "I write the information technology section. Put yourself in my shoes—some guy you don't know comes to visit and explains how a secret government agency to deal with time travelers from another universe has lost a bunch of atom bombs accidentally-on-purpose because they want the time travelers to plant them in our cities—what would you do? Ask him when he last took his prescription? *Show him the door*, by any chance?"

Fowler still stared at him, but after a second Agent Judt nodded. "Your point is taken," he said softly. "Nevertheless . . ."

"You want to wait until he makes contact again, be my guest." Steve shuddered. "He might be a fruitcake, or he might be the real thing; that's not my call. I assume you guys can tell the difference?"

"We get fruitcakes too," Judt assured him. Riccardo was being no help: He just stood there in front of the beige partition, eyes vacant, nodding along like a pod person. "But we don't usually get them so close to an actual, uh, *incident.*"

"Act of war," Fowler snarled quietly. "Or treason."

Fleming didn't ask for anonymity, Steve reminded himself. Which left: handing a journalistic source over to the FBI. Normally a huge no-no, utterly immoral and unjustifiable, except . . . this wasn't business as usual, was it? "I'll help you," Steve said quietly. "I want to see you catch whoever did it. But I don't think it's Fleming you want. He said he was trying to get the word out. If he planted the bombs, why spin that cock-and-bull story in the first place? And if he didn't plant them, but he knew where the bombs were, why *wouldn't* he tell me?"

"Leave the analysis to us," suggested Agent Judt. "It's our speciality." He pointed at the dictaphone. "I need to take that, I'm afraid. Jack, if you'd like to stay with Mr. Schroeder just in case the phone rings? I'm going to bring headquarters up to speed, get some backup in." He looked pointedly at Riccardo. "You didn't hear any of this, Mr. Pirello, but it would be very helpful to me if you could have someone in your building security department provide Agent Fowler and me with visitor badges, and warn the front desk we're expecting colleagues."

Riccardo scuttled away as soon as Judt broke eye contact. Then he turned back to Steve. "Just wait here with Jack," he said reassuringly.

"What if Fleming phones? What do I do?" Steve demanded.

"Answer it," said Fowler, in a much more human tone of

voice. "Record it, and let me listen in. And if he wants to set up a meet—go for it."

In a cheap motel room on the outskirts of Providence, Mike Fleming sat on the edge of an overstuffed mattress and poured a stiff shot of bourbon into the glass from the bathroom. His go bag sat on the luggage rack, leaking the dregs of his runaway life: a change of underwear, a set of false ID documents, the paperwork for the hire car in the parking lot—hired under a false name, paid for with a credit card under that name. The TV on the chest of drawers blatted on in hypermanic shock, endless rolling reruns of a flash reflecting off the Potomac, the collapsing monument—for some reason, the White House seemed to be taboo, too raw a nerve to touch in the bleeding subconscious of a national trauma. He needed the bourbon, as a personal anesthetic: It was appallingly bad tradecraft, he knew, but right now he didn't feel able to face reality without a haze of alcohol.

Mike wasn't an amateur. He'd always known—always—that a job could blow up in his face. You didn't expect that to happen, in the DEA, but you were an idiot if you didn't take precautions and make arrangements to look after your own skin. It was surprisingly easy to build up a false identity, and after one particular assignment in Central America had gone bad on him with extreme prejudice (a local chief of police had turned out to be the brother-in-law of the local heroin wholesaler) he'd carefully considered his options. When Pete Garfinkle had died, he'd activated them. It made as much sense as keeping his gun clean and loaded—especially after Dr. James had earmarked him for a one-way ticket into fairyland. They weren't forgeries, they were genuine, legal ID: He didn't use the license to get off speeding tickets, and he paid the credit card bill in full every time he used it. They were simply an insurance policy for dangerous times, and ever since he'd gotten back home after the disastrous expedition into Niejwein a couple of months ago, he'd been glad of the driving license and credit card taped inside a video cassette's sleeve in the living room.

From Steve Schroeder's office he'd taken the elevator down to street level, caught a bus, switched to the Green Line, changed train and commuter line three times in thirty minutes, then hopped a Chinatown bus to New York, exiting early and ultimately ending up in a motel in Providence with a newly hired car and a deep sense of foreboding. Then, walking into the motel front desk, he'd seen the endless looping scenes of disaster on CNN. It had taken three times as long as usual to check in. One of the two clerks on duty was weeping, her shoulders shaking; the other was less demonstrative, but not one hundred percent functional. "Why do they *hate* us?" the weeping one moaned during a break in her crying jag. "Why won't they leave us alone?"

"Think Chemical Ali did it?" Three months ago it would have been Saddam, before his cousin's palace coup on the eve of the invasion.

"Who cares?"

Mike had disentangled himself, carefully trying not to think too hard about the scenes on the TV. But once he got to his room, it hit him.

I tried to do something. But I failed.

A vast, seething sense of numbness threatened to swallow him. *This can't be happening, there must be some way out of here, some way to get to where this didn't happen.* But it *had* happened; for better or worse—almost certainly for worse—Miriam's enemies had lashed out at the Family Trade Organization in the most brutal way imaginable. Not one, but two bombs had gone off in D.C. Atomic bombs, the all-time nightmare the DHS had been warning about, the things Mike had been having nightmares about for the year since Matthias walked into a DEA office in downtown Boston with a stolen ingot of plutonium in his pocket.

No way of knowing if Schroeder had taken him seriously. He'd felt the argument slipping away, Schroeder's impatience visibly growing as he tried to explain about the Clan, and about the FTO project to wrap them up and then to infiltrate and attack their home bases. He hadn't even gotten as far as his contact with Miriam's mother, Olga the ice princess, the business about negotiation. He could see Schroeder's attention drifting. And if he couldn't convince one man who'd known Miriam and wondered where she'd gotten to, what hope was there?

Maybe if I hadn't asked the colonel, weeks ago, he speculated. Colonel Smith was Air Force, on secondment to FTO by way of a posting with NSA. He understood chains of command and accountability and what to do about illegal orders. Not like that shadowy spook-fucker, Dr. James. *But they blew up my car.* They'd *expected* him to run somewhere. Smith might already be dead. *If I'd smuggled some of the tapes out*—tapes of conversations in hochsprache, recorded by someone with access to the Clan's innermost counsels—but that was nuts, too. The whole setup in that office was designed to prevent classified materials from going AWOL.

Where do I go, now?

Tired and sweaty and stressed and just a little bit numb from the bourbon, Mike sank back against the headboard and stared at the TV screen. Two diagonal columns of smoke, one of them almost forming the classic mushroom, the other bent and twisted out of recognizable shape. Again and again, the Washington Monument's base blasted sideways out from under it, the peak falling. Helicopter footage of the rubble, now, eight- and nine-story office blocks stomped flat as if by a giant's foot. Preliminary estimates of the death toll already saying it was worse than 9/11, much worse. Anchormen and women looking shocked and almost human under their makeup, idiotically repeating questions and answers, hunting for meaning in the meaningless. Interviews with a survivor on a gurney, bandaged around one side of their head, medevac'd to a hospital in Baltimore.

What's left that I can do?

The vice president, somber in a black suit—someone had found a mourning armband for him somewhere—mounting a stage and standing behind a lectern. Balding, jowly, face like thunder as he answered questions in a near-constant waterfall of flashbulb flickering. Promising to find the culprits and punish them. Make them pay. This man whom the Clan's consigliere had named as their West Coast connection. A whey-faced Justice Scalia stepping forward to administer the oath of office. President WARBUCKS. Dire warnings about the Middle East. Appeals for national unity in the face of this terrorist threat. Promises of further legislation to secure the border. State of emergency. State of complicity.

Where can I run?

Mike lifted his glass and took another mouthful. Knowing too much about the Family Trade Operation was bad enough; knowing too much about the new president's darker secrets was a one-way ticket to an unmarked roadside grave, sure enough. And the hell of it was, there was probably no price he could pay that would buy his way back in, even if he *wanted* in on what looked like the most monstrously cynical false-flag job since Hitler faked a Polish army attack on his own troops in order to justify the kickoff for the Second World War. *I need to be out of this game,* he realized blearily. Preferably in some way that would defuse the whole thing, reduce the risk of escalation. *Stop them killing each other, somehow.* It seemed absurdly, impossibly utopian, as far beyond his grasp as a mission to Mars. So he took another sip of bourbon. He had a lot of driving to do tomorrow, and he needed a good night's sleep beforehand, and after what he'd seen today . . . it was almost enough to make him wish he smoked marijuana.

Even revolutions need administration: And so the cabinet meeting rooms in the Brunswick Palace in New London played host to a very different committee from the nest of landowning aristocrats and deadwood who'd cluttered John Frederick's court just three months earlier. They'd replaced the long, polished mahogany table in the Green Receiving Room with a circular one, the better to disguise any irregularities of status, and they'd done away with the ornate seat with the royal coat of arms; but it was still a committee. Sir Adam Burroughs presided, in his role as First Citizen and Pastor of the Revolution; as for the rest of them . . .

Erasmus arrived late, nearly stepping on the heels of Jean-Paul Dax, the maritime and fisheries commissioner. "My apologies," he wheezed. "Is there a holdup?"

"Not really." Dax stepped aside, giving him a sharp glance. "I see your place has moved."

"Hmm." Burgeson had headed towards his place at the right of Sir Adam's hand, but now that he noticed, the engraved nameplates on the table had been shuffled, moving him three seats farther to the right. "A mere protocol lapse, nothing important." He shook his head, stepping over towards his new neighbors: Maurits Blanc, commissioner of forestry, and David McLellan, first industrial whip. "Hello, David, and good day to you."

"Not such a good day. . . ." McLellan seemed slightly subdued as Erasmus sat down. He directed his gaze at the opposite side of the round table, and Erasmus followed: *Not much chivalry on display there,* he noticed. A tight clump of uniforms sat to the left of Sir Adam: Reynolds, along with Jennings from the Justice Directorate, Fowler from Prisons and Reeducation, and a thin-faced fellow he didn't recognize—who, from his attitude, looked to be a crony of Reynolds's. A murder of crows, seated shoulder-to-shoulder: What kind of message was *that*?

"Is Stephen feeling his oats?" Erasmus murmured, for McLellan's ears only.

"I have no idea." Burgeson glanced at him sharply: McLellan's expression was fixed, almost ghostly. Erasmus would have said more, but at that precise moment Sir Adam cleared his throat.

"Good morning, and welcome. I declare this session open. I would like to note apologies for absence from the following commissioners: John Wilson, Electricity, Daniel Graves,

Munitions—" The list went on. Erasmus glanced around the table. There were, indeed, fewer seats than usual—a surprise, but not necessarily an unwelcome one: the cumbersome size of the revolutionary cabinet had sometimes driven him to despair.

"Now, to the agenda. First, a report on the rationing program. Citizen Brooks—"

Erasmus was barely listening—making notes, verging on doodles, on his pad—as the discussion wandered, seemingly at random, from department to department. He knew it was intentional, that Sir Adam's goal to was to insure that everyone had some degree of insight into everyone else's business—*transparency*, he called it—but sometimes the minutiae of government were deathly boring; he had newspapers and widecasters to run, a nagging itch to get out in front and cultivate his own garden. Nevertheless he sat at ease, cultivating stillness, and trying to keep at least the bare minimum of attention on the reports. Tone was as important as content, he often felt: You could often tell fairly rapidly if someone was trying to pull the wool over your eyes, simply by the way they spun out their words.

It was halfway through Fowler's report that Erasmus began to feel the first stirrings of disquiet. "Construction of new reeducation centers is proceeding apace"—Fowler droned portentously, like a well-fed vicar delivering a slow afternoon sermon—"on course to meet the goal of one center per township with a population in excess of ten thousand. And I confidently expect my department to be able to meet our labor obligation to the Forestry Commission and the Departments of Mines and Transport—"

Did I just hear that? Burgeson blinked, staring at Fowler and his neighbors. *Did I just hear the minister for prisons boast that he was supplying labor quotas to mines and road-building units?* The skin on the back of his neck crawled. Yes, there were a lot of soldiers in the royalist camp, and many prisoners of war—and yes, there was a depression-spawned crime wave—but handing a profit motive to the screws stuck in his throat. He glanced around the table. At least a third of the commissioners he recognized had done hard time in the royal labor camps. Yet they just sat there

while Fowler regurgitated his self-congratulatory litany of mana-
cles refastened and windows barred. *That can't be what's going
on,* he decided. *I must have misheard.*

Next on the agenda was Citizen Commissioner Reynolds's
report—and for this, Erasmus regained his focus and listened attentively. Reynolds wasn't exactly a rabble-rousing firebrand, but
unlike Fowler he had some idea about pacing and delivery and the
need to keep his audience's attention. "Thank you, citizens. The
struggle for hearts and minds continues"—he nodded at Erasmus,
guilelessly collegiate—"and I would like to congratulate our colleagues in propaganda and education for their sterling work in
bringing enlightenment to the public. However, there remains a
hard core of wreckers and traitors—I'd place it at between two
and eight percent—who cleave to the discredited doctrine of the
divine right of kingship, and who work tirelessly and in secret to
undermine our good works. The vast majority of these enemies
work outside our ranks, in open opposition—but as the party has
grown a hundredfold in the past three months, inevitably some of
them have slipped in among us, stealthy worms crawling within
to undermine and discredit us.

"A week ago, Citizens Fowler, Petersen, and I convened an
extraordinary meeting of the Peace and Justice Subcommittee.
We agreed that it was essential to identify the disloyal minority
and restrain them before they do any more damage. To that end,
we have begun a veterinarian process within our own departments. Security is particularly vulnerable to infiltration by saboteurs and former revenants of the Crown Polis, as you know, and
I am pleased to say that we have identified and arrested no fewer
than one hundred and fifty-six royalist traitors in the past three
days. These individuals are now being processed by tribunals of
people's legates appointed by the Department of Law. I hope to
report at the next cabinet meeting that the trials have been con-
cluded and my department purged of traitors; when I can make
such an announcement, it will be time to start looking for op-
portunities to carry the fight to the enemy." Reynolds smiled

warmly, nodding and making eye contact around the table; there was a brief rumble of agreement from all sides.

Erasmus bobbed his head: but unlike his neighbors, he was aghast. Among the books Miriam Beckstein had lent him the year before, he had been quite taken aback by one in particular: a history of revolution in the East, not in the French Empire-in-being in the Russias, but in a strange, rustic nation ruled by descendants of Peter the Great. The picture it painted, of purges and show trials followed by a lowering veil of terror, was one of utmost horror; he'd taken some comfort from the realization that it couldn't happen here, that the bizarre ideology of the Leninists was nothing like the egalitarian and democratic creed of the Levelers. *Was I wrong?* he wondered, watching Citizen Commissioner Reynolds smiling and acknowledging the congratulations of his fellow commissioners with a sense of sickness growing in his belly: *Is corruption and purgation a natural product of revolutions? Or is there something else going on here?*

His eyes narrowing, Erasmus Burgeson resolved to order some discreet research.

It wasn't a regular briefing room: They'd had to commandeer the biggest lecture theater in the complex and it was still packed, shoulder-to-shoulder with blue and brown uniforms. Security was tight, from the Bradleys and twitchy-fingered National Guard units out on the freeway to the military police patrols on the way in. Everyone knew about the lucky escape the Pentagon had had, if only via the grapevine. The word on the floor was that the bad guys were aiming for a trifecta, but missed one—well, they *mostly* missed: Half a dozen guards and unlucky commuters were still awaiting burial in a concrete vault with discreet radiation trefoils once Arlington got back to normal. But nobody in the lecture theater was inclined to cut them any slack. The mood, Colonel Smith reflected, was hungry. He tried to put it out of his mind as he walked to the podium and tapped the mike.

"Good morning, everyone. I'm Lieutenant Colonel Eric Smith, lately of the air force, seconded to NSA/CSS Office of Unconventional Programs, and from there to an organization you haven't heard of until now. I've been instructed to bring you up to speed on our existence, mission, and progress to date. I'll be happy to take your questions at the end, but I'd be grateful if you could hold on to them for the time being. Just so you know where we're going, this is about the attack yesterday, and what we—all of us—are going to be dealing with over the next months and years."

He hit the remote button to bring up the first slide. The silence was broken by a cough from the audience; otherwise, it was total.

"For the past year I've been seconded to a black ops group called the Family Trade Organization, FTO. FTO is unlisted and draws on assets from Air Force, NSA, FBI, CIA, DEA, NRO, and the national laboratories. We're tasked with responding to a threat which was only identified thirteen months ago. That's when this man walked into a DEA office in Boston and asked for witness protection."

Click. A new slide, showing a polyethylene-wrapped brick of white powder, and a small metal ingot, side by side on a worktop. "He was carrying a kilogram of China White and a hundred-gram lump of plutonium 239, which we subsequently confirmed had been produced in one of our own breeders. This got our attention, but his story was so crazy that DEA nearly wrote him off as a kook—they didn't take the plutonium brick seriously at first. However, it checked out."

Click. Surveillance video, grainy black-and-white, showing a view of a jail cell. A prisoner is sitting on the edge of a plastic bench, alone. He glances around. Then, after a few seconds, he rolls back his left sleeve to reveal some kind of tattoo on his wrist. He raises it in front of his face. Abruptly, the cell is empty.

"Our witness claimed to be a member of a group or tribe of illegal aliens with the ability to travel between worlds. The place of origin of these aliens was initially unknown, but backward. They can will themselves between their own world—or location—and ours, by staring at a special knotwork design. They speak a language not familiar to anyone in the linguistics department at NSA, but related to low German. And they use this ability to smuggle narcotics."

Click. A slide showing an odd, crude knotwork design.

"DEA would have written source GREENSLEEVES off as a nut, but they raided one of his suggested locations and hit paydirt—a major transfer location for a cocaine distribution ring they'd been hunting for two years. At this point they began following up his leads and arrested a number of couriers. One of whom you just saw pulling a vanishing trick in front of a spy camera in a locked cell."

Click. A windowless laboratory, white glove boxes and racks of electronics bulking beside workbenches.

"The initiative came from DEA but was escalated rapidly with the backing of OSP and NSA, to establish a cross-disciplinary investigative unit. About five months ago our collaborations at Livermore confirmed that there is indeed a physical mechanism at work here. What we're looking at is not teleportation, but some sort of quantum tunneling effect between our world and a world very much like our own—a parallel universe. Other worlds are also believed to exist—many of them."

Click. Video from a camera bolted to the rear bulkhead of a helicopter's flight deck, grainy and washed out from beneath by the low light level radiance spilled from the instrument consoles: a view of darkened ridgelines.

"Project ARMBAND is now delivering prototype transfer units that can displace aircraft—or limited-scale ground forces—to what we have confirmed is this other world. There's virtually no radio traffic or sign of advanced civilization other than stuff that these—the hostiles call themselves the Clan—have stolen from us. Our intelligence take is that this is a primitive version of our own world, one where the dark ages were very dark. The Clan, people with a biologically mediated ability to tunnel through into our world and back again—we don't know where they came from, and neither do the prisoners we've been able to question. But they exist within a high mediaeval civilization along the east coast of North America, former Viking colonies. They're not Christian: Christianity and Islam are unknown in their world. They've been using their access to us to build up their own power back home."

Click. Aerial photographs of a small city. Forests loom in an untamed blanket beyond the edge of town. Only a couple of narrow roads wind between the trees. Smoke rises from chimneys. There are walls, meandering along the hilltops around the center. Some way outside them, there is a small harbor.

"This is the capital city of the local power where the Clan holds most authority, a small state called Niejwein, located roughly where downtown Boston is. Four months ago we were able to use our captured prisoners to transport a SPECOPS forward recon team into position. We've confirmed this story six ways: I'd like to emphasize this, we have an intelligence briefing on the enemy culture and you'll find it in your in-tray when you check your email. What we're dealing with is a hostile power considerably more primitive and less well organized than Afghanistan, but sitting physically right on our doorstep—collocated with us geographically, but accessible only by means of ARMBAND devices or at will to the Clan's members."

Click. An olive-drab cylinder approximately the size of a beer keg, with a green box strapped to it and connected by fat wires.

"This is an FADM, field atomic demolition munition. Third-generation descendant of the W53 tactical weapon. Twelve of them were supposed to be in storage in Pantex. Source GREENSLEEVES claimed to have stolen and emplaced one in downtown Boston as insurance when he walked in and asked for witness protection—" Smith paused. "May I continue?" He leaned close to the mike but kept his tone mild: Most of the audience outranked him considerably.

"Thank you. There was an accident subsequently when GREENSLEEVES panicked and tried to escape custody, and

GREENSLEEVES was killed; and there was some question over whether he was in fact lying. A routine inventory check reported that all the FADMs were present and accounted for. However, a month ago FTO personnel located and subsequently disarmed a device in downtown Boston, confirming that the FADM audit report was faulty. This triggered a PINNACLE EMPTY QUIVER and a full-up inspection, in the course of which it became apparent that no less than six FADMs had been stolen from Pantex at some time in the preceding three years. FADMs are on the inactive inventory and the plant was following standard asset risk management procedures for the weapon storage areas, with layered security, patrols and sensors, and secure vaults. Unfortunately our existing ARM failed to take into account the possibility that extradimensional narcoterrorists might appear inside the storage vaults, remove the weapon assemblies from their carriers, and replace them with dummies."

Smith paused. There was no point continuing right now—not with the muttering wave of disbelief and outrage—and besides, his throat was becoming sore. He raised his water bottle, then tapped the mike again.

"If I may continue? Thank you. Those of you tasked with nuclear weapons security know more about the consequences of that particular event than I do; to those who aren't, we're in the process of upgrading our risk management model and temporarily escalated security is already in place for those parts of the inventory which suffer from compromised ARM. We're not going to lose any more nukes, period.

"Meanwhile, the background to this particular empty quiver event is that DEA's initial approach to the Clan was that they were a major narcotics ring—narcoterrorists on the same scale as the Medellín Cartel, with an additional twist. Estimates of their turnover are in the four-to-six-billion-dollar-per-year range, and a membership in excess of a thousand individuals—and should be dealt with accordingly. What became apparent only later was that the scope of the threat, intrusions from another world, a parallel universe, is unprecedented and carries with it many unknown unknowns, if I may steal a phrase from the top. What we failed to appreciate at first was that the Clan were effectively a parallel government within their own nation, but not *the* government—an analogy with al-Qaeda and the Taliban in Afghanistan is apposite—and that the local authorities wanted rid of them. The situation was highly unstable. I am informed that negotiations with the Clan for return of the stolen weapons were conducted, but internal factional disputes resulted in the, the consequences we've all witnessed this week."

Which was flat-out half-truths and lies, but the real story wasn't something it was safe to talk about even behind locked doors in Crypto City: Smith's boss, Dr. James, had anticipated a response, but not on this scale. Calculations had been botched, as badly as the decision in early 2001 to ignore the festering hatred in the hills around Kabul. "We need to get the hard-liners to talk to us, not the liberals," Dr. James had explained. Nobody had anticipated that the hard-liners' idea of a gambit would be a full-dress onslaught—or if they had, they were burying the evidence so deep that even thinking that thing was a life expectancy-limiting move.

"I can't discuss the political response to the current situation," Smith continued, speaking into a hair-raising silence, "but I've been told I can mention the legal dimension. Other FTO officials are briefing their respective departments today. As of now, FTO and the existence of the extradimensional threat are no longer super-black, although the content of this briefing remains classified. The briefing process is intended to bring everyone up to speed before the orders start coming down. I've been told to alert you that a military response is inevitable—the president is meeting with the survivors of the House of Representatives and there is a briefing going on behind closed doors right now—and the War Powers Act has been invoked. White House counsel and the attorney general's office agree that the usual treaty obligations requiring a UN mandate for a declaration of war do not apply to territory physically located within our own national borders, and *posse comitatus* does not apply to parallel universes—this remains to be confirmed by the Supreme Court, but we anticipate a favorable outcome."

As three of the four Justices who died in the attack were from the liberal side of the bench—by sheer bad luck, they'd been attending an event at GWU that morning—this was an extreme understatement: The new Supreme Court, when it could be sworn in, would be handpicked to make Chief Justice Scalia happy.

Smith took a deep breath. "So, to summarize: We have been attacked by a new kind of enemy, using our own stolen weapons. But we've been studying them covertly, and we've got the tools to reach out and touch them. And we're going to show them *exactly* what happens when you mess with the United States." He stared straight at one of the generals in the front row, who had been visibly containing himself for several minutes. "Thank you for your patience. Now are there any questions?"

The floodgates opened.

The day after his failed attempt to leak all over Steve Schroeder's news desk, Mike Fleming deliberately set out to tickle the dragon's tail. He did so in the full, cold foreknowledge that he was taking a huge personal risk, but he was running short on alternatives.

Driving from motel to strip mall and around and about by way of just about any second-rate road he could find that wasn't an interstate or turnpike, Mike watched the news unfold. The sky was blue and empty, contrail-free except for the occasional track of a patrolling F-15; as on 9/11, they'd shut down all civilian aviation. The fire this time had not come from above, but few people knew that so far and as gestures went, grounding the airliners was a trivially easy way to signal that something was being done to protect the nation. It was the old security syllogism: *Something must be done, this is something, ergo this must be done.* Mike drove slowly, listening to the radio. There were police checkpoints on roads in and out of D.C.; the tattered remnants of Congress and Supreme Court were gathering at an Undisclosed Location to mourn their dead and witness the somber inauguration of the new president, a sixty-something former business tycoon from Wyoming. A presidential address to the nation scheduled for the evening: unreassuring negatives leaking from the Pentagon, *This isn't al-Qaeda, this isn't the Iranians, this is something new.* The pro-forma groundswell rumble of rage and fury at yet another unheralded and unannounced cowardly attack on the sleeping giant. The nation was on the edge of its nerves, terrified and angry. Muslim-Americans: scared. Continuity of Government legislation was being overhauled, FEMA managers stumbling bleary-eyed to the realization that the job they'd been hired for was now necessary—

At a pay phone in the back of a 7-Eleven, Mike pulled out a calling card and began to dial, keeping a nervous eye on his wrist-watch. He listened briefly, then dialed a PIN. "*Hello. You have no new messages.*"

He hung up. "Shit," he muttered, trudging back towards the front of the shop, trying hard not to think of the implications, not hurrying, not dawdling, but conserving the energy he'd need to carry him through the next day. He was already two miles away as the first police cruiser pulled up outside with its lights flashing, ten minutes too late: driving slowly, mind spinning as he tried to come up with a fallback plan that didn't end with his death.

If only Miriam's mother had left a message, or Olga the ice princess, he'd have more options open—but they hadn't, and without a contact number he was out in the cold. The only lines he could follow led back into an organization answering to a new president who had been in cahoots with the Clan's worst elements and wanted the evidence buried, or to a news editor who hadn't believed him the first time round—and who knew what Steve would think, now that the White House was a smoking ruin?

I blew it, he thought bleakly. *Dr. James has likely declared me a rogue asset already.* Which was technically correct—as long as one was unaware that James himself was in it up to his eyes. The temptation to simply drive away, to take his papers and find a new life in a small town and forget he'd ever been Mike Fleming, was intense. *But it wouldn't work in the long term,* he realized. The emergency administration would bring in the kind of internal ID checks that people used to point to when they wanted to denounce the Soviets. They'd have to: It wasn't as if they could keep world-walkers out by ramping up the immigration service. *What can I do?*

His options seemed to be narrowing down. *Work within the organization* had gone out the window with that car bomb: The organization wanted him gone. *Talk to Iris Beckstein*—about what? *Talk to the press*—no, that had seemed like a good idea yesterday: funny how rapidly things changed. He could guess what would happen if he fixed up another meeting with Steve Schroeder any time soon. Steve would try to verify his source, be coopted, spun some line about Mike being a conspirator, and reel him in willingly; and Mike had no tangible evidence to back up his claims. *Try to turn a coworker*—look how well that had worked for Pete Garfinkle. Pete had confessed misgivings to Mike; shortly thereafter he'd been put in a situation that killed him. Mike had confessed misgivings to Colonel Smith; shortly thereafter—*join up the dots.* The whole organization was corrupt, from the top down. For all he knew, the bombs—his knuckles whitened upon the steering wheel—did WARBUCKS have big enough balls to deliberately maneuver the Clan into giving him everything he wanted, on a plate? To have helped them get their hands on the bombs, and then to have provoked them into attacking the United States? Not a crippling attack, but a beheading one, laying the groundwork for a coup d'état?

The scale of his paranoia was giving Mike a very strange sensation, the cold detachment of a head trip into a darkened wilderness of mirrors: the occupational disease of spies. *If you can't trust your friends, the only people left to trust are your enemies,* he reminded himself. Miriam had tried to warn him; that suggested, at a minimum, something to hope for. *But FTO'll be watching her house. And her mother's. In case anyone shows.*

He forced himself to relax his grip on the wheel and pay attention to his surroundings as a pickup weaved past him, horn blaring. *How* many *watchers?* Maintaining full surveillance on a building was extremely expensive—especially if nobody had bothered to look in on it for months.

An ephemeral flash of hope lit up the world around him. If FTO had been watching Miriam's house before, they might well have pulled out already—and yesterday's events would have shaken things up even more. *But what if they're wrong?* He remembered Matthias's advice, from months ago: *They think like a government. And Miriam's important to them. She's an insider— otherwise she wouldn't have been able to warn me. Would we put a watch on a cabinet official's house if we knew enemies had it under surveillance? Even if we were under attack?* Trying to work through that line of thought threatened to give him a headache, but it seemed to be worth checking out. Best case, there'd be a Clan security post discreetly watching her place, and nobody else. Worst case, an FTO surveillance team—but knowing how FTO worked in the field, he'd have a good chance of spotting them. *Find Miriam. Try to cut a deal: Warn her faction about the spy, about WARBUCKS's plans—in return, try to get them to hand over the murderers. Maybe find some way to cut a deal.*

I just hope I'm not too late.

Leaking everywhere

In a stately house four miles outside Niejwein, two noble ladies sat beside an unlit hearth, awkwardly eyeing each other. Between their angled chairs an occasional table stood like a frontier fence, surmounted by the border tower of a fortified wine decanter. The afternoon sun slanting through the lattice window stained the wood-paneled walls with a deep golden warmth; a pair of fat flies buzzed in erratic circles below the ceiling, swooping and tracing out the lines of their confinement.

"Have you been keeping well?" asked the older of the pair, her age-spotted eyelids drooping as she watched her sixty-two-year-old visitor. "Do you have any complaints?" She spoke abruptly, her tone brusque.

The younger one snorted. "Only the obvious, Mother." The last word came out with an odd emphasis, falling just short of making an insult of it. "Your hospitality is impeccable but, I hope you'll excuse me for putting it so crudely, oppressive. I would ask, though, is my maid Mhara unharmed?"

The dowager frowned, her crow's-feet wrinkles deepening. "I do not know." She extended a shaky hand and tugged on a braided bell cord. A discreet servants' door opened behind her. "My daughter inquires of her maid."

"Yes, my lady." The attendant bowed his head.

"Was she taken? If so, is she well?"

"She, ah, escaped, my lady. After she shot one of the dragoons in the, ah, thigh."

"Well then." The dowager gave her daughter a wintry smile. "Satisfied?"

Her daughter stared back at her for a long moment, then nodded fractionally. "Satisfied."

"Go away," the dowager announced to the air. The servants' door opened and closed again, restoring the illusion of privacy. "Such a show of compassion," she added, her tone of voice dripping with irony.

"There's no show about it, *Mother*." Patricia Thorold-Hjorth, herself dowager duchess and mother to the queen-widow, stared back at her own dam, the duchess Hildegarde. "We've bled ourselves white in your lifetime. Every one of us of the true blood who dies, especially the women, is a score fewer grandchildren to support our successors. If you don't feel that—"

She stopped, as Hildegarde's palm rattled the crystal on the table. "*Of course* I feel that!" the duchess exploded. "I've known that since long before I whelped you, you ungrateful child. I've known that ever since my sister—" She stopped, and reached for a glass of wine. "Damn you, *you're* old enough to know better, too."

Hildegarde stopped. They sat in silence for a minute, eyeing each other sidelong. Finally Patricia spoke. "I assume you didn't bring me here for a friendly mother-daughter chat."

"I brought you here to save your life, girl," Hildegarde said harshly.

Patricia blinked. "You did?"

"If you were elsewhere, I could not insure that certain of the more enthusiastic members of the conservative club would leave you be," the dowager pointed out. "And I feel some residual family loyalty to this day, whatever you may think of me."

"Eh. Well, if you say so. Do you expect that will make Helge think better of you?"

"No." The dowager stared at her daughter. "But it will be one less thing for me to take to my grave." For a moment her eyes unfocussed, staring vaguely into some interior landscape. "You corrupted her most thoroughly. My congratulations would be in order, were the ultimate effect not so damaging."

Patricia reached slowly for the other wineglass. "Why should I thank you for saving my life?" she asked. "Are your faction planning a return to the bad old days? Cousin killers?"

"No. Not really." Hildegarde took a sip from her glass. "But it was necessary to break the back of your half-brother's organization, to buy time while we deal with the harvest he was about to bring in from the field. Test-tube babies, what an idea. I gather I should thank you for helping deal with it—Dr. ven Hjalmar was quite effusive in his praise for your assistance. But in any case: The program is secure, as is our future. We shall make sure that the infants are raised by trustworthy families, to know their place within the Clan—better than your wildcat, anyway—and in the next generation our numbers will increase fivefold."

Patricia nodded guardedly. "Where is the doctor?" she asked.

"Oh, who cares?" Hildegarde waved a shaky hand: "He doesn't matter now that the program records are destroyed."

"Really?" Patricia shook her head. Hildegarde's grasp of computers was theoretical at best, shaky at worst. "He's not tried to blackmail you?"

"No." Hildegarde's grin was not reassuring. "I think he might be afraid to show his face. Something to do with your hoyden."

"So you took action against Security?" Patricia nudged.

"Yes. I had to, to preserve the balance. I know you harbor Anglischprache ideas about 'equality' and 'freedom,' but you must understand, we are *not* a meritocracy—we live or die by our bloodlines. Certainly Angbard had the right idea thirty years ago, to clamp a lid on the feuding, but his solution has become a monster. There are young people who pledge their loyalty to the Security directorate, would you believe it? If he was allowed to bring the, the changelings into his organization, within a generation we'd be done for. This way is better: With the Security organization cut back to its original status, and other threats dealt with, we can resume our traditional—" Patricia was whey-faced. "What is it?"

"*Other* threats. *What* other threats?"

"Oh, nothing important." Hildegarde waved the back of her hand dismissively, prompting a fly to dodge. "We sent a message to the Anglischprache leadership, one that they won't ignore. Once we've got them out of our hair—"

"A message the Anglischprache won't ignore? What kind of message?"

"Oh, we used those bombs Oliver had lying about." Hildegarde sniffed. "How else do you deal with a hostile king? They'll make the point quite well: Once the new Anglischprache president-emperor ascends the throne, he won't be under any illusions about the consequences of threatening us. We'll talk to him, I'm sure. We've done it before: This will just set negotiations off on the right foot."

"*Sky Father . . .*" Patricia stared at her mother, aghast, then raised her wineglass and knocked it back in a single swallow. "Those were atomic weapons," she said slowly. "Where were they set?"

"Oh, some white palace, I gather," Hildegarde said dismissively. "In a town named after a famous soldier."

"Oh dear Trickster Cousin," Patricia muttered under her breath. "You said 'used.' I suppose it's too much to hope that you misspoke, and there's still time—"

Hildegarde stared at her daughter, perplexed. "Of course not. This was yesterday. Are you all right?"

"I—a moment." Patricia shrugged uncomfortably. "This is

not a criticism I speak now, but—I lived among them for nearly a third of a century, Mother. You did not. You don't know them the way I do." Patricia nodded at the decanter: Her mother reached for the bell-pull once more. "I'm telling you, you've misjudged them badly."

"We had to get rid of their current king-emperor somehow; he's an idiot." Hildegarde paused while her footman refilled both goblets and retreated. "His next-in-line is far more intelligent. He understands power and its uses."

"Granted. But their president is not a king, as we understand the term, he is merely a first citizen, elected by his people. They run everything by a system of laws."

"I know that—"

"The trouble is, simply attacking them on their home field is . . . it's a declaration of war. And *they don't know how to surrender*, Mother. They *can't*. There is no law in their constitution that says 'if attacked by an irresistible force it is permissible to offer a limited surrender: To do so invoke this clause.' Once they're at war, any leader who tries to stop it will be impeached—removed. It's like stabbing a hornets' nest: Every one you kill just makes the others angrier. I'm not making this up. The last time they lost a war, nearly thirty years ago, they left it to an unelected temporary regent to take the barrage of rotten fruit, and there are *still* people who think they could have won in Vietnam if only they'd fought harder. There are still many in the South who think they could have won the slaveowners' rebellion against the North, a century and a half ago. They're all quite mad, you know. Just now they're fighting two wars on the other side of the world, all because a ranting priest sent his idiot followers to blow up a couple of towers. *Two* wars—because they're not sure who did it." Patricia picked up her glass again. "Do you know how powerful these bombs are?" she asked. "I'm told they can be made more or less damaging—"

"Oh, I'm sure they used the most powerful available," Hildegarde said dismissively. "No point tapping your enemy on the head with a twig when there's a club to hand, is there? As you say, it only makes them angry. But the enemy's intentions, you must understand—they don't matter. What can they do to us? Certainly they may kidnap one or two of our own, ride them like mules, and they may even bring more of their bombs, but we are on our home ground here. We must be firm and deliver our ultimatum, and they must learn to leave us alone!"

"Mother." Patricia looked at Hildegarde: "You're not the only person who's been sending messages. I—at the rump Council's orders—I've been trying to negotiate with them for some time. They don't want to haggle; they want our total surrender. They sent a final démarche and cut me dead."

"Really." Hildegarde didn't bother to feign interest.

"They're working on a *machine*, Mother dearest. A machine that does what we do, a machine for walking between worlds. Yes, they told us this. Also that it might take months or years, but when they succeeded, they would come here, and how they would treat with us would depend entirely on how we treated with *them*."

"And you believed that?"

"Yes. As a matter of fact, I did—and do. You've never really lived among them. You don't know what they're capable of."

Hildegarde sniffed. "Well, it will probably never happen. And if it does, we'll think of something. But for now, our internal factional dispute is settled. The Security apparat is back in its box, we have found a satisfactory solution to Angbard's silly little breeding program, and we—you and I—are back on course to meet our braid's long-term goal. Your diversion has had no real long-term effect. That's always been your besetting problem—always wanting to hare off and do things your own way, even when it forces you to do something silly, like hide yourself away in a foreign scholar's hovel for thirty years instead of enjoying the rightful fruits due to one of your rank. I know, you're not going to apologize. I don't expect you to. Will you believe me if I tell you that I bear you no ill will? Or your daughter? Or *her* child, be they boy or girl? But you have been a sore trial to your elderly mother, these years, more even than the prodigal stepson. Even now. Not even asking why I wanted to see you."

There was an uncomfortable pause. "Why?" Patricia finally asked.

"Because I'm dying," Hildegarde said, so offhandedly that it took Patricia a moment to do a double take. "Nothing that the Anglischprache doctors can repair, I assure you—I have been poked and prodded by Drs. ven Skorzeman and ven Hjalmar, and they have attempted to convince me to visit the other side for blood treatments that will make my hair fall out and my gums bleed, to no avail. I am a goodly age, Patricia. I may even live to see a world-walking great-grandchild of mine take the throne, which is more than my half-sister managed. And I never managed to settle my affairs with Angelin. So there is a canker in my guts and I should not want to impose overlong on your patience, but I am an old and impatient woman and I ask you to indulge my sentiment."

Patricia stared at the dowager. "But Angelin refused to speak to you—"

"She might have eventually, had she not died at the hands of her own grandchild's men." Hildegarde turned unfocussed eyes on the window. "Which just goes to show the unwisdom of schooling our young in alien ways: Never forget that—we are foreigners wherever we live, whether we be ruler or servant. Angelin failed to look to Egon's schooling. She left him to go native. You . . . made the opposite error with Helge. I never took the time to set things right with my sister. So, I thought I should at least make a gesture . . . don't make me reconsider the wisdom of this meeting."

"Oh, Mother." Patricia put her wineglass down. "This is most harsh, this news." A hesitancy crept into her voice.

"Bear with me." Hildegarde raised a slightly shaky hand and closed her eyes, as Patricia picked up the decanter with both hands and refilled their glasses. "I have always acted for what I perceived to be the best interests of our braid. I had hoped you would understand that, and at least not stand in my way, but by poisoning my natural heir against me . . . well, it's too late to undo that." She opened her eyes and blinked rheumily at her daughter. "May you have better luck with your grandchild. Angelin's great-grandchild."

"If it arrives. Consanguinuity—"

"It will be all right, child. Helge and Creon were first cousins once removed, and Creon's ailment was a consequence of poisoning, not inbreeding. We risk worse with every twist of the braid. The hazard is minimal."

"Miriam won't see it that way, you know."

"*Miriam*—what an odd name. Where did you get it from?"

Patricia smiled tightly. "The same place I got Iris. And Beckstein. She answers to it, you know. You might have gotten better results from her if you'd called her by the name she prefers."

"Perhaps. But it's not her name, it's a disguise. Where would we be if people could pick and choose their name? Nobody need recognize their seniors—there would. be anarchy! Or another strong man like Angbard would grab everybody by the throat and rule by force majeure. A rogue, that boy. But listen, I have a few months, perhaps a year or two. And seeing that Angbard was ill, I decided to move now, to detach his slippery followers' fingers from the reins of power and hand them back to their rightful owner—a woman of the line, or a lord working as her agent, as is right and proper. *You*, Patricia. You have a grandchild in the great game, or you will soon—you will act in their name. Once the hangers-on and opportunists are purged, once Angbard's security apparatus is emptied of dangerous innovators and cut back to its original size and scope, you will inherit the full power of my position, and they'll love you. Complete freedom of action. I never had that, girl, but *you will*."

Patricia stared at Hildegarde for almost a minute. Presently, she closed her mouth. "You're not joking."

"You know me, girl. Do I ever joke?"

Patricia opened her mouth for a moment, then closed it again. "Let me get this straight. You had your granddaughter forcibly inseminated with your sister's grandson's sperm so that you could reassert our cadet branch's claim to the throne. You had me kidnapped and brought here so that we could kiss and make up. You're dying of cancer, so you decided to set up Miriam's kid for the throne by destroying Angbard's security organization, just as the old nobility are getting over the civil war and wondering what we're going to unleash on them next. And you nuked the White House, just to send a message to WARBUCKS. Am I missing anything?"

"Yes." Hildegarde looked smug. "Who do you think taunted Egon about his younger brother's marriage? Someone had to do it—otherwise we'd never have pried his useless ass off the throne! It would have set us back at least two generations."

Patricia picked up her wineglass and drained it for the second time. "Mother, I have a confession to make. Miriam once told me she thought you were a scheming bitch, and I'm afraid I defended your honor. I take it all back. You're completely insane."

"Let us pray that it runs in the family, then. As for your confession—consider yourself forgiven. I shall be relying on your cunning once I surrender to you, you realize." Hildegarde reached out and pulled the bell rope—"*More wine, damn your eyes!* I insist on getting drunk with my daughter at least once before I die. Yes, I'm insane. If insanity is defined by wanting to put my great-grandchild on the throne, I'm mad. If it's crazy to want to strangle the ghouls that crowd the royal crib and break the private army that threatens our autonomy, I'm all of that. I bent the Clan and the Kingdom to serve you and your line, Patricia, and I find at the end of my days that I regret nothing. So. Once you are in charge of the Clan, what do you think you will do with it?"

"I haven't made my confession yet, Mother." Patricia looked at the dowager oddly. "It would have been good to have had this heart-to-heart a little earlier—perhaps a year ago. I'm afraid we're both too late. . . ."

An hour after Miriam and her guards and allies arrived at the farmstead, the place was abuzz with Clan Security. There were

several safe transfer locations in the state forest, and one of Earl-
Major Riordan's first orders had been to summon every available
soldier—not already committed to point defense or the pursuit
of the renegade elements of the Postal Service and the Conservative Club—to establish a security cordon.

Miriam, sick at heart, sat in one corner of the command post,
listening—the fast, military hochsprache was hard to follow, and
she was catching perhaps one word in three, but she could follow
the general sense of the discussion—and watching as Riordan
took reports and consulted with Olga and issued orders, as often
as not by radio to outlying sites. The headquarters troops had set
up a whole bunch of card indexes and a large corkboard, star-
tlingly prosaic in a field headquarters in a fire-damaged farmhouse, and were keeping a written log of every decision Riordan
handed down. A hanging list of index cards had gone up on one
wall, each card bearing a name: Baron Henryk, Baron Oliver,
Dowager Duchess Thorold-Hjorth. Miriam carefully avoided
trying to read the handwritten annotations whenever a clerk updated one of them. Ringleaders they might be, and in some cases
bitter enemies, but they were all people she knew, or had known,
at court. A similar list hung on the opposite wall, and it was both
longer and less frequently updated—known allies and their disposition.

"Why not computerize?" she'd asked Brill, in a quiet moment when the latter had sat down on the bench beside her with
a mug of coffee.

"Where are we going to get the electricity to run the computer
from?" Brill replied, shrugging. "Batteries need charging, generators need fuel. Best not to make hostages to fate. Besides," she
glanced sidelong at the communications specialist bent over the
radio, "computers come with their own problems. They make
treachery easier. And it's a small enough squabble that we don't
need them."

"But the Clan—" Miriam stopped.

"We know all the main players. By name and by face. We

know most of our associates, too." The world-walkers, children of latent, outer-family lines, not yet fully integrated into the Clan of which they were branches. "We are few enough that this will be over—" Brill stopped. The communications specialist had stood up, hunching over his set. Suddenly he swore, and waved urgently at Olga. Olga hurried over; a moment later Riordan joined her.

"What's going on?" Miriam stood up.

"I don't know." Brill's face was expressionless. "Nothing good by the look of it."

Olga turned towards them, mouthed something. She looked appalled.

"Tell me," Miriam demanded, raising her voice against the general hubbub of urgent questions and answers.

Olga took two steps towards her. "I am very sorry, my lady," she said woodenly.

"It's Plan Blue?"

Olga nodded. "It is all over the television channels," she added softly. "Two nuclear explosions. In Washington."

For a moment everything in Miriam's vision was as gray as ash. She must have staggered, for Brilliana caught her elbow. "What." She swallowed. "How bad?"

"We do not know yet, my lady. That news is still in the pipeline. We have"—she gestured at the radio bench—"other urgent priorities right now. But there are reports of many casualties."

Miriam swallowed again. Her stomach clenched. "Was this definitely the work of, of the conservative faction?"

"It is reasonable to suppose so, but we can't be certain yet." Olga was peering at her, worried. "My lady, what do you—"

"Because if it was their doing, if it was anything to do with the Clan, then we are *fucked*." She could see it in her mind's eye, mushroom clouds rising over the Capitol, and a bleak vision of a future far more traumatic than anything she'd ever imagined. "We're about to lose all access to the United States. They won't rest until they've found a way to come over here and chase us down and kill us. There won't be anywhere we can run to in their world or this one that's far enough away for safety."

"Even if it was not Baron Hjorth's doing, even if we had nothing to do with it, we would not be secure," Brilliana pointed out. "We know that the vice president has reason to want us dead. This could be some other's work, and he would still send his minions to hunt us."

"Shit." Miriam swallowed again, feeling the acid tang of bile at the back of her mouth. "Think I'm going to throw up."

"This way, milady"—everyone was solicitous towards the mother-to-be, Miriam noted absentmindedly, up to and including making decisions on her behalf, as if she were a passive object with no will of her own—

It was raining outside, and the stench from the latrines round the side of the house completed the job that the news and the anxiety and the morning sickness had started. Her stomach cramped as she doubled over, spitting bile, and waited for the shooting pain in her gut to subside. Brill waited outside, leaving her a token space. *I'm alone,* she realized despondently. *Alone, surrounded by allies and sworn vassals, some of whom consider themselves my friends. I don't think any of them truly understand. . . .* Her thoughts drifted back towards the sketchily described horrors unfolding down south, and her stomach clenched again. By the time she finished, she found she had regained a modicum of calm. *They don't know what's going to happen,* she realized. *But I do.* Miriam had been living in Boston through the crazy days that followed 9/11. And she'd seen the glassy-eyed lockstep to the drumbeat of war that followed, seen the way everybody rallied to the flag. In the past few weeks and months, a tenuous skepticism had been taking hold, but nothing could be better calculated to extinguish it than a terrorist outrage to dwarf the fall of the Twin Towers. The only question was how long it would take the US military to gear up for an invasion, and she had an uneasy feeling that they were already living on borrowed time.

"Milady?" It was Brill.

"I'm better. For now." Miriam waved off her offered hand and took a deep breath of rain-cleansed air. "I'm going to lie down. But. I need to know how bad it is, what the bastards have done. And as soon as Riordan and Olga have a free minute I need to talk to them."

"But they're going to be—" Brill stopped. "What do you need to distract them with?"

"The evacuation plan," Miriam said bluntly.

"What plan—"

"The one we need to draw up *right now* to get everyone across to New Britain. Because if we don't"—she raised her head, stared across the seared fields towards the tree line at the edge of the cleared area—"we're dead, or worse. I know what my people— sorry, the Americans—are capable of. We don't stand a chance if we stay here. One way or another, the Clan is finished with the Gruinmarkt; this whole stupid cockamamie scheme to put a baby on the throne is pointless now. The only question is which direction we run."

A steady stream of couriers, security staff, and refugees trickled into the farmstead over the hours following Miriam's evacuation. By midafternoon, Earl Riordan had sent out levies to round up labor from the nearest villages, and by sunset a large temporary camp was taking shape, patrolled by guards with assault rifles. The farm itself was receiving a makeover in the shape of a temporary royal residence: However humble it might be by comparison with the palaces of Niejwein, it was far better than the tents and improvised bivouacs of the soldiers.

Despite her ongoing nausea, Miriam followed Riordan and Olga and their staff when they moved into a pavilion beside the farmhouse. "You should be lying down, taking things easy," Brilliana said, halfheartedly trying to divert her.

"The hell with that." Miriam glared at her. "These are my people, aren't they? I need to be here." *And I need to know . . .* The sense of dread gnawing at her guts was beyond awful.

In late afternoon, despite the apparent defection of most of the Clan postal office's lords to the traitors' side—at least, it was hard to put any other interpretation on their total failure to comply with the executive head of Clan Security's increasingly heated orders to report—they managed to establish a solid radio network with the other security sites in the Gruinmarkt; and the New York office was still sufficiently functional to arrange a three-hourly courier run with digital video tapes from the Anglischprache world's news feeds. Shortwave and FM didn't have the bandwidth to play back video, but the headlines off the wire services were more than enough to make Miriam sick to her stomach and leave Brilliana and Sir Alasdair anxious for her health.

> REUTERS: THIRD ATOMIC WEAPON FAILS TO DETO-
> NATE AT PENTAGON
>
> AP: FLIGHTS, STOCK MARKET TRADING SUSPENDED
> INDEFINITELY
>
> REUTERS: VICE PRESIDENT SWORN IN AS WHITE
> HOUSE CONFIRMED DESTROYED: PRESIDENT WAS
> "AT HOME"
>
> UPI: IRAN CONDEMNS "FOOLISH AND ILL-ADVISED"
> ATTACK
>
> REUTERS: SADR LEADS NIGHTTIME DEMONSTRA-
> TION IN BAGHDAD: MILLION PROTESTORS IN FIR-
> DOS SQUARE
>
> AP: PRESIDENT TO ADDRESS NATION

But there was even more important news.

At first there was nothing more than a knot of turmoil around the table where Olga and three clerical assistants were coordinating intelligence reports and updating the list of known survivors and victims of the coup attempt. "I don't believe it," said Sir Alasdair, making his way back towards Miriam. "It can't be a coincidence!" His expression was glazed, distant.

"What's happened?" Brill, who had been leaning over a clipboard crossing off the names of couriers who had made too many crossings for the day, looked up at the tone in Miriam's voice.

"The duke," said Sir Alasdair. He cleared his throat. "I am very sorry, my lady. Your uncle. The latest report from the clinic says. Um. He went into cardiac arrest this morning."

"This *morning*?" Miriam caught Brilliana staring at her. She clutched the arm of her folding director's chair. "Can't be. Can't possibly be. Are they *sure*?" She swallowed. Angbard, the thin white duke: For over thirty years he'd been the guiding will behind the Clan Security operation, the hand that held the reins binding the disparate squabbling families together. Since his stroke two months ago his duties had been carved up and assigned to Olga and Riordan, but not without question or challenge: The Clan Council was not eager to see any individual ever again wield that much power. "He's dead?" She heard her voice rising and raised a hand to cover her mouth.

"If it's a coincidence I'll eat this table. I'm sorry, my lady," Sir Alasdair added, "but it can't possibly be an accident. Not with a revolt in progress and, and the other news. From the Americans."

"Brill, I'm sorry—" Miriam's voice broke. Angbard hadn't *felt* like an uncle to her—more like a scary Mafia godfather who, for no obvious reason, had taken a liking to her—but he'd been a huge influence on Brilliana. *And Olga,* Miriam reminded herself. *Shit.* "Is there any word on who killed him? Because when we find them—"

"It wasn't a killing, according to the clinic," Sir Alasdair reminded her. "Although it beggars belief to suppose it a coincidence, for now it must needs be but one more insult to avenge at our convenience. One of our doctors was in attendance, Dr. ven Hjalmar—"

"Shit. *Shit.*" Miriam clenched her fist. Brill was watching her, a dangerous light in her eyes.

Sir Alasdair paused. "Is there a problem?" he asked.

"Dr. ven Hjalmar is a wanted man," Brilliana said, her tone colorless.

"Very," Miriam added, her voice cracking. "Sir Alasdair. Should you or your men find Dr. ven Hjalmar . . . I will sleep better for knowing that he's dead."

Sir Alasdair nodded. "I'm sure that can be arranged." He paused. "Is there a reason?"

Brilliana cleared her throat. "A necessary and sufficient one that need not concern you further. Oh, and his murder of Duke Angbard should be sufficient, should it not?"

"Ah—really?" Sir Alasdair's eyebrow rose. "Well, if you say so—" He noticed Miriam's expression. "You're sure?"

"Very sure," she said flatly.

"In that case, I'll put the order out. By your leave." Sir Alasdair beat a hasty retreat.

Miriam glanced at Brill, trying to gather her wits. "Come on, I want to find out what's happening."

The card indexes, divided by faction members and known status, were growing in size and complexity—and a third list had joined the first two: known fatalities. Earl Riordan was deep in conversation with one of his lieutenants as Miriam approached him—"Then tomorrow morning, we shall relocate to Koudrivier House. Assign two lances to establish a security cordon and a third for courier and doppelganger duties. The rest of your men I want—my lady?" He straightened up. "What can I do for you?"

"My uncle is dead," Miriam managed, the words feeling strange in her mouth. *The uncle I never had time to get to know has been murdered.* . . . "Is my mother accounted for? Or my grandmother?"

Earl Riordan looked irritated for a moment, then thoughtful. "Your grandam is unaccounted for. Along with several of her friends, who appear to be involved in the insurrection." He turned to one of the clerks and asked a question in rapid hochsprache. "We shall find out about about her grace your mother shortly, I trust. Is there anything else?"

"Yes." Miriam gripped her hands tightly behind her back. "The duke is dead. How fast can we get a quorum of the Clan Council together? Just enough to confirm"—she caught Olga's head turning towards her, the warning look too late—"you as official head of Clan Security," she continued. "And an extraordinary meeting to discuss policy."

"We'll do that as soon as—" Riordan glanced at the map table across the aisle from his clerks. "We have a cabal of insurrectionists to arrest first—"

"No." The firmness in her voice surprised Miriam. Even though her guts were burning, acid bile and churning stress in her belly: *Can't stop now.* "I don't think you grasp how far this has gone. WARBUCKS has just been sworn in as president. You know he worked for the duke: This is a comprehensive clusterfuck. WARBUCKS wants to destroy us, destroy the evidence, and the fuckwit faction have just handed him the perfect excuse. The American military are going to find a way to come over here and they will kill *everybody*. You're thinking months or weeks. We probably don't have that long." Miriam stared at Riordan. He was not entirely an enigma, but she couldn't say that she knew him well; another of the younger generation, like Roland, educated to college level or higher in the United States, but bound to serve in the traditional family trade. "We just nuked the White House," she reminded him. "What would *you* do in their shoes?"

"I'd—" His expression would have been funny if the situation hadn't been so serious. "Oh. *Scheisse.*" A momentary expression of pure disgust flickered across his face. "What do you suggest?"

"We need to establish safe locations in New Britain right now, today. Get our people across there, start setting up an evacuation pipeline. You're right about suppressing the, the rebels—but we're not going back to business as usual over here. Never again. They won't give us time; if we want to survive we need to evacuate. There are folk I know who might be able to help us, if we can—"

Riordan raised a hand. "There will be no cutting and running," he said firmly. "Your point is well taken, but if we 'cut and run' while the houses are divided, our organization will . . . it won't remain viable. The rebels will harry us and our less loyal relatives will desert us, until there's nothing left. The Clan stands or dies as a group. But." He looked at Brilliana. "My lady, this world is not safe for her royal highness, not now, and probably not for some time. And she is quite right about the need for us to prepare an evacuation pipeline, against the hazard she so vividly identifies. Can you take her to New Britain and see to her safety?"

"Now wait a—" Miriam began, but Brill cut in before she could get going.

"Yes, I can do that." She nodded. "I'll need muscle. Sir Alasdair, her royal highness's household, a number of other people. And we'll need money."

"You've got it." Riordan took a deep breath. "My lady?" He looked back at Miriam. "The rebels want you under their thumb. If they have you, they hold the monarchy here. And they don't realize what they've unleashed in America. Your goal of preparing a, a fallback for us, in New Britain, is a worthy one, and my second-highest priority after rounding up the traitors. I see no reason for it not to be *your* highest priority. If nothing else, it puts you beyond the insurrectionists' easy reach—and the Americans', if your worries are realistic." He glanced at Brilliana. "Look after her and see that her orders in this enterprise are carried out. Make sure to keep me informed of your location: We may need to move the Continuity Council there as well, or at least hold audiences. If anyone obstructs you, you have my authority on this matter, on the orders of the Clan Security executive." To Miriam: "Is that what you desire, my lady?"

Miriam nodded, swallowed. The nausea was quite severe; she shoved it out of her mind. "I've got some plans already nailed down," she said. "Come on, Brill. Let's find somewhere to work. There's a list of people and things we need." She swallowed again, feeling a cramp in her belly. "Oh. Oh shit. I don't feel good. . . ."

(BEGIN RECORDING)

"Shalom, Mordechai."

"And you, my friend. This must be a fraught time for you; I can't say how much these outrages pain me, I can barely imagine how much worse it must be for you." (Pause.) "I assume this is not a casual visit?"

"No, I—I've been very busy, as you can imagine. I've got about an hour out of the office, though, and I think you need to know. First, tell me—the attacks. Who do you think carried them out?"

(Pause.) "If I tell you who I think did it, you'll assume it's inside information. And I can't give you inside information even if I have it to give, my friend. But I don't think it was the usual clowns, if that's what you're fishing for? Because they're simply incapable of pulling something like this off. Let me tell you, everyone in the Institute is doing their nut right now—"

"Oh *hell*. They haven't officially told your people, then? Who did it?"

"You *know* who did it? Who?"

(Slowly.) "You're going to think I'm nuts if you don't get this through official channels, I swear—they briefed everybody yesterday and this morning, half of us thought they were mad but they have evidence, Mordechai, hard evidence. It's a new threat, completely unlike anything we imagined."

"Really? My money was on a false-flag operation by the Office of Special Programs."

"No, no, it wasn't us. Well, the bombs were ours. They were stolen from the inactive inventory."

"*Stolen?* Tell me it's not true, Jack! Nobody 'just steals' special weapons like they're shoplifting a candy store—"

"Take a deep breath, man. There are other universes, parallel worlds, like ours but where things happened differently. Different people, different history. There's a secret project under Livermore building machines for transiting between parallel worlds: They've got the photographs to prove it. Way they briefed us—a bunch of, of drug lords from another dimension, can you believe it? Illegal aliens, emphasis on the alien, whatever. They stole half a dozen backpack nukes, they just *appeared inside* the secure storage cells and walked off with them! The White House has been studying the situation for a year now. Negotiations broke down, and this was their idea of a Dear John."

"Oy. From anyone else I would not believe it, Jack, but from you, I take it as gospel. Tell me, have you been working too hard lately?"

"Fuck off, I'm not jerking your chain. Listen, this is all over the internal chain. I expect you'll hear about it officially through diplomatic channels. It's a huge mess—a whole fucking sewage farm has hit the windmill. D.C. was blowback, just like al-Qaeda, let's not kid ourselves—and the president means to put an end to it, and do it hard and fast."

"What do you mean by hard and fast, in this context?"

"They've indented for a hundred and sixty B83s from Pantex, with an option on another two hundred in two weeks, that's what I mean. And the Fifth Bomb Wing have gone onto lockdown. I mean, everyone's on alert everywhere, but the Fifth have canceled all leave and there's a complete communications blackout. Half of them moved to Fairford in England for Iraq, and the grapevine says the rest are staging out there with B83s aboard, just to keep them out of enemy hands. I just saw orders reactivating the Seventy-second Bomb Squadron and pulling in ground staff."

"Out of *enemy*—what the fuck is going on?"

"Like I said, it's a whole new ballgame. These fuckers can just appear out of thin air, anywhere! Inside your security perimeter! My guess is that the Fifth Bomb Wing is being readied for a counterstrike mission into a, a parallel universe, just as soon as they can load up with B83s, fit the transit machines, and as soon as the U2s deliver accurate target maps. Keeping them overseas in England is a security measure: They can move sideways between worlds, show up inside the perimeter of our bases—but if the bombers aren't home they can't touch them. Watch for the KC-10s moving too. I tell you, they're getting ready for an attack on North America—just not *our* North America."

"Okay, Jack, I've got to hand it to you. You are either taking far more LSD than is good for you, or you have completely spoiled my afternoon, because you are just not imaginative enough to make up a story like that without chemical assistance. I say that as a compliment, by the way—an excessively active imagination is a liability in your line of work. I'm going to have to escalate this, and that's going to make my head hurt because my boss, it's going to make *his* head hurt. So I hope you won't take this the wrong way when I ask, what have you got for me? What concrete evidence have you got to back these claims up?"

(Rustling.) "It's classified, but not top-secret. I mean, this stuff is general dissemination for about a hundred thousand soldiers, as of this morning—it *was* top-secret, but they're realists, there's no way to keep a lid on something like this indefinitely. So I, uh, there's a classified briefing pack that I need to lock back in my office drawer tonight. I assume you've got a camera or something?"

"Of course. Jack, you're a mensch. Listen, I am just about to go to the toilet, I'll be back in a few minutes and your briefing pack can go right back to the office after lunch while I go find some headache pills before I call Tel Aviv. Are you sure this isn't just a prank to make Benny Netenyahu shit himself . . . ? No? Too bad. Because I'd love to be there to see his face when this lands on his desk."

(END RECORDING)

Oliver, Baron Hjorth—formerly Earl Hjorth, but the higher landed titles had been coming vacant with distressing frequency over the past year—had spent a sleepless night in a co-opted tax farmer's mansion in a country estate, near the site of Baltimore in the United States. Two stories up, under the eaves, the rooms were uncomfortably hot in the summer miasma; but they lent a good view of the approaches to the house, and more importantly, good radio reception for a location so far south of the Gruinmarkt.

In his opinion, it was only sensible to take precautions: He had played his part in the operation in good faith, but there was a significant risk that some ne'er-do-well or rakehell anarchist of the progressive creed might seek him out with murder in mind. So the baron sat in a sweltering servants' room, his head bowed beneath the roof beams, while next door his man Schuller poked at the scanner, waiting.

On the other side of the wall of worlds from this mansion there was a modest, suburban family home. In its car port waited a black Lincoln, fully fueled for the dash up I-95 to Boston. But once he took to the wide American highways he'd be trapped, in a manner of speaking; committed to Niejwein, by hook or by crook. He could be at the palace in a matter of hours, there to take charge of a troop of cavalry such as befitted a gentleman: but while he was on the road he'd be unable to listen in on the upstart Riordan's increasingly desperate messages.

Impatient and irritable with tiredness, Oliver stood—for perhaps the fifth time that morning—and walked to the window casement. Below him, a cleared slope ran downhill to the woodline: Nobody stirred on the dirt track leading to the house. *Good.* He glanced at the doorway. Schuller was a reliable man, one of the outer family world-walkers Riordan had sacked from Angbard's organization in the wake of the fiasco at the Hjalmar Palace. *Let's see what news . . .* Oliver walked to the doorway and shoved the curtain aside. "How goes it?" he demanded.

Schuller glanced up, then nodded—overfamiliarly, in Oliver's opinion, but fatigue made churls of all men—and shoved one headphone away from an ear. "Nothing for the past fifteen minutes, my lord. Before that, something garbled from Lady Thorold's adjutant. A call for reinforcements from their Millgartfurt station, where they reported word of an attack—cut short. Orders from Major Riordan's command post, demanding that all units hold their station and report by numbers. There were three responses."

"*Good.*" The baron laced his fingers together tightly. "What word from the Anglischprache?"

"Riordan told the post to keep reporting hourly on the attack; it is by all accounts chaos over there. All air flights are grounded, but the roads are open—outside of the capital, of course. They're clucking like headless chickens." Schuller's expression was stony. "As well they might. Fools."

"Did I pledge you for your opinions?" The baron raised an eyelid: Schuller recoiled slightly.

"No sir!"

"Then kindly keep them to yourself, there's a good chap. I'm trying to think." Oliver dabbed at his forehead, trying to mop away the perspiration. *The limousine is air-conditioned*, he reminded himself. "You have a log, yes? Let me see it." Schuller held up a clipboard. The pages were neatly hand-scribed, a list of times and stations and cryptic notes of their message content. "Careless of them. They're not encrypting."

"They are probably shorthanded, sir." Schuller looked up at the baron as he paged through the sheet. "Their traffic has been tailing off all morning."

"Well then." The baron smiled tightly as he saw the time stamps grow thinner, the broadcasts more desperate. "I think it's time to move headquarters. Tell Stanislaw and Poul we're moving, then hail Andrei and tell him to ready the troops to move this afternoon. Shut up shop and meet me downstairs in ten minutes: I must change first." It wouldn't do to be stopped and searched by the Anglische police while dressed as a Sudtmarkt cousin's guest, but he had a business suit laid out next door.

The plan was simple, as such things went: Baron Hjorth would transfer to the United States, drive north—covering a distance of hundreds of miles in a mere afternoon—and reemerge in the Gruinmarkt, on his own estate, with a bodyguard of cavalrymen in time to ride to the flag of the Postal Lords and her grace the dowager duchess. Who, if things were going to plan—as appeared to be the case—would have coaxed the Idiot's hoyden widow into a suitably well-guarded retreat and arranged for her confinement, in every sense of the word. Having managed the successful delivery of the atomic bombs to their targets (an expensive process, as Kurt and Jurgen could attest), he was, if nothing else, in line for the reward for a job well done. *Probably more of the same,* he thought, as he dressed in American fashion, mildly irritated by the lack of body servants. *The sacrifices we make. . . .*

Oliver made his way through the empty servants' quarters, passing the room recently vacated by Schuller, before descending by way of a back staircase and a dressing room to reach the main staircase. His men had dismissed most of the regular servants, banishing them to the village over the hill in the name of security. The great house was almost deserted, sweltering in the noon heat. Air-conditioning and the milder Northern climate beckoned, putting a spring in the baron's step. As he reached the bottom step, one shoe touching the mosaic floor of the central hall, he paused. It was, if anything, *too* quiet. "Poul?" he called quietly. "Stanislaw—"

"They won't be answering." Schuller stepped out of the shadows.

Oliver's left hand tightened on the handrail. "What is this?" His right hand was already shoving aside his jacket, reaching for the small of his back—

Schuller shot him. In the confines of the high-ceilinged room the blast of the shotgun was more than a noise, a deafening concussion that launched a screeching flight of frightened birds from the grounds outside. Oliver Hjorth collapsed, eyes staring, his chest flayed open as any victim of the blood-eagle. Schuller racked the pump on his weapon, ejecting the smoking cartridge, his eyes red-rimmed and tired, his face still expressionless. "Fucking aristocratic traitor," he muttered, inspecting the baron's body for any sign of residual life; but there was not so much as a toe-twitch, and the pool of blood was spreading evenly now, no longer spurting but beginning to soak into the rug at the center of the hall. Turning on his heel, Schuller walked slowly towards the front door of the hall; raising his left hand to stare at something cupped within his palm, he vanished. An instant later he reappeared in a linoleum-floored utility room, windowless. Walking over to the telephone, he dialed a number from memory: "Message to the major," he said, swallowing back bile. "Cuckoo Four has hatched three eggs. Cuckoo Four is going home."

There was a moment's delay, and then a woman's voice spoke: "Got that, and good luck. The major says you did well."

"Bye." He hung up, carefully unloaded his shotgun, and deposited it on the workbench. Then, taking a pair of car keys from his pocket, he headed for the carport. It would be a long drive for one man sticking religiously to the speed limit; but if he hurried, he could be back with his unit by sundown. Unlike the baron, Earl-Major Riordan didn't think of his agents as expendable embarrassments.

It took more than a war, a liquidity crisis, or even a revolution to stop the dogs. The morning after his father explained the new arrangement to him—the identity of their new political patron, the reason for backing ven Hjalmar, and the ruling council of elders' plans for the future—James Lee, his hat pulled down as low as his spirits, walked to the track to put some money on the greyhounds.

It was not, of course, entirely safe for a man with Asian features to walk these streets alone; but Lin, his favorite younger brother, was more than eager to get out of the house for a few hours. With smoked glasses and the beard he'd been cultivating of late, James didn't feel too out of place; and in addition to his cane, he had a pistol and a locket on a ribbon around his left wrist.

"Look—I'll put two shillings on Red Leinster in the next race," said Lin, pointing at one of the muzzled and hooded hounds, being led back to the kennels in the wake of a near-miss. "How about you?"

"Huh. Three and six on Bottle Rocket, I think." James glanced around, looking for a tout's man. "And a pint of mild."

"Make that two pints." Lin flashed him a brief grin. "What's gotten into you, brother? I haven't seen you this low since . . ." He trailed off.

James shook his head. Another glance: "Not in English," he said quietly. "Later, maybe."

"Oh." Slightly crestfallen, Lin subsided. But not for long: "Look! There's your bookmaker." He pointed excitedly, at a sharply dressed figure surrounded by a court of supplicants, and not a few stone-faced gentlemen with stout walking sticks—some of them doubtless concealing blades. "Are you going to—"

James shook his head. "Life's a gamble," he said quietly. A moment later his mood lifted. "Yes, I think I shall take a flutter." He worked his way over towards the bookmaker, Lin following along in his wake. A few minutes later, by way of a tap-man who dispensed mild straight into battered pewter pots from the back of a cask-laden dray, he made his way towards the back of the trackside crowd. The audience was abuzz with anticipation as the fresh dogs were led out to the stalls. "Which do you think is more important: filial obedience, or honor?" he asked.

Lin's eyes crossed briefly. "Uh. Beer?" he hazarded.

James shook his head minutely. "Imagine I'm being serious."

"Well, then." Lin took a gulp of the black beer. "This is a trick question, isn't it? Filial obedience, obviously, because that's where your honor comes from, right?"

"Wrong." James took a sip from his own mug. "And yes it *is* a trick question, but not the kind you're expecting. Let me see. Try this one: Why does honor come from filial obedience?"

"Because it does?" Lin rolled his eyes this time, making it clear that he was honoring his elder brother precisely inasmuch as the free beer required. "This is boring—"

"No it isn't," James said, quietly urgent. "Listen. Firstly, we obey because it's the right and traditional thing to do. Secondly, we obey because it is what we shall want for ourselves, when *we* are elders. And thirdly, we obey because the old farts are usually right, and they are making decisions with our family's best inter-ests in mind. They know what they're doing. Except when they *don't*. So let me rephrase: If you found out that the elders were do-ing something really stupid, *dangerously* stupid, and you couldn't talk them out of it—what would you do?"

A rattling clangor of gates and the shrill of a whistle: The dogs were off, bolting up the track in pursuit of the mechanical hare. "Oh brother." Lin was uncharacteristically quiet. "This isn't theoretical, is it?"

"No." Shouting and hoarse cheering rose on all sides as the crowd urged their hounds on. "They've bet the family's future on a wild black dog. *Our* future, Lin."

"They wouldn't do that," Lin said automatically. He raised his tankard, drank deeply as the gongs clashed and the crowd roared their approval. "Would they?" He wiped his mouth with the back of a hairless wrist.

"They would, and they did, with the best of intentions." James shook his head. "Huh, there goes my three and six. But looks like you lucked out."

"What have they done?" Lin asked as they queued to collect his winnings—not so much, for he'd bet on a favorite—from the men with clubs.

"Later." James waited vigilantly while his younger brother swapped his ticket for five shillings; the tout's men looked disapprovingly on, but made no move to pick a fight. They headed back to the dray for a refill, then over to the fence near the bleachers to watch. The racing dogs were kenneled, while dogs of another kind were brought out, along with a bear for them to bait in a wire-fenced enclosure in the middle of the track. "You met the enemy heir, Helge, Miriam. What did you think of her?"

Lin shook his head. "She's a crazy woman," he said admiringly. A shadow crossed his face. "I owe her, brother. It shames me to say."

"The elders sent you to kill her, and she ended up saving your life. That's a heavy obligation, isn't it? What if I said the elders have settled on a harebrained scheme to make us safe and rich—but one that will kill her? Where's your honor there, eh?"

"They wouldn't do that!" Lin glanced from side to side. "That would restart the war, wouldn't it?"

"They may not realize what they're doing," James said quietly. "They're entering into an arrangement with one of her enemies, though, a man who she told me had wronged her grievously. An-other of the cousins, their feuds are hard to keep track of . . . but what makes this different is that they're *also* talking to a govern-ment man." His younger brother's eyes were bulging with disbe-lief. "I know, I know. *I* think they've taken leave of their senses, you know the rules—but Dad and Uncle Huan are agreed. They figure the revolution's going to turn into a bloody civil war, and I think they're probably right about that—and they think we need political patronage to survive it. Well, that goes against the old rules, but they're the elders: They *make* the rules, and sometimes you have to throw out the old rules and bring in new rules. The trouble is, they're hoping to use a mad scheme of Dr. ven Hjal-mar's to breed extra world-walkers—don't ask me how it works, it's magic medicine from the other world the cousins go to—and they're hoping to use their political patron's offices to make it work. Ven Hjalmar is poison: Miriam hates him. And the patron they've picked—" James shook his head. "I don't trust him. Un-cle doesn't trust him either, but I think Uncle underestimates how untrustworthy he is. *And* ven Hjalmar. They'll cut a deal behind our backs and we'll be at their mercy."

"A deal. What sort of deal? What do they want us to do?" Lin stared at his elder brother.

"Assassination. Spying. Smuggling. What do *you* think the Leveler's secret Polis might want of us? And then they'll own us, match, lock, and trigger. But more importantly—the cousins will be looking for sanctuary here, and this will put them at our throat, and we at theirs: The Polis won't tolerate a different group of world-walkers beyond their control, once they learn of the cousins' existence. We'll be right back where we started, but this time under the thumb of the Polis—who despise us because we're children of the Inner Kingdom."

"We could go back there—" Lin stopped.

"Could we?" It was James's turn to raise an eyebrow. "Where would we be, if we couldn't move freely through New Britain? How would we prosper? And that's assuming we *can* go back there. What the cousins have stirred up—" He shook his head. "No, it wouldn't work. That's why I'm asking you: Which comes first, your honor or your filial loyalty?"

Lin stared for a few seconds; then his shoulders slumped. He took a deep mouthful of beer. "I defer to your elder wisdom," he finally said. Another pause. "What are you going to do?"

"I'm going to watch." James whistled tunelessly between his front teeth. "Hopefully I won't have to do anything. Hopefully Uncle is right and I am wrong. But if it turns out that Uncle Huan *isn't* right . . . will you obey him to the end, or will you do what's right for the family?"

Lin looked away. Then he looked back and nodded: a minute inclination of the head, but a significant one—the precise degree of submission that he might otherwise give his father. "What are you considering?"

"Nothing specific, as yet." James raised his tankard. "But if the elders' plans go astray—we'll see."

As he turned in to Miriam Beckstein's street, Mike Fleming felt an uncontrollable shudder ripple up the small of his back: an intense sensation of guilt, as if he'd done something unforgivable. Which was ridiculous. *Why do I feel like a stalker?* he wondered ironically. *I'm not the guy who's been lurking in the bushes with a phone and a camera for the past six months, hoping she'll come home.* He drove carefully up the road, not slowing and not staring at the houses, trying to tag the parked cars as memories battered for his attention.

Mike had a history: not uncommon. Single cop, married to the job. He had another history, too: dates, girlfriends, brief excursions into the alien world of domesticity that never quite seemed to gain traction. Four or five years ago he'd met a woman journalist—*how?* he could remember the where, but not the why—and asked her out, or maybe she'd asked him to ask her out, or something. And they'd gotten to know each other and she'd asked him home and then it all seemed to cool off, over the space of a couple of months.

Nothing new there; and he could easily have written it off. *She's a civilian, it wasn't going to work.* But for some reason, he hadn't gotten over her as easily as all that. He'd thought about looking her up. Seeing if he could make her change her mind. Then he realized he was getting into some creepy headspace, and asked himself if that was really who he wanted to be, took a vacation and went on a cruise, drank too much, and had a couple of one night stands. Which seemed to fix things, but he'd teetered on the fine edge of obsession for a few weeks, and now here he was driving down her street, and it felt weird. Creepy. Blame FTO for sucking him in and Miriam for concealing her secret other life from him—assuming that was what she'd been doing?—but this felt *wrong*. And what he was going to do next was even more wrong.

Burgling Ex-Girlfriend's House 101: First make sure there's nobody watching it, then make sure there's nobody home. Mike took a long loop around the neighborhood, killing five minutes before he turned back and drove down the street in the opposite direction. One parked car had departed; of the remaining ones, two were occupied, but hadn't been on his first pass. Ten minutes later, he made a third pass. A truck had parked up, with two workmen sitting inside, eating their lunch or something. Someone was messing with the trunk of another parked car. The two that had been occupied earlier were vacant. *If there's a watch they're using a house or a camera.* But not sitting in a car, waiting to pounce.

Mike pulled in, several doors down from Miriam's. He'd stopped at a Kinkos on his way. Now he hung a laminated badge around his neck, and stuck a fat day planner under his left arm. The badge bore a photograph but gave a false name and identified him as working for a fictional market research company, and the bulging day planner's zipped compartment held tools rather than papers, but to a casual bystander . . . well.

Now came the tricky part. He climbed out of his car and locked it; stretched; then walked up the street, trying not to hobble. He paused at the first door he came to, deliberately trying to look bored. There was a doorbell: J & P SUTHERLAND. He pushed it, waited, hoping nobody was in. If they were, he had a couple of spiels ready; but any exposure was a calculated risk. After a minute he pushed the buzzer again. The Sutherlands were obviously out; check one house off the list—he ritually made a note on the pad clipped to the back of his planner—and move on.

As Mike moved up the road, ringing doorbells and waiting, he kept a weather eye open for twitching curtains, unexpected antennae. A bored Boston grandmother at one apartment threatened to take too much interest in him, but he managed to dissuade her with the number-two pitch: was she satisfied with her current lawn-care company. (For telecommuting techies, the number-one pitch was a nonstick-bakeware multilevel marketing scheme. Anything to avoid having to actually interview anybody.) Finally he reached Miriam's doorstep. The windows were grimy, and the mailbox was threatening to overflow: good. *So nobody's renting.* He rang the doorbell, stood there for the requisite minute, and moved on.

This was the moment of maximum danger, and his skin was crawling as he slowly walked to the next door. If FTO *was* watching the Beckstein house, they'd be all over him if they suspected he was trying to make contact. But they *wouldn't* be all over a random street canvasser, and Mike had taken steps to not look like Mike Fleming, rogue agent and wanted man, from his cheap suit to the shaven scalp and false mustache. It wouldn't fool a proper inspection, but if he had to do that he'd already lost; all he had to do was look like part of the street furniture.

Three doors. Nobody coming out of the houses opposite, no sedan cruising slowly down the road towards him. His mind kept circling back to the ingrained grime on the windows, the crammed mailbox. *Let them have dropped the watch,* he prayed. A 24×7 watch on a person of interest was a costly affair: It took at least five agents working forty hours a week to minimally cover a target, and if they were expecting it and taking evasive measures—jumping next door's backyard fence, for example—you could double or triple that watch before you had a hope of keeping the cordon intact. Add management and headquarters staff and vacation and sick leave and you could easily use up twenty personnel—call it a cool million and a half per year in payroll alone. And Miriam hadn't been back, that much he was fairly sure of. Another sixty seconds passed. Mike made an executive decision: *There's no watch. Party time!*

The houses adjacent to the Beckstein residence were all vacant. Mike turned and walked back to the next one over, then rang the doorbell again. When there was no response, he shrugged; then instead of going back to the sidewalk he walked around the building, slowly, looking up at the eaves. (Cover story number three: Would you like to buy some weatherproof gutter lining?)

The fence between their yard and the next was head-high, but they weren't tidy gardeners and there was no dog; once he was out of sight of the street it took Mike thirty seconds to shove an empty rainwater barrel against the wooden wall and climb over it, taking care to lower himself down on his good leg. The grass in Miriam's yard was thigh-high, utterly unkempt and flopping over under its own weight. Mike picked himself up and looked around. There was a wooden shed, and a glass sliding door into the living room—locked. *Think like a cop. Where would she leave it?* Mike turned to the shed immediately. It had seen better days: The concrete plinth was cracked, and the window hung loose. He carefully reached through the window opening, slowly feeling around the frame until his questing fingers touched a nail and something else. He stifled a grin as he inspected the keyring. This was almost *too* easy. *What am I missing?* he wondered. A momentary premonition tickled the edge of his consciousness. *Miriam has enemies in the Clan, folks like Matthias. Oh.* Matthias had an extra-special calling card. Mike looked at the sliding door, then shook his head. So it wasn't going to be easy. Was it?

The key turned in the lock. Mike opened his case and removed a can of WD40, and sprayed it into the track at the bottom of the door. Then he took out another can, and a long screwdriver.

First, he edged the door open a quarter of an inch. Then he slowly ran the screwdriver's tip into the gap, and painstakingly lifted it from floor to ceiling. It met no resistance. *Good.* It was a warm day, and the cold sweat was clammy across his neck and shoulders and in the small of his back as he widened the entrance. Still nothing. *Am I jumping at shadows?* When the opening was eighteen inches wide, Mike gave the second spray can a brisk shake, then pointed it into the room, towards the ceiling, and held the nozzle down.

Silly String—quick-setting plastic foam—squirted out and drifted towards the floor in loops and tangles. About six inches inside the doorway, at calf level to a careless boot, it hung in midair, draped over a fine wire. Mike crouched down and studied it, then looked inside. The tripwire—now he knew what to look for—ran to a hook in the opposite side of the doorframe, and then to a green box screwed to the wall.

Mike stepped over the wire. Then he breathed out, and looked around.

The lounge-cum-office was a mess. Some person or persons unknown had searched it, thoroughly, not taking pains to tidy up afterwards; then someone else had installed the booby box and tripwire. It was dusty inside, and dark. *Power's probably out,* he realized. A turf'n'trap sting gone to seed, long neglected by its intended victim: *Better check for more wires.* Before touching anything, he pulled on a pair of surgical gloves. A poke at a desk lamp confirmed that the power was out—no surprises there. Hunting around in the sea of papers that hands unseen had dumped on the office floor was going to take some time, but seemed unavoidable: Empty sockets in a main extension block under the desk, and an abandoned palmtop docking station, suggested the absence of a computer and other electronic devices. Mike checked the rest of the house briefly, squirting Silly String before going through each doorway: There was another wire just inside the front door, beyond a toppled-over bookcase, but there were no other traps as far as he could see.

Getting down to work on the office, he wondered who'd turfed the scene. The missing computer was suggestive; going by the empty shelves and the boxes on the floor, it didn't take long to notice that all the computer media—Zip disks, CD-ROMs, even dusty old floppy disks—were missing. "Huh," he said quietly. "So they were looking for files?" Miriam was a journalist. It was carelessly done, as if they'd been looking for something specific—and the searchers weren't cops or spooks. Cops searching a journalist's office wouldn't leave a scrap of paper behind, and spooks wouldn't want the subject to know they were under surveillance. "Fucking amateurs." Mike took heart: It made his job that bit easier, to know that the perps had been looking for something specific, not trying to deny information to someone coming after.

Fumbling through the pile of papers, sorting them into separate blocks, Mike ran across a telephone cable. It was still plugged in, and tracing it back to the desk he discovered the handset, which had fallen down beside the wall. It was a fancy one, with a built-in answerphone and a cassette tape. Mike pocketed the tape, then went back to work on the papers. Lots of cuttings from newspapers and magazines, lots of scribbled notes about articles she'd been working on, a grocery bill, invoices from the gas and electric—nothing obviously significant. The books: There was a pile of software manuals, business books, some dog-eared crime thrillers and Harlequin romances, a Filofax—

Mike flipped it open. "Bingo!" It was full of handwritten names, numbers, and addresses, scribbled out and overwritten and annotated. Evidently Miriam didn't trust computers for everything; either that, or he'd latched on to a years-out-of-date organizer. But a quick look in the front revealed a year planner that went as far forward as the current year. *Why the hell didn't they take it?* he wondered, looking around. "Huh." Assuming the searchers were from the Clan . . . would they even know what a Filofax *was*? It looked like a book, from a distance; perhaps someone had told the brute squad to grab computers, disks, and

any loose files on her desk. *They don't think like cops* or *spooks.*
He looked round, at the green box on the wall above the door, and
shuddered. *Time to blow.*

Outside, with the glass door shut and the key back on its nail
in the shed, he glanced at the fence. His leg twinged, reminding
him that he wasn't ready for climbing or running. There was a
gap between the fence and the side of the house, shadowy; he
slipped into it, his fat planner (now pregnant with Miriam's Filofax) clutched before him.

There was a wooden gate at the end of the alley, latched shut
but not padlocked. He paused behind it to peer between the ver-
tical slats. A police car cruised slowly along the street, two officers inside. *Two?* Mike swore under his breath and crouched
down. The car seemed to take forever to drive out of sight. Heart
pounding, Mike checked his watch. It was half past noon, near
enough exactly. He straightened up slowly, then unlatched the
gate and limped past the front of the house as fast as he could,
then back onto the sidewalk outside. He fumbled the key to his
rental car at first, sweat and tension and butterflies in his stomach making him uncharacteristically clumsy, but on the second
try, the door swung open and he slumped down behind the steering wheel and pulled it to just as another police car—or perhaps
the same one, returning—swung into the street.

Mike ducked. *They're not running a stakeout but they've got
regular surveillance,* he told himself. *Believe it, man.* Adding the
Beckstein residence to a regular patrol's list of places of interest
would cost FTO virtually nothing—and they'd missed spotting
him by seconds. He stayed down, crouched over the passenger
seat as the cruiser slowly drove past. They'd be counting heads,
looking for the unexpected. His cover was good but it wouldn't
pass a police background check if they went to town on him—and
they would, if they found Miriam's purloined Filofax. Ten seconds passed, then twenty. Mike straightened up cautiously and
glanced in the rearview mirror. The cops were nearing the end of
the road. Thirty seconds; they paused briefly, then hung a left, and

Mike breathed out. *Okay, back to the motel,* he told himself. *Then we'll see what we've got here. . . .*

BEGIN RECORDING

"My fellow Americans, good evening.

"It pains me more than I can say to be speaking to you to-night as your president. There are no good situations in which a vice president can take the oath of office; we step into the boots of a fallen commander in chief, hoping we can fill them, hoping we can live up to what our dead predecessor would have expected of us. It is a heavy burden of responsibility and, God willing, I shall do my utmost to live up to it. I owe nothing less to you, to all our citizens and especially to the gallant men and women who serve the cause of freedom and democracy in our nations armed forces; and I say this—I shall not sleep until our enemies, the enemies who murderously attacked us a week ago, are hunted down wherever they hide and are destroyed.

"In time of war—and this is nothing less—it is the job of the commander in chief to defend the republic, and it is the job of the vice president to stand ready to serve, which is why I have nominated as my replacement a man well-qualified to fight for freedom: former Secretary of Defense Rumsfeld. I trust that his appointment to this post, vacated by my succession, will be approved by the house. The future of the republic is safe in his hands.

"But I can already hear you asking: Safe from whom?

"In the turmoil and heroism and agony of the attacks, it was difficult at first for us to ascertain the identity of our enemies. We have many enemies in the Middle East, from al-Qaeda and the terrorists in Iraq and Afghanistan, to the mullahs of Tehran, and naturally our suspicions first fell in those quarters. But they are not our only enemies; and the nature of the attack made it hard to be sure who was responsible. The two atomic bombs that exploded in our capital, and the third that misfired in the Pentagon visitors lot, were stolen from our own stockpile. This was not only a cowardly and heinous act of nuclear terrorism, but a carefully planned one.

However, we have identified the attackers, and we are now preparing to deal with them as they have dealt with us.

"There is no easy way for me to explain this because the reality lies far beyond our everyday experience, but the scientists of our national laboratories assure me that this is true: We live in what they call a multiverse, a many-branched tree of reality. Scientists at Los Alamos have for a year now been probing techniques for traveling to other universes—to other versions of this, our own Earth. They had hoped to use this technique for peaceful ends, to solve the environmental and climatic problems that may arise in future decades. But we have discovered, the hard way, that we are not alone.

"Some of the alternate earths we have discovered are inhabited. And in one of these, at least, the inhabitants are hostile. Worse: They, too, have the technological tools to travel to other universes. The enemy who attacked us is the government of a sovereign nation in another America, a Godless feudal despotism ruled by terror and the lash. They know no freedom and they hate our own, for we are a living refutation of everything they hold to be true. Agents of this enemy have moved unseen among us for a generation, and indeed they have been active in the narcotics trade, using it to fund their infiltration of our institutions, their theft of our technologies. They are followers of an alien ideology and they seek to bring us down, and it is to that end that they stole at least six atomic weapons from their storage cells on military bases—gaining access from another unseen universe even as our guards vigilantly defended the perimeter fences.

"We have a name for this enemy: They call themselves the Clan, and they rule a despotic kingdom called Gruinmarkt. And we know what to do to them, for they attacked us without warning on the sixteenth of July, a date that will live in infamy with 9/11, and 12/7, for as long as there is a United States of America.

"To you of the Clan, the cabal of thieves and drug smugglers who have attacked America, I have a simple message: If you surrender now, without preconditions, I will guarantee you a fair trial before the military tribunals now convened at

Guantánamo Bay. Only those of you who are guilty of crimes against the United States need fear our justice. But you should think fast. This offer expires one week from today. And then, in the words of my predecessor, Harry S Truman, you face prompt and utter annihilation.

"Think about it.

"Good night, and God bless America."

END RECORDING

BED REST

I t was beyond belief, how far things could change in just a week.

Sir Huw, beanpole-skinny and a bit gawky, reined his horse in and dismounted painfully while he was still a hundred yards short of the farmstead. He stretched, trying to iron the kinks out of his thigh and calf muscles.

"Is this it, bro?" rumbled the man-mountain driving the cart and pair behind him. "In the middle of nowhere?"

Huw glanced around. "On the other side, we're near Edison," he said. "I'll go first. We're expected, but . . ." No point saying it: *The guards are jumpy.* Because this week and forevermore, *all* the guards were jumpy. *Probably expecting Delta Force to drop in,* Huw mused idly. Not, in his estimate, that likely just yet—although in the long run it couldn't be ruled out. Anxiety battled caution, and set his feet in motion. "I wonder how Her Majesty is."

"Nearly three months gone by now," chirped another voice from the back of the cart, emanating from beneath a blanket that covered its passenger and a mound of wheeled luggage—all Tumi branded, expensive but ultralightweight ballistic nylon. "Sick as a mule on a coaster." Huw didn't look round: Trust Elena to interpret it as a political question. Because Miriam's pregnancy *was* political—and that was all it was. "Did you pack the books?"

"Yes." Huw had, in fact, packed the books. Two hundred kilograms of them, paper that was worth far more than its weight in gold, or cocaine, where they were going. The Rubber Bible, the Merck Manual, the US Pharmacopoeia; and more recondite references, science and engineering and medicine all, with a side order of mathematics and maps. They weighed a bundle, but when he'd messaged ahead to ask if they should go digital, the reply had been a terse *no*. Which made a certain sense. CD-ROMs and computers weren't durable enough for what Miriam was planning—if, in fact, he was reading her intentions aright.

Huw walked towards the farmyard, leading his horse. It was a hedge-laird's place; the hearth smoke of a small village rose beyond it, and he could see stooped backs in the fields, some of them pausing and turning to stare at the visitors. But then two guards stepped out in front of him from the barn, and he stopped. The middle-aged sergeant raised a hand: "Who hails?" The other stood by tensely, his rifle pointed at the ground before Huw's feet.

"Sir Huw Thoms, lieutenant by order of his grace, accompanied by Hulius Thoms and the lady Elena of Holdt, in the service of the Council." He halted; his horse exhaled noisily, neck drooping.

"Approach and be identified." Huw took a step forward. The sergeant peered at him, then glanced at a clipboard cautiously. "You are welcome, sir."

Huw stood where he was. "The password of the day is 'banquet,'" he stated. "*Now* can we come in? The horses are tired."

The armsman with the rifle relaxed visibly as his sergeant

nodded. "Very good, sir, the countersign is 'mullet.'" He gestured tiredly towards the stables. "We'll be pleased to sort you
out. Sorry about the precautions—you can't be too careful these
days."

Huw grimaced, then waved a hand at the machine gun dug
in just inside the tree line, ready to enfilade the approach to the
farm. "Any rebels try you so far?"

"Not yet, sir. Ah, your companions. If you don't mind—"

Elena and Yul climbed down from the cart and consented to
be inspected and compared to their photographs. "Is it that bad?"
She asked brightly, shaking out her skirts.

"Some of Lord Ganskwert's retainers attacked the house at
Doveswood last night, using a carriage and disguises to cover their
approach. Three dead, plus the traitors of course. We can't be too
careful."

"Indeed." Elena grinned alarmingly, and flashed the sergeant
a glimpse of what she had inside her capacious shoulder bag. He
blanched. "Sleep tight!" She added, "We're on your side!"

"Lightning Child, can't you keep it to yourself for even a
minute?" Huw complained. To the sergeant: "We won't be staying
overnight—we're wanted by Her Majesty, as soon as possible."

"Ah, we'll do our best, sir. I'll have to confirm that first."
His tone didn't brook argument.

"We can wait awhile," Huw conceded. "Got to sort out the
horses first, grab something to eat if possible, that sort of thing."

"There is bread and sausages in the kitchen. If you'd like
to wait inside I can have my men deal with your mounts? I take
it they're security livery?"

"Yes," Huw confirmed. "All yours." He handed his reins to
the man. "We'll be inside if you need us."

"Excellent," added Yul, following his elder brother towards
the farm building.

Huw and his small team had been well away from the excite-
ment when the putsch by the conservatives and the lords of the
Postal Service broke; following up a task assigned to him by
Angbard, Duke Lofstrom, back before his stroke—the urgency

of which had only become greater since. Huw had been in a rented house outside Macon, recovering from an exploration run, when Elena had erupted into the living room shouting about something on the television and waking up Yul (who had a post-walk hangover of doom). He'd begun to chastise her, only to fall silent as the mushroom cloud, red-lit from within, roiled skyward behind a rain of damaged-camera static.

They'd spent the first hour in shock, but then had come Riordan's Plan Black; and that had presented Huw with a problem, because they were nearly a thousand miles from the nearest evacuation point. Flights were grounded; police and national guard units were hogging the highways. It had taken them three days to make the drive, avoiding interstates and major cities. Finally they'd reached the outskirts of Providence and crossed over, taking another four days to finish the journey from Huw's family estates to this transit point, barely seventy miles away. A thousand miles—two hours by air. Or three days by back roads in the United States. Seventy miles—four days, in the Gruinmarkt. It was an object lesson in the source of the Clan's power—and a warning.

They didn't have long to wait; true to his word, the sergeant ducked in through the kitchen door barely half an hour later. "By your leave, sir, we have confirmed your permission to travel. If you are ready to go now . . . ?"

"I suppose so," said Yul, reluctantly setting aside a mug of game soup and a half-eaten cornbread roll. Elena was already on her feet, impatient; Huw set down his wine—a half-drained glass, itself exotic and valuable in this place—and stood.

"Have you got a level stage?" he asked. "We need to take the cart's contents."

"We have something better, sir." The guard turned and headed towards the barn. Huw followed him. Opposite the stalls—he saw a lad busily rubbing down the horses—someone had installed a raised platform, planks stretched across aluminum scaffolding. A ramp led up to it, and at the bottom—

"That's a *good* idea," Elena said admiringly.

Three big supermarket trolleys waited for them, loaded up with bags. "The regular couriers will bring them back once you unload them," said the sergeant. He picked up his clipboard. "In view of the current troubles we have no postmaster, but I'm keeping score. For later."

"All right." Huw set his hands to one of the trolleys and pushed it up the ramp. "What's the other side like?"

"It's in a cellar." The sergeant looked disapproving. "Good thing too. You don't want to be seen coming and going over there—it's a real zoo. But you'll be safe enough here." He caught Huw's raised eyebrow and nodded. "I'll go first, see if I don't." He climbed onto the platform and waited while Yulius and Elena pushed their laden trolleys up the ramp. "Here, you let me take that one, young miss. Why don't you ride for once?" Laying one hand on the trolley's metal frame, he reached up and tugged a cord leading to a blind on the opposite wall. The blind rose—

The basement was brick-walled, and the ceiling low, but the Clan's surveyors had done their job well and the raised floor was a perfectly level match for the platform in the barn. As Huw hauled the first of his suitcases out of the trolley, trying to ignore the nausea and migrainelike headache, he heard voices from the top of the staircase: Elena, and someone else, someone familiar and welcome.

"My lady Brilliana," he said. He deposited his case beside the top step—the cellar stairs surfaced in what seemed to be a servants' pantry—and bowed. "I'm glad to see you."

"Sir Huw! How wonderful to see you, too." She smiled slightly more warmly than was proper: Huw held himself in check, ignoring the impulse to hug her to him. He'd been worried about her for the past week; to find her here, her hair in blond curls, dressed after last year's New London mode, lifted a huge weight from his heart. Brilliana was an officer of the duke's intelligence directorate and the queen-widow's chief of staff—and something more to Huw. She held out her hand, and, somewhat daringly, he bent to kiss it. "Have you had a troublesome time?" she asked, gripping his fingers.

"Not as bad as some." Huw straightened up, then gestured at the bags: "I bought the books Miriam wanted. And a few more besides. Yul is"—footsteps creaked on the stairs and he stepped aside as his brother hauled two more suitcases over the threshold—"here, too."

"And all these damned bits of paper," his brother complained, shoving the cases forward. "Lightning Child damn them for a waste of weight—" He stepped forward, out of the path of the sergeant from the other side of the transit post, who heaved another two bags towards Huw.

"Trig tables," Huw added. "Have you any idea how hard it is to find five-digit trigonometry tables in good condition? Nobody's printed them for years. I also threw in a couple of calculators—I found a store with old stock HP-48GXs and a thermal printer, so I bought the lot. They take rechargeable batteries so the only scarce resource is the thermal paper," he added defensively. "I'm still running the one I bought for my freshman year—they run forever."

"Oh, Huw." Brill shook her head, still smiling. "Listen, I'm sure it's a good idea! It's just"—she glanced over her shoulder—"we may not be able to resupply at will, and you know how easily computers break."

"These aren't computers; they're programmable calculators. But they might as well be mainframes, by these people's standards." He was burbling, he realized: a combination of post-world-walking sickness and the peculiar relief of finding Brill alive and well in the wake of the previous week's events. "Sorry. Been a stressful time. Is Miriam—"

"She's in bed upstairs. Resting." An unreadable expression flickered across Brill's face. "I'll give you the tour, if you like. Who else . . . ?"

"Me, ma'am." The sergeant reappeared, carrying two more suitcases, wheezing somewhat. "One more to go, sirs, ladies."

"No need to overdo it, Marek, the last cases will wait half an hour if you want to put your feet up." Brill's concern was obvious: "You've already been over today, haven't you?"

"Yes, ma'am, but it needs moving and we're shorthanded—"

"You'll be even more shorthanded if you work yourself into a stroke! Go and sit yourself down in the parlor with a mug of beer and a pill until your head clears. Go on, I'll get Maria to look after you—" Brill dragged the sergeant out of the servants' stairwell, seemingly by main force of will, then returned to lead Huw into the downstairs lounge. "He's right that they're badly undermanned over there, but he insists on trying to do everything," she said apologetically. "There's too much of that around here."

"Too much of it *everywhere*!" Elena said emphatically. "Why, if I hadn't forced Huw to let me drive—but how is her royal highness?" She looked at Huw: "Won't she want to—"

"Yes, how is she?" Huw began, then stopped. Brill's expression was bleak. "Oh. Oh *shit*."

"The lady Helge is perfectly all right." Brilliana's voice was emotionless. "But she's very tired and needs time to recover."

"Recover from what?" Yul chipped in before Elena could kick his ankle.

"Her express instructions are that you are to tell no one," Brill continued, looking Huw straight in the eye. "Nobody is going to leave this house who cannot keep his or her mouth shut, at least until it no longer matters."

"Until *what* matters?" Yul asked, head swiveling between Brilliana and Huw with ever-increasing perplexity.

"Was it spontaneous?" Huw demanded.

Brill nodded reluctantly. "The day of the putsch."

"Let me see her?" demanded Elena. "My mother was midwife to the district nobility when I was young and she taught me—"

Yul stood by, crestfallen and lost for words. "Give me your locket," Brill said to Elena. "And you too," she added to Yul. She spared Huw but a brief narrow-eyed glance that seemed to say, *If I can't trust you, then who?* "You're not to tire her out, mind," she added for Elena's benefit. "If she's sleeping, leave her be." Then she turned towards the door to the owner's rooms. "Leave the cases for now, Huw. Let me fill you in on what's been going wrong here. . . ."

In the end, there was no siege: The house surrendered without a shot being fired, doors and windows flung wide, a white flag running up the pole that rose from the apex of the steeply pitched roof.

That wouldn't have been enough to save the occupants, of course. Riordan was not inclined towards mercy: In the wake of a hard-fought civil war against the old nobility, it was quite obvious to one and all that the Clan divided must fall, and this rebellion could be seen as nothing but the blackest treachery. But by the same token, the families were weak, their numbers perilously low—and acts of gratuitous revenge would only weaken them further, and risk sowing the seeds of blood feud to boot. "Arrest everyone," he'd instructed his captain on the ground, Sir Helmut: "You may hang Oliver Hjorth, Griben ven Hjalmar, or"—a lengthy list of confirmed conspirators—"out of hand, and you may deal as you wish with anyone who resists, but we must avoid the appearance of revenge at all costs. We can afford to spare those who did not raise arms against us, and who are guilty only of following their sworn liege—and their dependents."

Helmut's mustache quivered. "Is this wise, sir?" he asked.

"It may not be wise, but it is *necessary*," Riordan retorted. "Unless you think we should undertake our enemies' work for them by cutting each other's throats to the last?"

And so: This was the third great holding of a rebel family that Sir Helmut had ridden into in two days. And they were getting the message. At the last, the house of Freyn-Hankl, a minor outer family connected with the Hjorth lineage, the servants had risen up and locked their upstart landowners in the wine cellars, and sued for mercy. Sir Helmut, mindful of his commanding officer's advice, had rewarded them accordingly, then sent them packing to spread the word (before he discreetly executed his prisoners—who had, to be fair, poisoned the entire staff of the local Security post by treachery). Facing the open windows and doors of the summer house at Judtford, with his soldiers going in and coming out at will, he was pleased with the outcome of this tactic. Whether or not it was wise or necessary, it was certainly proving to be effective.

"Sir! If you please, to the drawing room." A startled-looking messenger boy, barely in his teens, darted from the front door.

Sir Helmut stared at him. "In whose name?" he demanded.

"Sir! Two duchesses! One of them's the queen's mum, an' the other is hers! What should we do with them, Jan wants to know?"

Sir Helmut stared some more, until the lad's bravado collapsed with a shudder. Then he nodded and glanced over his shoulder. "Sammel, Karl, accompany me," he snapped. The two soldiers nodded and moved in, rifles at the ready. "Lead me to the ladies," he told the messenger. "Let's see what we've got."

The withdrawing room was dark, and cramped with too much overstuffed furniture, and it smelled of face powder and death. Flies buzzed near the ceiling above the occupants, a pair whom Sir Helmut could not help but recognize. One of them was sleeping. "What happened here?" he demanded.

The younger of the pair—the one who was mother to the queen-widow—looked at him from beneath drooping eyelids. "Was 'fraid you wouldn't get here," she slurred.

"What—"

"Poison. In tha' wine. Sh-she started it." A shaking hand rose slowly, pointed at the mounded fabric, the shriveled, doll-like body within. "Tha' coup. 'S'hers. Did it for Helge, she said."

"But—" Helmut's eyes took in the empty decanter, the lack of motion. "Are you drunk, or—"

"Dying, prob'ly." She wheezed for a second or two; it might have been laughter. "Poisoned the wine with pure heroin. The trade of queens."

"I see." Helmut turned to the wide-eyed messenger lad: "You. Run along and fetch a medic, *fast*." To the duchess: "There's an antidote. We'll get you—"

"No." Patricia closed her eyes for a long moment. "Ma, Hilde-Hildegarde. Started this all. Leave her. No trial. As for me . . ." She subsided, slurring. A rattling snort emanated from the other chair and Helmut glanced at the door, before leaning to listen to the old woman's chest.

Helmut rose and, turning on his heel, strode towards the door. *Crone save me,* he subvocalized. The messenger was coming, a corpsman following behind. "I have two heroin overdoses for you," Helmut told him. "Forget triage; save the younger one first if at all possible."

"Heroin overdose?" The paramedic looked startled. "But I don't have—are you sure—"

"Deliberate poisoning. Get to it." Helmut stepped aside as the medic nodded and went inside. Helmut breathed deeply, then turned to the messenger. "Here." He pulled out his notepad and scribbled a brief memo. "Tell comms to radio this to Earl-Major Riordan in day code purple, stat." The lad took the note and fled. Helmut stared after him for a moment then shook his head. *What a mess.* Poisoning and attempted matricide versus kidnapping: petty treason versus high treason. How to weigh the balance? "Jester's balls, if only I'd been delayed an hour on the road. . . ."

Miriam lay in bed, propped up on a small mountain of pillows, staring blankly at the floral-patterned wallpaper behind the water jug on the dresser and thinking about death.

I never wanted it. So why am I feeling so bad? she wondered. *What the hell is* wrong *with me?*

It wasn't as if she'd wanted to have a baby: Griben ven Hjalmar's artificial insemination was, if not actual rape, then certainly morally equivalent. He—his sponsors (she shied away from thinking about them)—had wanted an heir to the throne. They'd specifically wanted *her* to bear the heir, and not trusting her to willingly have intercourse with the man they were forcing her to marry—a man who was so badly damaged by a poisoning incident in his childhood that he could barely talk—they had held her captive and committed a most unspeakable act upon her person. The irony of which was that her thirty-something womb was still fertile, but the marriage had been a most signal failure, disrupted by Prince Creon's elder brother in a spectacularly bloody putsch that ignited an all-out civil war in the Gruinmarkt. By the time the dust settled, Miriam had been three weeks pregnant, the entire royal family was dead . . . and she was carrying the heir to the throne, acknowledged by all who had survived the lethal betrothal ceremony.

She had not taken the news well; only Huw's cunning offer to help her obtain a termination—if that was what she willed—had kept her from running, and not stopping until she arrived at the nearest available abortion clinic. As the immediate rage and humiliation and dread faded, she began to reevaluate the situation: not from an American woman's perspective, but with the eyes of a Clan noblewoman catapulted headlong into the middle of a fraught political dilemma. *I don't have to love it. I don't have to raise it. I just have to put up with eight months of back pain and morning sickness and get it out of my body. And in return . . .* they'd promised her the moon on a stick: a seat at the highest table, as much power and wealth as anyone in that godforsaken mediaeval nightmare of a country could have, and most important of all, *security*. Security for herself, for her mother, for her friends. A chance to fix some of the things that were wrong with the Clan, from the inside, working with allies. Even a chance to try and do something about the bigger picture: to jump-start the process of dragging the Gruinmarkt towards modernity.

She'd signed a fraught compromise with her conscience. Perhaps she was just rationalizing her situation, even succumbing to Stockholm syndrome—the tendency of the abducted to empathize with their kidnappers—and while she hated what had been done to her, she was no longer eager to dispose of the unwanted pregnancy. She'd done it before, many years ago; it had been difficult, the situation looming no less inconveniently in a life turned upside down, but she'd persevered. She'd even, a year ago, harbored wistful thoughts about finding a Mr. Right and—

Her body had betrayed her.

I'm thirty-five, damn it. Not an ideal age to be pregnant, especially in a mediaeval backwater without rapid access to decent medical care. Especially in the middle of a civil war with enemies scheming for her demise, or worse. She'd been stressed, anxious, frightened, and still in the first trimester: and when the cramps began she'd ignored them, refusing to admit what was happening. *And now it's not going to happen.* The royal dynasty that had ruled the Gruinmarkt for the past century and a half had bled out in a bedpan in New Britain, while the soldiers watched their maps and the nobles schemed. It wasn't much worse than a heavy period (aside from the pain, and the shock, and the sudden sense of horror as a sky full of cloud-castle futures evaporated). But it was a death sentence, and not just for the dynastic plans of the conservative faction.

She'd managed to hold her face together until she was away from Riordan's headquarters, with Brill's support. Ridden piggyback across to a farmhouse in the countryside outside small-town Framingham—not swallowed by Boston's suburbs, in New Britain's contorted history—that Sir Alasdair had located: abandoned, for reasons unclear, but not decayed.

"We've got to keep you away from court, my lady," Brill explained, hollow-eyed with exhaustion, as she steered her up the staircase to an underfurnished bedroom. It had been a day since the miscarriage: a day of heavy bleeding, with the added discomfort of a ride in an oxcart through the backwoods around Niejwein. She'd begun shivering with the onset of a mild fever, not taking it all in, anomalously passive. "When word gets out all hell will follow soon enough, but we can buy time first. Miriam? How do you feel?"

Miriam had licked her lips. "Freezing," she complained. "Need water." She'd pulled the bedding over her shoulders, curling up beneath without removing her clothes.

"I'll get a doctor," Brill had said. And that was about the last thing Miriam remembered clearly for the next forty-eight hours.

Her fever banished by bootleg drugs—amoxycillin was eerily effective in a world that hadn't been overexposed to antibiotics—she lay abed, weak but recovering. Brilliana had held the center of her world, drafting in her household staff as they surfaced after the coup, organizing a courier link to the Niejwein countryside, turning her muttered suggestions into firm orders issued in the name of the security directorate's highest office. *I don't deserve these people,* Miriam thought vaguely. Depression stalked her waking hours incessantly, and her mood fluctuated from hour to hour: She couldn't tell from moment to moment whether she was relieved or bereft. *Why do they put up with me? Can't do anything right. Can't build a business, can't have a baby, can't even stay awake—*

There was a knock at the door.

She cleared her throat. "Enter." Her voice creaked like a rusting hinge, underused.

The door opened. "Miriam?"

She turned her head. "Ah! Sir Huw." She cleared her throat again. "Sorry. Not been well." Huw was still wearing Gruinmarkt-casual: leather leggings, linen blouson. She saw another face behind him: "And, and Elena? Hello, come on in. Sorry I can't be more hos, hospitable." She tried to sit up.

"Your Majesty!" trilled Elena. Miriam tried not to wince. "Oh, you look so ill—"

"It's not that bad," she interrupted, before the girl—*Girl? By Clan standards she's overdue to be married*—started gushing. "I had a fever," she added, to Huw. "Caught something nasty while I was having the miscarriage. Or maybe I miscarried because . . ." She trailed off. "How have you been?" she added. *When at a loss for small talk, ask a leading question.* That was what her mother, Iris—or Patricia, to her long-lost family—had brought her up to do. Once, it had made for a career—

Huw took a deep breath. "We found more," he said, holding up three fingers. "And two viable knots. Then all hell broke loose and we only just got here." He grinned, much too brightly.

"*Three* worlds?" Miriam raised an eyebrow.

"Yes!" Elena bounced up and down on the linen press she'd taken for a seat. She, too, was wearing native dress from the

Clan's home world; she and Huw would have faded right into the background at any Renaissance Faire, if not for the machine pistol poking from her shoulder bag. "Three! It was very exciting! One of them was so warm Yul nearly fainted before he could get his oxygen mask off! The others—"

Huw cleared *his* throat, pointedly. "If I may? *That* one was subtropical, humid. Lots of cycads and ferns, very damp. We didn't see any people, or any animal life for that matter—but insects. Big dragonflies, *that* big." He held his hands a foot apart. "I was pretty light-headed by the time we left. I want to measure the atmospheric gas mix—think it's way on the high side of normal, oxygen-wise. Like the carboniferous era never ended, or came back, or something. And then there was another cold pine-forest world. Again, no life, no radio transmissions, no sign of people." He shook his head.

"The third?" Miriam pushed herself up against the pillows, fascinated.

"We nearly died," Elena said very quietly.

"You nearly—" Miriam stopped. "Huw, I thought you were taking precautions? Pressure suits, oxygen, guns?"

"We were. *That* one's inhabited—but not by anything alive." He clammed up. "Miriam. Uh. Helge. My lady. What's going on? Why are we here?"

Miriam blinked. "Inhabited? By what?"

"Robots, maybe. Or very fast minerals. Something surprised Yul so he shot it, and it ate his shotgun. After that, we didn't stick around. Why are we here? The major said you were in charge of, of something important—"

"I need to get out of bed." Miriam winced. "This wasn't part of the plan. Huw, we're here to make contact with the government. Official contact, and that means I need to be in there doing it."

"*Official* contact?" His eyes widened.

"Yes." She took a deep breath. "We're finished in the United States. The Clan, I mean. Those mindless thugs in the postal arm, Baron Hjorth, my grandmother—they've completely wrecked any hope of us *ever* going back, much less normalizing relations. The US will follow us, to the ends of the universe. Ends of *every* universe, perhaps. Certainly they had agents in the Gruinmarkt . . . Riordan's not stupid, he saw this coming. That's what we're doing here. We're to open negotiations with the Empire of New Britain and sue for asylum. They've got problems too, stuff we can help with—the French, that is, the Bourbon monarchy in St. Petersburg. We've got access to science and technology that's half a century ahead of anything they've got in the laboratory here, much less widely deployed. That gives us a bargaining tool, much better than a suitcase full of heroin." She chuckled softly. It made her ribs hurt. "You know all the Roswell, Area 51, alien jokes? Crashed flying saucers, secret government labs full of alien technology? We're going to be their aliens. Except there's a slight problem."

"A problem." Huw's expression was a sight. "I can see several potential problems with that idea. What kind of problem do you find worrying enough to single out?"

"We're not the only people who've had a coup d'état." Miriam sat up, bracing her arms against the headboard of the bed. "The king's under arrest, the country is in a state of crisis, and the contacts I'd made are high up in the new government. Which may sound like a great opportunity to you, but I'm not sure I like what they're doing with it. And before we can talk to them we need to square things with the cousins."

"The cousins—"

"Yes. Or they'll assume we're breaking the truce. Tell me, Huw—have you ever met James Lee?"

The huge, wooden radio in the parlor of the safe house near Framingham was tuned permanently to Voice of England, hissing and warbling the stentorian voice of Freedom Party–approved news as and when the atmospheric conditions permitted. The morning of the day after his arrival, Huw opened it up and marveled at the bulky tubes and rat's nest of wires within. It was a basic amplitude-modulated set, the main tuning capacitor fixed firmly in position by a loop of wire sealed with a royal crest in solder: comically easy to subvert, *if* the amateur engineer had been partial to five years in a labor camp. Huw shook his head, then added a crate of pocket-sized Sony world-band receivers to his next supply run shopping list, along with a gross of nicad batteries and some solar-powered chargers.

"How do you use it?" asked Brilliana, looking at it dubiously.

"You plug it back in"—Huw demonstrated, clipping the battery wire to the bulky lead-acid cell that filled much of the radio's plinth—"and turn it on like so." Hissing static filled the room.

She frowned. "It sounds horrible. How do you tune it?"

"You don't. I mean, we can adjust it slightly, within a permitted frequency range." Huw straightened up. "But the state owns the airwaves." Someone was talking in portentious tones through the wrong end of a trombone. "Welcome to the pre-transistor era, when radio engineers needed muscles."

"What use is a radio you can't—"

Miriam stopped in the doorway. "Wait!" She held up a hand, frowning. She was looking better this morning, Huw decided: There was color in her cheeks and she'd bothered to get dressed in native drag, something like an Indian shalwar suit, only with frightening amounts of embroidery. "Can you turn that up?"

"I guess." Huw tweaked the fine-tuning pot, then cranked up the volume.

"I know that voice!" Miriam stared at the radio, her eyes wide. "It's Erasmus!"

"Really?" Brill nodded, then cocked her head. "I suppose it might be."

"—Our enemies. Only through unceasing vigilance can we insure our safety in the face of the brutal attacks of the aristocratic gang and their lickspittle toadies. But be of good heart: They are a minority, and they swim against the current of history. The slave owners and gangmasters and mercantilists cannot bully us if we stand firm against them. The party is the backbone of the people, and we shall bear the full weight of the struggle against totalitarian monarchism on your behalf—"

"Yes, I think you're right," Brilliana said thoughtfully. "He's wordy enough. . . ."

"Jesus." Miriam swayed slightly. "It's too early for this. Is there any coffee?"

"In the kitchen, I think." Brill raised an eyebrow at Huw. "Enough with the radio," she said. Huw could take a hint: He switched it off, and waited for the glowing tubes to fade to gray before he followed them towards the waiting pot.

Miriam was sitting on one of the two chairs, her hands clutching an earthenware mug of black coffee. The kettle still steamed atop the coal-fired cast-iron cooking range. "He's on the *radio*," she said, as if she didn't quite believe it. "Voice of England. That's the official news channel, isn't it? He must have made it to California and come back. This will make everything so much simpler." Her hands were shaking slightly. "But it also means we need to talk to the cousins now, not later."

"It's too dangerous." Brill looked mulish. "Travel, I mean! There are roving gangs, and we don't have a car, or—"

"They don't use cars here," Miriam pointed out. "At least not the way they do in our—my—America. There are trains. We're about three miles outside city limits and there's a railway station. You can catch a train to, to—where are the Lees? Do we have an address for them in Boston? If the service is running right now, and if they aren't demanding travel papers. But there's a small-scale civil war going on. They don't—neither side—have the resources to lock down travel, except across contested borders. We're on the east coast city belt here, the paper says it's all Freedom Party territory—"

"You've got newspapers?" Huw demanded, incredulity getting the better of him.

"Yes, why wouldn't we?" Miriam was nonplussed. "They don't have domestic television, Huw, no internet either. How do you expect they get their news?"

"But, but—there's a civil war going on!"

"Yes, but that's not stopping the local papers. We get visitors, Huw. We've had knife-grinders and pan-sellers and we get a book merchant who carries the weekly paper. As far as our neighbors know, we're a bunch of squatters who moved in here when the farmer and his family ran away—they're royalists, he was a snitch, apparently. They don't mind having us around: Alasdair and Erik saw off a gang of hobos—probably deserters—the day before yesterday. So we, we try to keep informed. And we're trying to fit in." She frowned. "Got to get you some local clothes."

"I'll sort him out." Brill rose and poked at the firebox in the range cautiously. Huw winced. Between the summer warmth and an active fire the kitchen was unpleasantly warm, although Miriam still looked as if she was cold. "There's a lot of work involved in establishing a safe house," she said, looking at Huw speculatively. "I've got a list. If you want to stick around, make yourself useful—"

"No," said Miriam. Brill looked at her. "I need to see Erasmus. In person." She tapped a finger on the table. "We need to send a message to James Lee, fix up a conference." Another tap. "And we need to get as many of our people as possible over here right now. And set up identities for them." A third finger-tap. "Which feeds back to Erasmus. If he'll help us out, *all* our immediate troubles here go away."

"And if he doesn't?" Asked Brill.

"Then we're so screwed it isn't funny." Miriam took a sip of coffee. "So we're not going to worry about that right now. I'm not well enough to travel today, but I'm getting better. Huw? I want you and Yul—you're the expeditionary research team, aren't you?—to go into Framingham today. Yeah, I know, so find him some clothes, Brill. I'll give you a couple of letters to post, Huw, and a shopping list. Starting with a steamer. We've got gold, yes? More of the shiny stuff than we know what to do with. So we're going to spend some of it. Get a steamer—a truck, not a passenger car—and buy food and clothing, anything that's not nailed down, anything you can find from thrift stores.

Some furniture, too, chairs and beds if you can get them, we're short on stuff here, but that's a secondary consideration." She was staring past him, Huw realized, staring into some interior space, transcribing a vision. "Along the way you're going to post those letters, one to James Lee, one to Erasmus."

She cleared her throat. "Now here's the hard bit. If you're stopped by Freedom Riders, drop my name—Miriam Beckstein—and say I'm working for Erasmus Burgeson and Lady Margaret Bishop. Remember that name: Margaret Bishop. It'll get their attention. If it doesn't get their attention, *don't* resist if they take you into custody, but make sure you emphasize that you're working for me and I'm working for their bosses—Lady Bishop and Erasmus know about me, and about the Clan, at least in outline. Then get the hell away. You know how to do it, you've got your temp tats, yes?"

Huw cleared his throat. "Do you want that to happen?" *Or is this just micromanagement due to nerves?*

"No." Miriam shook her head. "We want to make contact at the highest level, which means ideally we go straight to Erasmus. But if things go wrong, we *don't* want to start out with a firefight. Do you see where I'm going here?"

"Six different directions at once, it seems." Huw rolled his eyes. "Yeah, I *think* I get it. These people are going to be our patrons, so don't start the relationship by shooting the servants, right?"

"That's about it." Miriam paused. "If you run into real trouble, don't hang around—just world-walk. We can afford to try again later; we can't afford to lose you."

"Conflicting mission objectives: check." *Click.* Yul shoved another cartridge into the magazine he was filling. "Flashing wads of money around in the middle of a revolution while guilty of looking foreign." *Click.* "Micromanaging boss trying to run things on impulse." *Clack.* He squeezed down on the last cartridge with a quiet grunt, then laid the magazine aside. "Have I missed anything, bro?"

"Yes." It was either the coffee or pre-op nerves: Huw was annoyed to find his hands were shaking slightly as he checked the battery level on the small Pentax digital camera. "We've got a six-month deadline to make BOLTHOLE work." (BOLTHOLE was the name Brill had pinned on the current project; a handy identifier, and one that anticipated Miriam's tendency to hatch additional projects.) "Then all the hounds of Hel come belling after our heels. And that's before the Americans—"

"I don't see what you and Her Maj are so worked up about, bro. They can't touch us." Yulius stood, shrugging his coat into shape.

"We disagree." Huw slid the camera into an inner pocket of his own jacket. "You haven't spent enough time over there to know how they think, how they work." He stood up as Yul stowed his spare magazines in a deep pocket. "Come on, let's go." He slung a small leather satchel across his chest, allowed it to settle into place, then gave the strap a jerk: Nothing rattled.

It was a warm day outside, but the cloud cover threatened rain for the afternoon. Huw and Yul headed out into the run-down farmyard—now coming into a modicum of order as Helge's armsmen cleared up after the absent owners—then down the dirt track to the highway. The road into town was metaled but only wide enough for one vehicle, bordered by deep ditches with passing places every quarter mile. "They make good roads," Yul remarked as they walked along the side. "Not as good as the Americans, but better than us. Why is that?"

"Long story." Huw shook his head. "We're stuck in a development trap, back home."

"A what trap?"

A rabbit bolted for safety ahead of them as the road curved; birds peeped and clattered in the trees to either side like misconfigured machinery. "Development. In the Americans' world there are lots of other countries. Some of them are dirt-poor, full of peasants. Sort of like home, believe it or not. The rich folks can import automobiles and mobile phones but the poor are just like they've always been. The Americans were that way, two hundred years ago—somewhere along the way they did something right. You've seen how they live today. Turns out—they've tried it a lot, in their world—if you just throw money at a poor country and pay for things like roads and schools, it doesn't automatically *get better*. The economists have a bunch of theories about why, and how, and what you need to do to make an entire nation lift itself up by its own bootstraps . . . but most of them are wrong. Not surprising, really; mostly economists say what the rich people who pay them want to hear. If they knew for sure, if there was one true answer, there'd be *no* underdeveloped nations. *We'd* have developed, in the Gruinmarkt, too, if there was a well-defined recipe. It's probably some combination of money, and institutions like the rule of law and suppression of corruption, and education, and a work ethic, and fair markets, and ways of making people feel like they can better themselves—social inclusion. But nobody knows for sure."

A high stone wall appeared alongside the road, boundary marker to a country estate. "People have to be able to produce a bit more than they consume, for one thing. And for another, they have to know that if they *do* produce it—well, what does a lord do if his peasants are growing more food than they need?"

Yul shrugged. "What do you expect me to say, bro? They're his tenants!"

"Well, yeah, but." They passed a spiked iron gate, head-high and closed, behind which a big house squatted with sullenly shuttered windows. The wall resumed. "Here's the thing. Our families became rich, and bought titles of nobility, and married into the aristocracy. And after a generation or two they *were* noble houses. But we're still stuck in a sea of peasants who don't make anything worth shit, who don't generate surpluses because they know some guy in a suit of armor can take it away from them whenever he likes. We've got towns and artisans and apothecaries and some traders and merchants and they're . . . you've seen the Americans. They're not smarter than us. They don't work harder than the peasants on your father's land. They're not—most of them—rich because they inherited it. But two hundred years ago things over there took a strange turn, and now they're overwhelmingly wealthy. These people are . . . they're better off than us: not as good as the Americans, but doing well, getting better. So *what are they doing right?*"

Huw stopped. The wall had come to an end, and ahead of them the road ran straight between a burned-out strip of row houses and a cleared field; but a group of four men had stepped into the highway in front of them, blocking the way ahead. They had the thin faces and hungry eyes of those who had been too long between hot meals.

"Yer bag. Give it 'ere," said the thinnest, sharpest man. He held out a hand, palm-up. Huw saw that it was missing two fingers. The men to either side of the speaker, hard-faced, held crudely carved shillelaghs close by their sides.

"I don't think so," replied Huw. He smiled. "Would you like to reconsider?" From behind his left shoulder he heard a rip of Velcro as Yul freed up his holster.

"They's the strangers wot moved on ole Hansen's farm," the skinny man—barely more than a teenager—at the left of the row hissed sharply.

The speaker's eyes flickered sideways, but he showed no sign of attention. "Git 'em, lads," he drawled, and the highwaymen raised their clubs.

Yul drew and fired in a smooth motion. His Glock cracked four times while Huw was pursuading his own weapon to point the right way. The two club-men dropped like sacks of potatoes. The skinny lad's jaw dropped; he turned and bolted into the field.

"Aw, *shit*," said the sharp-faced speaker. He sounded disgusted, resigned even, but he didn't run. "Yez party men, huh?" Huw strained to make the words out through a combination of ringing ears, the thunder of his own heartbeat, and the man's foreign-sounding accent.

"That's right!" He kept his aim on the highwayman's chest.

Yul stayed out of his line of fire, performing an odd, jerky duck-walk as he scanned the sides of the road for further threats. "And you are . . . ?"

"Down on me luck." Abruptly, the highwayman sat down in the middle of the road and screwed his eyes shut fiercely. "G'wan shoot me. Better'n'starvin' to death like this past week. I'm ready."

"No. You're not worth the bullet." Huw stared at the high-wayman over the sights of his pistol. A plan came to him. "You are under arrest for attempted robbery. Now, we can do this two different ways. First way is, we take you for trial before a people's court. They won't show you any mercy: Why should they? You're a highwayman. But the other way—if you want to make yourself useful to us, if you're very *useful*, my colleague and I can accidentally look the other way for a few seconds."

"Forget it, citizen. He's a villain: Once a villain always a vil-lain. Let's find a rope—" Yul was just playing bad cop. Probably.

"What do ye want?" The highwayman was looking from Yul to Huw and back again in fear. "Yer playin' with me! Yer mad!"

"Dead right." Huw grinned. "On your feet. We're going into town and you're going to walk in front of us with your hands tied behind your back. The people's foe. And you know what? I'm going to ask you for directions and you're going to guide us truthfully. Do it well and maybe we won't hand you over to the tribunal. Do it badly—" He jerked his neck sideways. "Under-stand?"

The highwayman nodded fearfully. It was, Huw reflected, a hell of a way to hire a tour guide.

Framingham was a mess. From burned-out farmsteads and cot-tages on the outskirts of town to beggarmen showing their war wounds and soup kitchens on the curbsides, it gave every indica-tion of being locked in a spiral of decline. But there were no fur-ther highwaymen or muggers; probably none such were willing to risk tangling with two openly armed men escorting a prisoner before them. Huw kept his back straight, attempting to exude unconscious authority. *We're party men, Freedom Riders. If nobody here's* seen *such before* . . . well, it would work right up until they ran into the real thing; and when that happened, they could world-walk.

"We're going to the main post office," Huw told the prisoner. "Then to"—he racked his memory for the name they'd plucked from a local newssheet's advertising columns—"Rackham's bookmaker. Make it smart."

The main post office was a stone-fronted building in a dusty high street, guarded by half a dozen desperadoes behind a barricade of beer casks from a nearby pub. Rackham's was a quarter mile past it, down a side street, its facade boarded over and its door barred.

They turned into an alleyway behind the bookmaker's. "You have ten seconds to make yourself invisible," Huw told his shivering prisoner, who stared at him with stunned disbelief for a moment before taking to his heels.

"Was that clever?" asked Yul.

"No, but it had to be done," Huw told him. "Or were you really planning on walking into a people's tribunal behind him?"

"Um. Point, bro." Yul paused. "What do we do now?"

"We sell this next door." Huw tightened his grip on the satchel, feeling the gold ingots inside. "And then we go to the post office and post a letter."

"But it's not running! You saw the barricades? It's the Freedom Party headquarters."

"That's what I'm counting on," Huw said calmly—more calmly than he felt. "They've got a grip on the mass media—the phones, the email equivalents, the news distribution system. They're not stupid, they know about controlling the flow of information. Which means they're the only people who can get a message through to that friend of Miriam's—the skinny guy with the hat. Remember the railway station?" Brilliana had coopted Huw and his team, dragged them on what seemed at first like a wild goose chase to a one-platform stop in the middle of nowhere. They'd arrived in the nick of time, as Miriam's other pursuers—a political officer and a carload of police thugs—had surrounded the ticket office where she and Erasmus Burgeson were barricaded inside. "The problem is getting their attention without getting ourselves shot. Once we've got it, though . . ." He headed towards the bookmaker's, where a pair of adequately fed bouncers were eyeing the passersby. ". . . We're on the way."

The committee watched the presidential address, and the press conference that followed it, in dead silence.

The thirty-two-inch plasma screen and DVD player were alien intrusions in the wood-and-tapestry-lined audience room at the west of the royal palace. The portable gasoline generator in the antechamber outside throbbed loudly, threatening to drown out the recorded questions, played through speakers too small for a chamber designed for royal audiences in an age before amplification. The flickering color images danced off the walls, reflecting from the tired faces of the noble audience. Many of them still wore armor, camouflage surcoats over bulletproof vests and machine-woven titanium chain mail. They were the surviving officers of the Clan's security organization, and such of the Clan's other leaders as were deemed trustworthy, ignorant of or uninvolved in the abortive putsch mounted by the lords of the postal corvee. Wanted men, one and all.

Finally, Olga paused the DVD—recorded off-air by one of the few communications techs Riordan had ordered to stay behind in Cambridge. She looked around the semicircle of faces opposite, taking in their expressions, ranging from blank incomprehension to shock and dismay. "Does anyone have any questions, or can I move on to present our analysis?" she asked. "Strictly questions, no comment at this time."

A hand went up at the back. Olga made eye contact and nodded. It was Sir Ulrich, one of the progressive faction's stalwarts, a medic by training. "Can they do it?" he asked.

"You heard him." Olga's cheek twitched. Dread was a sick sensation in the pit of her stomach. "Let me remind you of WARBUCKS's history; he's a hawk. He was one of the main sponsors of the Project for a New American Century, he's the planner behind the Iraq invasion, and he's an imperialist in the old model. What most of you don't know is that back in the 1980s he was one of our main commercial enabling partners in the Western operation. And he's gone public about our existence. Getting back to your question: He's defined the success of his presidency in terms of his ability to take us down. The Americans will follow their king-emperor unquestioningly—as long as he delivers results. BOY WONDER used Iraq as a rallying cry after 9/11; WARBUCKS has pinned the target on us."

"So you think—" Ulrich paused. "Sorry."

"It's quite all right." Olga gestured at the front rank. "My lord Riordan, I yield the floor."

Riordan walked to the front of the room. "Thank you, Lady ven Thorold," he started. Then he paused, and looked around at his audience. "I'm not going to tell you any comforting lies. We have lost"—he raised a folio and squinted at it—"thirty-nine world-walkers of our own, and sixty-six of the conservative faction. Eleven more are in custody, awaiting a hearing. Most of them we can do naught with but hang as a warning. Remaining to us in the five great families"—he swallowed—"we have a total of four hundred and sixteen who can world-walk regularly, and another hundred and nineteen elderly and infants. Twenty-eight womenfolk who are with child and so must needs be carried. In our offshoots and cadet branches there are perhaps two thousand three hundred relatives, of whom one thousand and seven hundred or thereabouts are married or coming into or of child-bearing age. One hundred and forty one of their children are world-walkers."

He stopped, and exchanged the folio for a hip flask for a moment.

"The American army is largely occupied overseas, for which we should be grateful. They have more than six hundred thousand men under arms, and five hundred warships, and with their navy and air forces their military number two warriors for every peasant in the Gruinmarkt. Our account of Baron Hjorth's treachery is that he purloined no less than four but certainly no more than six of their atomic bombs. That leaves them with"—he consulted the folio—"ah, *six thousand* or thereabouts, almost all of which are more powerful than those Oliver Hjorth absconded with." He closed the folio and stared at his audience.

"In strategic terms, the technical term for our predicament is: *fucked*.

"The only ray of hope is the possibility that their new king-emperor is bluffing about their ability to visit destruction upon our heads. But our analysis is that there is no way that he could afford to threaten us politically unless he has the capability to follow through, so the Anglischprache probably *do* have a world-walking ability. It might be a matter of captured cousins, but I doubt it. There's the destruction of the Hjalmar Palace to consider, and they had Special Forces soldiers scouting around Niejwein as long ago as the betrothal feast between Prince Creon and Her Majesty. We know therefore that they had the ability to maintain a small scouting force over here four months ago. That implies they could not, back then, send a major expeditionary force across at that time. What they can do now—"

A hand went up in the front row. Riordan stopped. "Your grace," he said, with labored and pointed patience.

"Believe them," Patricia Thorold-Hjorth called tiredly from her wheelchair. She clasped her hands on top of her walking stick and frowned, her face still haggard. The medic's intervention had kept her breathing, but the poisoning had taken its toll. "During the late civil war, I was—with the express consent of my late brother—negotiating with the current president. His agent broke off communications with a sudden ultimatum: our immediate surrender in return for our lives. He spoke of a mechanical contrivance for world-walking, for moving vehicles. One of my daughter's protégés was tasked by my brother with investigating the nature and limitations of world-walking, and has made a number of discoveries; in particular, some wheeled contrivances can—under some circumstances—be carried along." A muttering spread through her audience. "And to this date, four more worlds have been discovered, and two new knots." The muttering grew louder.

"Silence!" shouted Riordan. "Damn you, I will hear one speaker at a time!" He looked at the dowager. "You have more?"

"Not much." She looked pensive. "Wheelbarrows—it was suppressed by the lords of the post, I presume, during the civil war. Too much risk of a few young things going over the wall, if they realized how few bodies it would take to start a rival operation; we would have faced dissolution within months. But there is no obvious size limit; the limit was imposed by the exclusion problem, the risk of wheels intersecting with matter in the other world. Given a suitably prepared staging area, machined to high precision, who knows what they could send. Tanks? Helicopters? And we are on their doorstep. These people sent a hundred thousand soldiers halfway around the world. What can they send an hour's drive down the road?"

"I don't think we need worry about that just yet," Riordan declared, trying to regain control of the briefing. "But." He paused a moment, looking around the anxious faces before him. "At a minimum, we face teams of special forces and possibly backpack atomic bombs, like the ones that have already been used. At worst, if they have truly worked out how to travel between worlds, we may see a full-scale invasion. I think the latter is a very real threat, and we have the example of their recent adventure in the distant land of Iraq to learn from. If we sit and wait for them to come to us, we will be defeated—they outnumber all the Eastern kingdoms, not just the Gruinmarkt, by thirty bodies to one, and look what they did to Iraq. This is not a matter for chivalrous denial; it is a fight *we cannot win*."

He gestured in the direction of Baron Horst of Lorsburg, one of the few conservatives to have been conclusively proven to have been on the outside of the coup attempt—a tiresomely business-minded fellow, fussy and narrowly legalistic. "Sir, I believe you wish to express an opinion?"

Lorsburg removed his bifocals and nervously rubbed them on his shirt sleeve. "You appear to be saying that Clan Security can't protect us. Is that right?"

"Clan Security can't take on the United States government, no, not if they develop world-walking machines." Riordan nodded patiently. "Do you have something more to say?"

Lorsburg hunkered down in his seat. "If you can't save us, what good *are* you?" he asked querulously.

"There's a difference between saying we can't win a direct fight, and not being able to save you. We probably *can* save the Clan—but not if we sit and wait for the Anglischprache to come calling. What we can't save are the fixed assets: our estates and vassals. Anything we can't carry. We are descended from migrant tinkers and traders, and I am afraid that we will have to become such again, at least for a while. Those of you who think the American army will not come here are welcome to go back to your palaces and great houses and pretend we can continue to do business as usual. You might be right—in which case, the rest of us will rejoin you in due course. But for the time being, I submit that our best hope lies elsewhere.

"We could cross over to America, and live in hiding among a people who hate and fear us. The Clan has some small accumulated capital; the banking committee has invested heavily in real estate, investment banks, and big corporations over the past fifty years. We would be modestly wealthy, but no longer the rulers and lords of all we survey, as we are here; and we would live in fear of a single loose-tongued cousin unraveling our network, by accident or malice. Our modest wealthy existence could only survive if all of us took a vow of silence and held to it. And I leave to your imagination the difficulty of maintaining our continuity, the braids—

"But there is a better alternative. My lady ven Thorold?"

Olga stood up. "I speak not as the director of intelligence

operations, but as a confidant of the queen-widow," she said, turning to face the room. "As we have known for some time, there are other worlds than just this one and that of the Anglisch-prache. Before his illness, Duke Lofstrom detailed a protégé of Helge's to conduct a survey. Helge has continued to press for these activities—we now know of four other worlds beyond the initial three, but they are not considered suitable for exploita-tion. If you desire the details, I will be happy to describe them later. For the time being, our best hope lies in New Britain, where Her Majesty is attempting to establish negotiations with the new revolutionary government—" Uproar.

"I say! *Silence!*" Riordan's bellow cut through the shouting. "I'll drag the next man who interrupts out and horse-whip him around the walls! Show some respect, damn you!"

The hubbub subsided. Olga waited for the earl to nod at her, then continued. "*Unlike* the Anglischprache of America, we have *good contacts* with the revolutionaries who have formed the pro-visional government of New Britain. We have, if nothing else, a ne-gotiable arrangement with our relatives there; I'm sure a diplomatic accommodation can be reached." She stared at Lorsburg, who was looking mulishly unconvinced. "Her Majesty is a *personal friend* of the minister of propaganda. We supplied their cells in Boston with material and aid prior to the abdication and uprising. Unlike the situation in the United States, we have no history of large-scale law-breaking to prejudice them against us; nothing but our aristo-cratic rank in the Gruinmarkt, which we must perforce shed in any case if we abandon our way of life here and move to a new world." She paused, voluntarily this time: Lorsburg had raised a hand. "Yes? What is it?"

"This is well and good, and perhaps we would be safe from the Americans there—for a while. But you're asking us to aban-don everything, to take to the roads and live like vagabonds, or throw ourselves on the mercy of a dubious cabal of regicidal peasants! How do you expect us to subsist in this new world? What shall we do?"

"We will have to work." Olga smiled tightly. "You are quite

right; it's not going to be easy. We will have to give up much that we have become accustomed to. On the other hand, we will be alive, we will be able to sleep without worrying that the next knock on the door may be agents of the state come to arrest us, and, as I said, there is a *business plan*. Nobody will hold a gun to your heads and force you to join those of us who intend to establish first a refuge and then a new trade and source of wealth in New Britain—if you wish to wait here and guard your estates, then I believe the Council will be happy to accede to your desires. But there is one condition: *If* the Americans come, we don't want you spilling our plans to their interrogators. So I am going to ask everyone to leave the room now. Those of you who wish to join our plan, may come back in; those who want no truck with it should go home. If you change your minds later, you can petition my lord the earl for a place. But if you stay for the next stage of this briefing you are committing yourselves to join us in New Britain—or to the silence of the grave."

WAR TRAIN ROLLING

holed up back in a motel room with a bottle of Pepsi and a box of graham crackers, Mike opened up his planner and spread his spoils on the comforter—room service had tidied the room while he'd been burglarizing Miriam's booby-trapped home. He was still shaking with the aftermath of the adrenaline surge from the near-miss with the police watch team. *Thirty seconds and they'd have made me.* Thirty seconds and—*Stop that,* he scolded himself. *You've got a job to do!*

Two items sat on the bed: a cassette and a bulging organizer, its edges rounded and worn by daily use. He added the remaining contents of his shopping bag, spoils of a brief excursion into a Walgreens: a cheap Far Eastern walkman, and a box of batteries. "Let's get you set up," he muttered to the machine, then did a double take. *Talking to myself. Huh.* It wasn't a terribly good sign. It had been a couple of days—since his abortive meeting with Steve Schroeder—since Mike had exchanged more words with anyone than it took to rent a car. It wasn't as if he was a gregarious type, but hanging out here with his ass on the line had him feeling horribly exposed. And there were loose life-ends left untied, from Oscar the tomcat (who had probably moved in with the neighbors who kept overfeeding him by now) to his dad and his third wife (whom he didn't dare call; even if they weren't in custody, their line was almost certainly on a fully-staffed watch by now). "The time to throw in the towel is when you start talking back to yourself, right? Oh no it isn't, Mike. . . ." The batteries were in, so he hit the playback button.

A beep, then a man's voice: "Miriam? Andy here. Listen, a little bird told me about what happened yesterday and I think it sucks. They didn't have any details, but I want you to know if you need some freelance commissions you should give me a call. Talk later? Bye."

Mike paused, then rewound. *Andy* went on his notepad, along with *freelance commissions*. Probably nothing useful, but . . .

Click. "Hi? Paulette here, it's seven-thirty, listen, I've been doing some thinking about what we dug up before they fired us. Miriam, honey, let's talk. I don't want to rake over dead shit, but there's some stuff I need to get straight in my head. Can I come around?"

He sat up. *Fired*, he wrote on his pad, and underlined the word twice. This Paulette woman had said *we*. So Miriam had been fired. "When?" That was the trouble with answerphones; the new solid-state ones had timestamps, but the old cassette ones were less than useful in that department. On the other hand, she hadn't wiped these messages. So they'd arrived pretty close to whatever had brought her into contact with the Clan.

Next message: a man's voice, threatening. "Bitch. We know where you live. Heard about you from our mutual friend Joe. Keep your nose out of our business or you'll be fucking sorry."

Mike stopped dead, his shoulders tense. *Joe*, he wrote, then circled the name heavily and added a couple of question marks. *Not Clan?* he added. The Clan weren't in the cold-call trade; concrete overcoats and car bombs were more their style. Still, coming on top of Paulette's message this was . . . suggestive. Miriam had been fired from her job, along with this Paulette woman, for digging up something. "She's a journalist, it's what she does." Next thing, there was a threatening phone call. Some time not long later, Miriam disappeared. Some time after that, her house was systematically searched for computers and electronic media, by someone who wasn't interested in old paperwork. And then it was booby-trapped and staked out by the FTO. . . . "Stop right there!" Mike flipped the organizer open and turned to the address divider. "Paulet, Paulette, Powell-et? How do you spell it, it's a first name. . . ."

He read for a long time, swearing occasionally at Miriam's spidery handwriting and her copious list of contacts—*She's a journalist, it's what she does*—until he hit paydirt a third of the way through: *Milan, Paulette. Business intelligence division, the Weatherman.* That was where Miriam had worked, last time he looked. "Bingo," Mike muttered. There was a cell number *and* a street address out in Somerville. He made a note of it; then, systematic to the end, he went back to the cassette tape.

The next message was a call from Steve Schroeder—his voice familiar—asking Miriam to get in touch. It was followed by an odd double beep: some kind of tape position marker, probably. Then the rest of the tape: a farrago of political polls, telesales contacts, and robocalls that took Mike almost an hour to skim. He took notes, hoping some sort of pattern would appear, but nothing jumped out at him. Probably the calls were exactly what they sounded like: junk. Which left him with a couple of names, one of which seemed promising, and a conundrum. Someone had threatened Miriam, right after she'd been fired for stumbling over something. Was it Clan-related? And was this Paulette woman involved? "There's only one way to find out," Mike told himself unhappily. His stomach rumbled. "Time to hit the road again."

The coded electrogram from Springfield followed a circuitous course to Erasmus Burgeson's desk.

Huw's bluff had worked; the cadre at the post office were inexperienced and undisciplined, excited volunteers barely out of the first flush of revolutionary fervor, more enthusiastic than efficient. There was no command structure as such, no uniforms and no identity papers, and as yet very little paranoia: The threats they expected to defend the post office against were the crude and obvious violence of counterrevolutionary elements, fists and guns rather than the sly subtlety of wreckers and saboteurs from within. This was not—yet—a revolution that had begun to eat its offspring.

When Huw claimed to be part of a small reconnaissance cell in the countryside and asked to send a message to the stratospheric heights of the party organization, he was met at first with gapejawed incomprehension and then an eagerness to oblige that was almost comically servile. It was only when he and Yul prepared to slip away that anyone questioned the wisdom of allowing strangers to transmit electrograms to New London without clearance, and by the time old Johnny Miller, former deputy postmaster of the imperial mail (now wearing his union hat openly), expressed the doubtful opinion that perhaps somebody ought to have detained the strangers pending the establishment of their bona fides, Huw and Yul were half a mile down the road.

Despite deputy postmaster Miller's misgivings, the eightyword electrogram Miriam had so carefully crafted arrived in the central monitoring and sorting hall at Breed's Hill, whereupon an eagle-eyed (and probably bored) clerk recognized the office of the recipient and, for no very good reason, stamped it with a PARTY PRIORITY flag and sent it on its way.

From Breed's Hill—where in Miriam's world one of the key battles of the American War of Independence had been fought—the message was encrypted in a standard party cypher and flashed down cables to the Imperial Postal Headquarters building on Manhattan Island, and thence to the Ministry of Propaganda, where the commissioner on duty in the message room saw its high priority and swore, vilely. Erasmus was not in town that day; indeed, was not due back for some time. But it was a PARTY PRIORITY cable. What to do?

In the basement of the Ministry of Propaganda were numerous broadcasting rooms; and no fewer than six of these were given over to the letter talkers, who endlessly recited strings of words sapped of all meaning, words chosen for their clarity over the airwaves. So barely two hours after Huw and Yul had shown the cadre in Springfield two clean pairs of heels, a letter talker keyed his microphone and began to intone: "Libra, Opal, Furlong, Opal, Whisky, Trident"—over the air on a shortwave frequency given over to the encrypted electrospeak broadcasts of the party's network, a frequency that would be echoed by transmitters all over both Western continents, flooding the airwaves until Burgeson's radio operator could not help but receive it.

Which event happened in the operator's room on board an armored war train fifty miles west of St. Anne, which stood not far from the site of Cincinatti in Miriam's world. The operator, his ears encased in bulky headphones, handed the coded message with his header to the encryption sergeant, who typed it into his clacking, buzzing machine, and then folded the tape and handed it off to a messenger boy, who dashed from the compartment into the train's main corridor and then along a treacherous, swaying armored tunnel to the command carriage where the commissioner of state propaganda sat slumped over a pile of newspapers, reading the day's dispatches as he planned the next step in his media blitz.

"What is it now?" Erasmus asked, glancing up.

The messenger boy straightened. "Sor, a cript for thee?" He presented the roll of tape with both hands. "Came in over the airwaves, like."

"I see." The train clanked across a badly maintained crossing, swaying from side to side. Erasmus, unrolling the tape, drew the electric lamp down from overhead to illuminate the mechanical scratchings as he tried to focus on it. It had been under at least three pairs of eyeballs since arriving here; over the electrograph, that meant . . . He blinked. *Miriam? She's* here? *And she wants to talk?* He wound back to the header at the start of the message that identified the sending station. *Springfield.* Burgeson chuckled humorlessly for a moment. HAVE INTERESTING PROPOSAL FOR YOU RE TECHNOLOGY TRANSFER AND FAMILY BUSINESS. To put that much in an uncoded message was a giveaway: It reeked of near-panic. She'd said something about her relatives being caught up in a civil war, hadn't she? *Interesting.*

Burgeson reached out with his left hand and yanked the bell rope, without taking his eyes off the message tape. A few seconds later Citizen Supervisor Philips stuck his head round the partition. "You called, citizen?"

"Yes." Burgeson shoved the newspaper stack to one side, so that they overflowed the desk and drifted down across the empty rifle rack beside it. "Something urgent has come up back East. I need to be in Boston as soon as possible."

"Boston?" Philips raised a thin eyebrow. "What about the campaign, citizen?"

"The campaign can continue without me for a couple of days." Burgeson stared at Philips. Dried-out and etiolated, the officer resembled a praying mantis in a black uniform: but he was an efficient organizer, indeed had pulled together the staff and crew for this campaign train at short notice. "We've hit New Brentford and Jensenville in the past two days, you've seen how I want things done: Occupy the local paper's offices, vet the correspondents, deal with any who are unreliable and promote our cadres in their place. Continue to monitor as you move on." The two-thousand-ton armored war train, bristling with machine guns and black-clad Freedom Riders, was probably unique in history in having its own offset press and typesetting carriage; but as Erasmus had argued the point with Sir Adam, this was a war of public perception—and despite the technowizardry of the videography engineers, public perceptions were still shaped by hot metal type. "Keep moving, look for royal blue newspapers and insure that you leave only red freedom-lovers in your wake."

"I think I can do that, sir." Philips nodded. "Difficult cases . . . ?"

"Use your discretion." *Here, have some rope; try not to*

hang yourself with it. "I'll be back as soon as I can. Meanwhile, when's the next supply run back to Lynchburg departing?"

"If it's Boston you want, there's an aerodrome near Raleigh that's loyal," Philips offered. "I'll wire them to put a scout at your disposal?"

"Do that." Burgeson winced. Flying tended to make him airsick, even in the modern fully-enclosed mail planes that had been coming in recently. "I need to be there as soon as possible."

"Absolutely, citizen. I'll put the wheels in motion at once." And, true to his word, almost as soon as Philips disappeared there came an almighty squeal of brakes from beneath the train.

The past week had been one long nightmare for Paulette Milan.

She'd been a fascinated observer of Miriam's adventures, in the wake of the horrible morning a year ago when they'd both lost their jobs; and later, when Miriam had sucked her into running an office for her—funneling resources to an extradimensional business start-up—she'd been able to square it with her conscience because she agreed with Miriam's goals. If the Clan, Miriam's criminal extended family, could be diverted into some other line of business, that was cool. And if some of their money stuck to Paulie's fingertips in the form of wages, well, as long as the wages weren't coming in for anything illegal on her part, that was fine, too.

But things hadn't worked out. First Miriam had vanished for nearly six months—a virtual prisoner, held under house arrest for much of that time. The money pipeline had slammed shut, leaving Paulie looking for a job in the middle of a recession. Then things got worse. About six weeks ago Miriam's friends— or co-conspirators, or cousins, or whatever—Olga and Brill had turned up on her doorstep and made her the kind of offer you weren't allowed to refuse if you knew what was good for you. There was a fat line of credit to sweeten the pill, but it left Paulie looking over her shoulder nervously. You didn't hand out that kind of money just to open an office, in her experience. And there had been dark hints about internal politics within the Clan, a civil war, and the feds nosing around.

All of this was *bad*. Capital-B bad. Paulie had grown up in a neighborhood where the hard men flashed too much cash around, sometimes checked into club fed for a few years at a time, and snitches tended to have accidents . . . she'd thought she had a good idea what was coming until she'd turned on the TV a few days ago and seen the rising mushroom clouds. Heard the new president's broadcast, glacial blue eyes twinkling as he came out with words that were still reverberating through the talk shows and news columns ("PENTAGON SPOKESMAN: PRESIDENT 'NOT IN-SANE,'" as the *Globe* had put it).

It made her sick to her stomach. She'd spent the first two days in bed, crying and throwing up on trips to the bathroom, certain that the FBI were going to break down her door at any moment. The stakes she'd signed up for were far higher than she'd ever imagined, and she found she hated herself for it: hated her earlier moment of pecuniary weakness, her passive compliance in following Miriam down her path of good intentions, her willingness to make friends and let people influence her. She'd caught herself looking in the bathroom cabinet at one point, and hastily shut it: The temptation to take a sleeping pill, or two, or enough to shut it out forever, was a whispering demon on her shoulder for a few hours. "What the fuck can I *do*?" She'd asked the bourbon bottle on the kitchen table. "What the *fuck* can I do?"

Today . . . hadn't been better, exactly; but she'd awakened in a mildly depressive haze, rather than a blind panic, knowing that she had two options. She could go to the feds, spill her guts, and hope a jail cell for the rest of her life was better than whatever the Clan did to their snitches. Or she could keep calm and carry on—she'd seen a foreign wartime poster with that line, once—carry on doing what Miriam had asked of her: sit in an office, buy books and put them in boxes, buy *stuff* (surveying tools, precision atomic clocks, laboratory balances: What did she know?) and stash it in a self-storage locker ready for a courier collection that might never arrive.

Get up. Drink a mug of coffee, no food. Go to the office. Order supplies. Repackage them with an inventory sheet, to meet the following size and weight requirements. Drive them to the lockup. Consider eating lunch and feel revulsion at the idea so do some more work, then go home. Keep calm and carry on (it beats going to Gitmo). Try not to think . . .

Paulette drove home from the rented office suite in a haze of distraction, inattentive and absentminded. The level of boxes in the lockup had begun to go down again, she'd noticed: For the first time in a week there'd been a new manilla envelope with a handwritten shopping list inside. (She'd stuffed it in her handbag, purposely not reading it.) So someone was collecting the consignments. Her fingers were white on the steering wheel as she pulled up in the nearest parking space, half a block from her front door. She was running short on supplies, but the idea of going grocery shopping made her feel sick: Anything out of the routine scared her right now.

She unlocked the front door and went inside, switched the front hall light on, and dumped her handbag beside the answering machine. It was a warm enough summer's day that she hadn't bothered with a jacket. She walked through into the kitchen to start a pot of coffee, purposely not thinking about how she was going to fill the evening—a phone call to Mother, perhaps, and a movie on DVD—and that was when the strange man stepped out behind her and held up a badge.

"Paulette Milan, I'm from the DEA and I'd—"

She was lying down, and dizzy. He was staring at her. Everything was gray. His mouth was moving, and so was the world. It was confusing for a moment, but then her head began to clear: *I fainted?* She was looking up at the living room ceiling, she realized. There was something soft under the back of her head.

"Can you hear me?" He looked concerned.

"I'm." She took a couple of breaths. "I'm. Oh God."

"I'm sorry, I didn't mean to scare you like that—are you all right? Listen, do you have a heart condition—" *No. No.* She must have shaken her head. "Do you know Miriam Beckstein?"

Paulie swallowed. "Shit."

Everything, for an instant, was crystal clear. *I'm from the DEA. Do you know Miriam Beckstein?* The next logical words had to be, *You're under arrest.*

"I need to talk to her; her life's in danger."

Paulie blinked. *Does not compute.* "You're from the DEA," she said hesitantly. Pushed against the carpet. "I fainted?"

"Uh, yes, in the kitchen. I never—I carried you in here. I'm sorry, I didn't mean to scare you. I wanted to talk, but I was afraid they might be watching."

Watching? "Who?" she asked.

"The FTO," he said. *Who?* she wondered. "Or the Clan."

The brittle crystal shell around her world shattered. "Oh, them," she said carelessly, her tongue loosened by shock. "They ring the front doorbell. Like everyone else." Bit by bit, awareness was starting to return. Chagrin—*I can't believe I fainted*—was followed by anxiety—*Who is this guy? How do I know he's DEA? Is he a burglar?*—and then fear: *Alone with a strange man.*

The strange man seemed to be going out of his way to be non-threatening, though. "Do you want a hand up?" he asked. "Figure you might be more comfortable on the sofa—" She waved him away, then pushed herself upright, then nodded. Things went gray again for a moment. "Listen, I'm not, uh, here on official business, exactly. But I need to talk to Miriam—" She rose, took two steps backwards, and collapsed onto the sofa. "Are you sure you're okay?"

"No," she heard herself say, very distinctly. "I'm *not* okay. Who are you, mister, and what are you doing in my house?"

He hunkered down on the balls of his feet so that he was at eye level to her. "Name's Fleming, Mike Fleming. I used to know Miriam. She's in a whole bunch of trouble; if you know what she's been doing this past year, you'd know that—if you know about the Clan, you're in trouble, too. That goes for me, also." He paused. "Want me to go on?"

"You're." She stopped. "Why did you tell me you're DEA?"

"I was, originally—still carry a badge they issued. I'd prefer you not to phone them just yet to verify that. See, I'm willing to put my neck on the line. But I want to get to the truth. You know about the Clan?"

Paulie shook her head. "If I say anything, you know what those people will do?" She was saying too much, she vaguely recognized, but something about this setup smelled wrong.

"Which people? The Clan, or the Family Trade Organization?" Fleming paused. "I'm not in a position to arrest you for anything—I'm not here on official business. I need to talk to Miriam—"

"Wait." Paulette tried to pull herself together. "The *what* organization? You want to talk to her? About what?"

Fleming looked at her quizzically. "The FTO is a cross-agency operation to shut down the Clan. I was part of it until, uh, about a week ago. It was an attempt to get all the agencies whose lines the Clan crossed to sing from the same hymn book. I came in from the DEA side when source GREEN—a Clan defector called Matthias—walked in the door. I've seen Miriam, about three months ago, in a palace in a place called Niejwein—want me to go on?"

Oh Jesus, save me—he's the real thing. She shook her head numbly. "What do you want?"

"Like I said, I need to talk to Miriam. She's in terrible danger—FTO has been penetrated. The president used to work with the Clan, back in the eighties and early nineties. He's the one behind this mess, he deliberately goaded them into using those nukes, and there's worse to come. He's running FTO. All the oil in Texas—*every* version of Texas—that's what he's after, that and a state of emergency at home to give him carte blanche to do whatever the hell he likes. I've tried to put out a warning via the press, but my contact didn't believe me until the attacks, and now—"

"You went to the press?" Paulette stared at him as if he'd grown a second head. "What did you have?"

"Nothing!" His frustration was visible.

"But you found me," she pointed out.

"Yeah, after I turfed her house. Which is under police watch *and* booby-trapped; I found an old planner of hers, played back the answering-machine tape—"

"Shit." She tried to stand, failed for a moment, then got her suddenly shaky knees to behave. "There was a tape?" *If you found me,* they *could find me.*

"Relax. Those agencies you're thinking about don't talk to each other at that level. You're probably safe, for now."

Probably safe and her cousin *Don't worry* had helped many a girl get pregnant, in Paulie's opinion, and when the canoodling in question might lead to the queue for the execution chamber at Gitmo rather than a hospital delivery room, chancing it was not on her roadmap. "No, forget that: If they catch you they'll backtrack to me. Thanks a million, Mr. Fleming, you just doubled my chances of not getting out of this alive. I didn't ask for this shit! It just landed on my lap!" Her heart was hammering, she could feel her face flushing: Fleming was leaning away from her sudden vehemence. "Fucking goodfellas, I grew up in their backyard, you know what I'm saying? The old generation. You kept your nose out of their business and didn't do nothing and they'd mostly leave you alone, especially if you knew their cousin's wife or walked their sister's dogs or something. But if you crossed them it wouldn't be any fucking horse's head at the end of your bed, no fucking wreath at your funeral; you wouldn't *have* a funeral, there wouldn't be anything to bury. There were rumors about the meat-packing plant, about the cat and dog food. And the cops weren't much better. Shakedown money every Tuesday, free coffee and bagels at the corner, and you better hope they liked your face. And that was the *local* cops, and the old-time *local* hoods, who didn't shit in their backyard 'case someone took exception, you know where I'm coming from?"

Fleming just squatted on his heels and took it, like a giant inflatable target for all her frustration. "Yes, I know where you're from," he said quietly when she ran down. "Keep a low profile and don't rock the boat and you think maybe you can get by without anyone hurting you. But where *I'm* coming from—that's not an option anymore. It's not Miriam's fault that she's descended from them and has their ability, not her fault about those bombs—she tried to warn me. There are back channels between governments: That was before my boss's boss decided to burn me. No; what *I'm* telling *you* is that we're caught in the middle of a fight that's been fixed, and if I don't get to talk to Miriam, a lot of people are going to die. The new president wants the Clan dead, because it's a necessary condition to cover up his own past connection with them: He ran their West Coast heroin-distribution arm for about seven years. He's had his fingers deep into their business since then, he's the one who nudged them into acquiring nukes and then prodded them into using them, and he's just been sworn in—we probably don't have much time to get the warning out. So are you going to help me? Or are you going to sit in your foxhole and stick your fingers in your ears and sing 'La la la, I can't *hear* you'?"

"You're telling me it's the *president's* fault?" She stared. Fleming didn't *look* mad—

"Yes. I know where too many bodies are buried, that's why they tried to car bomb me four days ago. FTO itself is still secret: I know enough to blow the operation sky high. Black underground prisons on US soil, captured Clan members being forced to act as mules with bombs strapped to their necks, vivisection on subjects to find out what makes them tick, helicopters with black boxes containing bits of brain tissue—don't ask me how they got them—that can travel to the Gruinmarkt. There's an invasion coming, Ms. Milan, and they've been gearing up to attack the Clan in their own world for at least six months."

"Call me Paulie," she said automatically.

"It's not even the first time our government's considered setting off nukes on our own territory to justify an attack on someone else. Back in the early seventies, we figure Nixon—there was a bomb in Boston, you see, GREENSLEEVES planted it as a blackmail backup before he defected, and we ran across an older device while we were looking for his: a big one, the kind you air-dropped from a B52 when you wanted to flatten Moscow. It dated to 1972, just before Nixon showed up in Beijing to make nice. Turns out it was his Plan B: Get rid of a bunch of useless liberals and wave the bloody flag at the Commies. They didn't do it then, but they've gone and done it now, with the fall guy's fingerprints all over the throwdown."

Paulie opened her mouth, then shut it again.

Fleming sighed. "I can see we're going to be here some time," he said. "Any chance of a coffee?"

Two days after Huw and Yul hiked into Springfield to post a letter at great personal peril (two days in which six more ClanSec world-walkers and a full half-ton of requisitioned supplies reached the safe house, two days during which the neighbors kept a remarkably low profile), Miriam was sitting in the makeshift living room, single-mindedly typing up her to-do list, when something strange happened.

With no warning, the bulky wooden cabinet in the corner of the room crackled into life. "This is the emergency widecast network. Repeat, this is the emergency widecast network. The following message is for Miss Beckstein, last known in Springfield. Will Miss Beckstein please go to the shop in Boston where her sick friend is waiting for her. Repeat—"

The repetition of the message was lost in a clatter. "Shit!" Miriam applied some other choice words as she bent to pick up the dropped laptop and check it for damage.

"What's happened?" Brill called from the direction of the kitchen.

"Dropped my—we've got contact!"

"What?" A second later Brill pushed the door wide open.

"The radio." Miriam pointed at it. "Huw didn't say there's an emergency station! Erasmus wants to see me. In Boston."

Brill looked at her oddly. Miriam realized she was cradling the laptop as if it were cut-glass. "Are you sure—"

"This is the emergency widecast network. Repeat—"

"I told you!"

{185}

"Okay." Brill nodded, then paused to listen. Her face tightened as she unconsciously clenched her jaw. "Oh yes. It worked. Well, my lady, you got what you wanted. What do we do now?"

"I'd think it was obvious—"

The other door opened; it was Sir Alasdair. "Hello? I heard shouting?"

Miriam stood up, shut the laptop's lid, and placed it carefully on the side table. "We're going to Boston," she announced. "Erasmus has made contact—"

Alasdair cleared his throat. "Made contact how—"

"Now look here!" Miriam and Huw both stopped dead. "Have I your full attention?" Brilliana demanded. "Because as your loyal retainer I think we should consider this with care. My lady, what do you intend to do? Need I remind you these are dangerous times?"

"No." Miriam looked at Sir Alasdair, who was watching Brilliana with the patience of a hound. "But this is exactly what we should have expected, isn't it? Erasmus is high in their ministry of propaganda, and we didn't tell him where I was. How else would he contact me, but a broadcast? So now the ball's back on our side of the court. I need to go visit him at the shop, because that's where he'll be. Unless you've got any better ideas?" Alasdair cleared his throat again. "Yes?" she asked.

"My lady d'Ost." He glanced at Brill. "What is your threat assessment?"

"Hard to say. Getting there—dangerous because all travel in this land is risky in the season of civil war. Once there . . . I do not believe Burgeson means ill of my lady; he is as close to a friend, in fact, as any in the world."

"But?" His word hung in the air for a few short seconds.

"Assuming the message is from Burgeson," Brilliana said reluctantly. "There is no word of his disposition. Should he be the victim of an internal plot, this might be a trap. I'd think unlikely, but stranger things happen. And then, should he in fact be the speaker—what then?"

"Wait a minute." Miriam raised a hand. "The idea is to

make contact. Then put my proposal to him and see what he thinks is achievable. At that point, once we've got a channel, it's down to diplomacy."

"And capabilities." Alasdair lowered himself onto one of the wooden dining chairs Huw and Yul had scared up in the furniture-hunting expedition. "Their expectation of our abilities must view us as a potential threat, just as the Americans do. They will want to know why we seek refuge here. If we tell them the unvarnished truth—"

"We *must*." Miriam was forceful. "Yeah, we may have to admit the Clan fucked up royally in the United States. But you know something? It's nothing but the truth. If we tell them we fucked up and we want to start afresh and turn over a new leaf, it's not only believable—it's true, and they'll get the same story from everyone they ask. If we start telling white lies or trying to bamboozle them . . . how many of our people have to remember to tell the same lie? *Someone* will get confused and let something slip over a glass of wine, and then Erasmus's people get to let their suspicions run riot. And let me remind you this country is in the middle of a revolution? Maybe they're going to come out of it peacefully, but most revolutions don't—we have a chance to try and influence that if we're on the inside, but we won't have a leg to stand on unless we're like Caesar's wife, above re-proach. So my goal is simple: get us *in* with the temporal authorities, so deeply embedded that we're indispensable within months."

"Indispensable?"

"I've been doing some reading." Miriam turned tired eyes on Alasdair. "Revolutions eat their young, especially as they build new power structures. But they *don't* eat the institutions that prop them up. Secret police, bureaucrats, armies—that's the rule. They may hang the men at the top, and go hard on their external ene-mies, but the majority of the rank and file keep their places. I think we can come up with a value proposition that they can't ig-nore, one that would scare the crap out of them if we didn't *very obviously* need their help."

Sir Alasdair looked at Brill. "Do you understand her when she starts talking like this?" he grumbled.

"No. Isn't it great?" Brill flashed him a grin. "You can see why the duke, may he rest peacefully, wanted her for a figurehead upon the throne. My lady. What do you propose to do? Let us say we get you to Boston to meet with your man. What do you need?"

"I've got a list," said Miriam, picking up the laptop. "Let's get started. . . ."

BEGIN RECORDING

"—Latest news coming in from Delhi, the Pakistani foreign minister has called off negotiations over the cease fire on the disputed Kashmir frontier—"

(*Fast forward*)

"—Artillery duels continuing, it looks like a long, tense night for the soldiers here on the border near Amritsar. Over to you in the studio, Dan."

"Thank you, Bob Mancini, live from the India-Pakistan border region near the disputed Kashmir province, where the cold war between the Indian and Pakistani militaries has been running hot for the past month. A reminder that the catastrophic events of 7/16 didn't stop the shooting; may in fact have aggravated it, with rumors flying that the quantum effect used by the attackers is being frantically investigated by military labs all over the world, we go to our military affairs expert, Erik Olsen. Hello, Erik."

"Hello, Dan."

"Briefly, what are the implications? Mr. Mukhtar's accusation that the Indian secret service is sneaking saboteurs across the border via a parallel universe is pretty serious, but is it credible? What's going on here?"

"Well, Dan, the hard fact is, nobody knows for sure who's got this technique. We've seen it in action, it's been used against us to great effect—and nobody knows who's got it. As you can imagine, it's spoiling a lot of military leaders' sleep. If you can carry a nuclear weapon across time lines and have it materialize in a city, you can mount what's called a first strike, a decapitation stroke: You can take out an enemy's missiles and bombers on the ground before they can launch. Submarines are immune, luckily—"

"Why are submarines immune, Erik?"

"You've got to find them first, Dan, you can't materialize a bomb inside a submarine that's underwater unless you can find it. Bombers that are airborne are pretty much safe as well. But if they're on the ground or in dry dock—it upsets the whole logic of nuclear deterrence. And India and Pakistan both have sizable nuclear arsenals, but no submarines, they're all carried on bombers or ground-launched missiles. Into the middle of a hot war, the conflict over Kashmir with the artillery duels and machine gun attacks we've been hearing about these past weeks, it's not new—they've fought four wars in the past thirty years—the news about this science-fictional new threat, it's upset all the realities on the ground. India and Pakistan have both got to be afraid that the other side's got a new tool that makes their nuclear arsenal obsolete, the capability to smuggle nukes through other worlds—and they're already on three-minute warning, much like we were with the USSR in the fifties except that their capital cities are just five minutes apart as the missile flies."

"But they wouldn't be crazy enough to start a nuclear war over Kashmir, would they?"

"Nobody ever wants to be the first to start a nuclear war, Dan, that's not in question. The trouble is, they may think the other side is starting one. Back in 1983, for example, a malfunctioning Russian radar computer told the Soviets that we'd launched on them. Luckily a Colonel Petrov kept his head and waited for more information to come in, but if he'd played by the rule book he'd have told Moscow they were under attack, and it's anyone's guess what could have happened. Petrov had fifteen minutes' warning. Islamabad and New Delhi have got just three minutes to make up their minds, that's why the Federation of American Scientists say they're the greatest risk of nuclear war anywhere in the world today."

"But that's not going to happen—"

(*Fast forward*)

"Oh Jesus." (*Bleeped mild expletive.*) "This can't be—oh. I'm waiting for Bob, Bob Mancini on the India-Pakistan border. We're going over live to Bob, as soon as we can raise him. Bob? Bob, can you hear me? . . . No? Bob? We seem to have lost Bob. Our hearts go out to him, to his family and loved ones, to everyone out there. . . .

"That was the emergency line from the Pentagon. America is not, repeat *not*, under attack. It's not a repeat of 7/16, it's . . . it appears that one of the Pakistani army or the Indian air force have gone—a nuclear bomb, a hydrogen bomb on Islamabad, other explosions in India. Amritsar, New Delhi, Lahore in Pakistan. I'm Dan Rather on CBS, keeping you posted on the latest developments in what are we calling this? World War Two-point-five? India and Pakistan. Five large nuclear explosions have been reported so far. We can't get a telephone line to the subcontinent.

"Reports are coming in of airliners being diverted away from Indian and Pakistani airspace. The Pentagon has announced that America is not, repeat *not*, under attack, this is a purely local conflict between India and Pakistan. We're going over live to Jim Patterson in Mumbai, India. Jim, what's happening?"

"Hello Dan, it's absolute chaos here, sirens going in the background, you can probably hear them. From here on the sixth floor of the Taj Mahal Palace Hotel there's traffic gridlocked throughout the city as people try to flee. In just a minute we're going down into the basements where" (*Click.*)

"Jim? Jim? We seem to have lost Jim. Wait, we're getting— oh no. No."

END RECORDING

Τbε vιεω ϝroϖ ϝorτy τbουsanὁ ϝεετ

I don't know if this will work," said Paulette. "I've never done it before."

"Don't worry, they'll have set this up to be fail-safe. Believe me, we had enough trouble cracking their communication security—they know what they're doing. You may not get an immediate answer, but they'll know you paged them."

"I don't know how you can sit there and be so calm about it!"

Mike shrugged. "I've had a long time to get used to the idea," he said. Not exactly true: He'd had a couple of weeks. But the stench of bureaucratic excess, the penumbra of the inquisition, had clouded his entire period of service at the Family Trade Organization. "Sometimes you can smell it when the place you work, when there's a bad atmosphere? When people are doing stuff that *isn't quite right*? But nobody says anything, so you think it's just you, and you're afraid to speak out."

Paulie nodded. "Like Enron."

"Like—more than Enron, I guess; like the CIA in the early seventies, when they were out of control. Throwing people out of helicopters in Vietnam, mounting coups in South America. It's like they say, fish rot from the head down."

She lifted the phone handset she'd been gripping with bony fingers and hesitantly punched in an area code, and then a number. "We did an in-depth on Enron. It was just unbelievable, what was going on there." The phone rang, unanswered; she let it continue for ten seconds, then neatly ended the call. "What's next?"

Mike consulted the handwritten list she'd given him. "Second number, ring for four seconds, at least one minute after ending the first call." She didn't need him to do this: She could read it herself, easily enough. But company helped. "The hardest part of being a whistle-blower is being on your own, on the outside. Everybody telling you to shut the hell up, stop rocking the boat, keep your head down and work at whatever the wise heads have put in front of you. Hmm. Area code 414—"

Paulie dialed the second number, let it ring for four seconds, then disconnected. "I did an interview with Sherron Watkins, you know? When the whole Enron thing blew up. She said that, too, pretty much." She stabbed the phone at him. "Harder to blow the whistle on these guys, let me tell you. Much harder."

"I know it." He stared at the third number on the list. "On the other hand, they're not your regular gangsters: They think like a government."

"Some folks say, governments *are* gangsters. A bunch of guys with guns who demand money, right?"

"There's a difference of approach. Gangsters aren't part of the community. They don't put anything back into it, they don't build roads and schools, they just take the money and run. Governments think differently. At least, working ones do."

"But the Clan take money out of *our* communities. They don't spend it on *us*, do they? From our point of view they're like gangsters."

"Or an empire." Mike turned the thought around, examining

it from different angles. "Like the Soviet Union, the way they drained resources from outlying territories." There was something not quite right with the metaphor, if he could just figure it out. "Oh, next number time. Area code is 506—"

They worked down the list over the course of an hour, as the jug of coffee cooled and the evening shadows lengthened outside. There were five numbers to call for varying lengths of time, at set minimum intervals; the third had an annoying voice menu system to navigate, asking for a quotation for auto insurance, and the fifth—answered in an Indian call center somewhere—was the only one with human interaction required: "Sorry, wrong number."

The whole tedious business was necessary for several reasons. A couple of random numbers to make traffic analysis harder; a couple of flags to say *I need to talk* and *I am not under duress*; and words spoken into a recording device to prove that the contact was, in fact, Paulette Milan, and not an agent in an FTO office. There were other rituals to perform: the curtains to be left undrawn in the spare bedroom but drawn in the main, a light to be left on inside the front door. Rituals of tradecraft, the magic rite of summoning spies, impenetrable to outsiders but practiced for good reason by those on the inside. *Someone sets up a small but highly professional intelligence agency. Question: Where do they get their training? Given that we know their soldiers use the USMC as a finishing school* . . . Mike pondered for a moment, then winced. Every one of the possible answers that came to mind was disturbing.

Finally they were done. "I should hear back within twenty-four hours," Paulie said diffidently. She paused. *What now?* he wondered.

"I've been staying in a motel." It would be racking up another night's charges. The idea of driving back there to spend another night in silence abruptly made him nauseous. "Don't get me wrong, but I think I should be here if they come unexpectedly—"

She looked at him thoughtfully, then nodded. "You can use the spare bedroom if you like. There's spare bedding in the closet."

"Thank you." To fill the potentially awkward silence he added, "I feel like I'm imposing on you." He'd had his fill of silence: Silence concealed lies. "Can I buy you dinner?"

"Guess so." The set of her shoulders relaxed slightly. "Where did you meet Miriam, the first time?"

The sky was overcast, and the muggy onshore breeze blew a stink of fish guts and coal smoke across the streets, gusting occasionally to moan and rattle around the chimney stacks—the barometer was falling, a rain front threatening to break the summer heat.

Driving sixty miles over the poor-quality roads in a pair of steamers with leaf-spring suspensions had taken them the best part of four hours, but they'd started early and the purposeful-looking convoy had apparently convinced the more opportunistic highwaymen to keep a low profile. The only delays they encountered were a couple of checkpoints manned by volunteer militias, and as these were mostly concerned with keeping the starving robber gangs out of their suburbs, Miriam's party were waved through—a rapid progress doubtless greased by the low-denomination banknotes interleaved between the pages of the inkjet-forged Vehicle Pilot's Warrants that Huw and Alasdair presented when challenged. It was, perhaps, for the best that the militiamen's concupiscience avoided the need for a search: much better to hand over a few hundred million New Crown notes than to risk a brisk and very one-sided exchange of gunfire.

"Did you see that?" Brill asked Miriam indignantly as they left the second checkpoint: "Half of them were carrying pitchforks! And the one with the bent nose, his tines were rusty!"

There were few obvious signs of revolution as they drove through the outskirts of Boston. More men and women in the streets, perhaps, hanging out in small groups; but with the economy spiraling into a true deflationary depression and unemployment nearing fifty percent, that was hardly surprising. There were soup kitchens, true, and the street cars bore banners proclaiming that the People's Party would feed the needy at certain listed locations—but there were also fishmongers and grocery stalls with their wares laid out in front, and the district farmer's market they passed was the usual chaos of handcarts and wagons piled high with food. *Someone* was keeping things moving, between town and country—a good sign, as far as Miriam could tell.

And then they were into familiar streets and the second car turned off, heading for its prearranged rendezvous point. "I'll get out here and walk the rest of the way," Miriam said quietly as they sat behind a streetcar that had stopped for a horse-drawn wagon to unload some crates. "You know the block. I'll remember to press once every ten minutes while things are going well."

"Check it now," said Brilliana, holding up her own earpiece.

"Check." Miriam squeezed her left hand, inside a coat pocket. Brill's unit beeped. "Okay, we're in business."

Brilliana caught her arm as she opened the door. "Take care, my lady. And if you sense trouble—"

"There won't be any trouble," Miriam said firmly. *Not with Sir Alasdair and his team watching my back.* If there was any trouble, if she was walking into a baited trap rather than a safe meeting, things would get spectacularly messy for the troublemakers. It wasn't just a matter of them having modern automatic weapons, two-way radios, and the ability to world-walk out of danger: Alasdair had cherry-picked the best men he could find in Clan Security for her bodyguard, and they'd planned and rehearsed this meeting carefully. "I'll be fine."

There was an alleyway, off the high street between two shuttered shopfronts; partway along it stood a tenement with its own shuttered frontage, and the three gilt balls of a pawnbroker hanging above the doorway. Miriam walked back along the pavement and turned in to the alleyway. There were no obvious watchers, nor loitering muggers. She marched up to the door beside the wooden shuttered window and yanked the bell-pull.

A few seconds later the door opened. "Come in, come in!" It was Erasmus, his face alight with evident pleasure. Miriam drew a deep breath of relief and stepped across the threshold. "How have you been?" he asked. "I've been worried—"

The door swung to behind her, and she took a step forward, ending up in his arms with her chin on his shoulder. He hugged her gingerly, as if afraid she might break. "It's been crazy," she confessed, hugging him back. "I've missed you too." Erasmus let go and straightened up awkwardly. "There's been a lot happening, much of it bad."

"Indeed, yes—" He took a step back, into the shadowy interior of the shop. "Excuse me." He turned and pushed a button that had been screwed crudely to the wall beside the door. A buzzer sounded somewhere below, in the cellars. "An all-clear sign. Just a precaution." He shrugged apologetically. "Otherwise they won't let me out of their sight."

Miriam glanced round. "I know that problem." The shop was just as she'd last seen it, albeit dustier and more neglected. But there was a light on in the back room, and a creaking sound. "Do you want to talk in front of company?"

"We'll be in the morning room upstairs, Frank," Erasmus called through the doorway, his voice a lot stronger than when she'd first met him.

"Are you sure?" Frank, staying unseen in the back room, had a rough voice.

"You've got the exit guarded. You've got the area covered. I will personally vouch for Miss Beckstein's trustworthiness; without her I wouldn't be alive for you to nanny me. But your ears are not safe for this discussion. Do you understand?"

Frank chuckled grimly. "Aye, citizen. But all the same, if I don't hear from you inside half an hour, I'll be coming up to check on you by and by. It's what Sir Adam would expect of me."

Erasmus shrugged apologetically at Miriam. "This way," he mouthed, then turned and opened the side door onto the tenement stairwell. Halfway up the staircase he added, "I should apologize for Frank. But he's doing no less than his duty. Even getting this much time to myself is difficult."

"Uh, yes." Miriam waited while Erasmus opened the door to the morning room. Dust sheets covered the piano and the villainous, ancient sofa. He stripped the latter one off, sneezing as he shook it out and cast it atop the piano stool. "My, I haven't been back here in months."

Miriam sat down carefully. Then, remembering, she reached into her pocket and pulled out the walkie-talkie. "Miriam here. Stand down, repeat, stand down. Over." She caught Erasmus staring at the device. "I have guards, too." It beeped twice, Brill acknowledging; she slid it away. "Please, sit down," she asked, gesturing at the other side of the sofa.

"You have a habit of surprising me." Erasmus folded himself into the far corner. "Please don't stop."

"Not if I can help it." She tried to smile, belying the tension in her stomach. "How's it going, anyway?"

"How's what going?" He waved a hand at the piano, the dusty fly-specked windows, the world beyond. "I never thought I'd live this long. Never thought I'd see the end of the tyranny, either. Nor that Sir Adam would come back and form a government, much less that he'd ask me to—well. How about yourself? What has happened to you since we last met? Nothing too trying, I hope?" His raised eyebrow was camouflage, she realized. *He's worried. About me?* She pushed the thought aside.

"Madness—bedlam," she translated. "Let me see if I can explain this. . . . I told you about the Clan? My relations?" He nodded. "Things went bad, very fast. You know what I was trying to do, the business. Brake pads, disk brakes. Their conservatives— they spiked it. Meanwhile, they tried to shut me up. Apparently a full-scale civil war broke out back home. And the conservative faction also discovered that the other—you know the world I came from isn't the one the Clan live in?—that other America, they found out about the Clan. To cut a long story short, the Clan conservatives tried to decapitate the American government, and at the same time, tried to kill the progressive faction. They failed on both counts. But now the US military are winding up for war on the Clan, and it looks like they might be able to build machinery for moving their weapons between worlds. It's not magic, Erasmus, it's some kind of physical phenomenon, and their scientists—they're better than you can imagine."

Burgeson shook his head. "This isn't making much sense—"

"I'm telling it wrong." She screwed up her eyes and took a deep breath. "Erasmus, let me start again?"

"For you, anything." He smiled briefly.

"Okay." She opened her eyes and exhaled. "The Clan exists as a family business, trading between worlds. A group of us—several hundred—believe that we have irrevocably fouled up our relationship with the world of the United States. That the United States military will soon have the power to attack the Gruinmarkt. Nowhere in the world the Clan lives in is safe. We are fairly certain that the US military doesn't know about *your* world, or at least has no way of reaching it directly—you can't get there from here without going via the Gruinmarkt. So I've got a proposal for you. We need somewhere to live—somewhere relatively safe, somewhere we haven't shat in the bed. Somewhere like New Britain. In return, we can offer you . . . well, my people have been busy grabbing all the science and engineering references they can get their hands on.

"The United States is sixty to eighty years ahead of you, although it might as well be two hundred—we can't promise to bridge that gap instantly, but we *can* show your engineers and scientists where to look. Right now you've got a hostile French empire off your shore. There are strategies and weapons technologies we can look up in the American history books that are decades ahead of anything the French—or your—navy can muster. And other stuff; see what their economists say, for example, or their historians."

"Ah." Erasmus nodded to himself. "That's an interesting idea." He paused. "What do your aristocratic cousins say about this idea? You are aware that we have recently held a revolution against the idea of autocracy and the landed gentry . . . ?"

"The ones you're worried about won't be coming, Erasmus. We're on the edge of a permanent split. The people who're listening to me—the progressives—the United States had their revolution more than two hundred years ago, remember that history I gave you?" He nodded. "For decades, the Clan has been educating its children in the United States. I'm unusual only in degree—my mother went the whole way, and raised me there from infancy. There's a pronounced split between the generation that has been exposed to American culture, education, and ideas, and the backwoods nobility of the Gruinmarkt; the Clan has found it increasingly hard to hold these two factions together for decades now. And those are the people I'd be bringing—those Clan members who'd rather be live refugees in a progressive republic than dead nobles clinging to the smoking wreckage of the old order. People whose idea of a world they'd like to live in is compatible with your party's ideology. All they want is a reasonable expectation of being able to live in peace."

"Oh, Miriam." Erasmus shook his head. "I would be very happy if I could offer you the assurance you want. Unfortunately" —she tensed—"I'd be lying if I said I could." He held out his hand towards her. She stared at it for a moment, then reached out and took it. "There is *no* certainty here. *None.* Those books you gave me, the histories of your America, they offer no reassurance. We are at war with an internal enemy who will show us no quarter if we lose, and our people are hungry, angry, and desperate. This is a governance of emergency. We hold the east coast and the west, and the major cities, but some of the small towns—" He shook his head. "The south, the southern continent, the big plantations there—the fighting is bloody and merciless. You shouldn't expect aid or comfort of us, Miriam. It's going to get a lot worse before it gets better. One of your American wise men said, the tree of liberty has to be watered with the blood of patriots. He wasn't exaggerating. My job is to, to try and hide what goes into the watering can. To put a good face on murder. You shouldn't expect too much of me."

Miriam stared at him for a long moment. "All right." She pulled on his hand gently. "Let's forget the living-in-peace bit. Can you protect us if we deliver? During the crisis, I mean. We help you develop the industrial mechanisms to defeat your external enemies. Can you, in return, keep the police off us?"

"The police, Reynolds and his Internal Security apparatus—" His expression clouded. "As long as I'm not arrested myself, *that*

I can manage. I've got leverage. Bentley and Crowe owe me, Williams needs my support—but best if it comes from the top, though, from Sir Adam and with the approval of the steering committee of the People's Council. Would be best if we kept it under wraps, though, especially if your first task is to build new factories for the war effort. Hmm."

There was a creak from outside the morning-room door, then a throat-clearing: "Be you folks decent?"

Erasmus's head whipped round. "Yes, everything is fine," he called.

"Just so, just so." It was Frank, the unseen bodyguard. He sounded amused.

"You can go away now," Erasmus added sharply.

A moment later Miriam heard a heavy tread descending the stairs, no longer stealthy. She looked at Erasmus. "Does he think we're—"

Erasmus looked back at her. "I don't *know* he thinks that, but it would make a good cover story, wouldn't you agree?"

"If we—" She stopped, feeling her ears heat. *Sitting on the sofa, holding hands.* She hadn't given much thought to that sort of thing—not since Roland's death. She let go of his fingers hastily.

"I'll need to make inquiries," said Erasmus. He let his hand fall. "Meanwhile, that big house you bought—I'll see it's left alone. If you follow me."

Miriam swallowed. "How long?" she asked, trying to regain control.

"You called me back from a, a marketing campaign. I'll have to see it's running smoothly. Then report to the Council, and talk to certain people. It could take months."

"I'm not sure we've got months."

"If you can come up with concrete proposals, I can probably hasten the process. Nothing too amazing, but if you can think of something concrete: smaller telautographs, better aircraft engines . . . ?"

"We can do that." Miriam swallowed. "I can have a written proposal ready next week." *That sort of target should be easy enough,* she thought: Someone had mentioned a flyer in the Clan who'd smuggled an ultralight into the Gruinmarkt against orders. *Find him, tell him what's needed, and pull the trigger.* Even a Second World War–era fighter plane would make an impressively futuristic demo in the skies above New London. "Let's meet here again. Next week?"

He nodded conspiratorially. "Come at the same time. I'll have something for you."

"I'll do that," she said automatically, then thought, *What?* "What kind of something?"

"Documents. A warrant pass. A tele number to call on." Erasmus rose to his feet, then offered her a hand. She took it, levering herself out of the collapsed cushion.

"Do you really think Frank believes we're having an affair?"

He leaned close to her ear. "Frank reports regularly to Oswald Sartorius, who is secretary in charge of state intelligence. He doesn't realize I know, and I would appreciate your not telling him. It would be safest for you if Oswald thinks we are having an affair; that way you need only worry about being arrested if he decides to move on me, and he will believe you to be of more value alive than dead. If he learns you represent a power center . . . Oswald wants what's best for state intelligence; he is no more dangerous than a shark, as long as you stay out of the water."

Miriam froze, feeling his breath on her cheek. "Is it that bad?"

"I don't know." He sounded uncertain. "So please be careful."

"You're the second person who's said that to me today." It was disturbing: It meant more to her than she'd anticipated. "You be careful too."

"I will be." He gestured at the door. "After you. . . ."

BEGIN PHONE TRANSCRIPT

(Groggy.) "Yes? Who is this?"

"Sir? This is BLOWTORCH. Duty officer speaking. Can you confirm your identity, please?"

(Pause.) "I'm KINGPIN. Is this line secure—"

"Not yet sir, if you'd like to press button four on your secure terminal now—"

(Click.) "Okay, I'm scrambling. What time—Jesus, this had better be good. What's the call, son?"

"Sir, we've, uh, there's a medical alert over WARBUCKS."

"It's definitely medical? The usual problem?"

"Sir, it may be worse this time. Don Ensenat says it would be best if you were up and alert—"

"Damn. How bad is it?"

"Sir, we have, uh, the cardiac crash team are trying to resuscitate, but as of now WARBUCKS is medically unfit. They've got him in transit to PIVOT and there's an operating theater standing by, but it doesn't look good. Sir, we're trying to contact Chief Justice Scalia as per the new continuity of government provisions but it's four in the morning in New York where he's—"

"Son. Stop right there." (Rustling.) "I'm just waking up here. I'll be in the operations center in five minutes: Get a team ready to take me to PAVILION, ready to leave in fifteen. Keep me informed if there's any change in WARBUCKS's condition, if he recovers or . . . not."

"Yes, sir."

"He'll hang in there. He's a tough old bird."

"I sure hope so, sir. Hell of a thing. Is there anything else I can do for you?"

"No, son, just get me that transport."

"Thank you sir. Goodbye and God bless."

(Click.)

(Softly.) "Christ on a crutch."

END PHONE TRANSCRIPT

"Ah, Erasmus. Come in, sit down. How are you?"

"I'm well, citizen. Thank you." It was a small office, surprisingly cramped in view of the seniority of its occupant. Windowless, which was clearly one of the features that had commended it to Sir Adam's security detail. Burgeson lowered himself into a spindly court chair and laid his folio on the chief commissioner's desk. "There's no end of rushing about, it seems. I really ought to be back to my train, but, well. The matter of our alien friends came up again."

Sir Adam's expression blanked for a moment, assuming the vacuity of information overload. Then he blinked. "Ah. The Beckworth woman?"

"And her allies."

Sir Adam looked past Erasmus, to his bodyguard. "Seumas, if you could go and rustle up tea for two, please? I think we may be a while." He paused until the stout fellow had left the room. "I've got a session of the defense policy review board at three, but I can give you half an hour right now. Will that suffice?"

"I hope so." Erasmus held his hands together to keep from fidgeting. "They've got more than gold, as I believe I told you; did you have time to read the book?"

"Yes, as a matter of fact. . . ." The chief commissioner removed his spectacles and carefully laid them on the blotter in front of him. Gold-rimmed, they gleamed in the harsh radiance cast by the electrical chandelier overhead. "It was very strange. Erasmus, either this is a most remarkable confidence trick, or—"

Burgeson shook his head. "There's more than just books. I've seen some of their machines. Yes, they're very strange. Frighteningly advanced. They have guns that—I've seen a young lady with a gun the size of that pen box, Sir Adam, I've seen it mow down polis thugs like a sewing engine. A battery gun you could fit in your coat pocket."

"Aliens. With advanced technology. How much of a threat to us are they, in your estimate?"

Erasmus spread his hands wide. "I think they're an opportunity, if we handle them carefully."

"What kind of opportunity? And what kind of care do you have in mind?"

"They're in trouble, Sir Adam. Which gives us leverage. My understanding of their plight is admittedly incomplete, but you can rest easy: They are not from the United States and they did not invent these near-magical engines that they use. Rather, they are traders—ours is not the only world they can reach—and they have infiltrated the United States you read about and use it as a source of wealth. Mercantilists, in other words. They have historically been an irritant to their host—smugglers and criminals—and now the host has discovered their existence. Miss Beckstein is entangled in a progressive faction among them, modernizers and democrats if not actual levelers. They recognize the bankruptcy of their former position and would seek sanctuary. In return, they offer to—Miriam's term for it is *technology transfer*. They can stealthily filch the secrets of the United States' engineers and scientists, and bring them to us for development. More: They have for years been training their children in modern management techniques."

"Just so. Very well, how many of these refugees are they?"

"Miriam says two to three thousand, at the outside. Most of them cannot travel to the other world—there are only a few hundred who can—but they're blood relatives. Which suggests an angle, doesn't it?"

Sir Adam nodded. "What are they running from? Enemies at home, or this United States of America?"

"The latter. It appears they were careless and drew themselves to the attention of the authorities there. I have a distinct and unpleasant impression that the US authorities are building machines that can travel between other worlds, for purposes of invasion. In which case—"

"Hmm."

"Indeed."

"What do you intend to do with these people, Erasmus?"

"I think we have room for a couple of thousand refugees, and it's easy enough to be generous under the circumstances. We should keep them isolated and under wraps, of course. The ones who can't world-walk—as they call it—are as important as those who can: Apparently their children may acquire the trait. In the meantime, they can be used to compel cooperation. Sir

Adam: I propose to use the world-walking refugees to acquire a library of scientific and technological material stolen from the United States. It may also be necessary to recruit human resources, doctors, skilled professionals, a library of experts: voluntarily if possible, but otherwise—"

"You're talking about abduction."

The door opened: Seumas and a silent palace servant entered, bearing a tea trolley. Sir Adam and Erasmus waited patiently for them to leave; then Erasmus picked up where he'd left off.

"If necessary, and only in service to our war effort, but . . . yes, if push comes to shove. May I continue? I envisage setting up a network of design bureaux and academies around this library of the future. They will act as a shield around this resource, filtering it out into our own industries. The United States is, well . . . it's hard to say, but I think their world is between fifty and a hundred years ahead of us in some respects. We won't close the gap in a decade, or even two or three, because they're moving forward as well. But we can close the gap *faster than the French*. If nothing else, knowing what played-out mines to avoid pouring treasure and sweat into will help us. This is a strategic resource, Sir Adam."

The first citizen nodded, then raised one eyebrow. "You don't need to convince me further, Erasmus: It's preposterous on first hearing but the world is indeed a strange place. But let's see, when this hits the central committee . . . argue me this: Why *you*? Why Propaganda? Why not Industry? Give me ammunition."

Erasmus picked up his teacup. It's rim clattered against the saucer it was balanced on. "Firstly, because they know me. Miss Beckstein trusts me, and she is their figurehead or leader or at least highly influential among them. These people are not beholden to us and we can't hope to corral them if they take fright. Secondly, because I'm *not* Industry. What we learn from these aliens will have effects everywhere—Industry is only the beginning of it. The Schools of Health, for instance, and the Directorates of Agriculture and Transportation—they'll all be affected. The complex I propose to establish will not be building battleships or aerodynes or setting up experimental farms; it will merely provide scientific information on these topics. It is indubitably a subdivision of Propaganda—Information. And then there's the final thing. This, this *Clan*, they are not the only people who travel between worlds. The United States are building time machines and may stumble upon us one day; and there may be others. Our treatment of these refugees will set a precedent for future diplomatic contacts with other worlds—and also our treatment of refugees from elsewhere on this one. Do you really think that hock-fist Brunner, or perhaps Oswald the Ear, would handle the nuances of disclosure effectively?"

Sir Adam's smile was frozen. "Of course they wouldn't. Erasmus, you have convinced me of most of your case, but you're wrong on this last point."

"Really?"

"Yes. Because if these people are as valuable as you tell me, we can't possibly disclose their existence in public. Not now, not in twenty years' time. No, Erasmus. I'm counting on you to reel them in and put them in a deep, padded box—and build your institute and your complex of design bureaus and all the rest of the complicated machinery. We're not going to breathe a word of this to anyone, including the rest of the commission. Not the Peace and Justice puritans—they'll just find a way to use your world-travelers as a stick to stir up trouble. Not the Radicals: I've no idea what they'd do, but it'd probably be as stupid as those land-reform proposals they keep coming up with. And Foreign Affairs: If the Bourbon gets so much as a whisper that they exist, he can make them an offer that would bankrupt our coffers to match. No. This needs to be kept secret, so secret that nobody gets a whiff of their existence. And you're just the man to see that it happens, aren't you?

"These aliens must belong to us—and us alone. Make it so."

The morning after the night before: Mike Fleming jolted abruptly awake to the sensation of the world falling away beneath his back. His eyes flickered open from uneasy, distorted dreams of pursuit, a panicky sense of disorientation tearing at his attention. He glanced sideways beneath half-closed lids; the light filtering in through the thin curtains showed him a floral print hanging on pastel-painted walls, strange furniture, someone else's decor. The jigsaw pieces of memory began to fill themselves in. *Paulie Milan's spare room.* They'd ordered in a Chinese meal, sat up late talking. There ensued an uneasy tap-dance as he—unused to hospitality, living for too long without that kind of life—borrowed towels and bedding, showered, prepared for an uneasy night's sleep. (Which largely consisted of taking off his shoes and pants, but keeping his pistol close to hand and checking out the yard from an unlit window before lying down atop the comforter.) It felt strange to be consigned to the guest room, like a one night stand gone weirdly askew down some strange dimension of alienation. *Don't sleep too deep,* he'd warned himself, only to close his eyes on darkness and open them in daylight. *Well damn, but at least nobody tried to cut my throat in the night—*

He was up and standing with his back to the wall beside the door, pistol in hand, almost before he realized he'd moved. Something was amiss. His nostrils flared as he breathed in, then held his breath, listening: not to the sound of someone moving in the bathroom, or clattering in the kitchen, or voices on the radio, talking. *Not.* He'd slept through the normal noises of another person's morning. What he'd noticed was their absence, and it was infinitely more disturbing.

Voices on the radio? Talking? He could hear voices. *Who—*

Mike did a double take and closed his eyes. Tried to visualize the kitchen layout. Was there a—

Creak of a footstep on the landing. Then a tentative voice: "Mike? Are you awake yet?"

His muscles turned to jelly as he sagged, lowering the pistol. He'd been unaware of the tension in his neck and shoulders, the totality of focus, his heart hammering with a flashback to a cheap motel room in Tijuana that stank of stale cigarette smoke and claustrophobia. He pointed the gun at the floor beside him, letting its weight drag his wrist down. "Yeah?"

"We have a visitor. There's coffee in the kitchen. Do you want me to pour you one?"

Coffee plus visitor equals—"Yes." He glanced across the room to the bedside table where he'd left his holster. Coming down from the jittery adrenaline spike, he added, "I'll be down in a couple of minutes. Need to freshen up first."

"Okay." Paulie's footsteps receded down the stairs.

Mike let out a breath, quietly shuddering, still winding down. The radio, the sudden silence, whatever had triggered his ambush reflex—it was all right. Moving carefully, he placed the pistol beside the holster, then picked up his pants from where he'd hung them over the back of a chair. *A visitor* almost certainly meant one of Miriam's relatives. Paulette had admitted knowing a few of them: the ice princess, another woman called Brill. He dressed hurriedly, then slid the pistol in its holster into his trouser pocket, just in case. Not that he didn't trust Paulette—he trusted her enough to sleep under her roof—but experience had taught him not to make assumptions when dealing with the Clan.

He descended the stairs, carefully keeping his left hand on the rail, and glanced sideways through the kitchen doorway. The ice princess, Olga, was sitting at the breakfast bar drinking coffee. She nodded at him coolly. "Mr. Fleming."

The kitchen radio was babbling headline chatter about someone in hospital. His jaw tensed as he stepped inside the room. "Good morning." He noticed Paulette leaning against the kitchen worktop, her eyes worried. "Someone mentioned coffee." Paulette reached out and flicked off the radio as he glanced from side to side. A big leather shoulder bag gaping open on the table, something dark and angular inside it—she wouldn't come here unarmed—slatted blinds drawn down across the window onto the backyard—

"It's right here." Paulette gestured at a mug on the breakfast bar. Mike walked over and pulled a stool out, then sat down awkwardly opposite the ice princess.

"How does it feel to be one of the most wanted people in the world?" he remarked.

"Why ask me? Surely you already know." She kept a straight face, but the chill in her voice made his pulse speed.

"I didn't murder eighteen thousand people."

"Neither did I," said Olga. She took a mouthful of coffee, then put her mug down. "The people who did that are dead, Mr. Fleming. My people took them down. Do you have a *problem* with that?"

Mike opened his mouth, then closed it again.

"They didn't stop at detonating bombs in your capital city," Olga added. "They tried to murder everyone who stood in their way. A coup attempt." Her minute nod made his stomach shrink. "They tried to kill me, and Miriam, and everyone aligned with us. Luckily we had a tip-off. They failed; the last of the plotters was impaled yesterday morning."

"*Impaled?*" Paulette's expression was rigid.

"Oh yes. After the executioners blinded and castrated them," Olga added, and bowed her head. "My father was killed in the struggle, Mr. Fleming. I'd thank you not to place your *eighteen thousand dead* on my shoulders."

Mike almost asked which faction her father had belonged to; a vestigial sense of shame stilled his tongue for a few seconds. "I'm sorry to hear that," he said eventually.

"But impaling—" Paulette stopped.

"It was no better than they deserved. The traditional punishment for such high treason is to spread the wings of the blood-eagle, then quarter the parts," Olga added. "But that hasn't been practiced since my grandfather's time."

Mike stared at his mug of coffee, and dry-swallowed. This wasn't what he'd expected to hear. "You failed to stop them," he accused, knowing it signified nothing.

"You failed too. So we're even. Failures all round." The silence stretched on for half a minute. Finally Olga broke it. "Why did you call for help?"

Mike shuffled on his stool uncomfortably. "Did you find your mole?"

"We have more urgent problems right now." It was an evasion. Olga looked at Paulette. "Thank you for continuing to source provisions for us; it has been more useful than you can know, but there are some new arrangements I need to discuss with you. Things are going to be busy for a while. Mr. Fleming, there have been reports of contrails over the Gruinmarkt. We don't have much time for idle chatter. Do you know anything about them?"

"They've been planning some kind of incursion for at least six months," Mike told her. The secret, divulged, left him feeling naked. "I saw a spec-ops helicopter. This was planned before the bombs went off. They know where all the oil is, and you're a threat to national security. But since the bombs—now—I don't think they'll be satisfied with their original plans."

"Do you believe they'll use nuclear weapons?"

"Will they?" It was Mike's turn to frown. "They already did: that castle up near Concord. The question isn't whether, the question is when and how many." Stripped of the bloody shirt of *eighteen thousand dead*, these events acquired a logic of their own. "They'll kill a lot of people who have nothing to do with your extended family."

"Yes." Olga emptied her coffee mug. "And so, we are taking steps to leave, to put ourselves forever beyond contact with the US government. Those of us with any sense, that is. Some refuse to see the writing on the wall, as you would say. The Clan is breaking up, you know; a generation ago the mere suggestion of an open split would have been seen as treason."

"Where are you going?" asked Paulette.

"You've been there, I seem to recall. On a visit." Olga raised an eyebrow. "Excuse me for not describing it in front of Mr. Fleming. When we go—I am allowed to offer you a payoff in money, or asylum if you are afraid of the authorities here: We look after our friends. But it'll be a one-way trip."

"They'll come after you. They'll hunt you down wherever you run to," Mike predicted.

"Let them try." Olga shrugged. "Mr. Fleming, *I* didn't choose to fight the US government; I'm not Osama bin Laden. Your former vice president, he—well. We have a rule. When we do business with outsiders, we have a rule: *no politicians.* WARBUCKS quit politics, in the late eighties: That's when our West Coast subsidiary approached him—well. Water under the bridge. It was a serious oversight, but one we are in the process of rectifying. My question to you is, what are you going to do now? Paulette tells me your agency has tried to kill you. What do you *want*? I can give you money—we've got more than we know what to do with, we can't take it where we're going—or I can offer you asylum—"

"I want the files," said Mike.

"The. What?"

"Your files on WARBUCKS."

"Huh?" Paulette looked confusedly between them.

"WARBUCKS started this. I wouldn't be here now if I didn't know a deliberate provocation when I saw one. This is all happening because he wants to cover up his past complicity with the Clan, and because the existence of the Clan is now a matter of public record. An awful lot of people are going to die to cover up his secret." Mike's frustration sought a way out. "People who have nothing to do with your nasty little family trade, or with me, or with WARBUCKS. Listen, I don't much care for you. If it was business as usual I'd arrest you *right now* and put you away on racketeering, money laundering, and drugs charges. Oh, and the illegal firearm." He gestured at Olga's bag and she twitched a hand towards it; he shrugged. "But it's not business as usual—probably never will be, ever again. The man who you guys have fallen out with is *running my country.* He's corrupted *my* government, built a secret unaccountable agency with the capability to bypass the national nuclear command authority, disappeared people into underground prisons; you name it, he's done it. He's wiped his ass on the Constitution and it's all thanks to dirty drugs money: not directly, oh no, but you're complicit. I don't care *what* happens to you people—but I swore an oath to protect the constitution of the United States, and it looks like for the past year I've been working for an organization designed from the get-go to undermine it. So I want your files on WARBUCKS, now they're no use to you any more if you're serious about pulling out. I want the dirt. And if you won't give it to me, you're worse than I think you are—and my opinion of you is pretty low right now."

"What are you going to do with the files if we give them to you?" Olga asked slowly.

"Well, that depends." He glanced at Paulette. "I take it your work here is mostly done, or you wouldn't have told me even that much?" He didn't wait for a reply. "I need someone who knows how the press works. And I need ammunition. Someone's got to blow the lid on WARBUCKS before he eats the US government from inside—and I don't see anyone else volunteering."

"But—" Paulette stopped and looked bleakly at Olga.

"What?" Mike glanced between them.

"Do you want to tell him?" asked Olga.

Paulette shook her head wordlessly and reached across to flick on the radio.

"—Cardiac arrest on the way to Bethesda Naval Hospital. Doctors worked for three hours to try to resuscitate the president but he was declared dead at five-fourteen this morning. The vice president is meeting with advisors but is expected to appear at a press conference to make a statement imminently; we understand that Supreme Court Chief Justice Scalia is on his way to the vice president's location to administer the oath—"

"Fuck." Mike stared at the radio. All his carefully considered plans crumbled. *"Fuck."*

"That's two presidents in a month," said Olga. "I understand it's a stressful job."

"Jesus fuck." Paulette looked at Mike reproachfully. "Sorry," he muttered.

Olga was imperturbable: "Do you think your people will care about the misdeeds of KINGPIN's predecessor?"

Mike shook his head. "Fuck. Sorry." He stared at the radio. The presenter was babbling on about previous presidential emergency successions. "He's dead. Why did the bastard have to die *now*?"

"What will this new President do?" Olga leaned toward him.

"KINGPIN? He'll—" Mike chuckled weakly. "Oh dear god."

"WARBUCKS was KINGPIN's assistant, wasn't he?" Paulette blinked, her eyes watery. "Back in the Ford era, or something. They're more like partners, were more like partners, the past couple of years. Partners in crime—politics, not the Clan. KINGPIN is going to be just like WARBUCKS, only without the personal history."

Mike nodded. "You had a handle on WARBUCKS. KINGPIN is the same—only you've lost your handle."

"Oh." Olga sat motionless for a few seconds. "This fact needs to be reported."

"What are you going to do?" Mike asked.

"I'm going to tell certain people." Olga flashed him a bright, brittle smile. "I'm going to see if I can get you those papers—if you still want them. Then those of us with even half an ounce of self-preservation are going to run away very fast. . . ."

NEVER COMING BACK

The row of big town houses, set back behind high walls or hedges, had seen better days. Every other building showed boarded-up windows to the street, the blank-eyed, gape-doored stare of ruination and downfall. Some of them—some very few—had been squatted, but for the most part the Freedom Riders had kept the dusty workless poor out of the houses of the bourgeoisie, for this was not solely a revolution of the working class.

The big steamer huffed and bumped across last winter's pot-holes, then slowed as Yul wrestled with the wooden steering wheel, swearing at it as he worked the brake handle and tried to lever the beast between stone gateposts. Miriam sat up in the back, trying to see over his shoulders for a first glimpse of the house she'd bought in this city using smuggled Clan bullion, a little over a year ago. "Is it—" She swallowed her words as the front of the building came into view.

"It seems intact." Brilliana, next to her, nodded. "Let us examine it, my lady."

The boarded-up windows were still sealed, the front door barred and padlocked as one of her armsmen held the car's door open for Miriam. "By your leave, my lady?" Alasdair slid round in his jump seat. "I should go first."

Miriam bit back an irritated response. "Yes," she agreed. "Thank you." Sir Alasdair unfolded his legs and stood, interposing his not-inconsiderable frame between Miriam and the facade of the building.

"Wait," Alasdair rumbled without looking round as he moved forward. "Schraeder, left and rear. Yul, you stay with the car. Brunner, with me. . . ." They spread out around the house purposefully, their long coats still closed despite the summer humidity. It looked empty, but appearances could be deceptive and Sir Alasdair was not inclined to take risks with Helge's life, figurehead though her queen-widowship might be: He'd sworn an oath to protect her, and his people took such things seriously.

Miriam stared at the front door as Alasdair approached it, slowing on the steps, then bending close to peer at the door handle. Beside her, Brill shifted on the bench seat, one hand going to the earpiece tucked discreetly under her hat. "Clear behind," she said suddenly. "Schraeder's in."

I bought that house, Miriam told herself. Right now it looked as unfamiliar as her father—her adoptive father—had looked in the funeral parlor. Houses took as much of their character from the people who filled them as racks of meat on bone took from their animating personality. It had once been her home; but for the miscarriage she might now be looking to raise a child in it. But for now it was just a big neglected building, a cumbersomely inanimate corpse—

Alasdair interrupted her morbid stream of consciousness by straightening up. He unlocked the door, opened it slowly, and stepped inside.

"All clear," said Brill, tapping Miriam on the shoulder. "Let's go inside."

The house was much as Miriam had last seen it, only dusty and boarded-up, the furniture looming beneath dust sheets. "Who organized this?" she asked, pausing at the foot of the stairs.

"I did," said Brill. "When Baron Henryk assigned the business operation to Morgan I assumed they'd want you back sooner or later. Morgan didn't like it here, he preferred to spend as much time at home as he could."

"Right. This way." Miriam headed upstairs in the dark, a flashlight guiding her feet. Opposite the top of the stairs was the door to the main bedroom. She pushed it open, saw daylight: The upper windows at least were not boarded up. "I need a hand with this."

"With what—"

Miriam was already kneeling near the skirting board beside the bed. Stale dust and a faint smell of mouse piss wrinkled her nose. "In here. Here, hold this." She passed Brill the loose piece of woodwork. Behind it, the brickwork was visible. "Pass me your knife. . . ." It took a little work, but between them they levered the two half-bricks out of their niche. Then Miriam reached inside and grabbed. "Got it."

The black cloth bag was about the size of a boot, but much heavier. Miriam grunted and lifted it onto the bed.

"How much is it?" asked Brilliana.

"I'm surprised it's still here." Miriam untied the knotted drawstring then thrust her hand inside. "Yep, it's the real thing." The gold brick glinted in the afternoon light; she returned it to the bag hastily. "About six kilos of twenty-three-carat. It was worth a hell of a lot a year ago—God only knows what it's worth right now." Stuck in a deflationary cycle and a liquidity crash with a revolution on top, gold—with or without seigniorage—was enormously more valuable than it had been when it was merely what the coin of the realm was made of. The national treasury had been stripped bare to pay for the war: That was what had started the crisis.

She straightened up and dusted herself down. "Job number one for Alasdair is to get someone who knows what they're doing to hide this *properly*. We lucked out once, but sooner or later one of Erasmus's rival ministries will probably try and shake us down to see where the leverage is coming from. They won't believe the truth, and if they find this here we'll be for the chop. Revolutionary governments hate hoarders; it's a law of nature."

"I'll see to it, my lady—"

"That's another thing." Miriam glanced at the windows. "It's not 'my lady' anymore—I mean it. Drop the honorific, and tell everyone else: It's Miriam, or ma'am, but not 'my lady.' "

Brill's dismay was palpable. "But you *are* my lady! You are my liege, and I owe you an acknowledgment of that fact! This isn't the United States, this is—"

"This is a continent *in the grip of revolution*." Miriam walked towards the wardrobe and lifted one corner of its dusty shroud. "What do you know about revolutionary governments?"

"Not much; we hang rebels, my lady." Brill lifted back the top of the dust sheet from the bed, wrinkling her nose.

"Well, I've been doing some reading this week. Remember the books?" Miriam had given Brill a list of titles to order from Amazon. "There's a general pattern. First there's a crisis—usually fiscal, often military. The old government is discredited and a coalition of interests move in and toss the bums out. Then they start trying to govern as a coalition, and it goes to hell quickly because just changing the government doesn't solve the underlying crisis unless it was a crisis of legitimacy." Brill looked perturbed, as Miriam continued: "This means that the new government gets to try and fix the crisis at its weakest, and in conditions where it's very easy to replace them. Most postrevolutionary regimes are overthrown by their own hard-line radicals, the ones with the most blinkered ideological outlook—precisely because they're also the ones most willing to murder anyone who stands between them and a solution to the crisis."

She tugged the dust sheet down from the wardrobe and stepped aside.

"The revolution here was against the autocratic monarchy, but there's also a fiscal crisis and a war. They hit the trifecta—crisis of currency, conflict, and legitimacy in one go. The aristocracy, such as it is, gets its own legitimacy from the Crown—for centuries, John Frederick and his family have sold titles as a way of raising revenue—so anyone with a noble title is going to be automatically suspect to the hard-liners in the new government. And unless Sir Adam can end the war with France and fix the economy in, oh, about six months, the hard-liners are going to get restive." She turned worried eyes on Brilliana. "That's why I want everyone to stop using titles *immediately*. If I'm wrong, they'll get over it. But if I'm right . . ."

"I understand," Brill said tiredly. "There's no need to repeat yourself. Miriam. Ma'am." She peeled back the blankets and sheets that had stayed on the bed, exposing them to air for the first time in months. "What else is going to happen here?"

"I don't know. It depends on whether they tackle the economy, the war, or the constitutional problems—any or all of them." She opened the wardrobe, sniffed. "I think something died in here. Where's the flashlight?"

"Here." Brill waited while Miriam shoved aside the dresses on the rail and shone the beam around the interior of the wardrobe. "What do you think?"

"I think they'll have to execute the king, and a lot of his supporters, or the French would use him as an excuse to make mischief. And they won't rest with a revolutionary superpower on the other side of the world—Sir Adam Burroughs's Leveler ideology is an existential threat to any absolute monarchy, much like the Soviet Union was to the United States' capitalist system. Which leaves the economy." Miriam straightened up. "Lots of radical ministries jockeying for preeminence, a permanent emergency in foreign affairs, a big war effort. Central planning, maybe, lots of nationalization. They're going to have to industrialize properly if they're going to dig their way out of this mess. War spending is always a good way to boost an economy. And land reform, let's not forget the land reform—they'll probably expropriate the big slave plantations in South America, the duchies of the Midwest."

"My—Miriam, you can't sleep here: The bedding's mildewed."

"Wha—oh? Shit. There should be spare sheets in the laundry—" Miriam wound down. "Oh. No servants."

"I could hire bodies easily enough, if you think it necessary?"

"No." Miriam frowned. "Flashing around cash would be really dangerous right now. Huh. Need to know if the electricity's working . . . listen, let's go see if the office is intact and the power still works. If so, we ought to go look at the factory. Then I can electrograph Erasmus and tell him we're ready to start work whenever he comes up with those passes he was talking about."

In an office near the northern end of Manhattan, with a window overlooking the royal navy dockyard, Stephen Reynolds set aside the stack of death warrants at his left hand and stood, smiling warmly, as commissioners Jennings and Fowler walked in.

"Good morning, citizens." He gestured at the seats beside his desk as he walked around it, placing himself on the same side of the table as his visitors: "Nice to see you. Are you both well? Edward, is your wife—"

"She's fine," Jennings said, a trifle brusquely, then cleared his throat. "Nothing to worry about, and the would-be assassin is already in custody." As the citizen inquisitor supervising the Justice Directorate, Jennings (not to mention his family) had become accustomed to being the principal target of the regime's enemies (not to mention their surviving relatives). "I gather your people have identified his conspirators already."

"Ah, excellent." Fowler cleared his throat. "Time is short, I'm afraid: Got a meeting of the Construction Subcommittee to chair in an hour. You have something that calls for extreme measures?"

"Yes." Reynolds smiled again, concealing his minor irritation at being so preempted. "Alas, we have a minor problem. That fine fellow Mr. Burgeson is apparently trespassing on our turf. I've had a tipoff from certain sources"—*not* mentioning Elder Cheung and his magical powers, or his strange associate, the Dutch doctor—"that Erasmus is, not to put too fine a point on it, dealing with *persons of interest*. There's some question as to what he is doing; I haven't been able to get an informer into his organization. But the secrecy with which he is conducting his affairs is suggestive. Certainly it's not any activity that falls within the portfolio of the commissioner for state truth. I believe he is in league with wreckers and subversives, and I would appreciate the cooperation of your departments in, ah, distinguishing the sheep from the goats."

Jennings tilted his head on one side thoughtfully. "I'm sure we can work together on this matter—*if* Citizen Burgeson is acting against the best interests of the people." A caveat from Justice was to be expected.

Reynolds nodded. It didn't signify opposition as such, merely that Jennings knew exactly what was going on and had no intention of being strung up as a scapegoat for Reynolds's move against the rival directorate. "Of course," he said unctuously. "There must be proceedings with all due process to confirm or disprove guilt, absolutely! But I think it would be best if they were handled in the Star Court with all available speed, precision, and discretion"—in other words, secretly and hastily—"and the prisoners segregated. If there's actual subversion within the party's highest echelons, we will need to obtain absolute proof before we arrest a party commissioner. And if not—again, it would be best if it were handled quietly. The scope for embarrassment is enormous and it would reflect badly on the party as an institution."

Fowler shrugged. "It can be done, but it'll cost you," he said bluntly. "There's a new interrogation and processing block scheduled for development on Long Island. Or I could do you a prison hulk."

"A prison hulk?" Reynolds's eyes lit up: "Capital! That would be just the ticket!" After the initial shock, he'd paid close attention to Cheung's sales pitch—and spent time in subsequent meetings attempting to deduce the limitations of the world-walkers' abilities. A steam yacht with decent owner's quarters and a train with sleeping car were already on his department's budget—officially to make it easier for the commissioner for internal security to travel safely between offices, unofficially to insure his safety against world-walking killers. "Do you have anything offshore near the Massachusetts coastline? Preferably with an antimutiny plug?" (Explosive scuttling charges had proven a most effective tool in preventing prison mutinies under the ancien régime.)

"I think something along those lines can be provided." Fowler pulled out a notebook. "How many berths do you need, and when and where will the arrests take place?"

"Number: unknown, but not more than a thousand at the absolute maximum. More likely under a hundred in the first instance, then a flow of stragglers for processing. Somewhere within a couple of hours of Boston. To be moored in deep water—not less than thirty feet beneath the keel—and not less than a mile offshore. If you could set it up within the next two days I would be eternally grateful . . . ?"

"I'll see what we can do." Fowler put his notebook away. "I take it the detainees are, er, disposable?"

"If necessary." Reynolds nodded.

"I didn't hear that," Jennings said fastidiously.

"Of course not."

"Jolly good, then." Jennings stood. "I'll see that a circuit tribunal under Star Rules is at your men's disposal in Boston two days hence. Now if you don't mind, I have a dreadful pile of paperwork to catch up on . . . ?" He sighed. "These wreckers and subversives! I swear we're going to run out of rope before they're all hanged."

The fortified great house had seen better days: Its walls were fire-scorched, half the downstairs windows were bricked up, the hastily applied mortar still weeping salts across the stone blocks of its facade, and the stable doors had been crudely removed. But it was still inhabitable—which counted for something—and the ten-meter radio mast sprouting from the roofline made it clear who its inhabitants must be.

"You wanted to see me, sir."

The office on the second floor had once been a squire's wife's boudoir; it still smelled faintly of rosewater and gunpowder. The bed had been broken up for firewood and scrap, used to reinforce the shutters during the brief siege, and today the room was dominated by a green folding aluminum map table.

"Yes. Come in, sit down, make yourself comfortable. I've got Pepsi if you need a drink."

"That would be wonderful, sir."

Rudi sat tensely on the narrow edge of the camp chair while Earl-Major Riordan poured him a mug of foaming brown cola with his own hands. The lack of a batman did not escape his notice, but if Riordan wanted to preserve the social niceties . . . *It must be bad news,* he decided, a hollowness below his ribs waiting to be filled by the exotic imported beverage.

"I want to pick your brains about aircraft," Riordan said stiffly. "Think of this as an informal brainstorming session. Nothing we discuss is for ears beyond this room, by the way."

Really? Rudi leaned forward. "Brainstorming, sir?"

Riordan sighed. "Her Majesty"—he paused, and poked at a paper on his desk—"has written me a letter, and you're the man to answer it." He looked slightly pained, as if his lunch had disagreed with his digestion.

"Sir."

"You know about the *British*." They spoke hochsprache. "She is talking to them. She wants an aircraft. Something that can be built for them within two years and that outstrips anything they can imagine. Something for war."

"To be built *there*?" Rudi shook his head. "I thought they were stuck in the steam age?"

"They have aircraft. Two wings, spaced above each other like so"—Riordan gestured—"slow, lumbering things. Made of wood and sailcloth."

"Really?" Rudi perked up. "And Her Majesty wants to build something better? What for?"

"They've got a war on." Riordan finally sat down in the chair opposite, and Rudi relaxed slightly. "The French are blockading them, there is a threat of bombardment from aerial tenders off-shore. I told her to give the *British* something for their navy, one of those submarines—you've seen *Das Boot*? no?—but she says ships take too long. They understand not to expect too much of aircraft, so build something revolutionary." He took a deep breath. "Give me an eagle's view. What should I be asking?"

"Huh." Rudi rubbed his chin. It was itching; he hadn't had a chance to shave for three days, scurrying hither and yon trying to arrange bodies to haul across the ultralight parts he'd been buying. "What engines do they have? That's going to limit us. And metallurgy. Electronics . . . I assume they've got vacuum tubes? It'll have to be something from the nineteen-forties. A warbird. Two engines for range, if it's going offshore, and it needs to be able to carry bombs or guns." He paused. "You know a plane on its own isn't going to do much? It needs tactical doctrine, pilot training, navigation tools and radar if they can build it, ideally an integrated air defense—"

Riordan waved an impatient hand. "Yes, that's not the point. We need what Her Majesty calls a *technology demonstrator*."

"Can they do aluminum engine blocks?" Rudi answered his own question: "Maybe not, but aluminum goes back to the nineteenth century—we can work on them. Hmm. Engines will be a bottleneck, but . . . P-38? No, it's a pure fighter. Hard to fly, too. If they're still doing wood—" He stopped.

"Wood?" Riordan frowned.

"We'd need to work out how to produce the engines, and we'd need modern epoxy glues instead of the shit they had back then, but. But." Rudi shook his head. "I think I know what you want," he said.

"Do you?"

"The de Havilland Mosquito. The British built tons of them during the war, kept them flying until the nineteen sixties—it was originally a fast two-seat bomber, but they hung guns on it and used it as a fighter too. Made out of plywood, with two Merlin engines—they were a nineteen-thirties design, so the metallurgy might be up to it. Long range, fast; if they're still using biplanes it'll run rings around anything they've seen. If the metallurgy is better and quality control is up to it, I'd go for the P-51D, the Mustang. Faster, single-engined, similar range, more maneuverable. But for a first cut, I'd go for something made of wood with two engines. Safer that way."

Riordan nodded slowly. "Could you build one?"

"Could." Rudi carefully placed his half-full mug on the map table. He tried not to exhale Pepsi. "*Build* one?"

"For the British." Riordan wasn't smiling. "With unlimited resources, but a knife over your head."

"Urk." Rudi thought for a while. "Maybe. But I'd hedge my bets."

"How?"

"I'd start by talking to their existing aircraft designers. And bring the biggest damn library of metallurgy, electronics, materials, and aerodynamics textbooks I can find. The designs for those nineteen-forties warbirds—you can buy them on eBay for a couple of hundred dollars—CD-ROMs with just about everything on them, technical manuals, patents, blueprints, everything. But you'll probably take longer to build an exact replica of one from the blueprints than it would take a clued-up manufacturer on a war footing to invent a new one and build it from scratch. Much better to grab all the textbooks and histories, copies of *Jane's Aircraft*, manuals, ephemera—*everything*—and drop them in front of a team who're already used to working together. Hell, give them a history of air warfare and blueprints of the aircraft and they'll have a field day."

"Huh." Riordan's frown deepened. "That may not be possible."

"Oh." Rudi deflated slightly. "That would make it a lot harder. If we can only use Clan members, it's nearly impossible. There aren't even a dozen of us who know an aileron from a slotted flap. But we could do the liaison thing, act as librarians, figure out what a design team needs to know and get it for them. Hell. We could go recruiting, you know? Look for aerospace engineers in trouble with the law, offer them a bolt-hole and a salary and a blind eye if they'll work for us."

"Not practical. That last idea, I mean. But the liaison idea, hmm. Can you get me a list of names?"

"Certainly, sir. When do you need it by?" *But what about the ultralights?* he wondered.

"You have two hours. Here's a pad and a pen; Comms and Crypto are downstairs on the left if you need to ask any questions. You have my seal." Riordan tossed a heavily embossed metal ring on the table in front of Rudi. Rudi flinched, as if from a poisonous mushroom. "I'll be back at five and I need to send the answer to Her Majesty by six. Your task is to identify those of our people who you will need in order to help the *British* develop their aerospace sector. Oh, and remember to include runway construction, fuel and repair equipment and facilities, munitions, bombsights, gunsights, training, and anything else I've forgotten. That's a higher priority than your ultralight squadron, I'm afraid, but it's a much bigger job. The Pepsi's all yours."

Late afternoon of a golden summer day. On a low ridge overlooking a gently sloping vale, a party of riders—exclusively male, of gentle breeding, discreetly armed but not under arms—paused for refreshment. To the peasants bent sweating over sickle and sheaf, they would be little more than dots on the horizon, as distant as the soaring eagle high above, and of as little immediate consequence.

"I fear this isn't a promising site," said one of the onlookers, a hatchet-faced man in early middle age. "Insufficient cover— see the brook yonder? And the path over to the house, around that outcrop?—we'd stick out like pilliwinked fingers."

"Bad location for helicopters, though," said a younger man. "See, the slope of the field: makes it hard for them to land. And for road access, I think we can add some suitable obstacles. If the major is right and they can bring vehicles across, they won't have an easy time of it."

Earl Bentbranch hung back, at the rear of the party. He glanced at his neighbor, Stefan ven Arnesen. Ven Arnesen twined his fingers deep in his salt-and-pepper beard, a distant look on his face. He noticed Bentbranch watching and nodded slightly.

"Do you credit it?" Bentbranch murmured.

Ven Arnesen thought for a moment. "No," he said softly, "no, I don't." He looked at the harvesters toiling in the strip fields below. It didn't *look* like the end of the world as he knew it. "I can't."

"They may not come for a generation. If ever. To throw everything away out of panic . . ."

Ven Arnesen spared his neighbor a long, appraising look. "They'll come. Look, the harvest comes. And with it the poppies. Their war dead—their families used to wear poppies to remember them, did you know that?"

"You had your tenants plant dream poppies in the divisions."

"Yes. If the bastards come for us, it's the least I can do. Give it away"—he looked out across his lands, as far as the eye could see—"for free." He coughed quietly. "I'm too old to uproot myself and move on, my friend. Let the youngsters take to the road, walk the vale of tears as indigent tinkers just like our great-great-grandfathers' grandsires once more. These are my lands and my people and I'll not be moving. All this talk of *business models* and *refugees* can't accommodate what runs in my veins."

"So you'll resist?"

Ven Arnesen raised an eyebrow. "Of course. And you haven't made your mind up yet."

"I'm . . . wavering. I went to school over there, do you remember? I speak Anglische, I *could* up sticks and go to this new world they're talking of, I'd be no more or less of a stranger there than I was for seven years in Baltimore. But I could dig my own midden, too, or run to Sky Father's priests out of mindless panic. I could do any number of stupid or distasteful things, were I so inclined, but I don't generally do such things without good reason. I'd need a *very* good reason to abandon home and hearth and accept poverty and exile for life."

"The size of the reason becomes greater the older one gets," ven Arnesen agreed. "But I'm not convinced by this nonsense about resisting the American army, either. I've seen their films. I've spent a little time there. Overt resistance will be difficult. Whatever Ostlake and his cronies think."

"I don't think they believe anything else, to tell you the truth. If—when—they come, the Americans will outgun us as heavily as we outgunned the Pervert's men. And there will be thousands of them, tens of thousands. With *tanks* and *helicopters*. Sure, we'll kill a few of them. And that will make it worse, it'll make them angry. They're not good at dealing with locals, not good at native tongues. They'll kill and they'll burn and they'll raise every man's hand against them and their occupation, and it will still take a bloody five years of pain and tears and death before they'll even think about changing their approach. By which time—"

"Look." Ven Arnesen raised his arm and pointed.

"Where?"

"Look *up*." A ruler-straight white line was inching across the turquoise vault of the sky, etching it like a jeweler's diamond on glass. A tiny speck crawled through the air, just ahead of the moving tip of the line. "Is that what, what I think it is?"

"A contrail." Bentbranch's cheeks paled. "It's them."

"Are you sure? Could it be something else? Something natural—"

"No. Their *jets* make those cloud-trails, when they move through the sky."

"And they look down on us from above? Do you suppose they can see us now? Lightning Child strike them blind."

"I very much fear that they're anything but blind." Bentbranch looked away as the aircraft's course led it westwards, towards the sunset. "Though how much detail they can see from up there . . . well, that tears it, of course. They will be drawing up maps, my lord. And they care naught that we know their mind. I find that a singularly ominous sign. Do you differ, can I ask?"

"No." Ven Arnesen shook his head as he stared after the aircraft. "No." But Bentbranch was unable to discern whether he was answering the question or railing against the sign in the heavens.

Ahead of them, the main group of riders, Lord Ostlake and his men, had noticed the contrail; arms were pointing and there were raised voices. "We should warn them," Bentbranch said, nudging his horse forward. Ven Arnesen paid him no attention, but stared at the sky with nerve-struck eyes.

Out over the ocean in the east, the U-2's contrail was already falling apart, like the dreams of future tranquility that it had so carelessly scrawled across.

It would not take many more forty-thousand-foot overflights to update the air force's terrain maps.

The old woman had been reading a book, and it still lay open on her lap, but her attention was elsewhere. There was a discreet knock at the door. She looked up as it opened, and adjusted her spectacles, unsurprised at the identity of her visitor. "Yes?"

"Your grace." The door closed behind him. "I hope I'm not interrupting anything?"

"No, no . . ." She slid a bookmark into place, then carefully closed the book and placed it on the table beside her. "I've got plenty of time. All the time in the world."

"Ah, yes. Well, I'd like to apologize for leaving you to your own devices for so long. I trust you have been well-attended?"

"Young man, you know as well as I do that when one is in a jail cell, however well furnished, it does little good to grumble at the jailer."

"It might, if you harbor some hope of release. And might reasonably expect to be in a position of authority over your captor, by and by." He raised an eyebrow, and waited.

She stared at him grimly. "Release." She raised her right hand. It shook, visibly. She let it fall atop the book. "Release from what?" The palsy was worse than it had been for some time. "What do you think I have to look forward to, even if you give me the freedom of the city outside these walls? Without imported medicines my quality of life will be poor. I can't use that liberty you hint at." She gestured at the wheelchair she sat in. "This is more of a jail than any dungeon you can put me in, Riordan."

Rather than answering, the earl crossed the stone-flagged floor of the day room and, picking up the heavy armchair from beside the small dining table, turned it to face her. Then he sat, crossing one leg over the other, and waited.

After a while she sighed. "Credit me with being old enough to be a realist, kid." She paused. "I'm not going to see the right side of sixty again, and I've got multiple sclerosis. It's gaining on me. I'd like to go back home to Cambridge, where I hear they've got stuff like hot and cold running water and decent health care, but thanks to my dear departed mother and her fuckwitted reactionary idiots that's not a terribly practical ambition, is it? I'm too old, too ill, and too tired to cast off and start up anew in another world, Riordan. I did it the once, in my youth, but it was a terrible strain even with Angbard's connivance. Besides, you need me here in this gilded cage. Rule of law, and all that."

"The rule of law." Riordan leaned forward. "You've never been much for that, have you?"

Patricia's cheek twitched in something that might have been the ghost of a smile. "I've never been much of one for bending the neck to authority." She shook her head. "If I had been born to a lower estate I'd have been lucky to have made it to adulthood. As it is, the lack of highborn bloodlines taking precedence over mine—well. Easier to be rebellious when you're the daughter of a duke, not a slave. What did you want to talk to me about?"

Her attempt to wrong-foot Riordan failed. "To ask you what I should do with you, your grace."

Patricia smile widened. "Well, that's an *interesting* question, isn't it? I suppose it depends what you want to achieve."

"I want to keep our people alive." He crossed his arms. "What do *you* want?"

"Huh." Her smile slipped away. "It's come to that?"

"You know it has. I'm not going to charge you with petty treason, your grace; the only evidence against you is your own

word, and besides, the victim had abducted you and was a conspirator at *high* treason. To hold her poisoning against you would
be ungrateful, not to mention sending entirely the wrong message.
But there is a question to which I would like some answers."

"My brother?"

Riordan shook his head. "I know you didn't kill him. But
Dr. ven Hjalmar is missing. And so is a certain set of medical
records."

"A set of—" Patricia stopped dead. "What do you know
about them?"

"I've been reading Angbard's files." Riordan's tone was
quiet but implacable. "I know about the fertility clinics and the
substituted donor sperm. Five thousand unwitting outer-family
members growing up in the United States. The plan to approach
some of them and pay them to bear further children. I'm not stupid, Patricia. I know what that plan would mean to the old ladies
and their matchmaking and braid alliances. The files are missing, your grace. Do you happen to know where they are?"

She shook her head. "Not exactly, no."

"And inexactly?"

"I don't think I should answer that question. For your own
good."

Riordan made a fist of his left hand and laid it quietly down
on the table beside him. "*Why?*"

"It's an insurance policy, kid. *I* don't know exactly where the
records are, only where they're going to surface. Griben ven
Hjalmar—if you see him, shoot him on sight, I beg you. He may
have made off with a copy of the breeding program records too."

"Why?" repeated the earl. "I think you owe me at least an
explanation."

"Our numbers are low. If they dip lower, the trade—our old
trade—may no longer be viable. But at the same time, Angbard's
plan was destabilizing in the extreme. If Clan Security suddenly
acquired an influx of tractable, trained world-walkers with no
loyalty to family or braid—it would overbalance the old order,
would it not? We agree that much, yes?"

Riordan nodded reluctantly. "So?"

"So Hildegarde tried to smash the program, at least by seizing the infants and having them adopted. Griben was her cat's-paw. It was a power play and countermove, nothing more. But her solution would give us other problems. There is a reason why we are six high families and their clients, why each group numbers less than three hundred. An extended family—a clan, not *our* great collective Clan, but a normal grouping—is of that order, you know? Anthropologists have theories to explain why humans form groups of that size. Tribes, clans. We knit our six together into one bigger group, to permit the braiding of recessive genetic trait without excessive inbreeding. But if you triple our numbers—well, there was a reason we were susceptible to civil war eighty years ago. If a tribe grows too large it splinters along factional lines."

"But you're—" Riordan stopped. "Oh."

Patricia nodded. "Yes. If Hildegarde's idea—bring the newborn world-walkers into the Clan's client families and raise them among us—had worked, we'd have grown much too fast to maintain control. It would have set us up for another damaging civil war."

"Have you destroyed the records, then?"

She shook her head. "No need. We may even need them later. I leave that to the Council's future deliberations; but in the meantime, I took steps to insure that nobody would use them to breed an army of world-walkers. It has to be done openly, with the consent of the entire Clan, or not at all."

"I can live with that—if you can guarantee it."

"The problem is ven Hjalmar." She turned her face to the window. A beam of sunlight splashed through it, lengthening across the floor. "The sleazy little tapeworm's stolen a set of the records. And now he's gone missing. *You* know that Helge will hang him as soon as look at him. Put yourself in his shoes—where would you go?"

Riordan stared at her. "You think he'd defect to . . . who? The Lees?"

"I wouldn't bet against it. He might be lying low in America, but what's he going to do? He can't fake up a good enough identity to practice as an ob-gyn—the full academic and employment track record would be a *lot* harder than a regular cover—so he can't simply jump the wall and hide there, not unless he's willing to take a big cut in his standard of living. So he needs sponsorship. The breeding program is . . . well, it'd be more useful to the Lees than it is to us: They're not far from extinction, did you know that? They've got less than a hundred world-walkers. He might have gone to the US government a couple of weeks ago, but he can't do that now: They wouldn't need him once they get their hands on the breeding program records and they're in no mood to be accommodating. That leaves the Lee family, or maybe the authorities in New Britain, but the latter won't have a clue what he's offering them without a working demonstration."

"God-on-a-stick." Riordan ran one hand through his thin hair. "I'll point Olga after him. One more damn thing to worry about."

"I have a question." Patricia waited.

"Yes?"

"My daughter's *interest* in Roland last year." She licked suddenly dry lips. "And Olga was betrothed to him. And that nasty business Helge told me about, in the old orangery. Which was that to do with—WARBUCKS or the breeding program?"

"WARBUCKS—" For a moment Riordan looked confused. He shook his head. "Let me think. There was something about it in the files. The old man knew there was a leak; Olga was investigating. I think he may have set her on him—she was still under cover so she could run the fresh-faced ingenue pumping her fiancé—to see if he was the leak. *Someone* on the inside was still colluding with WARBUCKS after we officially cut him off, and Roland was considered unreliable. But you may be right. Economics was his big thing, wasn't it? If he was talking to ven Hjalmar . . ." He trailed off.

"A tame army of world-walkers," Patricia said tartly. "If Roland had been planning to defect, and if he could get his hands on the breeding-program records and take them to WAR-BUCKS, he could have named his own price, couldn't he? Was that why he had to die?"

Riordan gave her a flat stare. "You might think that, but I couldn't possibly comment."

Patricia met his gaze. After several long seconds she nodded, very slightly. "In any case, there are other plausible explanations. My mother, for example. There's no way she would have allowed her granddaughter to marry a mere *earl*. Not with a pliable prince on offer, and her own elder sister—the queen-mother—happy to matchmake for her grandson."

"That is true." Riordan inclined his head. Then he took a deep breath. "I find the weight of your half-brother's secrets inordinately onerous, my lady. I wish I could confide fully in you; it's only those matters concerning your bloodline which give me cause for hesitation. I hope you can forgive me—but can you put yourself in my place?"

Patricia nodded again. "I beg your forgiveness. I don't believe even for a moment that you might have arranged the liquidation of your elder brother Roland, not even on the duke's orders. I don't think Angbard would have given such a—but we live in paranoid times, do we not? And we *know* Dr. ven Hjalmar is a lying sack of shit who liked to incriminate other people."

"Indeed. Did I mention it was his signature on your brother's death certificate?"

"Was it really?" Patricia breathed.

"Yes. Really." Riordan cleared his throat. "Just so you understand what—who—we're dealing with here. I gather Helge has given her retainers certain orders in his regard. I'm inclined to declare him outlaw before Clan Security. If you, and the committee, concur?"

Patricia nodded emphatically. "Oh, yes."

They sat in contemplative silence for a minute.

"Are you sure I can't convince you to go to New Britain?" asked Riordan. "Your daughter could use your support."

"She's a grown woman who can make her own mistakes,"

Patricia said sharply. "And I'll thank you for not telling her what I had to do to give her that freedom." Softly: "I think it better for the older generation to retire discreetly, you know. Rather than fighting, kicking and screaming, against the bitter end."

"I'm certain they could take care of you, over there," the earl pointed out. "If you stay behind when the Americans come . . ."

"I'll die." She sniffed. "I've been there, to the other world, Frederick. It's backward and dangerous. With my condition it's just a matter of time. Did I tell you, my mother was dying? She thought she had a year to live. Didn't occur to her to ask how I was doing, oh no. If it had, and if she'd won, she might have outlived me, you know."

"You're not that ill, are you?"

"Not yet. But without my medication I will be. And when the Americans come, it won't matter whether I'm hale and hearty or on my deathbed. If I evacuate, those medicines I need to sustain me will run out by and by. And if I stay . . ." She fixed him with a gimlet stare. "I hope you're going to evacuate yourself before the end. My daughter doesn't need old dead wood like me clogging up her household and draining her resources; but a young, energetic lord of security is another matter."

Riordan stared right back at her. "This land is my land. And enough of my people are staying that I'd be derelict if I abandoned them."

"My mother said something like that. My mother was also a damned fool." Patricia took a deep breath. "She shot a man-eating tiger in the tip of its tail, where the wound is calculated to cause maximum pain and outrage, but to do no lasting harm. Do you really expect it not to bite?"

"Oh, it's going to bite all right." Riordan looked as resigned as a condemned man on his way to the scaffold. "You are correct, your grace. And I am encouraging every man and woman I meet to make their way to the evacuation points. But it's an uphill battle, and many of our less well-traveled cousins are skeptical. If I go, my powers of persuasion are vastly reduced. So, like the captain of a sinking ship, my station is on the bridge."

"Exactly." Patricia folded her hands. "But I'm not going anywhere, even if you throw wide the doors to this gilded cell. So why not let me help?"

On the other side of the sprawling metropolis, a steamer drove slowly along a road lined with big houses, set back behind the wire-topped fences and overgrown hedges of a mostly absent bourgeoisie. Those with royalist connections or a history with the Polis or sympathies with the Patriot Party had mostly decided that they had pressing business out of town, far from urban militias who might recognize them and Leveler Party commissioners who might think the city better off without their ilk.

Sitting in the back of the steamer, James Lee stared pensively at the padlocked gates from behind smoked glass pince-nez spectacles. There, but for the lubrication of certain palms and the careful maintenance of appearances, were his own family's estates; in time of civil war, nobody suffered quite like foreign merchants, despised for their race and resented for their imagined wealth. Only the Lee family's dedication to concealing their true nature had kept them from attracting the mob's attention so far. "This next," he called ahead to the chauffeur and his companion, a heavyset fellow with a nose that had been broken so many times that it was almost flat. "She's at home." There was a trickle of smoke from one chimney pot, no doubt a flue venting from the kitchen range.

The thick hedge fronting the Beckstein estate was unkempt and as bushy as its neighbors, but the gate wasn't chained shut— and the hut beside it showed signs of recent use. As the car hissed to a halt in the roadway, the hut's door opened and a fellow stepped out, making no attempt to conceal his breech-loading blunderbuss.

"Ahoy, the house," called the chauffeur.

The gatekeeper stayed well clear of the car. "Who calls?" he demanded.

James leaned forward to rap the head of his cane once on the back of the driver's partition, then opened the car door and stepped out. "James Lee," he said easily in hochsprache. The gatekeeper jumped. "I have come to visit my cousin, Helge of Thorold-Hjorth."

"Wait, if it pleases you." The gatekeeper raised his left hand and held something to his mouth, muttering. Then he shook his head, as if hearing an answer. His face froze. "Please wait . . . my lord, I am told that you are welcome here. But your men will please leave their arms in the vehicle." Two more men appeared, hurrying along the driveway from the direction of the house. "If that is acceptable . . . ?"

James nodded. "Take the car where he directs you and wait with it," he told his chauffeur.

"Are you sure?" the bodyguard asked edgily.

James smiled tightly. "We're safer here than we were on the way," he pointed out. Which was true: Three men who would be taken as foreigners driving an expensive motor through a British city in time of revolution—"They won't lay a finger on us, Chang. They don't know what we are capable of. And besides, I am an honored guest." He closed the car door and walked towards the gate as it swung open.

The house Miriam had purchased for her first foray into the business world in New Britain was large enough to conceal a myriad of sins, and James Lee was not surprised when the suspiciously unobsequious butler who met him at the front door rushed him into a parlor off to one side. "If you'd wait here, sir, her—my lady sends her apologies, and she will see you shortly." He began to move towards the door, then paused. "Can I fetch you anything? Tea, coffee, whisky?"

James smiled. "I am perfectly all right," he said blandly. The not-butler frowned, then bowed briskly and hurried out of the room. He was clearly unused to playing this role; his stockings were creased and his periwig lamentably disordered. James sat in the solitary armchair, glancing round curiously. Aside from the presence of the armchair and a small box attached to the wall close to one ceiling corner, there was nothing particularly unusual about the room—for a butler's pantry. *Someone is not used to entertaining,* he decided. *Now, what does that signify?*

As it happened, he didn't have long to wait. Barely ten minutes later, the not-butler threw the door open in a rush. "They're ready for you now," he explained. "In the morning room. If you'll follow me, sir."

"Certainly." James stood and followed the fellow out into a gloomy passage, then out into a wood-paneled hall and through a doorway into a daylit room dominated by a large mahogany table set out with nearly a dozen seats. *Dining table or conference table?* He nodded politely at the occupants, reserving a small smile for their leader. "Good morning, Your Majesty—your grace—however I should address you? I must say, I'm glad to see you looking so well." *Well* was questionable; she looked as if she had recently been seriously unwell, and was not yet back to full health.

She nodded. "Thank you, my lord baron. Uh—we are trying to make a practice of avoiding titles here; the neighbors are less than understanding. You may call me Miriam and I shall call you James, or Mr. Lee, whichever you prefer. Unless you insist on formalities?"

"As you wish." The not-butler stepped forward, drawing out a chair for him. "Perhaps you could introduce your companions? I don't believe we've all met."

"Sure. Have a seat—everybody? Brilliana I think you've met. This is Sir—uh, Alasdair, my—"

"Chief of security," the man-mountain rumbled mildly. He, too, sat down. "Your men are being taken care of with all due hospitality," he added.

"Thank you." *Message received.* James nodded and concentrated on remembering names as Miriam—the former Duchess Helge—introduced another five members of the six traitor brothers' families—*Stop that,* he reminded himself. It was a bad habit, born of a hundred and fifty and more years of tradition built on the unfortunate belief that his ancestor had been abandoned to his fate by his wicked siblings. A belief which might or might not be true, but which was singularly unhelpful in the current day and age. . . .

"I assume you're here because of my letter," Miriam finished after the naming of names. Then she simply sat back, watching him expectantly.

"Ah—yes." *Damn.* He hadn't expected quite such an abrupt interrogation. He smiled experimentally. "My father was most intrigued by it—especially by what it left unsaid. What is this threat you referred to?"

Miriam took a deep breath. "I don't want to mince words. The Clan fucked up."

Brilliana—Miriam's chief of staff, as far as he could tell—glanced at her liege. "Should you be telling—"

Miriam shook her head. "Leave this to me, Brill." She looked back at James Lee, her shoulders slumping slightly. "You know about our factional splits." He nodded cautiously. The blame game might be easy enough to play at this point; gods knew, his parents and grandparents had done their best to aggravate those disputes in decades past. "But you don't know much about the Clan's trade in the United States."

He cocked his head attentively. "No. Not having been there, I couldn't say."

More euphemisms; the Lee family knotwork enabled them to travel between the worlds of the Gruinmarkt and New Britain, while the Clan's knot had provided them with access to the semi-mythical United States.

"The US government discovered the Clan," Miriam said carefully. "The Clan has earned its power over there through criminal enterprise—smuggling. The US government sent them a message by means of an, a, a superweapon. The conservatives decided to send one right back using stolen weapons of the same class—and at the same time to decapitate the Clan security apparatus and council. Their coup failed, but they *really* got the attention of the US authorities. Like climbing over the railings at a zoo and stamping on the tail of a sleeping tiger."

James tried not to wince visibly. "But what can they do?"

"Quite a lot." Miriam frowned and glanced at the skinny young fellow called Huw. "Huw? Tell him about the project my uncle gave you."

Huw fidgeted with his oddly styled spectacles. "I was detailed to test other knotwork designs and to systematically explore the possibility of other worlds." He rested a hand on a strange device molded out of resin that lay on the table before him. "I can show you—"

"No," Miriam interrupted. "Just the summary."

"*Okay.* We found and visited three other worlds before the coup attempt—and identified fifteen different candidate knots that look promising. One of the worlds was accessible using your, the Lee family, knotwork from the United States. We found ruins, but very high-tech ruins. Still slightly *radioactive.*" James squinted slightly at the unfamiliar jargon. "The others were all stranger. Up-shot: The three worlds we know of are only the tip of an iceberg."

"Let me put Huw's high technology in perspective." Miriam's smile tightened with a moue of distaste: "He means high tech in comparison to the United States. Which is about as far ahead of New Britain as New Britain is ahead of the Gruinmarkt. There is strange stuff out there, and no mistake."

"Perhaps, but of what use is it?" James shrugged, trying to feign disinterest.

"Well, perhaps the fact that the United States government has threatened us, and appears to have the ability to build machines that can move between worlds, will be of interest to you?" Miriam looked at him expectantly.

"Not really. They can't find us here, after all." James crossed his arms. "Unless you've told them where to look . . . ?"

"We haven't—we wouldn't know who to talk to, or how." James froze.

"Why are you *here?*" Alasdair asked pointedly.

Miriam held up a warning hand. "Stop," she told him. Looking back at James: "Let me see. This *might* just be a social visit."

She looked amused. "But on balance, no, I don't think so. You're here to deliver a message."

James nodded.

"From your elders—" Miriam stopped, registering his expression. "Oh shit. You're *not* here on your uncle's behalf?"

"You are not the only people with a problem," James confessed ruefully. "I am afraid my elders have made an error of judgment, one that is in nobody's best interests—not ours, nor yours."

"An error—"

"Shut up, Huw." This from Brilliana. "What have they done, and what do you think we can do about it?"

"These are dangerous, turbulent times." James stopped, hunting for the least damaging way of framing his confession. *These are dangerous, turbulent people,* he reminded himself. *Who were until a year ago enemies of our blood.* "They sought a patron," he confessed.

"A patr—" Miriam stared at him. "Crap. You mean, they've gone public?"

"Yes." *Wait and see.* James crossed his arms.

"How public?" asked Miriam. "What have they done?"

"It started nearly a month ago." James met her eyes. "When they learned of the upheaval in the Eastern states, the elders became alarmed. Add your cousins' manifest difficulties with their own strange world, the America, and there was . . . cause for concern. My uncle sought advice on the wisdom of maintaining the rule of secrecy. His idea was that we should seek out a high-ranking minister within the provisional government, provide them with discreet services—ideally to the point of incrimination, to compel their cooperation later—and use their office to secure our safety. Does this sound familiar?"

They were all nodding. "Very," said Miriam. "We made the same mistake." She glanced sidelong at Brill. "Getting involved in local politics. Hmm."

"Don't blame *me,*" Brill said with some asperity.

"I'm not. But if the Council hadn't wanted to place a world-walker on the throne, or to do business with local politicians in Wyoming, we wouldn't be in this fix now."

Fascinating, thought James. There was familial loyalty on display here, and also a strangely familiar bitterness. He cleared his throat. "Then a defector from your own ranks showed up."

"Who?"

"A doctor—" He stopped. They were staring at him, as if he'd grown a second head. "—I believe you know him. Ven Hjalmar, he's called." *Their faces*—cold sweat sprang out in the small of his back. "Why? Is something wrong?"

"Please continue." Miriam's voice was flat.

"But you—"

"It's a personal matter." She made a cutting gesture. James took in the other signs: Sir Alasdair, Lady Brilliana—sudden focus, as attentive as hounds at the trail of a fox. "What happened?"

Suddenly lots of things slid into place. "You have reason to hate him?" *Good.* "He has convinced my uncle that it is necessary to conspire with a political patron, and to sell him a, a *breeding program* he says your families established in America. Preposterous nonsense, but . . ." He trailed off. Miriam's expression was deathly.

"He did, did he?"

"Yes—" James took a deep breath. "It's true? He's telling the truth? There *is* a breeding program? The American doctors can breed world-walkers the way a farmer breeds sheep?"

"Not *exactly* like that, but close enough for government work." Miriam made eye contact with Alasdair. "We're in so much shit," she said quietly. She looked back to James: "Which commissar is your uncle doing business with?"

"Commissioner Reynolds, overstaff supervisor in charge of the Directorate of Internal Security." James took no pleasure from their expressions. "A man I love even less than the doctor. He carries a certain stink; if I was a Christian I'd say he's committed mortal sins, and knows himself for one of the damned." He smiled crookedly. "I was in at their last meeting, yesterday; to my eternal shame my uncle believes my loyalty knows no limits, and I have not yet disabused him of this notion. Yesterday. The meeting . . . the doctor told Reynolds that your acquaintance Mr. Burgeson was trying to acquire world-walkers of his own. I'm not entirely sure whether he was telling the truth or not, and this is purest hearsay and gossip—I know nothing specific about your arrangements, my lady, and I don't want to. But if the doctor was telling the truth, you'd better warn your patron sooner rather than later. . . ."

RSS HEADLINE NEWS FEED:
UN SECRETARY GENERAL FLIES TO AFFECTED REGION: SE ASIA FACES "UNPRECEDENTED CRISIS": UN Secretary General Kofi Annan today flew to Chandrapur, temporary capital of India, to start talks with the emergency government about efforts to enforce the cease-fire and relieve human suffering in the fallout zone to the north and west of the country . . .

PRESIDENT RUMSFELD SWORN IN: President Donald H. Rumsfeld was today sworn into office as the 45th President of the United States of America. The oath was administered by Supreme Court Chief Justice Antonin Scalia in a somber ceremony conducted at an undisclosed location . . .

HANNITY: ARE LIBERALS ALIENS FROM ANOTHER UNIVERSE?: Sean Hannity says it's open season on liberals because they're obviously intruders from a parallel universe and therefore not genuine Americans . . .

DEPARTMENT OF DEFENSE ANNOUNCES SUSPENSION OF EXTRAORDINARY RENDITION: Prisoners will be processed by CIA interrogators instead under new regulations approved by Attorney General Woo . . .

SARS OUTBREAK: WHO QUARANTINES TORONTO, FLIGHTS DIVERTED: A World Health Organization spokesperson denied that the respiratory disease is spread by travelers from parallel timelines. Meanwhile, the outbreak in Ontario claimed its fourth . . .

SAUCERWATCH: GOVERNMENT TESTING UFOS AT GROOM LAKE: Observers who have seen curious shapes in the sky above Area 51 say the current cover story is an increasingly desperate attempt to divert attention from the truth about the alien saucer tech . . .

HOUSE MEETS TO REVIEW EMERGENCY BILL: Congress is meeting today to vote on the Protecting America from Parallel Universe Attackers (PAPUA) bill, described by former president Cheney (deceased) as "vital measures to protect us in these perilous times." The bill was drafted by the newly sworn-in president last week in the wake of . . .

COULTER: NOW IS THE TIME TO INTERN TRAITORS

RUSSIA: PUTIN DENOUNCES "AUTHORITARIAN CONSPIRACY": Russian President Vladimir Putin today denied former President Cheney's account of the terrorist nuclear attack on the Capitol, describing it as implausible and accusing US authorities of concocting a "fairy tale" to provide cover for a coup . . .

END (NEWS FEED)

The Final Countdown

The track from Kirschford down to the Linden Valley—which also defined the border of the duchy of Niejwein and Baron Cromalloch's ridings—was unusually crowded with carriages and riders this day. A local farmer out tending his herd might have watched with some surprise; the majority of the traffic was clearly upper-class, whole families of minor nobility and their close servants taking to the road in a swarm, as if some great festival had been decreed in the nearby market town of Glantzwurt. But there was no such god's day coming, nor rumor of a royal court tour through the provinces. The aristocracy were more usually to be found on their home estates, staying away from the fetid kennels of the capital at this time of year.

But there were no curious farmers, of course. The soldiers who had ridden ahead with the morning sunrise had made it grimly clear that this procession was not to be witnessed; and in the wake of the savagery of spring and early summer's rampage, those tenants who had survived unscathed were more than cooperative. So the hedgerows were mostly empty of curious eyes as the convoy creaked and squealed and neighed along the Linden Valley—curious eyes which might, if they were owned by unusually well-traveled commoners, recognize the emblems of the witch-families.

The Clan was on the move, and nothing would be the same again.

A covered wagon or a noble's carriage is an uncomfortable way to travel at the best of times, alternately chill and drafty or chokingly, stiflingly hot (depending on the season), rocking on crude leaf springs or crashing from rut to stone on no springs at all, the seats a wooden bench (perhaps with a thin cushion to save the noble posterior from the insults of the road). The horsemen might have had a better time of it, but for the dust clouds flung up by the hooves of close to a hundred animals, and the flies. To exchange a stifling shuttered box for biting insects and mud that slowly clung to sweating man and horse alike was perhaps no choice at all. But one thing they agreed: It was essential to move together, and the path of least resistance was, to say the least, unsafe.

"Why can't we go to 'merca, Ma?"

Helena ven Wu gritted her teeth as one carriage wheel bounced across a stone in the road. Tess, her second-youngest, was four years old and bright by disposition, but the exodus was taking its toll after two days, and the question came out as a whine. "We can't go there, dear. I told you, it's not safe."

"But it's where Da goes when he travels?"

"That's different." Helena rested a hand lightly on the crib. Markus was asleep—had, in fact, cried himself to sleep after a wailing tantrum. He didn't travel well. "We can't go there."

"But why can't we—"

The other occupant of the carriage raised her eyes from the book she had been absorbed in. "For Sky Lady's love, leave your ma be, Tess. See you not, she was trying to sleep?"

Helena smiled gratefully at her. Kara, her sister-in-law, was traveling with them of necessity, for her husband Sir Leon was already busied with the residual duty of the postal corvée; his young wife, her pregnancy not yet showing, was just another parcel to be transferred between houses in this desperately busy time. Not that Sir Leon believed the most outlandish warnings of the radical faction, but there was little harm in sending Kara for a vacation with her eldest brother's family.

Now Kara shook her head and raised an eyebrow at Helena. The latter nodded, and Kara lifted Tess onto her lap, grunting slightly with the effort. "Once upon a time we could all travel freely to America, at least those of us the Postal Service would permit, and it was a wondrous place, full of magic and treasure. But that's not where we're going, Tess. There are bad men in America, and evil wizards; they are hunting our menfolk who travel there, and they want to hunt us all down and throw us in their deepest dungeons."

The child's eyes were growing wider with every sentence. Helena was about to suggest that Kara lighten up on the story, but she continued, gently bouncing Tess upon her knee: "But don't worry, we have a plan. We're going on a journey somewhere else, to a new world like America but different, one where the k— where the rulers don't hate and fear us. We're going to cross over there and we'll be safe. You'll have a new dress, and practice your Anglischprache, and it'll be a great adventure! And the bad men won't be able to find us."

Tess looked doubtful. "Will the bad men get Da?"

Helena's heart missed a beat. "Of course not!" she said hotly. Gyorg ven Wu would be deep underground, shuffling between doppelgangered bunkers with a full wheelbarrow as often as the blood-pressure monitor said was safe: a beast of burden, toiling to carry the vital necessities of life between a basement somewhere in Massachusetts and a dungeon or wine cellar beneath a castle or mansion in the Gruinmarkt. Ammunition, tools, medicine, gold, anything that Clan Security deemed necessary. The flow of luxuries had stopped cold, the personal allowance abolished in the

wake of the wave of assassinations that had accompanied the hor-
ridness in the Anglischprache capital.

"Your da is safe," Kara reassured the child. "He'll come to
see us soon enough. I expect he'll bring you chocolate."

Helena cast her a reproving look—chocolate was an expensive
import to gift on a child—but Kara caught her eye and shook her
head slightly. The effect of the work *chocolate* in Tess was remarkable. "Want chocolate!" she exclaimed. "*All* the chocolate!"

Kara smiled over Tess's head, then grimaced as one of the front
wheels thumped over the edge of a rut and the carriage crashed
down a few inches. Markus twitched, clenched a tiny fist close to
his mouth uneasily as Helena leaned over him. "I wish we had a
smoother road to travel," she said quietly. "Or that we could walk
from nearer home."

"The queen's men have arranged a safely defended house,"
Kara observed. "They wouldn't force us to travel this way without good reason. She wouldn't let them."

"She?"

"Her Majesty." An odd look stole across her face, one part
nostalgia to two parts regret. "I was one of her maids. She was
very wise."

So you never tire of reminding us, Helena thought, but held
her tongue; with another ennervating day's drive ahead, there
was nothing to gain from picking a fight. Then Tess chirped up
again: "Tell me about the queen?"

"Surely." Kara ruffled her hair. "Queen Helge was the child
of Duke Alfredo and his wife. One day when she was younger
than your brother Markus, when her parents were traveling to
their country estates, they were set upon by assassins sent by—"

Helena half-closed her eyes and leaned against the wall of
the carriage, looking out through the open window at the tree
line beyond the cleared roadside strip. *I wonder if this is what it
was like for Helge's mother,* she wondered. *She escaped just
ahead of her attackers, didn't she? I wonder if we'll be so
lucky. . . .*

———

Arranging a meeting was much easier the second time round. Miriam handed Sir Alasdair a hastily scribbled note for the telautograph office to dispatch: NEED TO TALK URGENTLY TOMORROW AGREED LOCATION STOP. One of Alasdair's men, and then the nearest post office, did the rest.

Not that imperiously demanding a conversation with the commissioner for propaganda was a trivial matter; receiving it in New London only two hours after it was transmitted, Erasmus swore under his breath and, before departing for his evening engagement—dinner with Victor McDougall, deputy commissioner for press approval—booked a compartment on the morning mail train to Boston, along with two adjacent compartments for his bodyguards and a communications clerk. By sheer good luck Miriam had picked the right day: He could see her and, provided he caught the following morning's train for the return journey, be back in the capital in time for the Thursday Central Committee meeting. "This had better be worth it," he muttered to himself as he clambered into the passenger compartment of his ministerial car for the journey to McDougall's home. However, it didn't occur to him to ignore Miriam's summons. In all the time he'd known her, she'd never struck him as being one to act impetuously; if she said something was urgent, it almost certainly was.

Attending the meeting was also easier, second time round. The morning after James Lee's visit, Miriam rose early and dressed for a public excursion. She took care to look as nondescript as possible; to be mistaken for a woman of particular wealth could be as dangerous here as to look impoverished, and the sartorial class indicators were much more sharply defined than back in the United States. "I'm ready to go whenever you've got cover for me," she told Sir Alasdair, as she entered the front parlor. "Two guards, one car, and a walkie-talkie."

"Emil and Klaus are waiting." Sir Alasdair didn't smile. "They'll park two streets away and remain on call." He gestured at the side table: "Lady d'Ost prepared a handbag for you before she went out."

"There's no—" Miriam paused. "You think I'll need this?" She lifted the bag, feeling the drag of its contents—a two-way radio and the dense metallic weight of a pistol.

"I hope you won't." He didn't smile. "Better safe than unsafe."

The steamer drove slowly through the streets and neighborhoods of a dense, urban Boston quite unlike the city Miriam had known; different architecture, different street names, different shops and businesses. There were a few more vehicles on the roads today, and fewer groups of men loitering on street corners; they passed two patrols of green-clad Freedom Rider militiamen, red armbands and shoulder-slung shotguns matching their arrogant stride. Policing and public order were beginning to return to the city, albeit in a very different shape. Posters had gone up on some of the high brick walls: the stern-jawed face of a balding, white-haired man. CITIZEN BURROUGHS SAYS: WE WORK FOR FREEDOM! Miriam hunched her shoulders against an imperceptible chill, pushing back against the bench seat. Erasmus had spoken glowingly of Citizen Burroughs. She found herself wishing fervently for him to be right, despite her better judgment.

Miriam covered the last hundred yards, from the deceptive safety of the car to the door of Burgeson's tenement building, feeling naked despite the contents of her bag and the presence of her backup team. It was odd: She couldn't *see* any bodyguards or observers, but just knowing Erasmus wouldn't be able to travel alone left her feeling watched. This time, however, she had a key. After turning it in the lock, she hastily closed the door behind her and climbed the stairwell Burgeson's apartment shared with half a dozen other dwellings.

His front door was locked. Miriam examined it carefully—it had become a habit, a kind of neurotic tic she'd picked up in the year-plus since she'd discovered her distinctly paranoid heritage—then opened it. The flat was much as it had been on her last visit; dustier, if anything, sheets covering most of the furniture. Erasmus wasn't here yet. For no reason she cared to examine too closely, Miriam walked from room to room, carefully opening doors and looking within. The bedroom: dominated by a sheeted bed, walled with bookcases, a fireplace still unraked with spring's white ash caked and crumbling behind the grate. A former closet, a crude bolt added inside the door to afford a moment's privacy to those who might use the flushing toilet. The kitchen was big and empty, a tin bath sitting in one corner next to the cold coal-fired cooking range. There wasn't much here to hang a personality on, aside from the books: Burgeson kept his most valued possessions inside his head. The flat was a large one by local standards— family-sized, suitable for a prosperous shopkeeper and his wife and offspring. He must have rattled around in it like a solitary pea in a pod. *Odd,* she thought. *But then, he* was *married. Before the last clampdown.* The lack of personal touches . . . *How badly did it damage him?* She shivered, then went back to the living room, which with its battered piano and beaten-up furniture gave at least a semblance of domestic clutter.

It was distinctly unsettling to her to realize how much she didn't know. Before, when she'd been an unwilling visitor in the Gruinmarkt and an adventurer exploring this strange other-Boston in New Britain, she'd not looked too deep beneath surface appearances. But now—now she was probably going to end her days *living* in this nation on the other side of time—and the thought of how little she knew about the people around her troubled her.

Who are you dealing with and how do you know whether you can trust them? It seemed to be the defining paradox of her life for the past year or so. They said that blood was thicker than water, but in her experience her relatives were most likely to define themselves as enemies; meanwhile, some who were clearly supposed to be her enemies weren't. Mike Fleming should have shanghaied her to an interrogation cell; instead, he'd warned her off. Erasmus— she'd originally trusted him as far as she could throw him; now here she was, waiting for him anxiously in an empty apartment. And she'd wanted to trust Roland, but he'd been badly, possibly irreparably, broken. She sniffed, wrinkling her nose, eyes itching— whether from a momentary twist of sorrow or a whiff of dust rising from the sofa, she couldn't say.

The street door banged, the sound reverberating distantly up the stairwell. Miriam stood, moving her hand to the top of her handbag, just in case. She heard footsteps, the front door opening, familiar sounds—Burgeson breathed heavily, moved just so—and she stood up, just in time to meet him in the living-room doorway.

"You came," she said, slightly awkwardly.

"You called." He looked at her, head tilted sidelong. "I could hardly ignore you and maintain that cover story?"

"Yes, well—" She caught her lower lip between her teeth: *What will the neighbors say? "The commissioner is visiting his mistress again"?*—"I couldn't exactly come and fetch you, could I? Hey, get your breath back. Do you have time to stay?"

"I can spare a few hours." He walked past her and dragged a dust sheet off the battered sofa. "I really need to sell up. I'm needed in the capital almost all the time; can't stay here, can't run the shop from two hundred miles away." He sounded almost amused. "Can I interest you in a sherry?"

"You can." The thought of Erasmus moving out, moving away, disturbed her unaccountably. As he rummaged around the sideboard, she sat down again. "A sherry would be nice. But I didn't rattle your cage just for a drink."

"I didn't imagine you would." He found a bottle, splashed generous measures into two mismatched wineglasses, and brought one over to her. He seemed to be in high spirits, or at least energized. "Your health?" He sat down beside her and she raised her glass to bump against his. "Now, what motivated you to bring me to town?"

They were sitting knee-to-knee. It was distracting. "I had a visitor yesterday," she said carefully. "One of the, the other family. The Lees. He had some disturbing news that I thought you needed to know about."

"Could you have wired it?" He smiled to take the sting out of the question.

"I don't think so. Um. Do you know a Commissioner Reynolds? In Internal Security?" Nothing in his facial expression changed, but the set of his shoulders told her all she needed to know. "James Lee came to me because, uh, he's very concerned that his uncle, the Lee family's elder, is cutting a deal with Reynolds."

Now *Burgeson's* expression changed: He was visibly struggling for calm. He placed a hand on her knee. "Please, do carry on."

Miriam tried to gather her thoughts, scattered by the unexpected contact. "The Lees have had a defector, a renegade from our people. One with a price on his head, Dr. ven Hjalmar. Ven Hjalmar has stolen a list of—look, this is going to take a long time to explain, just take it from me, it's bad. If the Lees can get the breeding program database out of him, they can potentially give Reynolds a couple of thousand young world-walkers within the next twenty years. There are only about a hundred of them right now. I don't like the sound of Reynolds, he's the successor to the old Polis, isn't he?"

"Yes." Burgeson took a deep breath. "It's a very good thing you didn't wire me. Damn." He took another breath, visibly rattled. "How much do the Lees know? About your people?"

"Too much for comfort." Despite the summer humidity, Miriam shivered. "More to the point, ven Hjalmar is a murderous bastard who picked the losing side in an internal fight. I told you about what happened to, to me before I escaped—"

"He's the doctor you mentioned. Yes?" She felt him go tense.

"Yes."

"Well, that tells me all I need to know just now. You say he's met Stephen Reynolds?"

"That's what James Lee says. Listen, I'm not a reliable source; I don't usually bear grudges but if I run into the doctor again . . . and then there's the question of whether James was telling the—"

"Did he have any obvious reason to lie to you?" Burgeson looked her in the eye. "Or to betray confidences?"

Miriam took a sip from her glass. Now Erasmus knew, she felt unaccountably free. "I met him while I was being held prisoner. He was a hostage against his parents' behavior after the truce—yes, that's how the noble families in the Gruinmarkt do business. He helped me get away. I think he's hoping I can save his people from what he sees as a big mistake."

"Yes, well." He took his hand away: She felt a momentary flash of disappointment. "I'm sorry. He was right to be afraid. Reynolds is not someone I would want to put any great faith in. Do you know what the Lee elders have in mind?"

"Spying. People who can vanish from one place and reappear in another." Miriam shrugged. "They don't have access to the United States, at least not yet, not without the doctor—they don't have the technology transfer capability I can give you, and they don't have the numbers yet. But they *do* have a track record as invisible assassins." She shivered and put the glass down on the floor. "How afraid should I be?"

"Very." He took her hand as she straightened up, leaning close; his expression was foreboding. "He's having me followed, you know."

"What, he—"

"Listen." He leaned closer, pitching his voice low: "I've met men like Reynolds before. As long as he thinks I'm in town to see my mistress he'll be happy—he thinks he's got a hand on my neck. But you're right, he's dangerous, he's an empire-builder. He's got a power base in Justice and Prisons and he's purging his own department and, hmm, the books you lent me—made me think of Felix Dzerzhinsky or Heinrich, um, Hitler? Himmler. Expert bureaucrats who build machineries of terror inside a revolutionary movement. But he doesn't have absolute power yet. He may not even have realized how much power he has at his fingertips. Sir Adam doesn't realize, either—but I'm in a position to tell him. Reynolds isn't invulnerable but he *is* dangerous, and you have just given me a huge problem, because he is already watching me."

"You think he's going to use me as a lever against you?"

"It's gone too far for that, I'm afraid. If he knows about your relatives and knows about our arrangement, he will see me as a direct threat. He'll have to move fast, within the next hours or days. Your household is almost certainly under surveillance as an anomaly, possibly suspected of being a group of monarchists. Damn." He looked at her. "I really should inform Sir Adam immediately—if Stephen has acquired a secret cell of world-walking assassins, he needs to know. I wouldn't put a coup attempt beyond him. Normally we should stay here for two or three hours at least, as if we were having a liaison. If I leave too soon, that would cause alarm. But if he's moving against your people right now—"

"Wait." Miriam took his arm. "You're forgetting we have radios. . . ."

The morning had dawned bright with a thin cloudy overcast, humid and warm with a threat of summer evening storms to follow. Brilliana, her morning check on the security points complete, placed the go-bag she'd prepared for Helge on the table in the front guard room; then she went in search of Huw.

She found him in one of the garden sheds behind a row of tomato vines, wiring up a row of instruments on a rough-topped table from which the plant pots had only just been removed. He didn't notice her at first, and she stood in the doorway for a minute, watching his hands, content. "Good morning," she said eventually.

He looked up then, smiling luminously. "My lady. What can I do for you?"

She looked at the row of electronics. "It's a nice day for a walk into town. Will your equipment suffer if you leave it for a few hours?"

Obviously conflicted, Huw glanced at his makeshift workbench, then back at her. "I suppose—" He shook his head. Then he smiled again. "Yeah, I can leave it for a while." He rummaged in one of the equipment boxes by the foot of the table, then pulled a plastic sheet out and began to unfold it. "If you wouldn't mind taking that corner?"

They covered the electronics—Brilliana was fairly certain she

recognized a regulated power supply and a radio transceiver—
and weighted the sheet down with potsherds in case of rain and a
leaky roof. Then Huw wiped his hands on a swatch of toweling.
"This isn't a casual stroll, is it?" he asked quietly.

"No, but it needs to look like one." She eyed him up, evidently disapproving of his choice of jeans and a college sweat-
shirt. "You'll need to get changed first. Background story: You're
a coachman, I'm a lady's maid, and we're on a morning off work.
He's courting her and she's agreed to see the sights with him. I'll
meet you by the trades' door in twenty minutes."

"Are you expecting trouble?" He looked at her sharply.

"I'm not expecting it, but I don't want to be taken by surprise." She grinned at him. "Go!"

(An observer keeping an eye on the Beckstein household that
morning would have seen little to report. A pair of servants—he
in a suit, worn but in good repair, and she in a black dress,
clutch bag tightly gripped under her left elbow—departed in the
direction of the streetcar stop. A door-to-door seller visited the
rear entrance, was rebuffed. Two hours later, a black steamer—
two men in the open-topped front, the passenger compartment
hooded and dark—rumbled out of the garage and turned towards the main road. With these exceptions, the household carried on much as it had the day before.)

"Where are we going?" Huw asked Brilliana as they waited
at the streetcar stop.

"Downtown." She narrowed her eyes, gazing along the
tracks. "Boston is safer than Springfield, but still . . . I want to
take a look at the docks. And then the railway stations, north
and south both. It's best to have a man at my side: less risk of
unwelcome misunderstandings."

"Oh." He sounded disappointed. "What else?"

She unwound slightly; a moment later she slid her fingers
through his waiting hand. "I thought if there is enough time after that, we could visit the fair on the common."

"That's more like it."

"It'll look good to the watchers." She squeezed his thumb, then leaned sideways, against his shoulder. "Assuming there are any. If there aren't—by then we should know."

"Indeed." He paused. "I'm carrying, in case you were wondering."

"Good." With her free hand she shifted the strap of her bag higher on her shoulder. "Your knot . . . ?"

"On my wrist-ribbon."

"That too." She relaxed slightly. "Oh look, a streetcar."

They rode together in silence on the open upper deck, she sitting primly upright, he discreetly attentive to her occasional remarks. There were few other passengers on the upper level this morning, and none who might be agents or Freedom Riders; the tracks were in poor repair and the car swayed like a drunk, shrieking and grating round corners. They changed streetcars near Haymarket Square, again taking the upper deck as the tram rattled its way towards the back bay.

"What are we looking for?" asked Huw.

"Doppelganger prisons." Brill looked away for a moment, checking the stairs at the rear of the car. "They use prison ships here. If you were a bad guy and were about to arrest a bunch of world-walkers, what would you—"

Rounding the corner of a block of bonded warehouses, the streetcar briefly came in sight of the open water, and then the piers and cranes of the docks. A row of smaller ships lay tied up inside the harbor, their funnels clear of smoke or steam: In the water beyond, larger vessels lay at anchor. The economic crash, and latterly the state of emergency and the new government, had wreaked havoc with trade, and behind fences great pyramids and piles of break-bulk goods had grown, waiting for the flow of shipping to resume. Today there was some activity—a gang of stevedores was busy with one of the nearer ships, loading cartloads of sacks out of one of the warehouses—but still far less than on a normal day.

"What's that?" asked Brill, pointing at a ship moored out in the open water, past the mole.

"I'm not sure"—Huw followed her direction—"a warship?"

It was large, painted in the gray blue favored by the navy, but it lacked the turrets and rangefinders of a ship of the line; more to the point, it looked poorly maintained, streaks of red staining its flanks below the anchor chains that dipped into the water. Large, boxy superstructures had been added fore and aft. "That's an odd one."

"Can you read its name?"

"Give me a moment." Huw glanced around quickly, then pulled out a compact monocular. "HMS *Burke*. Yup, it's the navy." He shoved the scope away quickly as the streetcar rounded a street corner and began to slow.

"Delta Charlie, please copy." Brill had her radio out. "I need a ship class identifying. HMS *Burke*, Bravo Uniform Romeo—" She finished, waited briefly for a reply, then slid the device away, switching it to silent as the streetcar stopped, swaying slightly as passengers boarded and alighted.

"Was that entirely safe?"

"No, but it's a calculated risk. We're right next to the harbor and if anyone's RDFing for spies they'll probably raid the ships' radio rooms first; they don't have pocket-sized transmitters around here. I set Sven up with a copy of the shipping register. He says it's a prison ship. Currently operated by the Directorate of Reeducation. That would be prisons." She frowned.

"You don't know that it's here for us." Huw glanced at the staircase again as the streetcar began to move.

"Would you like to bet on it?"

"No. I think we ought to head back." Huw reached out and took her hand, squeezed it gently.

She squeezed back, then pulled it away. "I think we ought to make sure nobody's following us first."

"You think they might try to pick us up . . . ?"

"Probably not—this sort of action is best conducted at night—but you can never be sure. I think we should be on guard. Let's head back and tell Helge. It's her call—whether we have to withdraw or not, whether Burgeson can come up with a security cordon for us—but I don't like the smell of that ship."

Brilliana and Huw had been away from Miriam's house for almost an hour. Miriam herself had left half an hour afterwards.
An observer—like the door-to-door salesman who had impor-
tuned the scullery maid to buy his brushes, or the ticket inspector stepping repeatedly on and off the streetcars running up and
down the main road and curiously not checking any tickets—
would have confirmed the presence of residents, and a lack of
activity on their part. Which would be an anomaly, worthy of
investigation in its own right: A household of that size would require the regular purchase of provisions, meat and milk and
other perishables, for the city's electrical supply was prone to
brownouts in the summer heat, rendering household food chillers
unreliable.

An observer other than the ticket inspector and the salesman
might have been puzzled when, shortly before noon, they disappeared into the grounds of a large abandoned house, its windows
boarded and its gates barred, three blocks up the street and a
block over—but there were no other observers, for Sir Alasdair's
men were patrolling the overgrown acre of Miriam's house and
garden and keeping an external watch only on the approaches to
the front and rear. "If you go outside you run an increased risk of
attracting attention," Miriam had pointed out, days earlier. "Your
job is to keep intruders out long enough for us to escape into the
doppelganger compound, right?" (Which was fenced in with
barbed wire and patrolled by two of Alasdair's men at all times,
even though it was little more than a clearing in the back woods
near the thin white duke's country retreat.)

Sir Alasdair's men were especially not patrolling the city
around them. And so they were unaware of the assembly of a
battalion of Internal Security troops, of the requisition of a barracks and an adjacent bonded warehouse in Saltonstall, or the
arrival on railroad flatcars of a squadron of machine-gun carriers and their blackcoat crew. Lady d'Ost's brief radio call-in
from the docks was received by Sven, but although he went in

search of Sir Alasdair to give him the news, its significance was not appreciated: Shipping in the marcher kingdoms of the Clan's world was primitive and risky, and the significance of prison ships was not something Sir Alasdair had given much thought to.

So when four machine-gun-equipped armored steamers pulled up outside each side of the grounds, along with eight trucks—from which poured over a hundred black-clad IS militia equipped with clubs, riot shields, and shotguns—this came as something of a surprise.

Similar surprise was being felt by the maintenance crew at the farm near Framingham, as the Internal Security troops rushed the farmyard and threw tear-gas grenades through the kitchen windows; and in a block of dilapidated-looking shops fronting an immigrant rookery in Irongate—perhaps more there than else-where, for Uncle Huan had until this morning had every reason to believe that Citizen Reynolds was his protector—and at vari-ous other sites. But the commissioner for internal security had his own idea of what constituted protection, and he'd briefed his troops accordingly. "It is essential that all the prisoners be hand-cuffed and hooded during transport," he'd explained in the brief-ing room the previous evening. "Disorientation and surprise are essential components of this operation—they're tricky charac-ters, and if you don't do this, some of them will escape. You will take them to the designated drop-off sites and hand them over to the Reeducation Department staff for transport to the prison ship. I mentioned escape attempts. The element of surprise is es-sential; in order to prevent the targets from raising the alarm, if any of them try to escape you should shoot them."

Reynolds himself left the briefing satisfied that his enthusias-tic and professional team of Polis troops would conduct them-selves appropriately. Then he retired to the office of the chief of polis, to share a lunch of cold cuts delivered from the commis-sary (along with a passable bottle of Chablis—which had some-how bypassed the blockade to end in the polis commissioner's private cellar) and discuss what to do next with the doctor.

Huw's first inkling that something was wrong came when the streetcar he Brilliana were returning on turned the corner at the far end of the high street and came to a jolting stop. He braced against the handrail and looked round. "Hey," he began.

"Get *down*," Brill hissed. Huw ducked below the level of the railing, into the space she'd just departed. She crouched in the aisle, her bag gaping open, her right hand holding a pistol inside it. "Not a stop."

"Right." Taking a deep breath, Huw reached inside his coat and pulled out his own weapon. "What did you see?"

"Barricades and—"

He missed the rest of the sentence. It was swallowed up in the familiar hammering roar of a SAW, then the harsh, slow thumping of some kind of heavy machine gun. "*Shit.* Let's bail." He raised his voice, but he could barely hear himself; the guns were firing a couple of blocks away, and he flattened himself against the wooden treads of the streetcar floor. Brill looked at him, white-faced, spread-eagled farther back along the aisle. Then she laid her pistol on the floor and reached into her handbag, pulling out the walkie-talkie. Fumbling slightly, she switched channels. "Charlie Delta, Charlie Delta, flash all units, attack in progress on Zulu Foxtrot, repeat, attack in progress on Zulu Foxtrot. Over."

The radio crackled, then a voice answered, slow and shocky: "Emil here, please repeat? Over."

"Shit." Brill keyed the transmit button: "Emil, get Helge out of there right now! Zulu Foxtrot is under attack. Over and out." She looked at Huw: "Come on, we'd better—"

Huw was looking past her shoulder, and so he saw the head of the IS militiaman climbing the steps at the rear of the carriage before Brilliana registered that anything was wrong. Huw raised his pistol and sighted. The steps curled round, and the blackcoat wasn't prepared for trouble; as he turned towards Huw his mouth opened and he began to raise one hand towards the long gun slung across his shoulder.

Huw pulled the trigger twice in quick succession. "Go!" he shouted at Brill. "Now!"

"But we're—" She flipped open the locket she wore on a ribbon around her left wrist, for all the world like a makeup compact.

More machine-gun fire in the near distance. Shouting, distant through tinnitus-fuzzed ears still ringing from the pistol shots. Huw shoved his sleeve up his arm and tried to focus on the dial of the handless watch, swimming eye-warpingly close under the glass. The streetcar rocked; booted feet hammered on the stair treads. Brilliana rose to a crouch on her knees and one wrist, then disappeared. Something round and black bounced onto the floor where she'd been lying, mocking Huw. He concentrated on the spinning, fiery knot in his eyes until it felt as if his head was about to explode; then the floor beneath him disappeared and he found himself falling hard, towards the grassy ground below.

Behind him, the grenade rolled a few inches, then stabilized for a second before exploding.

The man behind the desk was tall, silver-haired, every inch the distinguished patriarch and former fighter pilot who'd risen to lead a nation. But it was the wrong desk; and appearances were deceptive. Right now, the second unelected president of the United States was scanning a briefing folder, bifocals drooping down his nose until he flicked at them irritably. After a moment he glanced up. "Tell me, Andrew." He skewed Dr. James with a stare that was legendary for intimidating generals. "This gizmo. How reliable is it?"

Dr. James's cheek twitched. "We haven't made enough to say for sure, sir. But of the sixteen ARMBAND units we've used so far, only one has failed—and that was in the first manufactured group. We've got batch production down and we can swear to ninety-five-percent effectiveness for eighteen hours after manufacture. Reliability drops steeply after that time—the long-term storable variant under development should be good for six months and self-test, but we won't be able to swear to that until we've tested it. Call it a year out."

"Huh." The president frowned, then closed the folder and placed it carefully in the middle of the desk. "CARTHAGE is going to take sixty-two of them. What do you say to that?"

Is that it? Dr. James lifted his chin. "We can do it, sir. The units are already available—the main bottleneck is training the air force personnel on the mobile biomass generators, and that's in hand. Also the release to active duty and protocol for deployment, but we're basically repurposing the existing nuclear handling protocols for that; we can relax them later if you issue an executive order."

"I don't want one of our planes failing to transition and executing CARTHAGE over domestic airspace, son. That would be unacceptable collateral damage."

Dr. James glanced sidelong at his neighbor: another of the ubiquitous blue-suited generals who'd been dragged on board the planning side of this operation. "Sir? With respect I think that's a question for General Morgenstern."

The president nodded. "Well, General. How are you going to insure your boys don't fuck up if the doctor's mad science project fails to perform as advertised?"

The general was the perfect model of a modern military man: lean, intent, gleaming eyes. "Mark-one eyeball, sir: that, and radio. The pilot flying will visually ascertain that there are no landmarks in sight, and the DSO will confirm transition by checking for AM talk-radio broadcasts. We've done our reconnaissance: There are no interstates or railroads in the target zone, and their urban pattern is distinctively different."

"That assumes daylight, doesn't it?" The president had a question for every answer.

"No sir; our cities are illuminated, theirs aren't, it's that simple. The operation crews will be tasked with activating the ARM-BAND units within visual range of known waypoints and will confirm that they're not in our world anymore before they button up."

"Heavy cloud cover?"

"Radio, sir. There's no talk radio in fairyland. No GPS signal either. No sir, they aren't going to have any problem confirming they're in the correct DZ."

The president nodded sagely. "Make sure they check their receivers before they transition. We don't want any systems failures."

"Yes sir. Is there anything else you want me to add?" Normally, Dr. James thought, handing the man a leading question like that might border on insolence, but right now he was in an avuncular, expansive mood; the bright and shiny gadgets were coming out of the cold warrior's toy box, and playing up to the illusion of direct presidential control over the minutiae of a strike mission was only going to go down well. *A very political general,* he told himself. *Watch him.*

"I think there is." The president looked thoughtful. "Doctor. Can you have a handful more ARMBAND units ready two days after the operation? We'll want them fitting to a passenger aircraft suitable for giving some, uh, *witnesses,* a ringside seat. It's for the review stand at the execution—diplomatic witnesses to show the Chinese and the Russians what happens if you fuck with the United States. It'll need to be an airframe that's ready for the boneyard, it'll need a filtered air system, good cabin visibility, and nothing too sensitive for commie eyes. Except ARMBAND, but you'll be keeping the guests out of the cockpit. General, if you could get your staff to suggest a suitable aircraft and minute my office on their pick, I'll see you get an additional order via the joint command." He smiled alarmingly. "Wish I was going along with it myself."

Refugees

The walkie-talkie in Miriam's bag squawked for attention.
"What's that?" Burgeson, startled, let go of her arm as she turned to the table.

"Bad news, I think." She pulled the radio out. "Mike Bravo, Mike Bravo, sitrep please, over."

A buzz of static, squelched rapidly: "Boss? Emil here. I just got a call from Delta Charlie. Zulu Foxtrot is under attack, repeat, the house is under attack. We're bringing the truck round, you need to get out now, over."

Miriam stared at Erasmus. "My house is under attack. Do you know anything about it?" She knew the answer before the words were finished: The widening of his eyes and the paleness of his face told her all she needed. "Damn. It's got to be Reynolds, hasn't it?"

"I need to get to the railway station." Erasmus stood up, unfolding sticklike limbs as he glanced at the window. "If he's doing this now, he means to be back in New London by nightfall, which means this is the start of something bigger. There's a Council of People's Commissioners—cabinet—meeting tomorrow morning. He'll either present the arrests as a fait accompli, and impeach me for treason and conspiracy on the spot, or go a step further and arrest the entire Mutual wing of the Council in the name of the Peace and Justice Committee. It'll be a coup in all but name: Either way, he takes me out and weakens Sir Adam enormously."

"What are you going to do?" Miriam positioned herself between Erasmus and the doorway. "Do you have a plan?"

"Yes, if I can get to the station." He smiled. "You should go into hiding, in your other world—they can't reach you there—"

"The hell I will." She picked up her bag and slung it over her shoulder, then the walkie-talkie. "Emil, Mike Bravo here. I'm coming out with a passenger. We need a ride. Over." She pushed the door open. "What's at the station?"

"I have a train to catch. Once I'm on it, Reynolds can't touch me and can't stop me from telling the truth."

"A train—"

"*My* train." His smile widened, sharkishly. "Steve has *no idea* what I'm capable of doing with it."

"You'll have to tell me on the way." She paused, by the door. "Reynolds knows you're here, right?"

"Yes. But Josh and Mark are waiting down in the shop and his men won't get past them silently—"

"Reynolds has the Lee family working for him: or some of them." She held up a hand, then stood still, listening.

"What are you—"

She walked across to the window casement and looked out along the alley, keeping her body in the shadows. "Do you hear a steamer?" she asked quietly.

"No. Why?"

"Because we *should* be hearing one by now." She grimaced. "Emil and Klaus were just round the corner. Do you have some way of calling your bodyguards?"

"The shop bell-pull in the hall—it works both ways. What are you thinking?" He pitched his voice low.

"That we're very isolated right now. I may be jumping at shadows, but if Reynolds is raiding my house, why isn't he here?"

"Oh dear." Erasmus returned to the sideboard. "In that case, we'd better go." A muffled click, and he turned around, holding a small pepperpot pistol. A barely glimpsed gesture made it vanish into a sleeve or a pocket. "For once, I'm not going to let you go first."

"I don't think"—they collided in front of the doorway—"so?"

"My apologies." Looking her in the eye, Erasmus added, "It would be best if my bodyguards saw me first."

"Maybe." Miriam stepped aside reluctantly. He crossed the hall and turned the key, then pulled the front door open as she followed him.

"Stop or I shoot!" Erasmus froze in the doorway. The teenager on the landing kept his pistol in Burgeson's face, but went wide-eyed as he looked past the older man and saw Miriam. "What are *you* doing here?"

Heart in mouth, she looked the youth in the eye: "Point the gun at someone else, Lin, or I will be *very angry* with you."

"I'm not supposed to do that." His voice was shaky. "I'm supposed to kill everyone in this apartment."

"Who told you to do that?" Miriam asked quietly.

"The man Elder Huan told me to obey without question." Erasmus stood stock-still as Lin stepped back a pace and lowered his pistol to waist level. "I didn't know you'd be here," he added, almost petulantly.

Pulse hammering, Miriam took a step forward and placed a hand on Erasmus's shoulder. "Everything is going to be all right," she said quietly. "Lin, I want you to meet Mr. Burgeson. He's a, a friend of mine." She could feel his shoulder through the cloth of his jacket, solid and real and seeming to her as delicate as a fine bone-china teacup caught in midfall; she felt faint, this was so close to Roland's end. "I will never forgive you if you kill him."

Lin nodded. "I am dishonored either way. But I won't shoot him. For your sake." His elders had once sent Lin to kill

Miriam. She, capturing him, had not only spared him, she'd sent him back to them with a truce offer.

"Did the man who sent you here wear a black coat, by any chance? A party commissioner called Reynolds?"

Lin shook his head. "Oh no," he said earnestly. "The doctor sent me." His nostrils flared with evident disdain: "Dr. ven Hjalmar."

"Would someone," Erasmus said quietly but forcefully, "explain to me what exactly is happening?"

"I think I can put it together," said Miriam. "Lin, Dr. ven Hjalmar is working with Commissioner Reynolds, isn't he? No need to confirm or deny anything—your brother and I had a conversation."

Lin nodded. "I was sent to remove a, a party radical who was opposed to our ends, in the doctor's words." He stared at Erasmus. "What will you do now?"

"Have you met Stephen Reynolds?" Erasmus asked quietly. "He isn't one for whom loyalty is a two-way street."

"I've discussed this with James," said Miriam. "Lin, I've been negotiating a, a deal with Mr. Burgeson here. It's similar to the arrangement your elders came to with the security commissioner."

"The difference is, I don't send death squads to murder my rivals," Erasmus added.

Miriam looked straight at Lin: "That's why I've been dealing with him. The arrangement can be extended to include your relatives. But not if you shoot him, or hand us over to the Internal Security directorate. Or Dr. ven Hjalmar."

Lin looked straight back at her. "You say this man is a friend of yours," he said. "Do you mean that? Are you claiming privilege of kinship? Or is it just a business arrangement to which no honor attaches?"

Miriam blinked. She tightened her grip on Erasmus's shoulder as she felt him breathe in, preparing to say something potentially disastrous—"Erasmus is a personal friend of mine, Lin. This isn't just business." Which was true, she realized as she said it; not that they had gotten up to anything, not that there was substance to the cover story Burgeson's bodyguards and enemies believed, but she could conceive of it, at some future time. "So yes, I claim privilege of kinship, and if you touch one hair on his head I'll claim blood feud on you and yours. Is that what you want?"

Lin looked away, then shook his head.

"Good. We understand each other, I hope? Do you and yours claim Dr. ven Hjalmar?"

Lin's eyes widened. "Not yet. Nan was talking about finding him a wife, but—"

"Then you have no claim if I declare him outlaw and anathema and deal with him accordingly?"

He began to smile. "If your arrangement for the security of your clan can stretch to some more bodies—none whatsoever. What do you have in mind?"

"First, I think we need to deliver Mr. Burgeson safely to South Station, where a train is waiting for him." She felt Erasmus preparing to speak again. "And then I, and my sworn retainers, have an appointment with Dr. ven Hjalmar, and possibly with Commissioner Reynolds. Would you like to come along?"

"It will be my pleasure," Lin said gravely. He looked directly at Erasmus. "If you'd both care to come downstairs, my cousins and I have a wagon waiting on the other side of the wall of worlds. We were to use it to dispose of the evidence, but I think it will work just as well with living passengers." He returned his pistol to a pocket holster, then raised an eyebrow. "Which platform do you want?"

The miracles of modern communication technology: With two-way radios, the survivors of Reynolds's simultaneous raids called in and made contact within an hour. Miriam, her head pounding, hugged Erasmus briefly. "Try to take care," she murmured in his ear.

"My dear, I have every intention of doing so." He grinned lopsidedly.

"What are you going to do?"

"Get to my train on time, with the help of these fine fellows."

Behind her, Lin was filling two of his fellows in on the turn events had taken. "Then I shall first signal Sir Adam. Stephen's gone too far this time—setting up a parallel arrangement with these cousins of yours and trying to frame me for subversion. I have my own supporters within the Freedom Guard; if necessary we can take it to the street." He looked worried. "But that has its own price. What do you intend?"

"I'm going to find my people," she told him. "And then we're going to take out the trash. Stay away from the old Polis headquarters building for a couple of hours, Erasmus. You might want to turn up later—around six, maybe—to take charge of the cleanup operation and to assemble a cover story." She bit her lip. "It's not going to be pretty. Reynolds is a problem, but the doctor is a worse one: a sociopath with the background and intellect to raise his own version of the Clan, given half a chance."

"You think your doctor is more important than Reynolds?"

"I know it." She looked him in the eye. "You and your boss can deal with Reynolds; he's an attack dog, but if you put a chain on his collar you can keep him under control. But ven Hjalmar doesn't wear a collar in the first place."

"Then you should take care," he said gravely. "I should be going. But . . . take care. I would very much like to see you again."

"You too." She leaned forward and, trying not to think too hard about her intentions, kissed him. She was aiming for his cheek, but he turned, and for a moment their lips touched. "Oh. Go on."

"Until this evening," he said, coloring slightly as he took a step backwards, turning towards the cart, his temporary chauffeurs, and the somnolent mule between the traces.

Miriam waited until he looked away, then walked over to Lin's side. "Let's do it," she said. "My people first; then the Polis building."

Three o'clock in the afternoon, and for Commissioner Reynolds the day was not going terribly well.

In the communications room downstairs the telautographs were buzzing and clattering like deranged locusts; telespeakers clutching their earpieces hammered away on their keyboards, transcribing incoming messages from the snatch squads and the delivery teams charged with ferrying the detainees to the *Burke*. Periodically one of the supervisors or overofficers would collate a list of the most important updates and hurry them upstairs, where Reynolds would receive them in stony silence.

"Ninety-six subjects isolated at Irongate and consigned for detention. Thirty-one confirmed as received by the *Burke*, the others still being in transit. Slow, too slow. Site B in Boston, heavy gunfire—damn you, man, what do you mean, *heavy* gunfire returned? That group has gun carriers! What's going on out there?"

The doctor, placidly munching on a desert platter, paused to dab at his lips with a napkin. "I told you to expect organized resistance from that crowd," he reminded Reynolds.

"What is Site B putting up against our people?" Reynolds demanded.

The overstaffofficer paled: "Sir, there is word of machine-gun fire from inside the grounds. Casualties are three dead and eight injured so far; the supervisor-lieutenant on site has cordoned off the area and our men are exchanging fire with the defenders. One of the gun carriers was damaged by some sort of artillery piece when it tried to force the front gates."

"*Damaged*, by god?" Reynolds glared at him. "This was how long ago? Why haven't you called on the navy?"

"Sir, I can't order a shore bombardment of one of our own cities! If you want to request one it has to go up to the Joint Command Council for authorization—"

Reynolds cut him off with a chopping gesture. "Later. They're pinned down for now, yes? What about Site C?"

"Site C was overrun on schedule, sir. One casualty, apparently self-inflicted—negligent discharge. Six prisoners consigned for detention and received by the *Burke*. Two dead, killed resisting arrest or attempting to flee."

"Good." Reynolds nodded jerkily. "Site S?"

"I don't have a report for Site S, sir." The overstaffofficer riffled through his message sheets, increasingly concerned. "Sir, by your leave—"

"Go. Find out what happened. Report back. Dismissed." Reynolds turned to ven Hjalmar as his adjutant made himself scarce. "Damn it, you'd almost think—"

"They have radio—telautograph, I think you call it? Between sites. Between people." Ven Hjalmar was clearly irritated. "I told you that timing was essential."

"But how can they have notified the—my men cut all the wires! The transmission wires are vulnerable, yes?"

"Transmission wires?" Ven Hjalmar squinted. "What, you mean for transmitting the wireless signal? They don't use wires for that—just a stub antenna, so big." He spread the fingers of one hand. "I think we may have found a regrettable source of confusion: Their radios—the telautograph sets—are pocket-sized. They'll all be carrying them, at least one per group when they're off base—"

"Nonsense." Reynolds stared at him. "Pocket *telautographs*? That's ridiculous."

"Really?" Ven Hjalmar pushed his chair back from the table. "I was under the impression that the Lee family had taught you that when visitors from other universes come calling it's a good idea to keep an open mind." He stood up. "Sitting around up here and trying to convey the appearance of being in charge of the situation is all very well, but perhaps it would be a good idea to take a more hands-on approach before the enemy get inside your decision loop—"

A deep thudding sound vibrated through the walls and floor, rattling the crockery and shaking a puff of plaster dust from the ceiling.

"Damn." Reynolds flipped open the lid of his holster and headed towards the door. "We appear to have visitors," he said dryly. He glanced back at ven Hjalmar. "Come along, now."

The doctor nodded and bent to pick up his medical bag, which he tucked beneath one arm, keeping a grip on the handle with his other hand. "As you wish."

The lights flickered as Reynolds marched out into the corridor. The two guards snapped to attention. "Follow me," he told them. "This fellow is with us." He strode towards the staircase leading down to the operations and communications offices below, just as a burst of rapid gunfire reverberated up the stairwell. "Huh." Reynolds drew his gun.

"We need to get to ground level as fast as possible," ven Hjalmar said urgently. "If we're at ground level I can get you out of here, but if we're—"

"The *enemy* are at ground level," Reynolds cut him off. "They appear to be—" He listened. More gunfire, irregular and percussive, rattled the walls like an out-of-control drummer. "We can stop them ascending, however." He gestured his guards forward, to take up positions to either side of the stairs. "We wait here until the communications staff have organized a barricade—"

"But we've got to get down!" Ven Hjalmar was agitated now. "If we aren't at ground level I can't world-walk, which means—"

But Commissioner Reynolds was never to hear the end of ven Hjalmar's sentence.

Sir Alasdair and his men—just two had stayed behind at Site B to keep the security militia engaged—had exfiltrated to the backwoods landscape of the Gruinmarkt. The vicinity of Boston was well-mapped, crisscrossed by tracks and occasional roads and villages: maps, theodolites, and sensitive inertial platforms had built up a good picture of the key landmarks over the months since Miriam had pioneered a business start-up a couple of miles from Erasmus Burgeson's pawnbroker shop (and Leveler quartermaster's cellar). The Polis headquarters building, not far from Faneuil Hall, was a site of interest to Clan Security; with confirmation from Lin Lee that Reynolds and ven Hjalmar were present, it took Sir Alasdair less than an hour to arrange a counterattack.

Robard ven Hjalmar was not a soldier; he had no more (and

no less) knowledge of the defensive techniques evolved by the Clan's men of arms over half a century of bloody internicine feuding than any other civilian. Stephen Reynolds was not a civilian, but had only an outsider's insight into the world-walkers. Both of them knew, in principle, of the importance of doppelgangering their safe houses—of protecting them against infiltration by enemy attackers capable of bypassing doors and walls by entering from the world next door.

However, both of them had independently made different—and fatal—risk calculations. Reynolds had assumed that because Elder Huan's "Eastern cousins" came from a supposedly primitive world, and had demonstrated no particular talent for mayhem within his ambit, the most serious risk they presented was the piecemeal violence of the gun and the knife. And ven Hjalmar had assumed that the presence of armed guards downstairs (some of them briefed and alert to the risk of attackers appearing out of nowhere in their midst) would be sufficient.

What neither of them had anticipated was a systematic assault on the lobby of the headquarters building, conducted by a lance of Clan Security troops under the command of Sir Alasdair ven Hjorth-Wasser—who had been known as Sergeant Al "Tiny" Schroder, at the end of his five years in the USMC—troops in body armor, with grenades and automatic weapons, who had spent long years honing their expertise in storming defended buildings in other worlds. Nor had they anticipated Sir Alasdair's objective: to suppress the defenders for long enough to deliver a wheelbarrow load of ANNM charges, emplace them around the load-bearing walls, and world-walk back to safety. Two hundred kilograms of ammonium nitrate/nitromethane explosives, inside the six-story brick and stone structure, would be more than enough to blow out the load-bearing walls and drop the upper floors; building codes and construction technologies in New Britain lagged behind the United States by almost a century.

It was an anonymous and brutal counterattack, and left Sir Alasdair (and Commissioner Burgeson) with acid indigestion and disrupted sleep for some days, until the last of the bodies pulled from the rubble could finally be identified. If either ven Hjalmar or Reynolds had realized in time that their location had been betrayed, the operation might have failed, as would the cover story: a despicable Royalist cell's attack on the Peace and Justice Subcommittee's leading light, the heroic death of Commissioner Reynolds as he led the blackcoats in a spirited defense of the People's Revolution, and the destruction of the dastardly terrorists by their own bombs. But it *was* a success. And as the cover-up operation proceeded—starting with the delivery of the captives held on board the *Burke* to a rather different holding area ashore, under the control of guards outside the chain of command of the Directorate of Internal Security—the parties to the fragile conspiracy were able to breathe their respective sighs of relief.

The worst was over; but now the long haul was just beginning.

It was a humid morning near Boston; with a blustery breeze blowing, and cloud cover lowering across the sky, fat drops of rain spattered across the sidewalk and speckled the gray wooden wall of the compound.

The wall around the compound had sprung up almost overnight, enclosing a chunk of land on the green outskirts of Wellesley—land which included a former Royal Ordnance artillery works, and a wedge of rickety brick row houses trapped between the works and the railroad line. One day, a detachment of Freedom Guards had showed up and gone door to door, telling the inhabitants that they were being moved west with their factory, moving inland towards the heart of the empire, away from threat of coastal invasion. There had been no work, and no money to pay the workers, for five months; the managers had bartered steel fabrications and stockpiled gun barrels for food to keep their men from starvation. Word that the revolutionary government did indeed want them to resume production, and had prepared a new home for them and would in due course feed and pay them, overcame much resistance. Within two days the district's life had drained away on flatbeds and boxcars, rolling west towards a questionable future. The last laborers to leave had pegged out the line of the perimeter; the first to arrive unloaded timber from the sidings by the arsenal and began to build the wall and watchtowers. They did so under the guns of their camp guards, for these men were prisoners, captured royalist soldiers taken by the provisional government.

After they'd built the walls of the prison they'd occupy, and the watchtowers and guardhouses for their captors, the prisoners were set to work building their own cabins on the empty ground between two converging railroad tracks. These, too, they built walls around. They built lots of walls; and while they labored, they speculated quietly among themselves about who would get the vacant row houses.

They did not have long to wait to find out.

Family groups of oddly dressed folk, who spoke haltingly or with a strong Germanic accent, began to arrive one morning. The guards were not obsequious towards them, exactly, but it was clear that their position was one of relative privilege. They had the haunted expressions of refugees, uprooted from home and hearth forever. Some of them seemed resentful and slightly angry about their quarters, which was inexplicable: The houses were not the mansions of rich merchants or professionals, but they were habitable, and had sound roofs and foundations. Where had they come from? Nobody seemed to know, and speculation was severely discouraged. After a couple of prisoners disappeared—one of them evidently an informer, the other just plain unlucky—the others learned to keep their mouths shut.

The prisoners were kept busy. After a few more carriage-loads of displaced persons arrived, some of the inmates were assigned to new building work, this time large, well-lit drafting offices illuminated by overhead skylights. Another gang found themselves unloading wagonloads of machine tools, lightweight precision-engineering equipment to stand beside the forges and heavy presses left behind by the artillery works. Something important was coming, that much was clear. But what?

"What is this—*hovel*?" demanded the tall woman with the babe in arms, pausing on the threshold. She spoke hochsprache, with an aristocratic Northern accent; the politicals in their striped shirts, burdened beneath her trunk, didn't understand her.

Heyne shrugged, then turned to the convicts. "Leave it here and report back to barracks," he told them, speaking English. He watched as they deposited the trunk, none too softly, and shuffled away with downturned faces. Then he gestured back into the open doorway. "It's where you're going to live for a while," he told her bluntly. "Be thankful; this nation's in the grip of revolt, but you've got a roof over your head and food on the table, and guards to keep you safe."

"But I—" Helena ven Wu stepped inside and looked around. Raw brick faced with patches of crumbling plaster stared back at her; bare boards creaked underfoot.

The other woman was more practical. "Help me move this inside?" she said, looking up at him as she bent over one end of the trunk. The boy, free of her hand, dashed inside and thundered up the stairs, shouting excitedly.

"Certainly, my lady." Heyne picked up the other end of the trunk and helped her maneuver it past the other woman. It gave them both a polite excuse to ignore her hand-wringing dismay.

"Is there any bedding? Or furniture?" she asked quietly.

"Probably not." They finished shoving the trunk against the inner wall of the front room, and Heyne straightened up. "The previous tenants shipped out a week since, and stripped their houses of anything worth taking. The matter's in hand, though. We've got plenty of labor from the politicals in the workshop. Tell me the basics you need and I'll put in an order for it." He looked around. "Hmm. They *really* stripped this one." Walking through into the kitchen, he tutted. "Complete kitchen set, table and chairs, pots, a stove if we can find one. Beds"—he glanced over his shoulder—"for three of you." Walking to the back, he stared through the grimy window into the yard. "Chamber pots. Let's check the outhouse."

Outside in the sunlight, Kara spoke quietly. "I know we're refugees, dependent on the generosity of strangers. But Helena can't be the first like this . . . ?"

Heyne glanced back at the terraced house and shook his head. "No, she isn't. Most people go through something like it, sooner or later; but they get over it eventually." He looked back at the outhouse. "Good, they left the toilet seat. My lady, I know this accommodation is not up to your normal standards, but the fact is, we're beginning again from scratch, with barely any resources. We're lucky enough that Her Majesty negotiated a settlement with the revolutionaries that gives us this compound, and resources to . . . well, I'm not sure I can talk about that. But we're welcome here for now, anyway, and we're not going to starve." He turned and headed back through the kitchen door, glanced through into the front room—where Helena was sitting on the trunk, rocking slowly from side to side—and then climbed the creaking staircase to the top floor and the two cramped bedrooms below the attic.

The young boy was still crawling around the empty south-facing bedroom, jumping up and down and making-believe in some exciting adventure. Heyne tested the windows. "The glass is all here and the windows open. Good."

"How long will we be here?" Kara asked bluntly.

"As long as they want to keep us." He shrugged. "You don't want to go back home, my lady." His eyes lingered a moment too long on her stomach. "Not now, maybe not ever."

"But my husband—"

"He'll make it out here." Heyne's tone brooked no argument, even though his words were spoken with the voice of optimism rather than out of any genuine certainty. "Don't doubt it."

"But if we can't go back"—she frowned—"what use are we to them?"

Heyne shook his head. "Nobody's told me yet. But you can be sure Her Majesty has something in mind."

Stumbling through workdays like nothing he'd ever seen before, walking in a numb haze of dread, Steve Schroeder had spent the weeks since 7/16 waiting for the other shoe to fall.

There was the horror of the day's events, of course, and then the following momentous changes. Agent Judt sitting in one corner of the office for the first week, a personal and very pointed reminder that he'd accidentally turned down the kind of scoop that came along once in a lifetime—a chance to interview Osama bin Laden on September the twelfth—and then the consequences as the scale of the atrocity grew clearer. Then the surreal speech by the new president, preposterous claims that had no place in a real-world briefing; he'd thought WARBUCKS was mad for half an hour, until the chairman of the Joint Chiefs came on-screen on CNN, gloomily confirming that the rabbit hole the new president had jumped down was in fact not a rabbit hole at all, but a giant looming cypher like an alien black monolith suddenly arrived in the middle of the national landscape—

And then the India-Pakistan war, and its attendant horrors, and the other lesser reality excursions—the Israeli nuclear strike on Bushehr, the riots and massacres in Iraq, China's ballistic nuclear submarine putting to sea with warheads loaded and the tense standoff in the Formosa Strait—and then the looking-glass world had shattered, breaking out of its frame: the PAPUA Act, arrests of radicals and cells of suspected parallel-universe sympathizers, slower initiatives to bring forward a national biometric identity database, frightening rumors about the military tribunals at Guantánamo that had so abruptly dropped out of the headlines—

One day, after a couple of apocalyptic weeks, Agent Judt wasn't there anymore. And when a couple of days later the president had his third and fatal heart attack and there was a *new* president, one who spoke of *known unknowns* and *unknown unknowns* and seemed to think Dr. Strangelove was an aspirational role model, there was a new reality on the ground. The country had gone mad, Steve thought, traumatized and whiplashed by meaningless attacks: 9/11 and strange religious fanatics in the Middle East had been bad enough, but what was coming next?

Flying saucers on the White House lawn? Not that there was any White House lawn for them to land on, anymore. (WARBUCKS had promised to rebuild, once the radiation died down, but that would take months or years.)

Two weeks after the attack, Steve went to see his HMO and came away with a prescription for Seroxat. It helped, a bit; which was why, on his way home from a day shift one evening, he was alert enough to realize he was being followed.

Downtown Boston was no place to commute on wheels. Like most locals, Steve relied on the T to get him in and out, leaving his truck in a car park beside a station. He didn't usually pay much attention to his fellow passengers—no more than enough to spot a seat and keep a weather eye open for rare-to-nonexistent muggers—but as he got off a Green Line streetcar at Kenmore to change lines something drew his attention to a man stepping off the carriage behind him. Something familiar about the figure, glimpsed briefly through the crowd of bodies, triggered a rush of unease. Steve shivered despite the muggy heat and hurried across the tracks behind the streetcar, heading for his own platform. *It can't be him,* he told himself. *He spooked and ran.* He looked around behind him, but the half-recognized man wasn't there anymore.

What to do? Steve shook his head and hunkered down, waiting for the C Line train to North Station.

He knew something was wrong about five seconds after his train began to squeal and shudder away from the platform; knew it from the hairs on the back of his neck and the slight dip of his seat as the man behind him leaned forward, putting his weight on the seat back. "Hello, Steve."

He tensed. "What do you want?" It was hot in the streetcar, but the skin in the small of his back felt icy cold.

"I'm getting off at the next stop; don't try to follow me. I think you might like to have a look at these files. There's an email address; mail me when you want to talk again." A cheap plastic folder bulging with papers thrust over the seat back beside him like an accusing affidavit. He caught it before it spilled to the floor.

"What if I don't want to talk to you?" he asked thinly.

The man behind him laughed quietly. "Give it to your FBI handler. He'll shit a brick."

The streetcar slowed; Steve, too frightened to look round as the man behind him stood up, clutched the folio to his chest. *Jesus, I can't just let him get away*—

Too late: The doors opened with a hiss of compressed air. Steve began to turn, caution chiding him—*He might be armed*—but he was too late. Mike Fleming, Beckstein's friend, had disappeared again. Steve subsided with another shudder. *Fleming knows too damn much,* he thought. He'd known about 7/16 before it happened. *What if he was telling the truth? What if it's an inside job?* The prospect was unutterably terrifying. The looking-glass world news nightmare that had engulfed everything around him a month ago was bad enough; the idea that there really was a conspiracy behind it, and his own government shared responsibility for it, left Steve feeling sick. This was a job for Woodward and Bernstein, not him. But Bob Woodward was dead—one of the casualties of 7/16—and as for the rest of it, there was no one else to do whatever needed doing. *I could phone Agent Judt,* he told himself. *I could.*

A week or two ago, before the latest wave of chaos, he'd probably have done so immediately. But the end-times chaos of the past month had unhinged his reflexive loyalty to authority just as surely as it had reinforced that of millions of others. He unzipped the folio and glanced inside quickly. There was a cover sheet, laser-printed; he began reading.

8/18

It is a little-known fact that, contrary to public mythology, the president of the United States of America lacks the authority to order a strategic nuclear attack. Ever since the dog days of the Nixon administration, when the drunken president periodically phoned his diminishing circle of friends at 3:00 A.M. to rail incoherently about the urgent need to nuke North Vietnam, the executive branch has made every effort to insure that any such decision can only be made stone-cold sober and after a lengthy period of soul-searching contemplation. An elaborate protocol exists: A series of cabinet meetings, consultations with the Joint Chiefs, discussions with the Senate Armed Services Committee, and quite possibly divine intervention, a UN Security Council Resolution, and the sacrifice of a black goat in the Oval Office at midnight are required before such a grave step can be placed on the table for discussion.

However . . .

Retaliation in the aftermath of an attack is *much* easier.

If WARBUCKS put the plan in motion, diverted superblack off-budget funds to the Family Trade Organization, jogged BOY WONDER's elbow to sign the presidential orders setting in motion the research program to build machines around slivers of vivisected neural tissue extracted from the brains of captured Clan world-walkers, then perhaps the blame might be laid at his door. But it was his successor in the undisclosed location, former mentor and then vice president by appointment, who organized the details of the strike and bullied the Joint Chiefs into drafting new orders for USSTRATCOM tasking them with a mission enabled by the new ARMBAND technology. And it was the Office of the White House Counsel who drafted legal opinions approving the use of nuclear weapons in strict retaliation against an extradimensional threat, confirming that domestic law did not apply to parallel instances of North American geography, and that the two still-missing SADM demolition devices were necessary and sufficient justification: that such an operation constituted a due and proportionate response in accordance with international law, and that the Geneva conventions did not apply beyond the ends of the Earth.

Complicity spread like a brown, stinking cloud through the traumatized rump of a Congress and Senate who were themselves the survivors of a lethal attack on the Capitol. WARBUCKS had insured that the opposition would vote the way they were told; the PAPUA bill was as efficient an enabling act as had been seen anywhere in the world since 1933. A few dissenters—pacifists and peaceniks mostly—spoke out against the far-reaching surveillance and monitoring regime, but the press and the public were in no mood to put up with their rubbish about the First, Second, and Fourth Amendments; with the nation clearly under attack, who cared if a few whining hippie rejects talked themselves into a holiday in Club Fed? Better that than risk them giving aid and comfort to enemy infiltrators with stolen nukes. Rolling out the new identity-card system would take a couple of years, and until it was in place there'd always be the risk that the person walking past you in the street was a soldier of the invisible enemy. An eager Congress voted an ever-increasing laundry list of surveillance and control orders through with unanimous consent, each representative terrified of being seen to be weak on security.

And when the president went before the House Armed Services Committee in secret session to present certain legal opinions and request their imprimatur upon his war plans—the full House having already voted to declare war on whoever had attacked the capital city—nobody dared argue that they were excessive.

Midmorning in Gloucestershire, England. It was a bright day at Fairford, and behind the high barbed-wire–topped fence the air base was a seething hive of activity. Officially a British RAF base, Fairford had for decades now provided a secure forward operating base for USAF aircraft staging out to the Arabian Gulf. Newly upgraded to provide a jumping-off point for operations in Iraq, boasting recently upgraded fuel bunkers and a runway so long that it was designated as a Space Shuttle transatlantic abort landing strip, for three weeks Fairford had been playing host to the B52s of the Fifth Bomb Wing, USAF.

The Clan couldn't reach them in England, ran the official thinking. Not without international travel on forged documents.

Now they were queueing up on the taxiways: The aircraft of the Fifth Bomb Wing had been ordered to fly home. But first they were going to make a little detour.

For the past week, C17s had been flying in nightly from Stateside, carrying anonymous-looking low-loaders, which were driven to the bomb storage cells and unloaded under the guns of twitchy guards. And for the past two days technicians had been double- and triple-checking the weapons, nervously working through the ringbound manuals. Yesterday there'd been a hiatus; but in the evening the ordnance crews had turned out again, and this time they were moving the bombs out to the dispersal bays, under guard. Finally, around midnight, a last C17 arrived, carrying a group of specialists and a trailer that, over the following hours, made the rounds of the readying air wing.

Nobody outside the base saw a thing. The British authorities could take a hint; the small and dispirited huddle of protesters, camped by the front gate to denounce the carpet-bombers of Baghdad, had been rounded up in a midnight raid, hauled off to police cells under the Terrorism Act, to be held for weeks without counsel or charge. The village nearby was cowed by a military police presence that hadn't been seen since the height of the Troubles: Newspaper editors received discreet visits from senior police officers that left them tight-lipped and shaken. Fairford, to all intents and purposes, had vanished from the map.

At 11:00 A.M. Zulu time, the first of thirty-six B52H Stratofortresses ran its engines up to full throttle and began its takeoff roll. It was a hot day, and the huge jet's wing tanks were gravid with jet fuel; it climbed slowly away, shaking the ground with a bellowing thunder like the onrushing end of the world.

The Atlantic Ocean was wide, and the jet streams blowing west-to-east over Ireland slowed the bombers as they climbed towards their cruising altitude of forty-eight thousand feet, high above the air corridors used by the regular midmorning stream of airliners heading west from the major European and Asian hubs. The operations planners had seen no reason to warn or divert those airliners; when CARTHAGE was complete they would, if anything, be safer.

Over the next seven hours the BUFFs shadowed the daily commuter herd, tracking along the great circle route that took them just south of Greenland's icy hinterlands before turning south towards Newfoundland and then on towards Maine. As they neared the coast, the bombers diverged briefly from the civil aviation corridor, skirting around Canadian airspace and then flying parallel to the regular traffic, but farther east, staying over deep water for as long as possible. It was more than just the diplomatic nicety of keeping aircraft engaged on this mission out of foreign airspace: If anything should go catastrophically wrong, better that the cargo should ditch in the Atlantic waters than scatter over land.

As they passed the southernmost end of Nova Scotia, the bombers finally turned west. The final encrypted transmission came in: Meteorological conditions over the target were perfect. Downstairs from the pilot and copilot, the defensive-systems operators were busy at last, running the activation checklist on their ARMBAND units—gray boxes, bolted hastily to the equipment racks lining the dark cave of the bomber's lower deck—and the differential GPS receivers to which they were connected by raw, hand-soldered wiring looms. Meanwhile, their offensive systems operators were running checklists of their own; checklists that required the pilot and copilot's cooperation, reading out numbers from sealed envelopes held in a safe on the flight deck.

A hundred miles due east of Portland, the bomber crews completed their checklists. It was nearing three o'clock in the afternoon on the eastern seaboard as they lined up. At a range of fifty miles, the largest city in Maine was spread out before them, glittering beneath the cloudless summer sky. An observer on the ground who knew what they were looking at—one with very sharp eyes, or a pair of binoculars—would have seen a loosely spaced queue of aircraft, cruising in echelon far higher than normal airliners. But there were no such observers. Nor did the civilian air traffic control have anything to say in the presence of the FBI agents who had dropped in on them an hour ago.

Overhead without any fuss, the bombers were going out.

Another day, another world.

In the marcher kingdoms of the North American eastern seaboard, life went on. A frontal system moving in from the north was bringing cooler, denser air southeast from Lake Ontario, and a scattering of high cloud cover warned of rainfall by evening. The daily U2 reconnaissance overflight had reported a strong offshore breeze blowing, carrying dust and smoke out to sea; it was expected to continue for at least twenty-four hours.

The wheat harvest was all but over, and rye, too; the peasants were still laboring with sickle and adze in their strip fields, and the granaries were filling, but an end to toil was in sight. Their lords and masters busied themselves with the summer hunt, wild boar and deer fat and heavy; the season of late-summer parties was in swing, as eligible daughters were paraded around before their fathers' friends' sons, and barons and dukes sought surcease from the stink of the cities by touring their estates and the houses of their vassals.

There was quiet unrest too. Among the hedge-lords, whispered rumor spoke of the upstart tinker families becoming absent neighbors. Houses were mysteriously empty, houses that had weathered the campaign by the late pretender and survived the subsequent wave of murders that had engulfed the Clan. Some spoke of strangeness; families with children sent away, the parents' bright-eyed cheer covering some grim foreboding. Rumors of tinker Clansmen in their cups maundering about the *end of the world*, grumbling about absent cousins trying to run before the storm surge while they, the heroic drunk, chose to stand firm against the boiling wave crests—

And the queen, Prince Creon's widowed pregnant wife, had not been seen in public for nearly two months.

The queen's absence was not in and of itself remarkable—she was pregnant, and a retreat from court engagements was not unexpected—but the totality of it attracted notice. She hadn't been seen by *anyone* except, it appeared, her mother. The dowager duchess (herself mysteriously absent for a period of decades) was in residence in Niejwein in one of the Clan's less badly damaged great houses, busying herself with the restoration of the Summer Palace (or rather, with commencing its reconstruction from the ground up, for its charred beams and shattered stones would not be fit for habitation anytime soon). And *she* had seen her daughter the queen-widow, and loudly testified to that effect—to her bouts of morning sickness and desire for seclusion. But. The queen hadn't been seen in public for weeks now, and people were asking questions. Where was she?

Now, high above the thin mares' tails, a curious thing can be seen in the heavens.

A row of strange straight clouds are rushing across the vault of the sky, quite unlike anything anyone remembers seeing in times gone by. True, for the past month or so the witch-clouds have been glimpsed from time to time, racing crisscross from east to west—but only one at a time.

Today, two rows of knife-straight clouds are ploughing southwest, as if an invisible god has drawn two eighteen-toothed combs across the horizon, one comb flying two thousand feet above the other. They cover the dome of the sky from side to side, for they are not close together; a knowledgeable observer would count twelve miles between teeth.

Flying just ahead of each tine is a B52H Stratofortress of Fifth Bomb Wing, Eighth Air Force, Air Combat Command. Thirty-five out of thirty-six aircraft carry in each bomb bay a rotary dispenser containing six B83 free-fall hydrogen bombs. The remaining bomber is gravid with a single device, a monstrous B53-Y1, a bloated cylinder that weighs over four tons and fills the BUFF's central bomb bay completely. This aircraft flies near the eastern edge of the upper group. It is intended to deliver the president's signature message to the enemy capital: shock and awe.

The track from Kirschford down to the Linden Valley was clear of tinker-lord traffic this afternoon. The flow of refugees had slackened to a trickle, for those who wanted to evacuate had for the most part already left. Helena ven Wu and her infants and sister-in-law had come this way a week before; while Gyorg was still occupied with the corvée, shuttling supplies between anonymous storage lockups in Boston and wine cellars in the Gruinmarkt, his dependents had achieved the tenuous sanctuary of a refugee camp in New Britain.

So none of them paused to look up, slack-jawed, as the first wave of bombers commenced their laydown.

A B83 hydrogen bomb isn't very large; it weighs about a ton, and looks exactly like most other air-dropped bombs. The weapons the Fifth Bomb Wing were delivering were equipped with parachutes which retarded their descent from altitude, so that it would take each bomb more than three minutes to descend to its detonation altitude of twenty thousand feet. Flying parallel courses spaced twelve miles apart, wingtip-to-wingtip, the aircraft began to drop their payload at one-minute intervals, seeding a furrow of hells twelvemiles apart. The distance between bombs was important; any closer, and the heat flash might ignite the Kevlar ribbon chutes of the other weapons.

Three minutes and twenty seconds. The trails arrowed south across the sky of the Gruinmarkt, a faint rumble of distant thunder disturbing the afternoon quiet; and then the sky lit up as the first row of eighteen hydrogen bombs, spanning the kingdom from sea to inland frontier, detonated at an altitude of just under four miles.

The flash of a single one-megaton hydrogen bomb, followed by a fireball which dims over a period of nearly a minute, is visible in good weather at a range of hundreds of miles—light from the flash is scattered by particles in the upper atmosphere, reflected around the curve of the earth. To an observer in Niejwein, the capital city located nearly two hundred miles south of the first row, the northern horizon would have begun to flicker and brighten as if a gigantic match had been held to the edge of the map. There was no sound; would be no sound for many minutes, for even though the shock waves from the detonations overtook the bombers, it would take a long time for the attenuated noise to reach the capital.

To an observer located closer to the bombing line, it would have been the end of the world.

The heat flash from a B83 detonating at twenty thousand feet is sufficient, in good weather, to ignite cardboard or cotton sheeting, heat damp pine needles to smoldering tinder, and char wood and flesh six miles from ground zero. The leading row of eighteen bombers were spaced close enough that over open ground no spot could remain unseared; only in the lee slope of a steep valley or the depths of a cellar or cave was there any hope of survival.

Peasants working in the fields might have glanced up as the sky flashed white above them; it would have been the last thing they saw through rapidly clouding eyes. Their skin reddened and crisped as the grain stubble and trees around them began to smoke; screaming and stumbling for cover, they blundered towards their houses or the tree line, limned in the flaring red burn of a billion leaves igniting simultaneously. There were some survivors of the initial flash: women spinning thread or weaving cloth, millers tending their wheels, even a lucky few sitting behind dry-stone walls or swimming in cool water pools. But as they looked up in confusion they saw the same thing in every direction around them: trees, plants, buildings, even cattle and people smoking and flaming.

And then the hammerblast of wind arrived from above, slamming into hedges and walls alike and splintering all before them.

The aircrew saw nothing of this. They flew on instruments, insulated blackout screens drawn across the cockpit windows to prevent reflected light from blinding their pilots. Perhaps they glanced at one another as shock waves buffeted the tail surfaces of the bombers, bumping and dropping them before the pilots regained full control authority; but if they did so, it was with no sympathy for the unseen carnage below. A president had been killed, more thousands murdered by emissaries from this world; their word for the task they were engaged in was *payback*.

Seventy seconds later, the second row of H-bombs reached their preset altitude and began to detonate, flashbulbs popping erratically on a wire two hundred and fifty miles wide. And seventy seconds after that, the process continued, weeping tears of incandescence across the burning coastline.

There were a lot of flashes.

———

It took the aircraft nearly twelve minutes to reach Niejwein, two-thirds of the way through their carpet-bombing run. And here, there were witnesses. Niejwein, with a population of nearly sixty thousand souls, was the biggest city within four hundred miles; proud palaces and high-roofed temples rose above a sprawling urban metropolis, home to dozens of trades and no fewer than four markets. And the people of Niejwein had due notice. The flickering brightness on the horizon had been growing for almost a quarter hour; and lately there had been a rumbling in the ground, an uneasy shuddering as if Lightning Child himself was shifting, uneasy in his bed of clay. A strange hot wind had set the bells of the temple of Sky Father clanging, bringing the priests stumbling from their sanctuary to squint at the northern lights in disbelief and shock.

And in the Thorold Palace, some of the residents realized what was happening.

At midafternoon, the dowager duchess Patricia was holding court, sitting in formal session in the east wing of the palace to hear petitions on behalf of her daughter. A merchant, Freeman Riss of Somewhere-Bridge, was bringing a complaint about the lord of his nearest market town, who, either in a fit of pique or for some reason Freeman Riss was reticent about disclosing, had banned said merchant from selling his wares in the weekly market.

At another time, this complaint might well have interested Dame Patricia—also known for the majority of her life as Iris Beckstein—as much for its value as leverage against the earl in question as for its merit as a case. But it was a hot afternoon, and sitting in the stiff robes of state beneath a row of stained-glass windows which dammed the air and cast flickering multicolored shadows across the bench before her, she was prone to distraction.

Riss was reciting, in a scratchy voice as if from memory, "And I deponeth thus, that on the third feastday of Sister Corn, the laird did send his armsmen to stand before my drover and his oxen and say—"

Patricia raised a shaky hand. "Stop," she said. Freeman Riss paused, his mouth open. "Surcease, we pray you." She squinted up at the windows. They were flickering. "We declare a recess. Your indulgence is requested, for we are feeling unwell." She closed her eyes briefly. *I hope it isn't another attack,* she worried; the MS hadn't affected her vision so far, but her legs had been largely numb all week, and the prickling in her hands was worsening. "Sergeant-at-arms—"

There was a banging and clattering from outside the room. The courtiers and plaintiffs began to talk, just as the door burst open. It was Helmut ven Rindt, lord-lieutenant and commander of the second troop of the Clan's security force, accompanied by six soldiers. Their camouflage surcoats sat uneasy above machine-woven titanium mail. "Your grace? I regret the need to interrupt you, but you are urgently required elsewhere."

"Really?" Iris stared at Helmut. *Not you, too?* The clenching in her gut was bad.

"Yes, your grace. If I may approach"—she nodded; Helmut stepped towards her raised seat, then continued to speak, quietly, in English—"we lost radio nine minutes ago. There's nothing but static, and there are very bright lights on the northern horizon. Counting them and checking the decay curves, it's megaton-range and getting closer. With your permission, we're going to evacuate *right now.*"

"Yes, you go on." She nodded approvingly, then did a slow double take as one of Helmut's troops marched forward. "Hey—"

The soldier bent to lift her from her throne in a fireman's carry.

Instant uproar among the assembled courtiers, nobles, and tradesmasters assembled in the room. "Stop him!" cried one unfortunate, a young earl from somewhere out to the northwest. "He laid hands on her grace!"

That did it. As the soldier lifted Patricia, she saw a flurry of bodies moving towards the throne, past the open floor of the chamber, which by custom was not entered without the chair's consent. "Hey!" she repeated.

Helmut grimaced: "Earl-Major Riordan's orders, your grace,

you and any other family we set eyes on. We are to leave none alive behind, and you'll not make a family-killer of me." Louder: "To the evac cellar, lads! Double time!"

The young earl, perhaps alarmed at the unfamiliar sound of Anglischprache, moved a hand to his hip. "For queen and country!" he shouted, and drew, lunging towards Helmut. Four more nobles were scarcely a step behind, all of them armed.

For palace guard duty, in the wake of the recent civil disorder, Earl-Major Riordan had begun to reequip his men with FN P90s. A stubby, oddly melted-looking device little larger than a flintlock pistol, the P90 was an ultracompact submachine gun, designed for special forces and armored vehicle crews. Helmut's men were so equipped, and as the misguided young blood ran at them they opened fire. Unlike a traditional submachine gun, the P90 fired low-caliber armor-piercing rounds at a prodigious rate, from a large magazine. In the stone-walled hall, the detonations merged into a continuous concussive rasp. They fired for three seconds: sufficient to spray nearly two hundred rounds into the crowd from less than thirty feet.

As the sudden silence rang in Patricia's numb and aching ears her abductor shuffled forward, carefully managing his footing as he slid across blood-slick flagstones. The wounded and dying were moaning and screaming distantly in her ears, behind the thick cotton-wool wadding that seemed to fill her head. The light began to flicker beyond the windows again, this time brightening the daylight perceptibly. Helmut led the way to the door, raising his own weapon as his guards discarded their empty magazines and reloaded; then he ducked through into the next reception room. Patricia looked down from the shoulder of her bearer, into the staring eyes of a dead master of stonemasons. He sprawled beside a lady-in-waiting, or the wife of a baron's younger son. *My people,* she thought distantly. *Mother dearest wanted me to look after them.*

They stumbled out of the cloister around the palace into the sunlit afternoon of a summer's day, onto the tidily manicured lawn within the walled grounds. Something was wrong with the shadows, she noticed, watching Helmut's feet: There were too many suns in the sky. "Don't look up," he shouted, loudly enough that she couldn't help but hear him and raise her eyes briefly. *Too many suns.*

The northern wall of the palace grounds was silhouetted with the deepest black, long shadows etched across the grass towards her, flickering and brightening and dimming. A moment of icy terror twisted at her guts as she saw that Helmut and his guard were hurrying towards one of the smaller outbuildings ahead. Its doorway gaped open on darkness. "What's that?" she asked.

"Gatehouse. There's a cellar, doppelgangered."

She saw other figures crawling antlike across the too-bright lawn. *Nukes,* she realized. *They must be using* all *the nukes.* For a moment she felt every second of her sixty-two years. "Put me down," she called.

"No." The response came from Helmut. Her bearer was panting hard, all but jogging. Her weight on his back was shoving him down: He had no more breath to reply than any other servant might.

They were nearly at the building. Helmut hung back, gestured at her rescuer. "*Now,*" he snarled. "Drop her and *go.*"

The man let Patricia slide to the ground, twisting to lay her down, then without pause rose and dashed forward to the entrance. Helmut knelt beside her. "Do you want to die?" he asked, politely enough.

Behind him the sky cracked open again. Getting closer. She licked dry lips. "No," she admitted. "But I deserve to."

"Lots of people do. It has nothing to do with their fate." He slid an arm beneath her and, grunting, levered her up off the ground and into his arms. "Arms round my neck." He stumbled forward, into the darkness, following his men—who hadn't bothered to wait.

"I failed them," she confessed as Helmut's boots thudded on the steps down into the cellar. "We drew this down on them."

"They're not our people. They never were." He grunted again, reaching the bottom. "We're not part of them, any more than we were part of the Anglischprache who're coming to kill us. And if you reached your age without learning that, you're a fool."

"But we had a duty—" She stopped, a stab of grim amusement penetrating the oppressive miasma of guilt. It was the same old argument, liberal versus conservative by any other name. "Let's finish this later."

"*Now* she talks sense." There was an overhead electric light at the bottom, dangling from the top of the vaulted arch of the ceiling. The stonework grumbled faintly, dislodging a shower of plaster and whitewash dust; shadows rippled as the bulb shivered on the end of its cord. Someone had nailed a poster-sized sheet of laminated paper against the wall, bearing an intricate knotwork design that made her eyes hurt. Helmut stepped forward onto the empty circle chalked on the floor. The guards had already crossed over. "I'll carry your grace," he told her. Then he turned to face the family sigil and focus.

"I'm not your grace anymore," Iris tried to say; but neither of them were there anymore when she finished the sentence.

Sixty miles north of Niejwein, the first wave of B52s finished unloading their rotary dispensers. Their crews breathed a sigh of relief as they threw the levers to close their bomb-bay doors, and the DSOs began the checklist to reactivate their ARMBAND devices for the second and final time. Meanwhile, the second wave of bombers smoothly took their place in the bomb line.

One of them, the plane with the single device in its front bay, flew straight towards the enemy city. With the target confirmed in visual range, her DSO keyed a radio transmitter—a crude, high-powered low-bandwidth signal that would punch through the static hash across the line of sight to the other aircraft in the force. To either side, the formation split, the neighboring aircraft following prearranged courses to give it a wide berth. Twelve miles was an acceptable safety margin for a one-megaton weapon, but not for the device this aircraft carried.

("I'm going to send them a message," the president had said. "Who?" his chief of staff replied, an ironic tilt to his eyebrow. "The Russians." The president smirked. "Who did you think I meant?")

The single huge bomb crammed into the special bomber's bay was a B53; at nine megatons, the largest H-bomb ever fielded by the US military: a stubby cylinder the size of a pickup truck. The bomber rose sharply as the B53 fell away from the bomb bay. A sequence of parachutes burst from its tail, finally expanding into three huge canopies as its carrier aircraft closed its bay doors and the flight crew ran the engines up to full thrust, determined to clear the area as fast as possible.

To either side of the heavyweight, the megaton bursts continued—a raster burn of blowtorch flames chewing away at the edge of the world. Behind the racing bomber force the sky was a wall of darkness pitted with blazing rage, domed clouds expanding and rising and flaring and dimming with monotonous precision every few seconds. The ground behind the nuclear frontal system was blackened and charred, thousands of square miles of forest and field caught in a single vast firestorm as the separate waves of incineration fanning out from each bomb intersected and reinforced each other. The winds rushing into the zone were already strengthening towards hurricane force; the bombers struggled against an unexpected sixty-knot jet stream building from the south.

Beneath its parachutes, the bulbous B53 slowly descended towards the city. The strobing flare of distant apocalypses flashed ruby highlights across its burnished shell as it twisted in the wind, drifting towards the roof of a well-to-do carpenter's house on the Sheepmarket Street to the south of the city. The carpenter and his wife and apprentices were standing outside, staring at the horizon in gape-jawed dismay. "If it be a thunderstorm it's an unseasonal huge one," he told his wife. "Better fetch in your washing—" He whirled at the crashing and crunching from the roof. "Who did that!" Instant rage caught him as he saw the deflating dome of a white parachute descend across the yard. "If that be your idea of a prank, Pitr—"

Niejwein, population just under sixty thousand, two and a half miles by one and a quarter, Niejwein, capital of the Gruinmarkt— all gone.

Wiped away as if a bullet had slammed through a map pasted across a target.

Niejwein: home to just under sixty thousand artisans and tradesmen and their families, and almost two hundred aristo- crats and their servants and hangers-on, and previously home to as many as ninety members of the Clan—of whom only eleven remained at this point—all brought to a laser-bright end by a flash of light from the heart of a star.

The boiling, turbulent fireball resulting from a surface lay- down expanded in a fraction of a second until it was over a mile in diameter. At its periphery, the temperature was over a hun- dred thousand degrees: Stone boiled, the bodies of man and ani- mal flashed into vapor. A short distance beyond it—out to five miles—the heat was enough to melt iron structures. Castles and palaces only a mile or two beyond the fireball, be their walls made of stone and never so thick as a man's body, slumped and then shattered on the shock wave like a house of cards before a hand grenade.

There would be no survivors in Niejwein. Indeed, there could have been no survivors in the open within fifteen miles, had not the other bombers of the strike force continued to plow their fields with the fires of hell.

It was not the intention of the planners who designed Opera- tion CARTHAGE to leave any survivors, even in subsurface cellars.

The firestorm raged steadily down the coast, marching at the pace of a speeding jet bomber. Behind it, the clouds boiled up into the stratosphere, taking with them tens of millions of tons of radioactive ash and dust. Already the sun was paling behind the funeral pyre.

In the aftermath, the people of the Gruinmarkt might well be the luckiest of all. It was their fate to be gone in a flash or burned in a fire: a brief agony, compared with the chill and starvation that were to follow all around their world.

Huw was in the shed near the far end of the vegetable garden, tightening the straps on his pressure suit, when Brilliana found him.

"What in Sky Father's name do you think you're doing?" she demanded.

She was, Huw realized abstractedly, even more pretty when she was angry: the brilliant beauty of a lightning-edged thundercloud. Not even the weird local fashions she wore in this place could change that. He straightened up. "What does it look like I'm doing?"

Yul chipped in: "He's getting ready to—"

Brill turned on him. "Shut up and get out," she said flatly, her voice dangerously overcontrolled.

"But he needs me to—"

"*Out!*" She waved her fist at him.

"Give us some space, bro," Huw added. "Don't worry, she won't shoot me without a trial."

"You think so?" She waited, fists on hips, until Hulius vacated the shed and the door scraped shut behind him. "You're not going to do this, Huw. I forbid it."

"*Someone* has to do it," he pointed out. "I've got the equipment and, more importantly, the experience to go into an uncharted world."

"It's *not* an uncharted world, it's *our* world. And you're not going. You don't need to go. That's an order."

"You're not supposed to give me orders—"

"Then it's an order from Helge—"

"—Isn't she busy visiting her special friend in New London right now?" Huw raised an eyebrow.

Brill glared at him. "It *will* be one, as soon as I tell her. Don't think I won't!"

"But if the Americans—"

"*Listen* to me!" She stepped in front of him, standing on her toes until he couldn't help but see eye-to-eye with her. "We got a report."

"Oh?" Huw backed down. Heroic reconnaissance into the unknown was one thing, but wasting resources was something else. "Who from? What's happened?"

"Patricia's guards came across. They wired us a report and Brionne's only just decrypted it. They were in the palace when the sky lit up, the entire horizon north of Niejwein. Helmut reported at least thirty thermonuclear detonations lighting up over the horizon, probably many more of them, getting progressively closer over the quarter hour before he issued the order to evacuate. They were carpet-bombing with H-bombs. *Now* do you understand why you're not crossing over?"

Huw looked puzzled. "How do you know they were H-bombs?"

"Hello?" Brill's nostrils flared as she squinted at him. "They lit up the sky from over the horizon *in clear daylight* and they took a minute to fade! What else do you think they might be?"

"Oh." After a moment, Huw unbuckled the fastener on his left glove. "Shit. More than thirty of them? Coming towards Niejwein?"

Brill nodded mutely.

"Oh." He sat down heavily on the stool he'd been using while Yul helped him into the explorer's pressure suit. "Oh shit." He paused. "We'll have to go back eventually."

"Yes. But not in the middle of a firestorm." Her shoulders slumped. "It was only a couple of hours ago."

"There's a firestorm?"

"What do *you* think?"

"We're stranded here."

"Full marks, my pretty one."

Huw looked up at her. "My parents were going to evacuate; I should find out if they made it in time. What about your—"

She avoided his eyes. "What do you think?"

"I'm sorry—"

"Don't be." She made a cutting gesture, but her eyes seemed to glisten in the afternoon light filtered through the hazy window glass. "I burned my bridges with my father years ago. And my mother would never think to stand up to him. *He* told her to stop writing to me. I've been dead to them for years."

"But if they're—"

"Shut up and think about your brother, Huw. At least you've got Yul. How do you think he feels?"

"He—" Huw worked at the chin strap of his helmet. "Shit. Where's Elena? Is she—"

"Turn your head. This way." She knelt and worked the strap loose, then unclipped it. Huw lifted the helmet off. "Better." She straightened up. A moment later Huw rose to his feet. He stood uncertainly before her. "I last saw Elena half an hour ago."

"Sky Father be praised."

"That's one way of putting it." She watched him uncertainly. "Do you understand what's happening to us?"

Huw took a breath. "No," he admitted. "You're sure they were hydrogen bombs—"

"Denial and half a shilling will get you a cup of coffee, Huw."

"Then we're all orphans. Even those of us whose parents came along."

"Yes." Brill choked back an ugly laugh. "Those of us who haven't been orphaned all along."

"But you haven't been—" He stopped. "Uh. I was going to ask you to, uh, but this is the wrong time."

"Huw." She was, she realized, standing exactly the wrong distance away from him: not close enough, not far enough. "I didn't hear that. If you were going to say what I think you meant to say. Yes, it's the wrong time for that."

He swallowed, then looked at her. A moment later she was in his arms, hugging him fiercely.

"If we're orphans there's nobody to force us together or hold us apart," he whispered in her ear. "No braids, no arranged marriages, no pressure. We can do what we want."

"Maybe," she said, resting her chin on his shoulder. "But don't underestimate the power of ghosts. And external threats."

"There are no ghosts strong enough to scare me away from you."

His sincerity scared her at the same time as it enthralled her. She twisted away from his embrace. "I need some time to myself," she said. "Time to mourn. Time to grow."

He nodded. A shadow crossed his face. "Yes."

"We don't know what we're getting into," she warned.

"True." He nodded, then looked away and began to work at the fasteners on his pressure suit.

She paused, one hand on the doorknob. "You didn't ask me your question," she said, wondering if it was the right thing to do.

"I didn't?" He looked up, confused, then closed his mouth. "Oh. But it's the wrong time. Your parents—"

"They're dead. Ask me anyway." She forced a smile. "Assuming we're not talking at cross-purposes."

"Oh! All right." He took a deep breath. "My lady. Will you marry me?" Not the normal turn of phrase, which was more along the lines of *May I take your daughter's hand in marriage?*

"I thought you'd never ask," she said lightly.

"But I thought you—" He shook his head. "Forgive me, I'm slow."

"I'm an orphan, over the age of majority," she reminded him. "No estates, no guardians, no braids, no dowry. You know I don't come with so much as a clipped groat or a peasant's plot?"

His smile was luminous. "Do I look like I care?"

She walked back towards him; they met halfway across the floor of the hut. "No. But I wasn't certain."

"For you, my lady"—they leaned together—"I'd willingly go over the wall." To defect from the Clan, to voluntarily accept outlawry and exile: It was not a trivial offer.

"You don't need to," she murmured. She kissed him, hard, on

the mouth: not for the first time, but for the first time on these new terms, with no thought of concealment. "Nobody now alive in this world will gainsay us." Her knees felt weak at the thought. "Not my father, nor your mother." Even if his mother had lived to enter this exile, she was unlikely to reject any Clan maid her son brought before her, however impoverished; they were, indeed, all orphans, all destitute. "No need to fear a blood feud anymore. All the Clan's chains are rusted half away."

"I wonder how long it'll take the others to realize? And what will they all do when they work it out . . . ?"

epilogue

"My fellow Americans, good evening.

"It is two months since the cowardly and evil attack on our great nation. Two months since the murder of the president along with eighteen thousand more of our fellow citizens. Two months since my predecessor and friend stood here with tears in his eyes and iron determination in his soul, to promise you that we would bring prompt and utter annihilation to the enemies who struck at us without warning.

"Many of you doubted WARBUCKS's word when he spoke of other worlds. He spoke of things that have been unknown—indeed, of unknown unknowns—threats to the very existence of our nation that we knew absolutely nothing of, threats so serious that the instability of the Middle East, or the bellicosity of Russia, dwindle into insignificance in comparison. The horrific tragedy that unfolded between India and Pakistan last month—and our hearts go out to all the survivors of that extraordinary spasm of international madness—demonstrates what is at stake here; as long as hostile powers exist in other timelines that overlap our geographical borders, we face the gravest of existential threats.

"But I am speaking to you tonight to tell you that one such existential threat has been removed: WARBUCKS's promise has been carried out, and we shall all sleep safer in our beds tonight.

"At half past two this afternoon, aircraft of the Fifth Bomb Wing overflew the land of the enemy who attacked us so savagely on July the sixteenth. And I assure you that our enemies have just reaped the crop that they sowed that day. Those that attacked us with stolen nuclear weapons have received, in return, a just and proportional measure of retribution. And they have learned what happens to assassins and murderers who attack this great nation. Gruinmarkt, the nest of world-walking thieves and narcoterrorists, is home to them no longer. We have taken the brand of cleansing fire and cauterized this lesion within our geographic borders. And they will not attack us again.

"This does not mean that the threat is over. We have learned that there exists a multiplicity of worlds in parallel to our own. Most of them are harmless, uninhabited and resource-rich. Some of them are inhabited; of these, a few may threaten our security. I have today issued an executive order to put in place institutions to seek out and monitor other worlds, to assess them for usefulness and threat—and to insure that never again does an unseen enemy take us by surprise in this way. Over the coming weeks and months, I will work with Congress to establish funding for these agencies and to create a legislative framework to defend us from these threats.

"Good night, and God bless America."

END RECORDING